The Doctor's Dilemma by Hesba Stretton

Hesba Stretton was the pen name of Sarah Smith who was born on July 27th 1832 in Wellington, Shropshire, the younger daughter of bookseller, Benjamin Smith and his wife, Anne Bakewell Smith, a devout Methodist. Although she and her elder sister attended the Old Hall school in town, they were largely self-educated.

Smith became one of the most popular Evangelical writers of the 19th century. She used her "Christian principles as a protest against specific social evils in her children's books." Her moral tales and semi-religious stories, mainly directed towards the young, were printed in huge numbers.

After her sister submitted, without her knowledge, a story on her behalf ('The Lucky Leg', was a bizarre tale of a widower who proposes to women with wooden legs) Smith became a regular contributor to Household Words and All the Year Round, two popular periodicals begun by Charles Dickens. Dickens would collaborate with many writers to produce his part-work stories. Smith writing under the pseudonym Hesba Stretton (created from the initials of herself and four surviving siblings: **H**annah, **E**lizabeth, **S**arah, **B**enjamin, **A**nna and the name of a Shropshire village; All Stretton) contributed a well-regarded short story, 'The Ghost in the Cloak-Room', as part of 'The Haunted House'. She would go on to write over 40 novels.

Her break out book was 'Jessica's First Prayer', published in the Sunday at Home journal in 1866 and the following year as a book. By the end of the century it had sold over one and a half million copies. To put that into context; ten times the sales of 'Alice in Wonderland'. The book gave rise to a strand of books about homeless children in Victorian society combining elements of the sensational novel and the religious tract bringing the image of the poor, under-privileged, child into the Victorian social conscious.

A sequel, 'Jessica's Mother', was published in Sunday at Home in 1866 and eventually as a book, some decades later, in 1904. It was translated into fifteen European and Asiatic languages as well as Braille, depicted on coloured slides for magic lantern segments of Bands of Hope programmes, and placed in all Russian schools by order of Tsar Alexander II.

Smith became the chief writer for the Religious Tract Society. Her experience of working with slum children in Manchester in the 1860s gave her books great atmosphere and, of course, a sense of authenticity.

In 1884, Smith was one of the co-founders, together with Lord Shaftesbury and others, of the London Society for the Prevention of Cruelty to Children, which then combined, five years later, with societies in other cities to form the National Society for the Prevention of Cruelty to Children. Smith resigned a decade later in protest at financial mismanagement.

In retirement in Richmond, Surrey, the Smith sisters ran a branch of the Popular Book Club for working-class readers.

Sarah Smith died on October 8th, 1911 at home at Ivycroft on Ham Common. She had survived her sister by eight months.

Index of Contents

THE DOCTOR'S DILEMMA

PART THE FIRST

CHAPTER THE FIRST

AN OPEN DOOR

I think I was as nearly mad as I could be; nearer madness, I believe, than I shall ever be again, thank God! Three weeks of it had driven me to the very verge of desperation. I cannot say here what had brought me to this pass, for I do not know into whose hands these pages may fall; but I had made up my mind to persist in a certain line of conduct which I firmly believed to be right, while those who had authority over me, and were stronger than I was, were resolutely bent upon making me submit to their will. The conflict had been going on, more or less violently, for months; now I had come very near the end of it. I felt that I must either yield or go mad. There was no chance of my dying; I was too strong for that. There was no other alternative than subjection or insanity.

It had been raining all the day long, in a ceaseless, driving torrent, which had kept the streets clear of passengers. I could see nothing but wet flag-stones, with little pools of water lodging in every hollow, in which the rain-drops splashed heavily whenever the storm grew more in earnest. Now and then a tradesman's cart, or a cab, with their drivers wrapped in mackintoshes, dashed past; and I watched them till they were out of my sight. It had been the dreariest of days. My eyes had followed the course of solitary drops rolling down the window-panes, until my head ached. Toward nightfall I could distinguish a low, wailing tone, moaning through the air; a quiet prelude to a coming change in the weather, which was foretold also by little rents in the thick mantle of cloud, which had shrouded the sky all day. The storm of rain was about to be succeeded by a storm of wind. Any change would be acceptable to me.

There was nothing within my room less dreary than without. I was in London, but in what part of London I did not know. The house was one of those desirable family residences, advertised in the Times as to be let furnished, and promising all the comforts and refinements of a home. It was situated in a highly-respectable, though not altogether fashionable quarter; as I judged by the gloomy, monotonous rows of buildings which I could see from my windows: none of which were shops, but all private dwellings. The people who passed up and down the streets on line days were all of one stamp, well-to-do persons, who could afford to wear good and handsome clothes; but who were infinitely less interesting than the dear, picturesque beggars of Italian towns, or the sprightly, well-dressed peasantry of French cities. The rooms on the third floor—my rooms, which I had not been allowed to leave since we entered the house, three weeks before—were very badly furnished, indeed, with comfortless, high horse-hair-seated chairs, and a sofa of the same uncomfortable material, cold and slippery, on which it was impossible to rest. The carpet was nearly threadbare, and the curtains of dark-red moreen were very dingy; the mirror over the chimney-piece seemed to have been made purposely to distort my features, and produce in me a feeling of depression. My bedroom, which communicated with this agreeable sitting-room by folding-doors, was still smaller and gloomier; and opened upon a dismal back-yard, where a dog in a kennel howled dejectedly from time to time, and rattled his chain, as if to remind me that I was a prisoner like himself. I had no books, no work, no music. It was a dreary place to pass a dreary time in; and my only resource was to pace to and fro—to and fro from one end to another of those wretched rooms.

I watched the day grow dusk, and then dark. The rifts in the driving clouds were growing larger, and the edges were torn. I left off roaming up and down my room, like some entrapped creature, and sank down on the floor by the window, looking out for the pale, sad blue of the sky which gleamed now and then through the clouds, till the night had quite set in. I did not cry, for I am not given to overmuch weeping, and my heart was too sore to be healed by tears; neither did I tremble, for I held out my hand and arm to make sure they were steady; but still I felt as if I were sinking down—down into an awful, profound despondency, from which I should never rally; it was all over with me. I had nothing before me but to give up, and own myself overmatched and conquered. I have a half-remembrance that as I crouched there in the darkness I sobbed once, and cried under my breath, "God help me!"

A very slight sound grated on my ear, and a fresh thrill of strong, resentful feeling quivered all through me; it was the hateful click of the key turning in the lock. It gave me force enough to carry out my defiance a little longer. Before the door could be opened I sprang to my feet, and stood erect, and outwardly very calm, gazing through the window, with my face turned away from the persons who were coming in; I was so placed that I could see them reflected in the mirror over the fireplace. A servant came first, carrying in a tray, upon which were a lamp and my tea—such a meal as might be prepared for a school-girl in disgrace.

She came up to me, as if to draw down the blinds and close the shutters.

"Leave them," I said; "I will do it myself by-and-by."

"He's not coming home to-night," said a woman's voice behind me, in a scoffing tone.

I could see her too without turning round. A handsome woman, with bold black eyes, and a rouged face, which showed coarsely in the ugly looking-glass. She was extravagantly dressed, and wore a profusion of ornaments—tawdry ones, mostly, but one or two I recognized as my own. She was not many years older than myself. I took no notice whatever of her, or her words, or her presence; but continued to gaze out steadily at the lamp-lit streets and stormy sky. Her voice grew hoarse with passion, and I knew well how her face would burn and flush under the rouge.

"It will be no better for you when he is at home," she said, fiercely. "He hates you; he swears so a hundred times a day, and he is determined to break your proud spirit for you. We shall force you to knock under sooner or later; and I warn you it will be best for you to be sooner rather than later. What friends have you got anywhere to take your side? If you'd made friends with me, my fine lady, you'd have found it good for yourself; but you've chosen to make me your enemy, and I'll make him your enemy. You know, as well as I do, he can't bear the sight of your long, puling face."

Still I did not answer by word or sign. I set my teeth together and gave no indication that I had heard one of her taunting speeches. My silence only served to fan her fury.

"Upon my soul, madam," she almost shrieked, "you are enough to drive me to murder! I could beat you, standing there so dumb, as if I was not worthy to speak a word to. Ay! and I would, but for him. So, then, three weeks of this hasn't broken you down yet! but you are only making it the worse for yourself; we shall try other means to-morrow."

She had no idea how nearly my spirit was broken, for I gave her no reply. She came up to where I stood, and shook her clinched hand in my face—a large, well-shaped hand, with bejewelled fingers, that could have given me a heavy blow. Her face was dark with passion; yet she was maintaining some control over herself, though with great difficulty. She had never struck me yet, but I trembled and shrank from her, and was thankful when she flung herself out of the room, pulling the door violently after her, and locking it noisily, as if the harsh, jarring sounds would be more terrifying than the tones of her own voice.

Left to myself I turned round to the light, catching a fresh glimpse of my face in the mirror—a pale and sadder and more forlorn face than before. I almost hated myself in that glass. But I was hungry, for I was young, and my health and appetite were very good; and I sat down to my plain fare and ate it heartily. I felt stronger and in better spirits by the time I had finished the meal; I resolved to brave it out a little longer. The house was very quiet; for at present there was no one in it except the woman and the servant who had been up to my room. The servant was a poor London drudge, who was left in charge by the owners of the house, and who had been forbidden to speak to me. After a while I heard her heavy, shambling footsteps coming slowly up the staircase, and passing my door on her way to the attics above; they sounded louder than usual, and I turned my head round involuntarily. A thin, fine streak of light, no thicker than a thread, shone for an instant in the dark corner of the wall close by the door-post, but it died away almost before I saw it. My heart stood still for a moment, and then beat like a hammer. I stole very softly to the door and discovered that the bolt had slipped beyond the hoop of the lock; probably in the sharp bang with which it had been closed. The door was open for me!

CHAPTER THE SECOND

TO SOUTHAMPTON

There was not a moment to be lost. When the servant came downstairs again from her room in the attics, she would be sure to call for the tea-tray, in order to save herself another journey; how long she would be up-stairs was quite uncertain. If she was gone to "clean" herself, as she called it, the process might be a very long one, and a good hour might be at my disposal; but I could not count upon that. In the drawing-room below sat my jailer and enemy, who might take a whim into her head, and come up to see her prisoner at any instant. It was necessary to be very quick, very decisive, and very silent.

I had been on the alert for such a chance ever since my imprisonment began. My seal-skin hat and jacket lay ready to my hand in a drawer; but I could find no gloves; I could not wait for gloves. Already there were ominous sounds overhead, as if the servant had dispatched her brief business there, and was about to come down. I had not time to put on thicker boots; and it was perhaps essential to the success of my flight to steal down the stairs in the soft, velvet slippers I was wearing. I stepped as lightly as I could—lightly but very swiftly, for the servant was at the top of the upper flight, while I had two to descend. I crept past the drawing-room door. The heavy house-door opened with a grating of the hinges; but I stood outside it, in the shelter of the portico; free, but with the rain and wind of a stormy night in October beating against me, and with no light save the glimmer of the feeble street-lamps flickering across the wet pavement.

I knew very well that my escape was almost hopeless, for the success of it depended very much upon which road of the three lying before me I should happen to take. I had no idea of the direction of any one of them, for I had never been out of the house since the night I was brought to it. The strong, quick running of the servant, and the passionate fury of the woman, would overtake me if we were to have a long race; and if they overtook me they would force me back. I had no right to seek freedom in this wild way, yet it was the only way. Even while I hesitated in the portico of the house that ought to have been my home, I heard the shrill scream of the girl within when she found my door open, and my room empty. If I did not decide instantaneously, and decide aright, it would have been better for me never to have tried this chance of escape.

But I did not linger another moment. I could almost believe an angel took me by the hand and led me. I darted straight across the muddy road, getting my thin slippers wet through at once, ran for a few yards, and then turned sharply round a corner into a street at the end of which I saw the cheery light of shop-windows, all in a glow in spite of the rain. On I fled breathlessly, unhindered by any passer-by, for the rain was still falling, though more lightly. As I drew nearer to the shop-windows, an omnibus-driver, seeing me run toward him, pulled up his horses in expectation of a passenger. The conductor shouted some name which I did not hear, but I sprang in, caring very little where it might carry me, so that I could get quickly enough and far enough out of the reach of my pursuers. There had been no time to lose, and none was lost. The omnibus drove on again quickly, and no trace left of me.

I sat quite still in the farthest corner of the omnibus, hardly able to recover my breath after my rapid running. I was a little frightened at the notice the two or three other passengers appeared to take of me, and I did my best to seem calm and collected. My ungloved hands gave me some trouble, and I hid them as well as I could in the folds of my dress; for there was something remarkable about the want of gloves in any one as well dressed as I was. But nobody spoke to me, and one after another they left the omnibus, and fresh persons took their places, who did not know where I had got in. I did not stir, for I determined to go as far as I could in this conveyance. But all the while I was wondering what I should do with myself, and where I could go, when it readied its destination.

There was one trifling difficulty immediately ahead of me. When the omnibus stopped I should have no small change for paying my fare. There was an Australian sovereign fastened to my watch-chain which I could take off, but it would be difficult to detach it while we were jolting on. Besides, I dreaded to attract attention to myself. Yet what else could I do?

Before I had settled this question, which occupied me so fully that I forgot other and more serious difficulties, the omnibus drove into a station-yard, and every passenger, inside and out, prepared to alight. I lingered till the last, and sat still till I had unfastened my gold-piece. The wind drove across the open space in a strong gust as I stepped down upon the pavement. A man had just descended from the roof, and was paying the conductor: a tall, burly man, wearing a thick water-proof coat, and a seaman's hat of oil-skin, with a long flap lying over the back of his neck. His face was brown and weather-beaten, but he had kindly-looking eyes, which glanced at me as I stood waiting to pay my fare.

"Going down to Southampton?" said the conductor to him.

"Ay, and beyond Southampton," he answered.

"You'll have a rough night of it," said the conductor—"Sixpence, if you please, miss."

I offered him my Australian sovereign, which he turned over curiously, asking me if I had no smaller change. He grumbled when I answered no, and the stranger, who had not passed on, but was listening to what was said, turned pleasantly to me.

"You have no change, mam'zelle?" he asked, speaking rather slowly, as if English was not his ordinary speech. "Very well! are you going to Southampton?"

"Yes, by the next train," I answered, deciding upon that course without hesitation.

"So am I, mam'zelle," he said, raising his hand to his oil-skin cap; "I will pay this sixpence, and you can give it me again, when you buy your ticket in the office."

I smiled quickly, gladly; and he smiled back upon me, but gravely, as if his face was not used to a smile. I passed on into the station, where a train was standing, and people hurrying about the platform, choosing their carriages. At the ticket-office they changed my Australian gold-piece without a word; and I sought out my seaman friend to return the sixpence he had paid to me. He had done me a greater kindness than he could ever know, and I thanked him heartily. His honest, deep-set, blue eyes glistened under their shaggy eyebrows as they looked down upon me.

"Can I do nothing more for you, mam'zelle?" he asked. "Shall I see after your luggage?"

"Oh! that will be all right, thank you," I replied, "but is this the train for Southampton, and how soon will it start?"

I was watching anxiously the stream of people going to and fro, lest I should see some person who knew me. Yet who was there in London who could know me?

"It will be off in five minutes," answered the seaman. "Shall I look out a carriage for you?"

He was somewhat careful in making his selection; finally he put me into a compartment where there were only two ladies, and he stood in front of the door, but with his back turned toward it, until the train was about to start. Then he touched his hat again with a gesture of farewell, and ran away to a second-class carriage.

I sighed with satisfaction as the train rushed swiftly through the dimly-lighted suburbs of London, and entered upon the open country. A wan, watery line of light lay under the brooding clouds in the west, tinged with a lurid hue; and all the great field of sky stretching above the level landscape was overcast with storm-wrack, fleeing swiftly before the wind. At times the train seemed to shake with the Wast, when it was passing over any embankment more than ordinarily exposed; but it sped across the country almost as rapidly as the clouds across the sky. No one in the carriage spoke. Then came over me that weird feeling familiar to all travellers, that one has been doomed to travel thus through many years, and has not half accomplished the time. I felt as if I had been fleeing from my home, and those who should have been my friends, for a long and weary while; yet it was scarcely an hour since I had made my escape.

In about two hours or more—but exactly what time I did not know, for my watch had stopped—my fellow-passengers, who had scarcely condescended to glance at me, alighted at a large, half-deserted station, where only a few lamps were burning. Through the window I could see that very few other persons were leaving the train, and I concluded we had not yet reached the terminus. A porter came up to me as I leaned my head through the window.

"Going on, miss?" he asked.

"Oh, yes!" I answered, shrinking back into my corner-seat. He remained upon the step, with his arm over the window-frame, while the train moved on at a slackened pace for a few minutes, and then pulled up, but at no station. Before me lay a dim, dark, indistinct scene, with little specks of light twinkling here and there in the night, but whether on sea or shore I could not tell. Immediately opposite the train stood the black hulls and masts and funnels of two steamers, with a glimmer of lanterns on their decks, and up and down their shrouds. The porter opened the door for me.

"You've only to go on board, miss," he said, "your luggage will be seen to all right." And he hurried away to open the doors of the other carriages.

I stood still, utterly bewildered, for a minute or two, with the wind tossing my hair about, and the rain beating in sharp, stinging drops like hailstones upon my face and hands. It must have been close upon midnight, and there was no light but the dim, glow-worm glimmer of the lanterns on deck. Every one was hurrying past me. I began almost to repent of the desperate step I had taken; but I had learned already that there is no possibility of retracing one's steps. At the gangways of the two vessels there were men shouting hoarsely. "This way for the Channel Islands!" "This way for Havre and Paris!" To which boat should I trust myself and my fate? There was nothing to guide me. Yet once more that night the moment had come when I was compelled to make a prompt, decisive, urgent choice. It was almost a question of life and death to me: a leap in the dark that must be taken. My great terror was lest my place of refuge should be discovered, and I be forced back again. Where was I to go? To Paris, or to the Channel Islands?

CHAPTER THE THIRD

A ROUGH NIGHT AT SEA

A mere accident decided it. Near the fore-part of the train I saw the broad, tall figure of my new friend, the seaman, making his way across to the boat for the Channel Islands; and almost involuntarily I made up my mind to go on board the same steamer, for I had an instinctive feeling that he would prove a real friend, if I had need of one. He did not see me following; no doubt he supposed I had left the train at Southampton, having only taken my ticket so far; though how I had missed Southampton I could not tell. The deck was wet and slippery, and the confusion upon it was very great. I was too much at home upon a steamer to need any directions; and I went down immediately into the ladies' cabin, which was almost empty, and chose a berth for myself in the darkest corner. It was not far from the door, and presently two other ladies came down, with a gentleman and the captain, and held an anxious parley close to me. I listened absently and mechanically, as indifferent to the subject as if it could be of no consequence to me.

"Is there any danger?" asked one of the ladies.

"Well, I cannot say positively there will be no danger," answered the captain; "there's not danger enough to keep me and the crew in port; but it will be a very dirty night in the Channel. If there's no actual necessity for crossing to-night I should advise you to wait, and see how it will be to-morrow. Of course we shall use extra caution, and all that sort of thing. No; I cannot say I expect any great danger."

"But it will be awfully rough?" said the gentleman.

The captain answered only by a sound between a groan and a whistle, as if he could not trust himself to think of words that would describe the roughness. There could be no doubt of his meaning. The ladies hastily determined to drive back to their hotel, and gathered up their small packages and wrappings quickly. I fancied they were regarding me somewhat curiously, but I kept my face away from them carefully. They could only see my seal-skin jacket and hat, and my rough hair; and they did not speak to me.

"You are going to venture, miss?" said the captain, stepping into the cabin as the ladies retreated up the steps.

"Oh, yes," I answered. "I am obliged to go, and I am not in the least afraid."

"You needn't be," he replied, in a hearty voice. "We shall do our best, for our own sakes, and you would be our first care if there was any mishap. Women and children first always. I will send the stewardess to you; she goes, of course."

I sat down on one of the couches, listening for a few minutes to the noises about me. The masts were groaning, and the planks creaking under the heavy tramp of the sailors, as they got ready to start, with shrill cries to one another. Then the steam-engine began to throb like a pulse through all the vessel from stem to stern. Presently the stewardess came down, and recommended me to lie down in my berth at once, which I did very obediently, but silently, for I did not wish to enter into conversation with the woman, who seemed inclined to be talkative. She covered me up well with several blankets, and there I lay with my face turned from the light of the swinging lamp, and scarcely moved hand or foot throughout the dismal and stormy night.

For it was very stormy and dismal as soon as we were out of Southampton waters, and in the rush and swirl of the Channel. I did not fall asleep for an instant. I do not suppose I should have slept had the Channel been, as it is sometimes, smooth as a mill-pond, and there had been no clamorous hissing and booming of waves against the frail planks, which I could touch with my hand. I could see nothing of the storm, but I could hear it: and the boat seemed tossed, like a mere cockle-shell, to and fro upon the rough sea. It did not alarm me so much as it distracted my thoughts and kept them from dwelling upon possibilities far more perilous to me than the danger of death by shipwreck. A short suffering such a death would be.

My escape and flight had been so unexpected, so unhoped for, that it had bewildered me, and it was almost a pleasure to lie still and listen to the din and uproar of the sea and the swoop of the wind rushing down upon it. Was I myself or no? Was this nothing more than a very coherent, very vivid dream, from which I should awake by-and-by to find myself a prisoner still, a creature as wretched and friendless as any that the streets of London contained? My flight had been too extraordinary a success, so far, for my mind to be able to dwell upon it calmly.

I watched the dawn break through a little port-hole opening upon my berth, which had been washed and beaten by the water all the night long. The level light shone across the troubled and leaden-colored surface of the sea, which seemed to grow a little quieter under its touch. I had fancied during the night that the waves were running mountains high; but now I could see them, they only rolled to and fro in round, swelling hillocks, dull green against the eastern sky, with deep, sullen troughs of a livid purple between them. But the fury of the storm had spent itself, that was evident, and the steamer was making way steadily now.

The stewardess had gone away early in the night, being frightened to death, she said, to seek more genial companionship than mine. So I was alone, with the blending light of the early dawn and that of the lamp burning feebly from the ceiling. I sat up in my berth and cautiously unstitched the lining in the breast of my jacket. Here, months ago, when I first began to foresee this emergency, and while I was still allowed the use of my money, I had concealed one by one a few five-pound notes of the Bank of England. I counted them over, eight of them; forty pounds in all, my sole fortune, my only means of living. True, I had besides these a diamond ring, presented to me under circumstances which made it of no value to me, except for its worth in money, and a watch and chain given to me years ago by my father. A jeweller had told me that the ring was worth sixty pounds, and the watch and chain forty; but how difficult and dangerous it would be for me to sell either of them! Practically my means were limited to the eight bank-notes of five pounds each. I kept out one for the payment of my passage, and then replaced the rest, and carefully pinned them into the unstitched lining.

Then I began to wonder what my destination was. I knew nothing whatever of the Channel Islands, except the names which I had learned at school—Jersey, Guernsey, Alderney, and Sark. I repeated these over and over again to myself; but which of them we were bound for, or if we were about to call at each one of them, I did not know. I should have been more at home had I gone to Paris.

As the light grew I became restless, and at last I left my berth and ventured to climb the cabin-steps. The fresh air smote upon me almost painfully. There was no rain falling, and the wind had been lulling since the dawn. The sea itself was growing brighter, and glittered here and there in spots where the sunlight fell upon it. All the sailors looked beaten and worn out with the night's toil, and the few passengers who had braved the passage, and were now well enough to come on deck, were weary and sallow-looking. There was still no land in sight, for the clouds hung low on the horizon, and overhead the sky was often overcast and gloomy. It was so cold that, in spite of my warm mantle, I shivered from head to foot.

But I could not bear to go back to the close, ill-smelling cabin, which had been shut up all night. I stayed on deck in the biting wind, leaning over the wet bulwarks and gazing across the desolate sea till my spirits sank like lead. The reaction upon the violent strain on my nerves was coming, and I had no power to resist its influence. I could feel the tears rolling down my cheeks and falling on my hands without caring to wipe them away; the more so as there was no one to see them. What did my tears signify to any one? I was cold, and hungry, and miserable. How lonely I was! how poor! with neither a home nor a friend in the world!—a mere castaway upon the waves of this troublous life!

"Mam'zelle is a brave sailor," said a voice behind me, which I recognized as my seaman of the night before, whom I had well-nigh forgotten; "but the storm is over now, and we shall be in port only an hour or two behind time."

"What port shall we reach?" I asked, not caring to turn round lest he should see my wet eyes and cheeks.

"St. Peter-Port," he answered. "Mam'zelle, then, does not know our islands?"

"No," I said. "Where is St. Peter-Port?"

"In Guernsey," he replied. "Is mam'zelle going to Guernsey or Jersey? Jersey is about two hours' sail from Guernsey. If you were going to land at St. Peter-Port, I might be of some service to you."

I turned round then, and looked at him steadily. His voice was a very pleasant one, full of tones that went straight to my heart and filled me with confidence. His face did not give the lie to it, or cause me any disappointment. He was no gentleman, that was plain; his face was bronzed and weather-beaten, as if he often encountered rough weather. But his deep-set eyes had a steadfast, quiet power in them, and his mouth, although it was almost hidden by hair, had a pleasant curve about it. I could not guess how old he was; he looked a middle-aged man to me. His great, rough hands, which had never worn gloves, were stained and hard with labor; and he had evidently been taking a share in the toil of the night, for his close-fitting, woven blue jacket was wet through, and his hair was damp and rough with the wind and rain. He raised his cap as my eyes looked straight into his, and a faint smile flitted across his grave face.

"I want," I said, suddenly, "to find a place where I can live very cheaply. I have not much money, and I must make it last a long time. I do not mind how quiet the place, or how poor; the quieter the better for me. Can you tell me of such a place?"

"You would want a place fit for a lady?" he said, in a half-questioning tone, and with a glance at my silk dress.

"No," I answered, eagerly. "I mean such a cottage as you would live in. I would do all my own work, for I am very poor, and I do not know yet how I can get my living. I must be very careful of my money till I find out what I can do. What sort of a place do you and your wife live in?"

His face was clouded a little, I thought; and he did not answer me till after a short silence.

"My poor little wife is dead," he answered, "and I do not live in Guernsey or Jersey. We live in Sark, my mother and I. I am a fisherman, but I have also a little farm, for with us the land goes from the father to the eldest son, and I was the eldest. It is true we have one room to spare, which might do for mam'zelle; but the island is far away, and very triste. Jersey is gay, and so is Guernsey, but in the winter Sark is too mournful."

"It will be just the place I want," I said, eagerly; "it would suit me exactly. Can you let me go there at once? Will you take me with you?"

"Mam'zelle," he replied, smiling, "the room must be made ready for you, and I must speak to my mother. Besides, Sark is six miles from Guernsey, and to-day the passage would be too rough for you. If God sends us fair weather I will come back to St. Peter-Port for you in three days. My name is Tardif. You can ask the people in Peter-Port what sort of a man Tardif of the Havre Gosselin is."

"I do not want any one to tell me what sort of a man you are," I said, holding out my hand, red and cold with the keen air. He took it into his large, rough palm, looking down upon me with an air of friendly protection.

"What is your name, mam'zelle?" he inquired.

"Oh! my name is Olivia," I said; then I stopped abruptly, for there flashed across me the necessity for concealing it. Tardif did not seem to notice my embarrassment.

"There are some Olliviers in St. Peter-Port," he said. "Is mam'zelle of the same family? But no, that is not probable."

"I have no relations," I answered, "not even in England. I have very few friends, and they are all far away in Australia. I was born there, and lived there till I was seventeen."'

The tears sprang to my eyes again, and my new friend saw them, but said nothing. He moved off at once to the far end of the dock, to help one of the crew in some heavy piece of work. He did not come hack until the rain began to return—a fine, drizzling rain, which came in scuds across the sea.

"Mam'zelle," he said, "you ought to go below; and I will tell you when we are in sight of Guernsey."

I went below, inexpressibly more satisfied and comforted. What it was in this man that won my complete, unquestioning confidence, I did not know; but his very presence, and the sight of his good, trustworthy face, gave me a sense of security such as I have never felt before or since. Surely God had sent him to me in my great extremity.

CHAPTER THE FOURTH

A SAFE HAVEN

We were two hours after time at St. Peter-Port; and then all was hurry and confusion, for goods and passengers had to be landed and embarked for Jersey. Tardif, who was afraid of losing the cutter which would convey him to Sark, had only time to give me the address of a person with whom I could lodge until he came to fetch me to his island, and then he hastened away to a distant part of the quay. I was not sorry that he should miss finding out that I had no luggage of any kind with me.

I was busy enough during the next three days, for I had every thing to buy. The widow with whom I was lodging came to the conclusion that I had lost all my luggage, and I did not try to remove the false impression. Through her assistance I was able to procure all I required, without exciting more notice and curiosity. My purchases, though they were as simple and cheap as I could make them, drew largely upon my small store of money, and as I saw it dwindling away, while I grudged every shilling I was obliged to part with, my spirits sank lower and lower. I had never known the dread of being short of money, and the new experience was, perhaps, the more terrible to me. There was no chance of disposing of the costly dress in which I had journeyed, without arousing too much attention and running too great a risk. I stayed in-doors as much as possible, and, as the weather continued cold and gloomy, I did not meet many persons when I ventured out into the narrow, foreign-looking streets of the town.

But on the third day, when I looked out from my window, I saw that the sky had cleared, and the sun was shining joyously. It was one of those lovely days which come as a lull sometimes in the midst of the equinoctial gales, as if they were weary of the havoc they had made, and were resting with folded wings. For the first time I saw the little island of Sark lying against the eastern sky. The whole length of it was visible, from north to south, with the waves beating against its headlands, and a fringe of silvery foam girdling it. The sky was of a pale blue, as though the rains had washed it as well as the earth, and a few filmy clouds were still lingering about it. The sea beneath was a deeper blue, with streaks almost like a hoar frost upon it, with here and there tints of green, like that of the sky at sunset. A boat with three white sails, which were reflected in the water, was tacking about to enter the harbor, and a second, with amber sails, was a little way behind, but following quickly in its wake. I watched them for a long time. Was either of them Tardif's boat?

That question was answered in about two hours' time by Tardif's appearance at the house. He lifted my little box on to his broad shoulders, and marched away with it, trying vainly to reduce his long strides into steps that would suit me, as I walked beside him. I felt overjoyed that he was come. So long as I was in Guernsey, when every morning I could see the arrival of the packet that had brought me, I could not shake off the fear that it was bringing some one in pursuit of me; but in Sark that would be all different. Besides, I felt instinctively that this man would protect me, and take my part to the very utmost, should any circumstances arise that compelled me to appeal to him and trust him with my secret. I knew nothing of him, but his face was stamped with God's seal of trustworthiness, if ever a human face was.

A second man was in the boat when we reached it, and it looked well laden. Tardif made a comfortable seat for me amid the packages, and then the sails were unfurled, and we were off quickly out of the harbor and on the open sea.

A low, westerly wind was blowing, and fell upon the sails with a strong and equal pressure. We rode before it rapidly, skimming over the low, crested waves almost without a motion. Never before had I felt so perfectly secure upon the water. Now I could breathe freely, with the sense of assured safety growing stronger every moment as the coast of Guernsey receded on the horizon, and the rocky little island grew nearer. As we approached it no landing-place was to be seen, no beach or strand. An iron-bound coast of sharp and rugged crags confronted us, which it seemed impossible to scale. At last we cast anchor at the foot of a great cliff, rising sheer out of the sea, where a ladder hung down the face of the rock for a few feet. A wilder or lonelier place I had never seen. Nobody could pursue and surprise me here.

The boatman who was with us climbed up the ladder, and, kneeling down, stretched out his hand to help me, while Tardif stood waiting to hold me steadily on the damp and slippery rungs. For a moment I hesitated, and looked round at the crags, and the tossing, restless sea.

"I could carry you through the water, mam'zelle," said Tardif, pointing to a hand's breadth of shingle lying between the rocks, "but you will get wet. It will be better for you to mount up here."

I fastened both of my hands tightly round one of the upper rungs, before lifting my feet from the unsteady prow of the boat. But the ladder once climbed, the rest of the ascent was easy. I walked on up a zigzag path, cut in the face of the cliff, until I gained the summit, and sat down to wait for Tardif and his comrade. I could not have fled to a securer hiding-place. So long as my money held out, I might live as peacefully and safely as any fugitive had ever lived.

For a little while I sat looking out at the wild and beautiful scene before me, which no words can tell and no fancy picture to those who have never seen it. The white foam of the waves was so near, that I could see the rainbow colors playing through the bubbles as the sun shone on them. Below the clear water lay a girdle of sunken rocks, pointed as needles, and with edges as sharp as swords, about which the waves fretted ceaselessly, drawing silvery lines about their notched and dented ridges. The cliffs ran up precipitously from the sea, carved grotesquely over their whole surface into strange and fantastic shapes; while the golden and gray lichens embroidered them richly, and bright sea-flowers, and stray tufts of grass, lent them the most vivid and gorgeous hues. Beyond the channel, against the clear western sky, lay the island of Guernsey, rising like a purple mountain out of the opal sea, which lay like a lake between us, sparkling and changing every minute under the light of the afternoon sun.

But there was scarcely time for the exquisite beauty of this scene to sink deeply into my heart just then. Before long I heard the tramp of Tardif and his comrade following me; their heavy tread sent down the loose stones on the path plunging into the sea. They were both laden with part of the boat's cargo. They stopped to rest for a minute or two at the spot where I had sat down, and the other boatman began talking earnestly to Tardif in his patois, of which I did not understand a word. Tardif's face was very grave and sad, indescribably so; and, before he turned to me and spoke, I knew it was some sorrowful catastrophe he had to tell.

"You see how smooth it is, mam'zelle," he said—"how clear and beautiful—down below us, where the waves are at play like little white children? I love them, but they are cruel and treacherous. While I was away there was an accident down yonder, just beyond these rocks. Our doctor, and two gentlemen, and a sailor went out from our little bay below, and shortly after there came on a thick darkness, with heavy rain, and they were all lost, every one of them! Poor Renouf! he was a good friend of mine. And our doctor, too! If I had been here, maybe I might have persuaded them not to brave it."

It was a sad story to hear, yet just then I did not pay much attention to it. I was too much engrossed in my own difficulties and trouble. So far as my experience goes, I believe the heart is more open to other people's sorrows when it is free from burdens of its own. I was glad when Tardif took up his load again and turned his back upon the sea.

CHAPTER THE FIFTH

WILL IT DO?

Tardif walked on before me to a low, thatched cottage, standing at the back of a small farm-yard. There was no other dwelling in sight, and even the sea was not visible from it. It was sheltered by the steep slope of a hill rising behind it, and looked upon another slope covered with gorse-bushes; a very deep and narrow ravine ran down from it to the hand-breadth of shingle which I had seen from the boat. A more solitary place I could not have imagined; no sign of human life, or its neighborhood, betrayed itself; overhead was a vast dome of sky, with a few white-winged sea-gulls flitting across it, and uttering their low, wailing cry. The roof of sky and the two round outlines of the little hills, and the deep, dark ravine, the end of which was unseen, formed the whole of the view before me.

I felt chilled a little as I followed Tardif down into the dell. He glanced back, with grave, searching eyes, scanning my face carefully. I tried to smile, with a very faint, wan smile, I suppose, for the lightness had fled from my spirits, and my heart was heavy enough, God knows.

"Will it not do, mam'zelle?" he asked, anxiously, and with his slow, solemn utterance; "it is not a place that will do for a young lady like you, is it? I should have counselled you to go on to Jersey, where there is more life and gayety; it is my home, but for you it will be nothing but a dull prison."

"No, no!" I answered, as the recollection of the prison I had fled from flashed across me; "it is a very pretty place and very safe; by-and-by I shall like it as much as you do, Tardif."

The house was a low, picturesque building, with thick walls of stone and a thatched roof, which had two little dormer-windows in it; but at the most sheltered end, farthest from the ravine that led down to the sea, there had been built a small, square room of brick-work. As we entered the fold-yard, Tardif pointed this room out to me as mine.

"I built it," he said, softly, "for my poor little wife; I brought the bricks over from Guernsey in my own boat, and laid nearly every one of them with my own hands; she died in it, mam'zelle. Please God, you will be both happy and safe there!"

We stepped directly from the stone causeway of the yard into the farm-house kitchen—the only sitting-room in the house except my own. It was exquisitely clean, with that spotless and scrupulous cleanliness which appears impossible in houses where there are carpets and curtains, and papered walls. An old woman, very little and bent, and dressed in an odd and ugly costume, met us at the door, dropping a courtesy to me, and looking at me with dim, watery eyes. I was about to speak to her, when Tardif bent down his head, and put his mouth to her ear, shouting to her with a loud voice, but in their peculiar jargon, of which I could not make out a single word.

"My poor mother is deaf," he said to me, "very deaf; neither can she speak English. Most of the young people in Sark can talk in English a little, but she is old and too deaf to learn. She has only once been off the island."

I looked at her, wondering for a moment what she could have to think of, but, with an intelligible gesture of welcome, she beckoned me into my own room. The aspect of it was somewhat dreary; the walls were of bare plaster, but dazzlingly white, with one little black silhouette of a woman's head hanging in a common black frame over the low, open hearth, on which a fire of seaweed was smouldering, with a quantity of gray ashes round the small centre of smoking embers. There was a little round table, uncovered, but as white as snow, and two chairs, one of them an arm-chair, and furnished with cushions. A four-post bedstead, with curtains of blue and white check, occupied the larger portion of the floor.

It was not a luxurious apartment; and for an instant I could hardly realize the fact that it was to be my home for an indefinite period. Some efforts had evidently been made to give it a look of welcome, homely as it was. A pretty china tea cup and saucer, with a plate or two to match, were set out on the deal table, and the cushioned arm-chair had been drawn forward to the hearth. I sat down in it, and buried my face in my hands, thinking, till Tardif knocked at the door, and carried in my trunk.

"Will it do, mam'zelle?" he asked, "will it do?"

"It will do very nicely, Tardif," I answered; "but how ever am I to talk to your mother if she does not know English?"

"Mam'zelle," he said, as he uncorded my trunk, "you must order me as you would a servant. Through the winter I shall always be at hand; and you will soon be used to us and our ways, and we shall be used to you and your ways. I will do my best for you, mam'zelle; trust me, I will study to do my best, and make you very happy here. I will be ready to take you away whenever you desire to go. Look upon me as your hired servant."

He waited upon me all the evening, but with a quick attention to my wants, which I had never met with in any hired servant. It was not unfamiliar to me, for in my own country I had often been served only by men; and especially during my girlhood, when I had lived far away in the country, upon my father's sheep-walk. I knew it was Tardif who fried the fish which came in with my tea; and, when the night closed in, it was he who trimmed the oil-lamp and brought it in, and drew the check curtains across the low casement, as if there were prying eyes to see me on the opposite bank. Then a deep, deep stillness crept over the solitary place—a stillness strangely deeper than that even of the daytime. The wail of the sea-gulls died away, and the few busy cries of the farm-yard ceased; the only sound that broke the silence was a muffled, hollow boom which came up the ravine from the sea.

Before nine o'clock Tardif and his mother had gone up-stairs to their rooms in the thatch; and I lay wearied but sleepless in my bed, listening to these dull, faint, ceaseless murmurs, as a child listens to the sound of the sea in a shell. Was it possible that it was I, myself, the Olivia who had been so loved and cherished in her girlhood, and so hated and tortured in later years, who was come to live under a fisherman's roof, in an island, the name of which I barely knew four days ago?

I fell asleep at last, yet I awoke early; but not so early that the other inmates of the cottage were not up, and about their day's work. It was my wish to wait upon myself, and so diminish the cost of living with these secluded people; but I found it was not to be so; Tardif waited upon me assiduously, as well as his deaf mother. The old woman would not suffer me to do any work in my own room, but put me quietly upon one side when I began to make my bed. Fortunately I had plenty of sewing to employ myself in; for I had taken care not to waste my money by buying ready-made clothes. The equinoctial gales came on again fiercely the day after I had reached Sark; and I stitched away from morning till night, trying to fix my thoughts upon my mechanical work.

When the first week was over, Tardif's mother came to me at a time when her son was away out-of-doors, with a purse in her fingers, and by very plain signs made me understand that it was time I paid the first instalment of my debt to her for board and lodgings. I was anxious about my money. No agreement had been made between us as to what I was to pay. I laid a sovereign down upon the table, and the old woman looked at it carefully, and with a pleased expression; but she put it in her purse, and walked away with it, giving me no change. Not that I altogether expected any change; they provided me with every thing I needed, and waited upon me with very careful service; yet now I could calculate exactly how long I should be safe in this refuge, and the calculation gave me great uneasiness. In a few months I should find myself still in need of refuge, but without the means of paying for it. What would become of me then?

Very slowly the winter wore on. How shall I describe the peaceful monotony, the dull, lonely safety of those dark days and long nights? I had been violently tossed from a life of extreme trouble and peril into a profound, unbroken, sleepy security. At first the sudden change stupefied me; but after a while there came over me an uneasy restlessness, a longing to get away from the silence and solitude, even if it were into insecurity and danger. I began to wonder how the world beyond the little island was going on. No news reached us from without. Sometimes for weeks together it was impossible for an open boat to cross over to Guernsey; even when a cutter accomplished its voyage out and in, no letters could arrive for me. The season was so far advanced when I went to Sark, that those visitors who had been spending a portion of the summer there had already taken their departure, leaving the islanders to themselves.

They were sufficient for themselves; they and their own affairs formed the world. Tardif would bring home almost daily little scraps of news about the other families scattered about Sark; but of the greater affairs of life in other countries he could tell me nothing.

Yet why should I call these greater affairs? Each to himself is the centre of the world. It was a more important thing to me that I was safe, than that the freedom of England itself should be secure.

CHAPTER THE SIXTH

TOO MUCH ALONE

Yet looking back upon that time, now it is past, and has "rounded itself into that perfect star I saw not when I dwelt therein," it would be untrue to represent myself as in any way unhappy. At times I wished earnestly that I had been born among these people, and could live forever among them.

By degrees I discovered that Tardif led a somewhat solitary life himself, even in this solitary island, with its scanty population. There was an ugly church standing in as central and prominent a situation as possible, but Tardif and his mother did not frequent it. They belonged to a little knot of dissenters, who met for worship in a small room, when Tardif generally took the lead. For this reason a sort of coldness existed between him and the larger portion of his fellow-islanders. But there was a second and more important cause for a slight estrangement. He had married an Englishwoman many years ago, much to the astonishment and disappointment of his neighbors; and since her death he had held himself aloof from all the good women who would have been glad enough to undertake the task of consoling him for her loss. Tardif, therefore, was left very much to himself in his isolated cottage, and his mother's deafness caused her also to be no very great favorite with any of the gossips of the island. It was so difficult to make her understand any thing that could not be expressed by signs, that no one except her son attempted to tell her the small topics of the day.

All this told upon me, and my standing among them. At first I met a few curious glances as I roamed about the island; but my dress was as poor and plain as any of theirs, and I suppose there was nothing in my appearance, setting aside my dress, which could attract them. I learned afterward that Tardif had told those who asked him that my name was Ollivier, and they jumped to the conclusion that I belonged to a family of that name in Guernsey; this shielded me from the curiosity that might otherwise have been troublesome and dangerous. I was nobody but a poor young woman from Guernsey, who was lodging in the spare room of Tardif's cottage.

I set myself to grow used to their mode of life, and if possible to become so useful to them that, when my money was all spent, they might be willing to keep me with them; for I shrank from the thought of the time when I must be thrust out of this nest, lonely and silent as it was. As the long, dismal nights of winter set in, with the wind sweeping across the island for several days together with a dreary, monotonous moan which never ceased, I generally sat by their fire, for I had nobody but Tardif to talk to; and now and then there arose an urgent need within me to listen to some friendly voice, and to hear my own speaking in reply. There were only two books in the house, the Bible and the "Pilgrim's Progress," both of them in French; and I had not learned French beyond the few phrases necessary for travelling. But Tardif began to teach me that, and also to mend fishing-nets, which I persevered in, though the twine cut my fingers. Could I by any means make myself useful to them?

As the spring came on, half my dullness vanished. Sark was more beautiful in its cliff scenery than any thing I had ever seen, or could have imagined. Why cannot I describe it to you? I have but to close my eyes, and my memory paints it for me in my brain, with its innumerable islets engirdling it, as if to ward off its busy, indefatigable enemy, the sea. The long, sunken reefs, lying below the water at high tide, but at the ebb stretching like fortifications about it, as if to make of it a sure stronghold in the sea. The strange architecture and carving of the rocks, with faces and crowned heads but half obliterated upon them; the lofty arches, with columns of fretwork bearing them; the pinnacles, and sharp spires; the fallen masses heaped against the base of the cliffs, covered with seaweed, and worn out of all form, yet looking like the fragments of some great temple, with its treasures of sculpture; and about them all the clear, lucid water swelling and tossing, throwing over them sparkling sheets of foam. And the brilliant tone of the golden and saffron lichens, and the delicate tint of the gray and silvery ones, stealing about the bosses and angles and curves of the rocks, as if the rain and the wind and the frost had spent their whole power there to produce artistic effects. I say my memory paints it again for me; but it is only a memory, a shadow that my mind sees; and how can I describe to you a shadow? When words are but phantoms themselves, how can I use them to set forth a phantom?

Whenever the grandeur of the cliffs had wearied me, as one grows weary sometimes of too long and too close a study of what is great, there was a little, enclosed, quiet graveyard that lay in the very lap of the island, where I could go for rest. It was a small patch of ground, a God's acre, shut in on every side by high hedge-rows, which hid every view from sight except that of the heavens brooding over it. Nothing was to be seen but the long mossy mounds above the dead, and the great, warm, sunny dome rising above them. Even the church was not there, for it was built in another spot, and had a few graves of its own scattered about it.

I was sitting there one evening in the early spring, after the sun had dipped below the line of the high hedge-row, though it was still shining in level rays through it. No sound had disturbed the deep silence for a long time, except the twittering of birds among the branches; for up here even the sea could not be heard when it was calm. I suppose my face was sad, as most human faces are apt to be when the spirit is busy in its citadel, and has left the outworks of the eyes and mouth to themselves. So I was sitting quiet, with my hands clasped about my knees, and my face bent down, when a grave, low voice at my side startled me back to consciousness. Tardif was standing beside me, and looking down upon me with a world of watchful anxiety in his deep eyes.

"You are sad, mam'zelle," he said; "too sad for one so young as you are."

"Oh! everybody is sad, Tardif," I answered; "there is a great deal of trouble for every one in this world. You are often very sad indeed."

"Ah! but I have a cause," he said. "Mam'zelle does not know that she is sitting on the grave of my little wife."

He knelt down beside it as he spoke, and laid his hand gently on the green turf. I would have risen, but he would not let me.

"No," he said, "sit still, mam'zelle. Yes, you would have loved her, poor little soul! She was an Englishwoman, like you, only not a lady; a pretty little English girl, so little I could carry her like a baby. None of my people took to her, and she was very lonely, like you again; and she pined and faded away, just quietly, never saying one word against them. No, no, mam'zelle, I like to see you here. This is a favorite place with you, and it gives me pleasure. I ask myself a hundred times a day, 'Is there any thing I can do to make my young lady happy? Tell me what I can do more than I have done."

"There is nothing, Tardif," I answered, "nothing whatever. If you see me sad sometimes, take no notice of it, for you can do no more for me than you are doing. As it is, you are almost the only friend, perhaps the only true friend, I have in the world."

"May God be true to me only as I am true to you!" he said, solemnly, while his dark skin flushed and his eyes kindled. I looked at him closely. A more honest face one could never see, and his keen blue eyes met my gaze steadfastly. Heavy-hearted as I was just then, I could not help but smile, and all his face brightened, as the sea at its dullest brightens suddenly tinder a stray gleam of sunshine. Without another word we both rose to our feet, and stood side by side for a minute, looking down on the little grave beneath us. I would have gladly changed places then with the lonely English girl, who had pined away in this remote island.

After that short, silent pause, we went slowly homeward along the quiet, almost solitary lanes. Twice we met a fisherman, with his creel and nets across his shoulders, who bade us good-night; but no one else crossed our path.

It was a profound monotony, a seclusion I should not have had courage to face wittingly. But I had been led into it, and I dared not quit it. How long was it to last?

CHAPTER THE SEVENTH

A FALSE STEP

A day came after the winter storms, early, in March, with all the strength and sweetness of spring in it; though there was sharpness enough in the air to make my veins tingle. The sun was shining with so much heat in it, that I might be out-of-doors all day under the shelter of the rocks, in the warm, southern nooks where the daisies were growing. The birds sang more blithely than they had ever done before; a lark overhead, flinging down his triumphant notes; a thrush whistling clearly in a hawthorn-bush hanging over the cliff; and the cry of the gulls flitting about the rocks; I could hear them all at the same moment, with the deep, quiet tone of the sea sounding below their gay music. Tardif was going out to fish, and I had helped him to pack his basket. From my niche in the rocks I could see him getting out of the harbor, and he had caught a glimpse of me, and stood up in his boat, bareheaded, bidding me good-by. I began to sing before he was quite out of hearing, for he paused upon his oars listening, and had given me a joyous shout, and waved his hat round his head, when he was sure it was I who was singing. Nothing could be plainer than that he had gone away more glad at heart than he had been all the winter, simply because he believed that I was growing lighter-hearted. I could not help laughing, yet being touched and softened at the thought of his pleasure. What a good fellow he was! I had proved him by this time, and knew him to be one of the truest, bravest, most unselfish men on God's earth. How good a thing it was that I had met with him that wild night last October, when I had fled like one fleeing from a bitter slavery! For a few minutes my thoughts hovered about that old, miserable, evil time; but I did not care to ponder over past troubles. It was easy to forget them to-day, and I would forget them. I plucked the daisies, and listened almost drowsily to the birds and the sea, and felt all through me the delicious light and heat of the sun. Now and then I lifted up my eyes, to watch Tardif tacking about on the water. There were several boats out, but I kept his in sight, by the help of a queer-shaped patch upon one of the sails. I wished lazily for a book, but I should not have read it if I had had one. I was taking into my heart the loveliness of the spring day.

By twelve o'clock I knew my dinner would be ready, and I had been out in the fresh air long enough to be quite ready for it. Old Mrs. Tardif would be looking out for me impatiently, that she might get the meal over, and the things cleared away, and order restored in her dwelling. So I quitted my warm nook with a feeling of regret, though I knew I could return to it in an hour.

But one can never return to any thing that is once left. When we look for it again, even though the place may remain, something has vanished from it which can never come back. I never returned to my spring-day upon the cliffs of Sark.

A little crumbling path led round the rock and along the edge of the ravine. I chose it because from it I could see all the fantastic shore, bending in a semicircle toward the isle of Breckhou, with tiny, untrodden bays, covered at this hour with only glittering ripples, and with all the soft and tender shadows of the headlands falling across them. I had but to look straight below me, and I could see long tresses of glossy seaweed floating under the surface of the sea. Both my head and my footing were steady, for I had grown accustomed to giddy heights and venturesome climbing. I walked on slowly, casting many a reluctant glance behind me at the calm waters, with the boats gliding to and fro among the islets. I was just giving my last look to them when the loose stones on the crumbling path gave way under my tread, and before I could recover my foothold I found myself slipping down the almost perpendicular face of the cliff, and vainly clutching at every bramble and tuft of grass growing in its clefts.

CHAPTER THE EIGHTH

AN ISLAND WITHOUT A DOCTOR

I had not time to feel any fear, for, almost before I could realize the fact that I was falling, I touched the ground. The point from which I had slipped was above the reach of the water, but I fell upon the shingly beach so heavily that I was hardly conscious for a few minutes. When I came to my senses again, I lay still for a little while, trying to make out where I was, and how I came there. I was stunned and bewildered. Underneath me were the smooth, round pebbles, which lie above the line of the tide on a shore covered with shingles. Above me rose a dark, frowning rock, the chilly shadow of which lay across me. Without lifting my head I could see the water on a level with me, but it did not look on a level; its bright crested waves seemed swelling upward to the sky, ready to pour over me and bury me beneath them. I was very faint, and sick, and giddy. The ground felt as if it were about to sink under me. My eyelids closed languidly when I did not keep them open by an effort; and my head ached, and my brain swam with confused fancies.

After some time, and with some difficulty, I comprehended what had happened to me, and recollected that it was already past mid-day, and Mrs. Tardif would be waiting for me. I attempted to stand up, but an acute pain in my foot compelled me to desist. I tried to turn myself upon the pebbles, and my left arm refused to help me. I could not check a sharp cry of suffering as my left hand fell back upon the stones on which I was lying. My fall had cost me something more than a few minutes' insensibility and an aching head. I had no more power to move than one who is bound hand and foot.

After a few vain efforts I lay quite still again, trying to deliberate as well as I could for the pain which racked me. I reckoned up, after many attempts in which first my memory failed me, and then my faculty of calculation, what the time of the high tide would be, and how soon Tardif would come home. As nearly as I could make out, it would be high water in about two hours. Tardif had set off at low water, as his boat had been anchored at the foot of the rock, where the ladder hung; but before starting he had said something about returning at high tide, and running up his boat on the beach of our little bay. If he did that, he must pass close by me. It was Saturday morning, and he was not in the habit of staying out late on Saturdays, that he might prepare for the services of the next day. I might count, then, upon the prospect of him running the boat into the bay, and finding me there in about two hours' time.

It took me a very long time to make out all this, for every now and then my brain seemed to lose its power for a while, and every thing whirled about me. Especially there was that awful sensation of sinking down, down through the pebbles into some chasm that was bottomless. I had never either felt pain or fainted before, and all this alarmed me.

Presently I began to listen to the rustle of the pebbles, as the rising tide flowed over them and fell back again, leaving them all ajar and grating against one another—strange, gurgling, jangling sound that seemed to have some meaning. It was very cold, and a creeping moisture was oozing up from the water. A vague wonder took hold of me as to whether I was really above the line of the tide, for, now the March tides were come, I did not know how high their flood was. But I thought of it without any active feeling of terror or pain. I was numbed in body and mind. The ceaseless chime of the waves, and the regularity of the rustling play of the pebbles, seemed to lull and soothe me, almost in spite of myself. Cold I was, and in sharp pain, but my mind had not energy enough either for fear or effort. What appeared to me most terrible was the sensation, coming back time after time, of sinking, sinking into the fancied chasm beneath me.

I remember also watching a spray of ivy, far above my head, swaying and waving about in the wind; and a little bird, darting here and there with a brisk flutter of its tiny wings, and a chirping note of satisfaction; and the cloud drifting in soft, small cloudlets across the sky. These things I saw, not as if they were real, but rather as if they were memories of things that had passed before my eyes many years before.

At last—whether years or hours only had gone by, I could not then have told you—I heard the regular and careful beat of oars upon the water, and presently the grating of a boat's keel upon the shingle, with the rattle of a chain cast out with the grapnel. I could not turn round or raise my head, but I was sure it was Tardif, and that he did not yet see me, for he was whistling softly to himself. I had never heard him whistle before.

"Tardif!" I cried, attempting to shout, but my voice sounded very weak in my own ears, and the other sounds about me seemed very loud. He went on with his unlading, half whistling and half humming his tune, as he landed the nets and creel on the beach.

"Tardif!" I called again, summoning all my strength, and raising my head an inch or two from the hard pebbles which had been its resting-place.

He paused then, and stood quite still, listening. I knew it, though I could not see him. I ran the fingers of my right hand through the loose pebbles about me, and his ear caught the slight noise. In a moment I heard his strong feet coming across them toward me.

"Mon Dieu! mam'zelle," he exclaimed, "what has happened to you?"

I tried to smile as his honest, brown face bent over me, full of alarm. It was so great a relief to see a face like his after that long, weary agony, for it had been agony to me, who did not know what bodily pain was like. But in trying to smile I felt my lips drawn, and my eyes blinded with tears.

"I've fallen down the cliff," I said, feebly, "and I am hurt."

"Mon Dieu!" he cried again. The strong man shook, and his hand trembled as he stooped down and laid it under my head to lift it up a little. His agitation touched me to the heart, even then, and I did my best to speak more calmly.

"Tardif," I whispered, "it is not very much, and I might have been killed. I think my foot is hurt, and I am quite sure my arm is broken."

Speaking made me feel giddy and faint again, so I said no more. He lifted me in his arms as easily and tenderly as a mother lifts up her child, and carried me gently, taking slow and measured strides up the steep slope which led homeward. I closed my eyes, glad to leave myself wholly in his charge, and to have nothing further to dread; yet moaning a little, involuntarily, whenever a fresh pang of pain shot through me. Then he would cry again, "Mon Dieu!" in a beseeching tone, and pause for an instant as if to give me rest. It seemed a long time before we reached the farm-yard gate, and he shouted, with a tremendous voice, to his mother to come and open it. Fortunately she was in sight, and came toward us quickly.

He carried me into the house, and laid me down on the lit de fouaille—a wooden frame forming a sort of couch, and filled with dried fern, which forms the principal piece of furniture in every farm-house kitchen in the Channel Islands. Then he cut away the boot from my swollen ankle, with a steady but careful touch, speaking now and then a word of encouragement, as if I were a child whom he was tending. His mother stood by, looking on helplessly and in bewilderment, for he had not had time to explain my accident to her.

But for my arm, which hung helplessly at my side, and gave me excruciating pain when he touched it, it was quite evident he could do nothing.

"Is there nobody who could set it?" I asked, striving very hard to keep calm.

"We have no doctor in Sark now," he answered. "There is no one but Mother Renouf. I will fetch her."

But when she came she declared herself unable to set a broken limb. They all three held a consultation over it in their own dialect; but I saw by the solemn shaking of their heads, and Tardif's troubled expression, that it was entirely beyond her skill to set it right. She would undertake my sprained ankle, for she was famous for the cure of sprains and bruises, but my arm was past her? The pain I was enduring bathed my face with perspiration, but very little could be done to alleviate it. Tardif's expression grew more and more distressed.

"Mam'zelle knows," he said, stooping down to speak the more softly to me, "there is no doctor nearer than Guernsey, and the night is not far off. What are we to do?"

"Never mind, Tardif," I answered, resolving to be brave; "let the women help me into bed, and perhaps I shall be able to sleep. We must wait till morning."

It was more easily said than done. The two old women did their best, but their touch was clumsy and their help slight, compared to Tardif's. I was thoroughly worn out before I was in bed. But it was a great deal to find myself there, safe and warm, instead of on the cold, hard pebbles on the beach. Mother Renouf put my arm to rest upon a pillow, and bathed and fomented my ankle till it felt much easier.

Never, never shall I forget that night. I could not sleep; but I suppose my mind wandered a little. Hundreds of times I felt myself down on the shore, lying helplessly, while great green waves curled themselves over, and fell just within reach of me, ready to swallow me up, yet always missing me. Then I was back again in my own home in Adelaide, on my father's sheep-farm, and he was still alive, and with no thought but how to make every thing bright and gladsome for me; and hundreds of times I saw the woman who was afterward to be my step-mother, stealing up to the door and trying to get in to him and me. Sometimes I caught myself sobbing aloud, and then Tardif's voice, whispering at the door to ask how mam'zelle was, brought me back to consciousness. Now and then I looked round, fancying I heard my mother's voice speaking to me, and I saw only the wrinkled, yellow face of his mother, nodding drowsily in her seat by the fire. Twice Tardif brought me a cup of tea, freshly made. I could not distinctly made out who he was, or where I was, but I tried to speak loudly enough for him to hear me thank him.

I was very thankful when the first gleam of daylight shone into my room. It seemed to bring clearness to my brain.

"Mam'zelle," said Tardif, coming to my side very early in his fisherman's dress, "I am going to fetch a doctor."

"But it is Sunday," I answered faintly. I knew that no boatman put out to sea willingly on a Sunday from Sark; and the last fatal accident, being on a Sunday, had deepened their reluctance.

"It will be right, mam'zelle," he answered, with glowing eyes. "I have no fear."

"Do not be long away, Tardif," I said, sobbing.

"Not one moment longer than I can help," he replied.

PART THE SECOND

CHAPTER THE FIRST

DR. MARTIN DOBRÉE

My name is Martin Dobrée. Martin or Doctor Martin I was called throughout Guernsey. It will be necessary to state a few particulars about my family and position, before I proceed with my part of this narrative.

My father was Dr. Dobrée. He belonged to one of the oldest families in the island—a family of distinguished pur sang; but our branch of it had been growing poorer instead of richer during the last three or four generations. We had been gravitating steadily downward.

My father lived ostensibly by his profession, but actually upon the income of my cousin, Julia Dobrée, who had been his ward from her childhood. The house we dwelt in, a pleasant one in the Grange, belonged to Julia; and fully half of the year's household expenses were defrayed by her. Our practice, which he and I shared between us, was not a large one, though for its extent it was lucrative enough. But there always is an immense number of medical men in Guernsey in proportion to its population, and the island is healthy. There was small chance for any of us to make a fortune.

Then how was it that I, a young man, still under thirty, was wasting my time, and skill, and professional training, by remaining there, a sort of half pensioner on my cousin's bounty? The thickest rope that holds a vessel, weighing scores of tons, safely to the pier-head is made up of strands so slight that almost a breath will break them.

First, then—and the strength of two-thirds of the strands lay there—was my mother. I could never remember the time when she had not been delicate and ailing, even when I was a rough school-boy at Elizabeth College. It was that infirmity of the body which occasionally betrays the wounds of a soul. I did not comprehend it while I was a boy; then it was headache only. As I grew older I discovered that it was heartache. The gnawing of a perpetual disappointment, worse than a sudden and violent calamity, had slowly eaten away the very foundation of healthy life. No hand could administer any medicine for this disease except mine, and, as soon as I was sure of that, I felt what my first duty was.

I knew where the blame of this lay, if any blame there were. I had found it out years ago by my mother's silence, her white cheeks, and her feeble tone of health. My father was never openly unkind or careless, but there was always visible in his manner a weariness of her, an utter disregard for her feelings. He continued to like young and pretty women, just as he had liked her because she was young and pretty. He remained at the very point he was at when they began their married life. There was nothing patently criminal in it, God forbid!—nothing to create an open and a grave scandal on our little island. But it told upon my mother; it was the one drop of water falling day by day. "A continual dropping in a very rainy day and a contentious woman are alike," says the book of Proverbs. My father's small infidelities were much the same to my mother. She was thrown altogether upon me for sympathy, and support, and love.

When I first fathomed this mystery, my heart rose in very undutiful bitterness against Dr. Dobrée; but by-and-by I found that it resulted less from a want of fidelity to her than from a radical infirmity in his temperament. It was almost as impossible for him to avoid or conceal his preference for younger and more attractive women, as for my mother to conquer the fretting vexation this preference caused to her.

Next to my mother, came Julia, my cousin, five years older than I, who had coldly looked down upon me, and snubbed me like a sister, as a boy; watched my progress through Elizabeth College, and through Guy's Hospital; and perceived at last that I was a young man whom it was no disgrace to call cousin. To crown all, she fell in love with me; so at least my mother told me, taking me into her confidence, and speaking with a depth of pleading in her sunken eyes, which were worn with much weeping. Poor mother! I knew very well what unspoken wish was in her heart. Julia had grown up under her care as I had done, and she stood second to me in her affection.

It is not difficult to love any woman who has a moderate share of attractions—at least I did not find it so then. I was really fond of Julia, too—very fond. I knew her as intimately as any brother knows his sister. She had kept up a correspondence with me all the time I was at Guy's, and her letters had been more interesting and amusing than her conversation generally was. Some women, most cultivated women, can write charming letters; and Julia was a highly-cultivated woman. I came back from Guy's with a very greatly-increased regard and admiration for my cousin Julia.

So, when my mother, with her pleading, wistful eyes, spoke day after day of Julia, of her dutiful love toward her, and her growing love for me, I drifted, almost without an effort of my own volition, into an engagement with her. You see there was no counter-balance. I was acquainted with every girl on the island of my own class; pretty girls were many of them, but there was after all not one that I preferred to my cousin. My old dreams and romances about love, common to every young fellow, had all faded into a very commonplace, everyday vision of having a comfortable house of my own, and a wife as good as most other men's wives. Just in the same way, my ambitious plans of rising to the very top of the tree in my profession had dwindled down to satisfaction with the very limited practice of one of our island doctors. I found myself chained to this rock in the sea; all my future life would probably be spent there; and Fate offered me Julia as the companion fittest for me. I was contented with my fate, and laughed off my boyish fancy that I ought to be ready to barter the world for love.

Added to these two strong ties keeping me in Guernsey, there were the hundred, the thousand small associations which made that island, and my people living upon it, dearer than any other place, or any other people, in the world. Taking the strength of the rope which held me to the pier-head as represented by one hundred, then my love for my mother would stand at sixty-six and a half, my engagement to Julia at about twenty and the remainder may go toward my old associations. That is pretty nearly the sum of it.

My engagement to Julia came about so easily and naturally that, as I said, I was perfectly contented with it. We had been engaged since the previous Christmas, and were to be married in the early summer, as soon as a trip through Switzerland would be agreeable. We were to set up housekeeping for ourselves; that was a point Julia was bent upon. A suitable house had fallen vacant in one of the higher streets of St. Peter-Port, which commanded a noble view of the sea and the surrounding islands. We had taken it, though it was farther from the Grange and my mother than I should have chosen my home to be. She and Julia were busy, pleasantly busy, about the furnishing of it. Never had I seen my mother look so happy, or so young. Even my father paid her a compliment or two, which had the effect of bringing a pretty pink flush to her white cheeks, and of making her sunken eyes shine. As to myself, I was quietly happy, without a doubt. Julia was a good girl, everybody said that, and Julia loved me devotedly. I was on the point of becoming master of a house and owner of a considerable income; for Julia would not hear of there being any marriage settlements which would secure to her the property she was bringing to me. I found that making love, even to my cousin, who was like a sister to me, was upon the whole a pleasurable occupation. Every thing was going on smoothly.

That was till about the middle of March. I had been to church one Sunday morning with these two women, both devoted to me, and centring all their love and hopes in me, when, as we entered the house on our return, I heard my father calling "Martin! Martin!" as loudly as he could from his consulting-room. I answered the call instantly, and whom should I see but a very old friend of mine, Tardif of the Havre Gosselin. He was standing near the door, as if in too great a hurry to sit down. His handsome but weather-beaten face betrayed great anxiety, and his shaggy mustache rose and fell, as if the mouth below it was tremulously at work. My father looked chagrined and irresolute.

"Here's a pretty piece of work, Martin," he said; "Tardif wants one of us to go back with him to Sark, to see a woman who has fallen from the cliffs and broken her arm, confound it!"

"For the sake of the good God, Dr. Martin," cried Tardif, excitedly, and of course speaking in the Sark dialect, "I beg of you to come this instant even. She has been lying in anguish since mid-day yesterday—twenty-four hours now, sir. I started at dawn this morning, but both wind and tide were against me, and I have been waiting here some time. Be quick, doctor. Mon Dieu! if she should be dead!"

The poor fellow's voice faltered, and his eyes met mine imploringly. He and I had been fast friends in my boyhood, when all my holidays were spent in Sark, though he was some years older than I; and our friendship was still firm and true, though it had slackened a little from absence. I shook his hand heartily, giving it a good hard grip in token of my unaltered friendship—a grip which he returned with his fingers of iron till my own tingled again.

"I knew you'd come," he gasped.

"Ah, I'll go, Tardif," I said; "only I must get a snatch of something to eat while Dr. Dobrée puts up what I shall have need of. I'll be ready in half an hour. Go into the kitchen, and get some dinner yourself."

"Thank you, Dr. Martin," he answered, his voice still unsteady, and his mustache quivering; "but I can eat nothing. I'll go down and have the boat ready. You'll waste no time?"

"Not a moment," I promised.

I left my father to put up the things I should require, supposing he had heard all the particulars of the accident from Tardif. He was inclined to grumble a little at me for going; but I asked him what else I could have done. As he had no answer ready to that question, I walked away to the dining-room, where my mother and Julia were waiting; for dinner was ready, as we dined early on Sundays on account of the servants. Julia was suffering from the beginning of a bilious attack, to which she was subject, and her eyes were heavy and dull. I told them hastily where I was going, and what a hurry I was in.

"You are never going across to Sark to-day!" Julia exclaimed.

"Why not?" I asked, taking my seat and helping myself quickly.

"Because I am sure bad weather is coming," she answered, looking anxiously through a window facing the west. "I could see the coast of France this morning as plainly as Sark, and the gulls are keeping close to the shore, and the sunset last night was threatening. I will go and look at the storm-glass."

She went away, but came back again very soon, with an increase of anxiety in her face. "Don't go, dear Martin," she said, with her hand upon my shoulder; "the storm-glass is as troubled as it can be, and the wind is veering round to the west. You know what that foretells at this time of the year. There is a storm at hand; take my word for it, and do not venture across to Sark to-day."

"And what is to become of the poor woman?" I remonstrated. "Tardif says she has been suffering the pain of a broken limb these twenty-four hours. It would be my duty to go even if the storm were here, unless the risk was exceedingly great. Come, Julia, remember you are to be a doctor's wife, and don't be a coward."

"Don't go!" she reiterated, "for my sake and your mother's. I am certain some trouble will come of it. We shall be frightened to death; and this woman is only a stranger to you. Oh, I cannot bear to let you go!"

I did not attempt to reason with her, for I knew of old that when Julia was bilious and nervous she was quite deaf to reason. I only stroked the hand that lay on my shoulder, and went on with my dinner as if my life depended upon the speed with which I dispatched it.

"Uncle," she said, as my father came in with a small portmanteau in his hand, "tell Martin he must not go. There is sure to be a storm to-night."

"Pooh! pooh!" he answered. "I should be glad enough for Martin to stay at home, but there's no help for it, I suppose. There will be no storm at present, and they'll run across quickly. It will be the coming back that will be difficult. You'll scarcely get home again to-night, Martin."

"No," I said. "I'll stop at Gavey's, and come back in the Sark cutter if it has begun to ply. If not, Tardif must bring me over in the morning."

"Don't go," persisted Julia, as I thrust myself into my rough pilot-coat, and then bent down to kiss her cheek. Julia always presented me her cheek, and my lips had never met hers yet. My mother was standing by and looking tearful, but she did not say a word; she knew there was no question about what I ought to do. Julia followed me to the door and held me fast with both hands round my arm, sobbing out hysterically, "Don't go!" Even when I had released myself and was running down the drive, I could hear her still calling, "O Martin, don't go!"

I was glad to get out of hearing. I felt sorry for her, yet there was a considerable amount of pleasure in being the object of so much tender solicitude. I thought of her for a minute or two as I hurried along the steep streets leading down to the quay. But the prospect before me caught my eye. Opposite lay Sark, bathed in sunlight, and the sea between was calm enough at present. A ride across, with a westerly breeze filling the sails, and the boat dancing lightly over the waves, would not be a bad exchange for a dull Sunday afternoon, with Julia at the Sunday-school and my mother asleep. Besides, it was the path of duty which was leading me across the quiet gray sea before me.

Tardif was waiting, with his sails set and oars in the rowlocks, ready for clearing the harbor. I took one of them, and bent myself willingly to the light task. There was less wind than I had expected, but what there was blew in our favor. We were very quickly beyond the pier-head, where a group of idlers was always gathered, who sent after us a few warning shouts. Nothing could be more exhilarating than our onward progress. I felt as if I had been a prisoner, with, chains which had pressed heavily yet insensibly upon me, and that now I was free. I drew into my lungs the fresh, bracing, salt air of the sea, with a deep sigh of delight.

It struck me after a while that my friend Tardif was unusually silent. The shifting of the sails appeared to give him plenty to do; and to my surprise, instead of keeping to the ordinary course, he ran recklessly as it seemed across the grunes, which lie all about the bed of the channel between Guernsey and Sark. These grunes are reefs, rising a little above low water, but, as the tide was about half-flood, they were a few feet below it; yet at times there was scarcely enough depth to float us over them, while the brown seaweed torn from their edges lay in our wake, something like the swaths of grass in a meadow after the scythe has swept through it. Now and then came a bump and a scrape of the keel against their sharp ridges. The sweat stood in beads upon Tardif's face, and his thick hair fell forward over his forehead, where the great veins in the temples were purple and swollen. I spoke to him after a heavier bump over the grunes than any we had yet come to.

"Tardif," I said, "we are shaving the weeds a little too close, aren't we?"

"Look behind you, Dr. Martin," he answered, shifting the sails a little.

I did not look behind us. We were more than half-way over the channel, and Guernsey lay four miles or so west of us; but instead of the clear outline of the island standing out against the sky, I could see nothing but a bank of white fog. The afternoon sun was shining brightly over it, but before long it would dip into its dense folds. The fogs about our islands are peculiar. You may see them form apparently thick blocks of blanched vapor, with a distinct line between the atmosphere where the haze is and where it is not. To be overtaken by a fog like this, which would almost hide Tardif at one end of the boat from me at the other, would be no laughing matter in a sea lined with sunken reefs. The wind had almost gone, but a little breeze still caught us from the north of the fog-bank. Without a word I took the oars again, while Tardif devoted himself to the sails and the helm.

"A mile nearer home," he said, "and I could row my boat as easily in the dark as you could ride your horse along a lane."

My face was westward now, and I kept my eye upon the fog-bank creeping stealthily after us. I thought of my mother and Julia, and the fright they would be in. Moreover a fog like this was pretty often succeeded by a squall, especially at this season; and when a westerly gale blew up from the Atlantic in the month of March, no one could foretell when it would cease. I had been weather-bound in Sark, when I was a boy, for three weeks at one time, when our provisions ran short, and it was almost impossible to buy a loaf of bread. I could not help laughing at the recollection, but I kept an anxious lookout toward the west. Three weeks' imprisonment in Sark now would be a bore.

But the fog remained almost stationary in the front of Guernsey, and the round red eyeball of the sun glared after us as we ran nearer and nearer to Sark. The tide was with us, and carried us on it buoyantly. We anchored at the fisherman's landing-place below the cliff of the Havre Gosselin, and I climbed readily up the rough ladder which leads to the path. Tardif made his boat secure, and followed me; he passed me, and strode on up the steep track to the summit of the cliff, as if impatient to reach his home. It was then that I gave my first serious thought to the woman who had met with the accident.

"Tardif, who is this person that is hurt?" I asked, "and whereabout did she fall?"

"She fell down yonder," he answered, with an odd quaver in his voice, as he pointed to a rough and rather high portion of the cliff running inland; "the stones rolled from under her feet, so," he added, crushing down a quantity of the loose gravel with his foot, "and she slipped. She lay on the shingle underneath for two hours before I found her; two hours, Dr. Martin!"

"That was bad," I said, for the good fellow's voice failed him—"very bad. A fall like that might have killed her."

We went on, he carrying his oars, and I my little portmanteau. I heard Tardif muttering. "Killed her!" in a tone of terror; but his face brightened a little when we reached the gate of the farm-yard. He laid down the oars noiselessly upon the narrow stone causeway before the door, and lifted the latch as cautiously as if he were afraid to disturb some sleeping baby.

He had given me no information with regard to my patient; and the sole idea I had formed of her was of a strong, sturdy Sark woman, whose constitution would be tough, and her temperament of a stolid, phlegmatic tone. There was not ordinarily much sickness among them, and this case was evidently one of pure accident. I expected to find a nut-brown, sunburnt woman, with a rustic face, who would very probably be impatient and unreasonable under the pain I should be compelled to inflict upon her.

It had been my theory that a medical man, being admitted to the highest degree of intimacy with his patients, was bound to be as insensible as an anchorite to any beauty or homeliness in those whom he was attending professionally; he should have eyes only for the malady he came to consider and relieve. Dr. Dobrée had often sneered and made merry at my high-flown notions of honor and duty; but in our practice at home he had given me no opportunities of trying them. He had attended all our younger and more attractive patients himself, and had handed over to my care all the old people and children—on Julia's account, he had said, laughing.

Tardif's mother came to us as we entered the house. She was a little, ugly woman, stone deaf, as I knew of old. Yet in some mysterious way she could make out her son's deep voice, when he shouted into her ear. He did not speak now, however, but made dumb signs as if to ask how all was going on. She answered by a silent nod, and beckoned me to follow her into an inner room, which opened out of the kitchen.

It was a small, crowded room, with a ceiling so low, it seemed to rest upon the four posts of the bedstead. There were of course none of the little dainty luxuries about it with which I was familiar in my mother's bedroom. A long, low window opposite the head of the bed threw a strong light upon it. There were check curtains drawn round it, and a patchwork-quilt, and rough, homespun linen. Every thing was clean, but coarse and frugal—such as I expected to find about my Sark patient, in the home of a fisherman.

But when my eye fell upon the face resting on the rough pillow I paused involuntarily, only just controlling an explanation of surprise. There was absolutely nothing in the surroundings to mark her as a lady, yet I felt in a moment that she was one. There lay a delicate, refined face, white as the linen, with beautiful lips almost as white; and a mass of light, shining, silky hair tossed about the pillow; and large dark-gray eyes gazing at me beseechingly, with an expression that made my heart leap as it had never leaped before.

That was what I saw, and could not forbear seeing. I tried to recall my theory, and to close my eyes to the pathetic beauty of the face before me; but it was altogether in vain. If I had seen her before, or if I had been prepared to see any one like her, I might have succeeded; but I was completely thrown off my guard. There the charming face lay: the eyes gleaming, the white forehead tinted, and the delicate mouth contracting with pain: the bright, silky curls tossed about in confusion. I see it now just as I saw it then.

CHAPTER THE THIRD

WITHOUT RESOURCES

I suppose I did not stand still more than five seconds, yet during that pause a host of questions had flashed through my brain. Who was this beautiful creature? Where had she come from? How did it happen that she was in Tardif's house? and so on. But I recalled myself sharply to my senses; I was here as her physician, and common-sense and duty demanded of me to keep my head clear. I advanced to her side, and took the small, blue-veined hand in mine, and felt her pulse with my fingers. It beat under them a low but fast measure; too fast by a great deal. I could see that the general condition of her health was perfect, a great charm in itself to me; but she had been bearing acute pain for over twenty-eight hours, and she was becoming exhausted. A shudder ran through me at the thought of that long spell of suffering.

"You are in very great pain, I fear," I said, lowering my voice.

"Yes," her white lips answered, and she tried to smile a patient though a dreary smile, as she looked up into my face, "my arm is broken. Are you a doctor?"

"I am Dr. Martin Dobrée," I said, passing my hand softly down her arm. The fracture was above the elbow, and was of a kind to make the setting of it give her considerable pain. I could see she was scarce fit to bear any further suffering just then; but what was to be done? She was not likely to get much rest till the bone was set.

"Have you had much sleep since your fall?" I asked, looking at the weariness visible in her eyes.

"Not any," she replied; "not one moment's sleep."

"Did you have no sleep all night?" I inquired again.

"No." she said, "I could not fall asleep."

There were two things I could do—give her an opiate, and strengthen her a little with sleep beforehand, or administer chloroform to her before the operation. I hesitated between the two. A natural sleep would have done her a world of good, but there was a gleam in her eyes, and a feverish throb in her pulse, which gave me no hope of that. Perhaps the chloroform, if she had no objection to it, would be the best.

"Did you ever take chloroform?" I asked.

"No: I never needed it," she answered.

"Should you object to taking it?"

"Any thing." she replied, passively. "I will do any thing you wish."

I went back into the kitchen and opened the portmanteau my father had put up for me. Splints and bandages were there in abundance, enough to set half the arms in the island, but neither chloroform nor any thing in the shape of an opiate could I find. I might almost as well have come to Sark altogether unprepared for my case.

What could I do? There are no shops in Sark, and drugs of any kind were out of the question. There was not a chance of getting what I needed to calm and soothe a highly-nervous and finely-strung temperament like my patient's. A few minutes ago I had hesitated about using chloroform. Now I would have given half of every thing I possessed in the world for an ounce of it.

I said nothing to Tardif, who was watching me with his deep-set eyes, as closely as if I were meddling with some precious possession of his own. I laid the bundle of splints and rolls of linen down on the table with a professional air, while I was inwardly execrating my father's negligence. I emptied the portmanteau in the hope of finding some small phial or box. Any opiate would have been welcome to me, that would have dulled the overwrought nerves of the girl in the room within. But the practice of using any thing of the kind was not in favor with us generally in the Channel Islands, and my father had probably concluded that a Sark woman would not consent to use them. At any rate, there they were not.

I stood for a few minutes, deep in thought. The daylight was going, and it was useless to waste time; yet I found myself shrinking oddly from the duty before me. Tardif could not help but see my chagrin and hesitation.

"Doctor," he cried, "she is not going to die?"

"No, no," I answered, calling back my wandering thoughts and energies; "there is not the smallest danger of that. I must go and set her arm at once, and then she will sleep."

I returned to the room, and raised her as gently and painlessly as I could, motioning to the old woman to sit beside her on the bed and hold her steadily. I thought once of calling in Tardif to support her with his strong frame, but I did not. She moaned, though very softly, when I moved her, and she tried to smile again as her eyes met mine looking anxiously at her. That smile made me feel like a child. If she did it again, I knew my hands would be unsteady, and her pain would be tenfold greater.

"I would rather you cried out or shouted," I said. "Don't try to control yourself when I hurt you. You need not be afraid of seeming impatient, and a loud scream or two would do you good."

But I knew quite well as I spoke that she would never scream aloud. There was the self-control of culture about her. A woman of the lower class might shriek and cry, but this girl would try to smile at the moment when the pain was keenest. The white, round arm under my hands was cold, and the muscles were soft and unstrung. I felt the ends of the broken bone grating together as I drew the fragments into their right places, and the sensation went through and through me. I had set scores of broken limbs before with no feeling like this, which was so near unnerving me. But I kept my hands steady, and my attention fixed upon my work. I felt like two persons—a surgeon who had a simple, scientific operation to perform, and a mother who feels in her own person every pang her child has to suffer.

All the time the girl's white face and firmly-set lips lay under my gaze, with the wide-open, unflinching eyes looking straight at me: a mournful, silent, appealing face, which betrayed the pain I made her suffer ten times more than any cries or shrieks could have done. I thanked God in my heart when it was over, and I could lay her down again. I smoothed the coarse pillows for her to lie more comfortably upon them, and I spread my cambric handkerchief in a double fold between her cheek and the rough linen—too rough for a soft cheek like hers.

"Lie quite still," I said. "Do not stir, but go to sleep as fast as you can."

She was not smiling now, and she did not speak; but the gleam in her eyes was growing wilder, and she looked at me with a wandering expression. If sleep did not come very soon, there would be mischief. I drew the curtains across the window to shut out the twilight, and motioned to the old woman to sit quietly by the side of our patient.

Then I went out to Tardif.

He had not stirred from the place and position in which I had left him. I am sure no sound could have reached him from the inner room, for we had been so still that during the whole time I could hear the beat of the sea dashing up between the high cliffs of the Havre Gosselin. Up and down went Tardif's shaggy mustache, the surest indication of emotion with him, and he fetched his breath almost with a sob.

"Well, Dr. Martin?" was all he said.

"The arm is set," I answered, "and now she must get some sleep. There is not the least danger, Tardif; only we will keep the house as quiet as possible."

"I must go and bring in the boat," he replied, bestirring himself as if some spell was at an end. "There will be a storm to-night, and I should sleep the sounder if she was safe ashore."

"I'll come with you," I said, glad to get away from the seaweed fire.

It was not quite dark, and the cliffs stood out against the sky in odder and more grotesque shapes than by daylight. A host of seamews were fluttering about and uttering the most unearthly hootings, but the sea was as yet quite calm, save where it broke in wavering, serpentine lines over the submerged reefs which encircle the island. The tidal current was pouring rapidly through the very narrow channel between Sark and the little isle of Breckhou, and its eddies stretching to us made it rather an arduous task to get Tardif's boat on shore safely. But the work was pleasant just then. It kept our minds away from useless anxieties about the girl. An hour passed quickly, and up the ravine, in the deep gloom of the overhanging rocks, we made our way homeward.

"You will not quit the island to-morrow," said Tardif, standing at his door, and scanning the sky with his keen, weather-wise eyes.

"I must," I answered; "I must indeed, old fellow. You are no land-lubber, and you will run me over in the morning."

"No boat will leave Sark to-morrow," said Tardif, shaking his head.

We went in, and he threw off his jacket and rolled up his sleeves, preparatory to frying some fish for supper. I was beginning to feel ravenously hungry, for I had eaten nothing since dinner, and as far as I knew Tardif had had nothing since his early breakfast, but as a fisherman he was used to long spells of fasting. While he was busy cooking I stole quietly into the inner room to look after my patient.

The feeble light entering by the door, which I left open, showed me the old woman comfortably asleep in her chair, but not so the girl. I had told her when I laid her down that she must lie quite still, and she was obeying me implicitly. Her cheek still rested upon my handkerchief, and the broken arm remained undisturbed upon the pillow which I had placed under it. But her eyes were wide open and shining in the dimness, and I fancied I could see her lips moving incessantly, though soundlessly. I laid my hand across her eyes, and felt the long lashes brush against the palm, but the eyelids did not remain closed.

"You must go to sleep," I said, speaking distinctly and authoritatively; wondering at the time how much power my will would have over her. Did I possess any of that magnetic, tranquillizing influence about which Jack Senior and I had so often laughed incredulously at Guy's? Her lips moved fast; for now my eyes had grown used to the dim light I could see her face plainly, but I could not catch a syllable of what she was whispering so busily to herself.

Never had I felt so helpless and disconcerted in the presence of a patient. I could positively do nothing for her. The case was not beyond my skill, but all medicinal resources were beyond my reach. Sleep she must have, yet how was I to administer it to her?

I returned, troubled and irritable, to search once more my empty portmanteau. Empty it was, except of the current number of Punch, which my father had considerately packed among the splints for my Sunday-evening reading. I flung it and the bag across the kitchen, with an ejaculation not at all flattering to Dr. Dobrée, nor in accordance with the fifth commandment.

"What is the matter, doctor?" inquired Tardif.

I told him in a few sharp words what I wanted to soothe my patient. In an instant he left his cooking and thrust his arms into his blue jacket again.

"You can finish it yourself, Dr. Martin," he said, hurriedly; "I'll run over to old Mother Renouf; she'll have some herbs or something to send mam'zelle to sleep."

"Bring her back with you," I shouted after him as he sped across the yard. Mother Renouf was no stranger to me. While I was a boy she had charmed my warts away, and healed the bruises which were the inevitable consequences of cliff-climbing. I scarcely liked her coming in to fill up my deficiencies, and I knew our application to her for help would be inexpressibly gratifying. But I had no other resource than to call her in as a fellow-practitioner, and I knew she would make a first-rate nurse, for which Suzanne Tardif was unfitted by her deafness.

CHAPTER THE FOURTH

A RIVAL PRACTITIONER

Mother Renouf arrived from the other end of the island in an incredibly short time, borne along by Tardif as if he were a whirlwind and she a leaf caught in its current. She was a short, squat old woman, with a skin tanned like leather, and kindly little blue eyes, twinkling with delight and pride. Yes, there they are, photographed somewhere in my brain, the wrinkled, yellow, withered faces of the two old women, their watery eyes and toothless mouths, with figures as shapeless as the bowlders on the beach, watching beside the bed where lay the white but tenderly beautiful face of the young girl, with her curls of glossy hair tossed about the pillow, and her long, tremulous eyelashes making a shadow on her rounded cheek.

Mother Renouf gave me a hearty tap on the shoulder, and chuckled as merrily as the shortness of her breath after her rapid course would permit. The few English phrases she knew fell far short of expressing her triumph and exultation; but I was resolved to confer with her affably. My patient's case was too serious for me to stand upon my dignity.

"Mother," I said, "have you any simples to send this poor girl to sleep? Tardif told me you had taken her sprained ankle under your charge. I find I have nothing with me to induce sleep, and you can help us if any one can."

"Leave her to me, my dear little doctor," she answered, a laugh gurgling in her thick throat; "leave her to me. You have done your part with the bones. I have no touch at all for broken limbs, though my father, good man, could handle them with any doctor in all the islands. But I'll send her to sleep for you, never fear."

"You will stay with us all night?" I said, coaxingly. "Suzanne is deaf, and ears are of use in a sick-room, you know. I intended to go to Gavey's, but I shall throw myself down here on the fern bed, and you can call me at any moment, if there is need."

"There will be no need," she replied, in a tone of confidence. "My little mam'zelle will be sound asleep in ten minutes after she has taken my draught."

I went into the room with her to have a look at our patient. She had not stirred yet, but was precisely in the position in which I placed her after the operation was ended. There was something peculiar about this which distressed me. I asked Mother Renouf to move her gently and bring her face more toward me. The burning eyes opened widely as soon as she felt the old woman's arm under her, and she looked up, with a flash of intelligence, into my face. I stooped down to catch the whisper with which her lips were moving.

"You told me not to stir," she murmured.

"Yes," I said; "but you are not to lie still till you are cramped and stiff. Are you in much pain now?"

"He told me not to stir," muttered the parched lips again, "not to stir. I must lie quite still, quite still, quite still!"

The feeble voice died away as she whispered the last words, but her lips went on moving, as if she was repeating them to herself still. Certainly there was mischief here. My last order, given just before her mind began to wander, had taken possession of her brain, and retained authority over her will. There was a pathetic obedience in her perfect immobility, united with the shifting, restless glance of her eyes, and the ceaseless ripple of movement about her mouth, which made me trebly anxious and uneasy. A dominant idea had taken hold upon her which might prove dangerous. I was glad when Mother Renouf had finished stewing her decoction of poppy-heads, and brought the nauseous draught for the girl to drink.

But whether the poppy-heads had lost their virtue, or our patient's nervous condition had become too critical, too full of excitement and disturbance, I cannot tell. It is certain that she was not sleeping in ten minutes' or in an hour's time. Old Dame Tardif went off to her bedroom, and Mother Renouf took her place by the girl's side. Tardif could not be persuaded to leave the kitchen, though he appeared to be falling asleep heavily, waking up at intervals, and starting with terror at the least sound. For myself I scarcely slept at all, though I found the fern bed a tolerably comfortable resting-place.

The gale that Tardif had foretold came with great violence about the middle of the night. The wind howled up the long, narrow ravine like a pack of wolves; mighty storms of hail and rain beat in torrents against the windows, and the sea lifted up its voice with unmistakable energy. Now and again a stronger gust than the others appeared to threaten to carry off the thatched roof bodily, and leave us exposed to the tempest with only the thick stone walls about us; and the latch of the outer door rattled as if some one outside was striving to enter. I am not fanciful, but just then the notion came across me that if that door opened we should see the grim skeleton, Death, on the threshold, with his bleached, unclad bones dripping with the storm. I laughed at the ghastly fancy, and told it to Tardif in one of his waking intervals, but he was so terrified and troubled by it that it grew to have some little importance in my own eyes. So the night wore slowly away, the tall clock in the corner ticking out the seconds and striking the hours with a fidelity to its duty, which helped to keep me awake. Twice or thrice I crept, with quite unnecessary caution, into the room of my patient.

No, there was no symptom of sleep there. The pulse grew more rapid, the temples throbbed, and the fever gained ground. Mother Renouf was ready to weep with vexation. The girl herself sobbed and shuddered at the loud sounds of the tempest without; but yet, by a firm, supreme effort of her will, which was exhausting her strength dangerously, she kept herself quite still. I would have given up a year or two of my life to be able to set her free from the bondage of my own command.

CHAPTER THE FIFTH

LOCKS OF HAIR

The westerly gale, rising every few hours into a squall, gave me no chance of leaving Sark the next day, nor for some days afterward; but I was not at all put out by my captivity. All my interest—my whole being, in fact—was absorbed in the care of this girl, stranger as she was. I thought and moved, lived and breathed, only to fight step by step against delirium and death, and to fight without my accustomed weapons. Sometimes I could do nothing but watch the onset and inroads of the fever most helplessly. There was no possibility of aid. The stormy waters which beat against that little rock in the sea came swelling and rolling in from the vast plain of the Atlantic, and broke in tempestuous surf against the island. The wind howled, and the rain and hail beat across us almost incessantly for two days, and Tardif himself was kept a prisoner in the house, except when he went to look after his live-stock. No doubt it would have been practicable for me to get as far as the hotel, but to what good? It would be quite deserted, for there were no visitors to Sark at this season, and I did not give it a second thought. I was entirely engrossed in my patient, and I learned for the first time what their task is who hour after hour watch the progress of disease in the person, of one dear to them.

Tardif occupied himself with mending his nets, pausing frequently with his solemn eyes fixed upon the door of the girl's room, very much as a patient mastiff watches the spot where he knows his master is near to him, though out of sight. His mother went about her household work ploddingly, and Mother Renouf kept manfully to her post, in turn with me, as sentinel over the sickbed. There the young girl lay whispering from morning till night, and from night till morning again—always whispering. The fever gained ground from hour to hour. I had no data by which to calculate her chances of getting through it; but my hopes were very low at times.

On the Tuesday afternoon, in a temporary lull of the hail and wind, I started off on a walk across the island. The wind was still blowing from the southwest, and filling all the narrow sea between us and Guernsey with boiling surge. Very angry looked the masses of foam whirling about the sunken reefs, and very ominous the low-lying, hard blocks of clouds all along the horizon. I strolled as far as the Coupée, that giddy pathway between Great and Little Sark, where one can see the seething of the waves at the feet of the cliffs on both sides, three hundred feet below one. Something like a panic seized me. My nerves were too far unstrung for me to venture across the long, narrow isthmus. I turned abruptly again, and hurried as fast as my legs would carry me back to Tardif's cottage.

I had been away less than an hour, but an advantage had been taken of my absence. I found Tardif seated at the table, with a tangle of silky, shining hair lying before him. A tear or two had fallen upon it from his eyes. I understood at a glance what it meant. Mother Renouf had cut off my patient's pretty curls as soon as I was out of the house. I could not be angry with her, though I did not suppose it would do much good, and I felt a sort of resentment, such as a mother would feel, at this sacrifice of a natural beauty. They were all disordered and ravelled. Tardif's great hand caressed them tenderly, and I drew out one long, glossy tress and wound it about my fingers, with a heavy heart.

"It is like the pretty feathers of a bird that has been wounded," said Tardif, sorrowfully.

Just then there came a knock at the door and a sharp click of the latch, loud enough to penetrate Dame Tardif's deaf ears, or to arouse our patient, if she had been sleeping. Before either of us could move, the door was thrust open, and two young ladies appeared upon the door-sill.

They were—it flashed across me in an instant—old school-fellows and friends of Julia's. I declare to you honestly, I had scarcely had one thought of Julia till now. My mother I had wished for, to take her place by this poor girl's side, but Julia had hardly crossed my mind. Why, in Heaven's name, should the appearance of these friends of hers be so distasteful to me just now? I had known them all my life, and liked them as well as any girls I knew; but at this moment the very sight of them was annoying. They stood in the doorway, as much astonished and thunderstricken as I was, glaring at me, so it seemed to me, with that soft, bright-brown lock of hair curling and clinging round my finger. Never had I felt so foolish or guilty.

"Martin Dobrée!" ejaculated both in one breath.

"Yes, mesdemoiselles," I said, uncoiling the tress of hair as if it had been a serpent, and going forward to greet them; "are you surprised to see me?"

"Surprised!" echoed the elder. "No; we are amazed—petrified! However did you get here? When did you come?"

"Quite easily," I replied. "I came on Sunday, and Tardif fetched me in his own boat. If the weather had permitted, I should have paid you a call; but you know what it has been."

"To be sure," answered Emma; "and how is dear Julia? She will be very anxious about you."

"She was on the verge of a bilious attack when I left her," I said; "that will tend to increase her anxiety."

"Poor, dear girl," she replied, sympathetically. "But, Martin, is this young woman here so very ill? We have heard from the Renoufs she had had a dangerous fall. To think of your being in Sark ever since Sunday, and we never heard a word of it!"

No, thanks to Tardif's quiet tongue, and Mother Renouf's assiduous attendance upon mam'zelle, my sojourn in the island had been kept a secret; now that was at an end.

"Is that the young woman's hair?" asked Emma, as Tardif gathered together the scattered tresses and tied them up quickly in a little white handkerchief, out of their sight and mine. I saw them again afterward. The handkerchief had been his wife's—white, with a border of pink roses.

"Yes," I replied to her question, "it was necessary to cut it off. She is dangerously ill with fever."

Both of them shrank a little toward the door. A sudden temptation assailed me, and took me so much by surprise that I had yielded before I knew I was attacked. It was their shrinking movement that did it. My answer was almost as automatic and involuntary as their retreat.

"You see it would not be wise for any of us to go about," I said. "A fever breaking out in the island, especially now you have no resident doctor, would be very serious. I think it will be best to isolate this case till we see the nature of the fever. You will do me a favor by warning the people away from us at present. The storm has saved us so far, but now we must take other precautions."

This I said with a grave tone and face, knowing all the while that there was no fear whatever for the people of Sark. Was there a propensity in me, not hitherto developed, to make the worst of a case?

"Good-by, Martin, good-by," cried Emma, backing out through the open door. "Come away, Maria. We have run no risk yet, Martin, have we? Do not come any nearer to us. We have touched nothing, except shaking hands with you. Are we quite safe?"

"Is the young woman so very ill?" inquired Maria from a safe distance outside the house.

I shook my head in silence, and pointed to the door of the inner room, intimating to them that she was no farther away than there. An expression of horror came over both their faces. Scarcely waiting to bestow upon me a gesture of farewell, they fled, and I saw them hurrying with unusual rapidity across the fold.

I had at least secured isolation for myself and my patient. But why had I been eager to do so? I could not answer that question to myself, and I did not ponder over it many minutes. I was impatient, yet strangely reluctant, to look at the sick girl again, after the loss of her beautiful hair. It was still daylight. The change in her appearance struck me as singular. Her face before had a look of suffering and trouble, making it almost old, charming as it was; now she had the aspect of quite a young girl, scarcely touching upon womanhood. Her hair had not been shorn off closely—the woman could not manage that—and short, wavy tresses, like those of a young child, were curling about her exquisitely-shaped head. The white temples, with their blue, throbbing veins, were more visible, with the small, delicately-shaped ears. I should have guessed her age now as barely fifteen—almost that of a child. Thus changed, I felt more myself in her presence, more as I should have been in attendance upon any child. I scanned her face narrowly, and it struck me that there was a perceptible alteration; an expression of exhaustion or repose was creeping over it. The crisis of the fever was at hand. The repose of death or the wholesome sleep of returning health was not far off. Mother Renouf saw it as well as myself.

CHAPTER THE SIXTH

WHO IS SHE?

We sat up again together that night, Tardif and I. He would not smoke, lest the scent of the tobacco should get in through the crevices of the door, and lessen the girl's chance of sleep; but he held his pipe between his teeth, taking an imaginary puff now and then, that he might keep himself wide awake. We talked to one another in whispers.

"Tell me all you know about mam'zelle," I said. He had been chary of his knowledge before, but his heart seemed open at this moment. Most hearts are more open at midnight than at any other hour.

"There's not much to tell, doctor," he answered. "Her name is Ollivier, as I said to you; but she does not think she is any kin to the Olliviers of Guernsey. She is poor, though she does not look as if she had been born poor, does she?"

"Not in the least degree," I said. "If she is not a lady of birth, she is one of the first specimens of Nature's gentlefolks I have ever come across."

"Ah, there is a difference!" he said, sighing. "I feel it, doctor, in every word I speak to her, and every step I walk with her eyes upon me. Why cannot I be like her, or like you? You'll be on a level with her, and I am down far below her."

I looked at him curiously. The slouching figure—well shaped as it was—the rough, knotted hands, the unkempt mass of hair about his head and face, marked him for what he was—a toiler on the sea as well as on the land. He understood my scrutiny, and colored under it like a girl.

"You are a better fellow than I am, Tardif," I said; "but that has nothing to do with our talk. I think we ought to communicate with the young lady's friends, whoever they may be, as soon as there are any means of communicating with the rest of the world. We should be in a fix if any thing should happen to her. Have you no clew to her friends?"

"She is not going to die!" he cried. "No, no, doctor. God must hear my prayers for her. I have never ceased to lift up my voice to Him in my heart since I found her on the shingle. She will not die!"

"I am not so sure," I said; "but in any case we should write to her friends. Has she written to any one since she came here?"

"Not to a soul," he answered, eagerly. "She told me she has no friends nearer than Australia. That is a great way off."

"And has she had no letters?" I asked.

"Not one," he replied. "She has neither written nor received a single letter."

"But how did you come across her?" I inquired. "She did not fall from the skies, I suppose. How was it she came to live in this out-of-the-world place with you?"

Tardif smoked his imaginary pipe with great perseverance for some minutes, his face overcast with thought. But presently it cleared, and he turned to me with a frank smile.

"I'll tell you all about it, Dr. Martin," he said. "You know the Seigneur was in London last autumn, and there was a little difficulty in the Court of Chefs Plaids here, about an ordonnance we could not agree over, and I went across to London to see the Seigneur for myself. It was in coming back I met with Mam'zelle Ollivier. I was paying my fare at Waterloo station—the omnibus-fare, I mean—and I was turning away, when I heard the man speak grumblingly. I thought it was at me, and I looked back, and there she stood before him, looking scared and frightened at his rough words. Doctor, I never could bear to see any soft, tender, young thing in trouble. If it's nothing but a little bird that has fallen out of its warm nest, or a lamb slipped down among the cliffs, I feel as if I could risk my life to put them back again in some safe place. Yes, and I have done it scores of times, when I dared not let my poor mother know. Well, there stood mam'zelle, pale and trembling, with the tears ready to fall in her eyes; just such a soft, poor, tender soul as my little wife used to be. You remember my little wife, Dr. Martin?"

I only nodded as he looked at me.

"Just such another," he went on; "only this one was a lady, and less able to take care of herself. Her trouble was nothing but the omnibus-fare, and she had no change, nothing but an Australian sovereign;

so I paid it for her. I kept pretty near her about the station while she was buying her ticket, for I overheard two young men, who were roaming up and down, say as they looked at her, 'Pas de gants, et des souliers de velours!' That was true; she had no gloves on her hands, and her little feet had nothing on but some velvet slippers, all wet and muddy with the dirty streets. So I walked up to her, as if I had been her servant, you understand, and put her into a carriage, and stood at the door of it, keeping off any young men who wished to get in—for she was such a pretty young thing—till the train was ready to start, and then I got into the nearest second-class carriage there was to her."

"Well, Tardif?" I said, impatiently, as he paused, looking absently into the dull embers of the seaweed fire.

"I turned it over in my own mind then," he continued, "and I've turned it over in my own mind since, and I can make no sort of an account of it—a young lady travelling without any friends in a dress like that, as if she had not had a minute to spare in getting ready for her journey. It was a bad night for a journey too. Could she be going to see some friend who was dying? At every station I looked out to see if my young lady left the train; but no, not even at Southampton. Was she going on to France? 'I must look out for her at the pier-head,' I said to myself. But when we stopped at the pier I did not want her to think I was watching her, only I stood well in the light, that she might see me when she looked round. I saw her stand as if she was considering, and I moved away very slowly to our boat, to give her the chance of speaking to me, if she wished. But she only followed me very quietly, as if she did not want me to see her, and she went down into the ladies' cabin in a moment, out of sight. Then I thought, 'She is running away from some one, or from something.' She had no shawls, or umbrellas, or baskets, such as ladies are always cumbered with, and that looked strange."

"How was she dressed?" I asked.

"She wore a soft, bright-brown jacket," he answered—"a seal-skin they call it, though I never saw a seal with a skin like that—and a hat like it, and a blue-silk gown, and her little muddy velvet slippers. It was a strange dress for travelling, wasn't it, doctor?"

"Very strange indeed," I repeated. An idea was buzzing about my brain that I had heard a description exactly similar before, but I could not for the life of me recall where. I could not wait to hunt it out then, for Tardif was in a full flow of confidence.

"But my heart yearned to her," he said, "more than ever it did over any bird fallen from its nest, or any lamb that had slipped down the cliffs. All the softness and all the helplessness of every poor little creature I had ever seen in my life seemed about her; all the hunted creatures and all the trapped creatures came to my mind. I can hardly tell you about it, doctor. I could have risked my life a hundred times over for her. It was a rough night, and I kept seeing her pale, hunted-looking face before me, though there was not half the danger I've often been in round our islands. I couldn't keep myself from fancying we were all going down to the bottom of the sea, and that poor young thing, running away from one trouble, was going to meet a worse—if it is worse to die than to live in great trouble. Dr. Martin, they tell me all the bed of the sea out yonder under the Atlantic is a smooth, smooth floor, with no currents, or tides, or streams, but a great calm; and there is no life down there of any kind. Well, that night I seemed to see the dead who have perished by sea lying there calm and quiet with their hands folded across their breasts. A great company it was, and a great graveyard, strewed over with sleeping shapes, all at rest and quiet, waiting till they hear the trumpet of the archangel sounding so that even the dead will hear and live again. It was a solemn sight to see, doctor. Somehow I came to think it would not be altogether a bad thing for the poor young troubled creature to go down there among them and be at rest. There are some people who seem too tender and delicate for this world. Yet if there had come a chance I'd have laid down my life for hers, even then, when I knew nothing much about her."

"Tardif," I said, "I did not know what a good fellow you are, though I ought to have known it by this time."

"No," he answered, "it is not in me; it's something in her. You feel something of it yourself, doctor, or how could you stay in a poor little house like this, thinking of nothing but her, and not caring about the weather keeping you away from home? But let me go on. In the morning she came on deck, and talked to me about the islands, and where she could live cheaply, and it ended in her coming home here to lodge in our little spare room. There was another curious thing—she had not any luggage with her, not a box nor a bag of any kind. She never knew that I knew, for that would have troubled her. It is my belief that she has run away."

"But who can she have run away from, Tardif?" I asked.

"God knows," he answered, "but the girl has suffered; you can see that by her face. Whoever or whatever she has run away from, her cheeks are white from it, and her heart sorrowful. I know nothing of her secret; but this I do know: she is as good, and true, and sweet little soul as my poor little wife was. She has been here all winter, doctor, living under my eye, and I've waited on her as her servant, though a rough servant I am for one like her. She has tried to make herself cheerful and contented with our poor ways. See, she mended me that bit of net; those are her meshes, though her pretty white fingers were made sore by the twine. She would mend it, sitting where you are now in the chimney-corner. No; if mam'zelle should die, it will be a great grief of heart to me. If I could offer my life to God in place of hers, I'd do it willingly."

"No, she will not die. Look there, Tardif!" I said, pointing to the door-sill of the inner room. A white card had been slipped under the door noiselessly—a signal agreed upon between Mother Renouf and me, to inform me that my patient had at last fallen into a profound slumber, which seemed likely to continue some hours. She had slept perhaps a few minutes at a time before, but not a refreshing, wholesome sleep. Tardif understood the silent signal as well as I did, and a more solemn expression settled on his face. After a while he put away his pipe, and, stepping barefoot across the floor without a sound, he stopped the clock, and brought back to the table, where an oil-lamp was burning, a large old Bible. Throughout the long night, whenever I awoke, for I threw myself on the fern bed and slept fitfully, I saw his handsome face, with its rough, unkempt hair falling across his forehead as it was bent over the book, while his mouth moved silently as he read to himself chapter after chapter, and turned softly the pages before him.

I fell into a heavy slumber just before daybreak, and when I awoke two or three hours after I found that the house had been put in order, just as usual, though no sound had disturbed me. I glanced anxiously at the closed door. That it was closed, and the white card still on the sill, proved to me that our charge had no more been disturbed than myself. The thought struck me that the morning light would shine full upon the weak and weary eyelids of the sleeper; but upon going out into the fold to look at her casement, I discovered that Tardif had been before me and covered it with an old sail. The room within was sufficiently darkened.

The morning was more than half gone before Mother Renouf opened the door and came out to us, her old face looking more haggard than ever, but her little eyes twinkling with satisfaction. She gave me a patronizing nod, but she went up to Tardif, laid a hand on each of his broad shoulders, and looked him keenly in the face.

"All goes well, my friend," she said, significantly. "Your little mam'zelle does not think of going to the good God yet."

I did not stay to watch how Tardif received this news, for I was impatient myself to see how she was going on. Thank Heaven, the fever was gone, the delirium at an end. The dark-gray eyes, opening languidly as my fingers touched her wrist, were calm and intelligent. She was as weak as a kitten, but that did not trouble me much. I was sure her natural health was good, and she would soon recover her lost strength. I had to stoop down to hear what she was saying.

"Have I kept quite still, doctor?" she asked, faintly.

I must own that my eyes smarted, and my voice was not to be trusted. I had never felt so overjoyed in my life as at that moment. But what a singular wish to be obedient possessed this girl! What a wonderful power of submissive self-control! she had cast aside authority and broken away from it, as she had done apparently, there must have been some great provocation before a nature like hers could venture to assert its own independence.

I had ample time for turning over this reflection, for Mother Renouf was worn out and needed rest, and Suzanne Tardif was of little use in the sick-room. I scarcely left my patient all that day, for the rumor I had set afloat the day before was sufficient to make it a difficult task to procure another nurse. The almost childish face grew visibly better before my eyes, and when night came I had to acknowledge somewhat reluctantly that as soon as a boat could leave the island it would be my bounden duty to return to Guernsey.

"I should like to see Tardif," murmured the girl to me that night, after she had awakened from a second long and peaceful sleep.

I called him, and he came in barefoot, his broad, burly frame seeming to fill up all the little room. She could not lift up her head, but her face was turned toward us, and she held out her small, wasted hand to him, smiling faintly. He fell on his knees before he took it into his great, horny palm, and looked down upon it as he held it very carefully with, tears standing in his eyes.

"Why, it is like an egg-shell," he said. "God bless you, mam'zelle, God bless you for getting well again!"

She laughed at his words—a feeble though merry laugh, like a child's—and she seemed delighted with the sight of his hearty face, glowing as it was with happiness. It was a strange chance that had thrown these two together. I could not allow Tardif to remain long; but after that she kept devising little messages to send to him through me whenever I was about to leave her. Her intercourse with Mother Renouf was extremely limited, as the old woman's knowledge of English was slight; and with Suzanne she could hold no conversation at all. It happened, in consequence, that I was the only person who could talk or listen to her through the long and dreary hours.

CHAPTER THE SEVENTH

WHO ARE HER FRIENDS?

At another time I might have recognized the danger of my post; but my patient had become so childish-looking, and her mind, enfeebled by delirium, was in so childish a condition, that it seemed to me I little more than tending some young girl whose age was far below my own. I did not trouble myself, moreover, with any exact introspection. There was an under-current of satisfaction and happiness running through the hours which I was not inclined to fathom. The winds continued against me, and I had nothing to do but to devote myself to mam'zelle, as I called her in common with the people about me. She was still so far in a precarious state that, if she had been living in Guernsey, it would have been my duty to pay to her unflagging attention.

But upon Friday afternoon Tardif, who had been down to the Creux Harbor, brought back the information that one of the Sark cutters was about to venture to make the passage across the Channel the next morning, to attend the Saturday market, if the wind did not rise again in the night. It was clear as day what I must do. I must bid farewell to my patient, however reluctant I might be, with a very uncertain prospect of seeing her again. A patient in Sark could not have many visits from a doctor in Guernsey.

She was recovering with the wonderful elasticity of a thoroughly sound constitution; but I had not considered it advisable for her even to sit up yet, with her broken arm and sprained ankle. I took my seat beside her for the last time, her fair, sweet face lying upon the pillow as it had done when I first saw it, only the look of suffering was gone. I had made up my mind to learn something of the mystery that surrounded her; and the child, as I called her to myself, was so submissive to me that she would answer my questions readily.

"Mam'zelle," I said, "I am going away to-night. You will be sorry to lose me?"

"Very, very sorry," she answered, in her low, touching voice. "Are you obliged to go?"

If I had not been obliged to go, I should then and there have made a solemn vow to remain with her till she was well again.

"I must go," I said, shaking off the ridiculous and troublesome idea. "I have been away nearly six days. Six days is a long holiday for a doctor."

"It has not been a holiday for you," she whispered, her eyes fastened upon mine, and shining like clear stars.

"Well," I repeated, "I must go. Before I go I wish to write to your friends for you. You will not be strong enough to write yourself for some days, and it is quite time they knew what danger you have been in. I have brought a pen and paper, and I will post the letter as soon as I reach Guernsey."

A faint flush colored her face, and she turned her eyes away from me.

"Why do you think I ought to write?" she asked at length.

"Because you have been very near death." I answered. "If you had died, not one of us would have known whom to communicate with, unless you had left some direction in that box of yours, which is not very likely."

"No," she said, "you would find nothing there. I suppose if I had died nobody would ever have known who I am. How curious that would have been!"

Was she amused, or was she saddened by the thought? I could not tell.

"It would have been very painful to Tardif and to me," I said. "It must be very painful to your friends, whoever they are, not to know what has become of you. Give me permission to write to them. There can scarcely be reasons sufficient for you to separate yourself from them like this. Besides, you cannot go on living in a fisherman's cottage; you were not born to it—"

"How do you know?" she asked, quickly, with a sharp tone in her voice.

It was somewhat difficult to answer that question. There was nothing to indicate what position she had been used to. I had seen no token of wealth about her room, which was as homely as any other cottage chamber. Her conversation had been the simple, childish talk of an invalid recovering from a serious illness, and had scarcely proved her to be an educated person. Yet there was something in her face and tones and manner which, as plainly to Tardif as to me, stamped this runaway girl as a lady.

"Let me write to your friends," I urged, waiving the question. "It is not fit for you to remain here. I beg of you to allow me to communicate with them."

Her face quivered like a child's when it is partly frightened and partly grieved.

"I have no friends," she said; "not one real friend in the world."

An almost irresistible inclination assailed me to fall on my knees beside her, as I had seen Tardif do, and take a solemn oath to be her faithful servant and friend as long as my life should last. This, of course, I did not do; but the sound of the words so plaintively spoken, and the sight of her quivering face, rendered her a hundredfold more interesting to me.

"Mam'zelle," I said, taking her hand in mine, "if ever you should need a friend, you may count upon Martin Dobrée as one as true as any you could wish to have. Tardif is another. Never say again you have no friends."

"Thank you," she answered, simply. "I will count you and Tardif as my friends. But I have no others, so you need not write to anybody."

"But what if you had died?" I persisted.

"You would have buried me quietly up there," she answered, "in the pleasant graveyard, where the birds sing all day long, and I should have been forgotten soon. Am I likely to die, Dr. Martin?"

"Certainly not," I replied, hastily; "nothing of the kind. You are going to get well and strong again. But I must bid you good-by, now, since you have no friends to write to. Can I do any thing for you in Guernsey? I can send you any thing you fancy."

"I do not want any thing," she said.

"You want a great number of things," I said; "medicines, of course—what is the good of a doctor who sends no medicine?—and books. You will have to keep yourself quiet a long time. You would like some books?"

"Oh, I have longed for books," she said, sighing; "but don't buy any; lend me some of your own."

"Mine would be very unsuitable for a young lady," I answered, laughing at the thought of my private library. "May I ask why I am not to buy any?"

"Because I have no money to spend in books," she said.

"Well," I replied, "I will borrow some for you from the ladies I know. We will not waste our money, neither you nor I."

I stood looking at her, finding it harder to go away than I had supposed. So closely had I watched the changes upon her face, that every line of it was deeply engraved upon my memory. Other and more familiar faces seemed to have faded in proportion to that distinctness of impression. Julia's features, for instance, had become blurred and obscure, like a painting which has lost its original clearness of tone.

"How soon will you come back again?" asked the faint, plaintive voice.

Clearly it did not occur to her that I could not pay her a visit without great difficulty. I knew how it was next to an impossibility to get over to Sark, for some time at least; but I felt ready to combat even impossibilities.

"I will come back," I said—"yes, I promise to come back in a week's time. Make haste and get well before then, mam'zelle. Good-by, now; good-by."

I was going to sleep at Vaudin's Inn, near to Creux Harbor, from which the cutter would sail almost before the dawn. At five o'clock we started on oar passage—a boat-load of fishermen bound for the market. The cold was sharp, for it was still early in March, and the easterly wind pierced the skin like a myriad of fine needles. A waning moon was hanging in the sky over Guernsey, and the east was growing gray with the coming morning. By the time the sun was fairly up out of its bed of low-lying clouds, we had rounded the southern point of Sark, and were in sight of the Havre Gosselin. But Tardif's cottage was screened by the cliffs, and I could catch no glimpse of it, though, as we rowed onward, I saw a fine, thin column of white smoke blown toward us. It was from his hearth, I knew, and, at this moment, he was preparing an early breakfast for my invalid. I watched it till all the coast became an indistinct outline against the sky.

CHAPTER THE EIGHTH

I was more than half-numb with cold by the time we landed at the quay, opposite the Sark office. The place was all alive, seeming the more busy and animated to me for the solitary six days I had been spending since last Sunday. The arrival of our boat, and especially my appearance in it, created quite a stir among the loungers who are always hanging about the pier. By this time every individual in St. Peter-Port knew that Dr. Martin Dobrée had been missing for several days, having gone out in a fisherman's boat to Sark the Sunday before. I had seen myself in the glass before leaving my chamber at Vaudin's, and to some extent I presented the haggard appearance of a shipwrecked man. A score of voices greeted me; some welcoming, some chaffing. "Glad to see you again, old fellow!" "What news from Sark?" "Been in quod for a week?" "His hair is not cut short!" "No; he has tarried in Sark till his beard be grown!" There was a circling laugh at this last jest at my appearance, which had been uttered by a good-tempered, jovial clergyman, who was passing by on his way to the town church. I did my best to laugh and banter in return, but it was like a bear dancing with a sore head. I felt gloomy and uncomfortable. A change had come over me since I left home, for my return was by no means an unmixed pleasure.

As I was proceeding along the quay, with a train of sympathizing attendants, a man, who was driving a large cart piled with packages in cases, as if they had come in from England by the steamer, touched his hat to me, and stopped the horse. It was in order to inform me that he was conveying furniture which we—that is, Julia and I—had ordered, up to our new house, the windows of which I could see glistening in the morning sun. My spirits did not rise, even at this cheerful information. I looked coldly at the cases, bade the man go on, and shook off my train by taking an abrupt turn up a flight of steps, leading directly into the Haute Rue.

I had chosen instinctively the nearest by-way homeward, but, once in the Haute Rue, I did not pursue it. I turned again upon a sudden thought toward the Market Square, to see if I could pick up any dainties to tempt the delicate appetite of my Sark patient. Every step I took brought me into contact with some friend or acquaintance, whom I would have avoided gladly. The market was sure to be full of them, for the ladies of Guernsey, like Frenchwomen, would be there in shoals, with their maidservants behind them to carry their purchases. Yet I turned toward it, as I said, braving both congratulations and curiosity, to see what I could buy for Tardif's "mam'zelle."

The square had all the peculiar animation of an early market where ladies do their own bargaining. As I had known beforehand, most of my acquaintances were there; for in Guernsey the feminine element predominates terribly, and most of my acquaintances were ladies. The peasant-women behind the stalls also knew me. Most of them nodded to me as I strolled slowly through the crowd, but they were much too busy to suspend their purchases in order to catechise me just then, being sure of me at a future time. I had not done badly in choosing the busiest street for my way home.

But as I left the Market Square I came suddenly upon Julia, face to face. It had all the effect of a shock upon me. Like many other women, she seldom looked well out-of-doors. The prevailing fashion never suited her, however the bonnets were worn, whether hanging down the neck or slouched over the forehead, rising spoon-shaped toward the sky, or lying like a flat plate on the crown. Julia's bonnet always looked as if it had been made for somebody else. She was fond of wearing a shawl, which hung ungracefully about her, and made her figure look squarer and her shoulders higher than they really were. Her face struck sharply upon my brain, as if I had never seen it distinctly before; not a bad face, but unmistakably plain, and just now with a frown upon it, and her heavy eyebrows knitted forbiddingly. A pretty little basket was in her hand, and her mind was full of the bargains she was bent upon. She was even more surprised and startled by our encounter than I was, and her manner, when taken by surprise, was apt to be abrupt.

"Why, Martin!" she ejaculated.

"Well, Julia!" I said.

We stood looking at one another much in the same way as we used to do years before, when she had detected me in some boyish prank, and assumed the mentor while I felt a culprit. How really I felt a culprit at that moment she could not guess.

"I told you just how it would be," she said, in her mentor voice. "I knew there was a storm coming, and I begged and entreated of you not to go. Your mother has been ill all the week, and your father has been as cross as—as—"

"As two sticks," I suggested, precisely as I might have done when I was thirteen.

"It is nothing to laugh at," said Julia, severely. "I shall say nothing about myself and my own feelings, though they have been most acute, the wind blowing a hurricane for twenty-four hours together, and we not sure that you had even reached Sark in safety. Your mother and I wanted to charter the Rescue, and send her over to fetch you home as soon as the worst of the storm was over, but my uncle pooh-poohed it."

"I am very glad he did," I replied, involuntarily.

"He said you would be more than ready to come back in the first cutter that sailed," she went on. "I suppose you have just come in?"

"Yes," I said, "and I'm half numbed with cold, and nearly famished with hunger. You don't give me as good a welcome as the Prodigal Son got, Julia."

"No," she answered, softening a little; "but I'm not sorry to see you safe again. I would turn back with you, but I like to do the marketing myself, for the servants will buy any thing. Martin, a whole cartload of our furniture is come in. You will find the invoice inside my davenport. We must go down this afternoon and superintend the unpacking."

"Very well," I said; "but I cannot stay longer now."

I did not go on with any lighter heart than before this meeting with Julia. I had scrutinized her face, voice, and manner, with unwonted criticism. As a rule, a face that has been before us all our days is as seldom an object of criticism as any family portrait which has hung against the same place on the wall all our lifetime. The latter fills up a space which would otherwise be blank; the former does very little else. It never strikes you; it is almost invisible to you. There would be a blank space left if it disappeared, and you could not fill it up from memory. A phantom has been living, breathing, moving beside you, with vanishing features and no very real presence.

I had, therefore, for the first time criticised my future wife. It was a good, honest, plain, sensible face, with some fine, insidious lines about the corners of the eyes and lips, and across the forehead. They could hardly be called wrinkles yet, but they were the first faint sketch of them, and it is impossible to obliterate the slightest touch etched by Time. She was five years older than I—thirty-three last birthday. There was no more chance for our Guernsey girls to conceal their age than for the unhappy daughters of peers, whose dates are faithfully kept, and recorded in the Peerage. The upper classes of the island, who were linked together by endless and intricate ramifications of relationship, formed a kind of large family, with some of its advantages and many of its drawbacks. In one sense we had many things in common; our family histories were public property, as also our private characters and circumstances. For instance, my own engagement to Julia, and our approaching marriage, gave almost as much interest to the island as though we were members of each household.

I have looked out a passage in the standard work upon the Channel Islands. They are the words of an Englishman who was studying us more philosophically than we imagined. Unknown to ourselves we had been under his microscope. "At a period not very distant, society in Guernsey grouped itself into two divisions—one, including those families who prided themselves on ancient descent and landed estates, and who regarded themselves as the pur sang; and the other, those whose fortunes had chiefly been made during the late war or in trade. The former were called Sixties, the latter were the Forties."

Now Julia and I belonged emphatically to the Sixties. We had never been debased by trade, and a mésalliance was not known in our family. To be sure, my father had lost a fortune instead of making one in any way; but that did not alter his position or mine. We belonged to the aristocracy of Guernsey, and noblesse oblige. As for my marriage with Julia, it was so much the more interesting as the number of marriageable men was extremely limited; and she was considered favored indeed by Fate, which had provided for her a cousin willing to settle down for life in the island.

Still more greetings, more inquiries, more jokes, as I wended my way homeward. I had become very weary of them before I turned into our own drive. My father was just starting off on horseback. He looked exceedingly well on horseback, being a very handsome man, and in excellent preservation. His hair, as white as snow, was thick and well curled, and his face almost without a wrinkle. He had married young, and was not more than twenty-five years older than myself. He stopped, and extended two fingers to me.

"So you are back, Martin?" he said. "It has been a confounded nuisance, you being out of the way; and such weather for a man of my years! I had to ride out three miles to lance a baby's gums, confound it! in all that storm on Tuesday. Mrs. Durande has been very ill too; all your patients have been troublesome. But it must have been awfully dull work for you out yonder. What did you do with yourself, eh? Make love to some of the pretty Sark girls behind Julia's back, eh?"

My father kept himself young, as he was very fond of stating; his style of conversation was eminently so. It jarred upon my ears more than ever after Tardif's grave and solemn words, and often deep thoughts. I was on the point of answering sharply, but I checked myself.

"The weather has been awful," I said. "How did my mother bear it?"

"She has been like an old hen clucking after her duckling in the water," he replied. "She has been fretting and fuming after you all the week. If it had been me out in Sark, she would have slept soundly and ate heartily; as it was you, she has neither slept nor ate. You are quite an old woman's pet, Martin. As for me, there is no love lost between old women and me."

"Good-morning, sir," I said, turning away, and hurrying on to the house. I heard him laugh lightly, and hum an opera-air as he rode off, sitting his horse with the easy seat of a thorough horseman. He would never set up a carriage as long as he could ride like that. I watched him out of sight, and then went in to seek my poor mother.

CHAPTER THE NINTH

A CLEW TO THE SECRET

She was lying on the sofa in the breakfast-room, with the Venetian blinds down to darken the morning sunshine. Her eyes wore closed, though she held in her hands the prayer-hook, from which she had been reading as usual the Psalms for the day. I had time to take note of the extreme fragility of her appearance, which, doubtless I noticed the more plainly for my short absence. Her hands were very thin, and her cheeks hollow. A few silver threads were growing among her brown hair, and a line or two between her eyebrows were becoming deeper. But while I was looking at her, though I made no sort of sound or movement, she seemed to feel that I was there; and after looking up she started from her sofa, and flung her arms about me, pressing closer and closer to me.

"O Martin, my boy! my darling!" she sobbed, "thank God you are come back safe! Oh, I have been very rebellious, very unbelieving. I ought to have known that you would be safe. Oh, I am thankful!"

"So am I, mother," I said, kissing her, "and very hungry into the bargain."

I knew that would check her hysterical excitement. She looked up at me with smiles and tears on her face; but the smiles won the day.

"That is so like you, Martin," she said; "I believe your ghost would say those very words. You are always hungry when you come home. Well, my boy shall have the best breakfast in Guernsey. Sit down, then, and let me wait upon you."

That was just what pleased her most whenever I came in from some ride into the country. She was a woman with fondling, caressing little ways, such as Julia could no more perform gracefully than an elephant could waltz. My mother enjoyed fetching my slippers, and warming them herself by the fire, and carrying away my boots when I took them off. No servant was permitted to do any of these little offices for me—that is, when my father was out of the way. If he was there, my mother sat still, and left me to wait on myself, or ring for a servant, Never in my recollection had she done any thing of the kind for my father. Had she watched and waited upon him thus in the early days of their married life, until some neglect or unfaithfulness of his had cooled her love for him? I sat down as she bade me, and had my slippers brought, and felt her fingers passed fondly through my hair.

"You have come back like a barbarian," she said, "rougher than Tardif himself. How have you managed, my boy? You must tell me all about it as soon as your hunger is satisfied."

"As soon as I have had my breakfast, mother, I must put up a few things in a hamper to go back by the Sark cutter," I answered.

"What sort of things?" she asked. "Tell me, and I will be getting them ready for you."

"Well, there will be some physic, of course," I said; "you cannot help me in that. But you can find things suitable for a delicate appetite; jelly, you know, and jams, and marmalade; any thing nice that comes to hand. And some good port-wine, and a few amusing books."

"Books!" echoed my mother.

I recollected at once that the books she might select, as being suited to a Sark peasant, would hardly prove interesting to my patient. I could not do better than go down to Barbet's circulating library, and look out some good works there.

"Well, no," I said; "never mind the books. If you will look out the other things, those can wait."

"Whom are they for?" asked my mother.

"For my patient," I replied, devoting myself to the breakfast before me.

"What sort of a patient, Martin?" she inquired again.

"Her name is Ollivier," I said. "A common name. Our postmaster's name is Ollivier."

"Oh, yes," she answered; "I know several families of Olliviers. I dare say I should know this person if you could tell me her Christian name. Is it Jane, or Martha, or Rachel?"

"I don't know," I said; "I did not ask."

Should I tell my mother about my mysterious patient? I hesitated for a minute or two. But to what good? It was not my habit to talk about my patients and their ailments. I left them all behind me when I crossed the threshold of home. My mother's brief curiosity had been satisfied with the name of Ollivier, and she made no further inquiries about her. But to expedite me in my purpose, she rang, and gave orders for old Pellet, our only man-servant, to find a strong hamper, and told the cook to look out some jars of preserve.

The packing of that hamper interested me wonderfully; and my mother, rather amazed at my taking the superintendence of it in person, stood by me in her store-closet, letting me help myself liberally. There was a good space left after I had taken sufficient to supply Miss Ollivier with good things for some weeks to come. If my mother had not been by, I should have filled it up with books.

"Give me a loaf or two of white bread," I said; "the bread at Tardif's is coarse and hard, as I know after eating it for a week. A loaf, if you please, dear mother."

"Whatever are you doing here, Martin?" exclaimed Julia's unwelcome voice behind me. Her bilious attack had not quite passed away, and her tones were somewhat sharp and raspy.

"He has been living on Tardif's coarse fare for a week," answered my mother; "so now he has compassion enough for his Sark patient to pack up some dainties for her. If you could only give him one or two of your bad headaches, he would have more sympathy for you."

"Have you had one of your headaches, Julia?" I inquired.

"The worst I ever had," she answered. "It was partly your going off in that rash way, and the storm that came on after, and the fright we were in. You must not think of going again, Martin. I shall take care you don't go after we are married."

Julia had been used to speak out as calmly about our marriage as if it was no more than going to a picnic. It grated upon me just then; though it had been much the same with myself. There was no delightful agitation about the future that lay before us. We were going to set up housekeeping by ourselves, and that was all. There was no mystery in it; no problem to be solved; no discovery to be made on either side. There would be no Blue Beard's chamber in our dwelling. We had grown up together; now we had agreed to grow old together. That was the sum total of marriage to Julia and me.

I finished packing the hamper, and sent Pellet with it to the Sark office, having addressed it to Tardif, who had engaged to be down at the Creux Harbor to receive it when the cutter returned. Then I made a short and hurried toilet, which by this time had become essential to my reappearance in civilized society. But I was in haste to secure a parcel of books before the cutter should start home again, with its courageous little knot of market-people. I ran down to Barbet's, scarcely heeding the greetings which were flung after me by every passer-by. I looked through the library-shelves with growing dissatisfaction, until I hit upon two of Mrs. Gaskell's novels, "Pride and Prejudice," by Jane Austin, and "David Copperfield." Besides these, I chose a book for Sunday reading, as my observations upon my mother and Julia had taught me that my patient could not read a novel on a Sunday with a quiet conscience.

Barbet brought half a sheet of an old Times to form the first cover of my parcel. The shop was crowded with market-people, and, as he was busy, I undertook to pack them myself, the more willingly as I had no wish for him to know what direction I wrote upon them. I was about to fold the newspaper round them, when my eye was caught by an advertisement at the top of one of the columns, the first line of which was printed in capitals. I recollected in an instant that I had seen it and read it before. This was what I had tried in vain to recall while Tardif was describing Miss Ollivier to me. "Strayed from her home in London, on the 20th inst., a young lady with bright-brown hair, gray eyes, and delicate features; age twenty one. She is believed to have been alone. Was dressed in a blue-silk dress, and seal-skin jacket and hat. Fifty pounds reward is offered to any person giving such information as will lead to her restoration to her friends. Apply to Messrs. Scott and Brown, Gray's Inn Road, E.C."

I stood perfectly still for some seconds, staring blankly at the very simple, direct advertisement under my eyes. There was not the slightest doubt in my mind that it had a direct reference to my pretty patient in Sark. I had a reason for recollecting the date of Tardif's return from London, the very day after the mournful disaster off the Havre Gosselin, when four gentlemen and a boatman had been lost during a squall. But I had no time for deliberation then, and I tore off a large corner of the Times containing that and other advertisements, and thrust it unseen into my pocket. After that I went on with my work, and succeeded in turning out a creditable-looking parcel, which I carried down to the Sark cutter.

Before I returned home I made two or three half-professional calls upon patients whom my father had visited during my absence. Everywhere I had to submit to numerous questions as to my adventures and pursuits during my week's exile. At each place curiosity seemed to be quite satisfied with the information that the young woman who had been hurt by a fall from the cliffs was an Ollivier. With that freedom and familiarity which exists among us, I was rallied for my evident absence and preoccupation of mind, which were pleasantly ascribed to the well-known fact that a large quantity of furniture for our new house had arrived from England while I was away. These friends of mine could tell me the colors of the curtains, and the patterns of the carpets, and the style of my chairs and tables; so engrossingly interesting to all our circle was our approaching marriage.

In the mean time, I had no leisure to study and ponder over the advertisement, which by so odd a chance had come into my hands. That must be reserved till I was alone at night.

CHAPTER THE TENTH

JULIA'S WEDDING-DRESS

Yet I found my attention wandering, and my wits wool-gathering, even in the afternoon, when I had gone down with Julia and my mother to the new house, to see after the unpacking of that load of furniture. I can imagine circumstances in which nothing could be more delightful than the care with which a man prepares a home for his future wife. The very tint of the walls, and the way the light falls in through the windows, would become matters of grave importance. In what pleasant spot shall her favorite chair be placed? And what picture shall hang opposite it to catch her eye the oftenest? Where is her piano to stand? What china, and glass, and silver, is she to use? Where are the softest carpets to be found for her feet to tread? In short, where is the very best and daintiest of every thing to be had, for the best and daintiest little bride the sun ever shone on?

There was not the slightest flavor of this sentiment in our furnishing of our new house. It was really more Julia's business than mine. We had had dozens of furnishing lists to peruse from the principal houses in London and Paris, as if even there it was a well-understood thing that Julia and I were going to be married. We had toiled through these catalogues, making pencil-marks in them, as though they were catalogues of an art exhibition. We had prudently settled the precise sum (of Julia's money) which we were to lay out. Julia's taste did not often agree with mine, as she had no eye for the harmonies of color—a singular deficiency among us, as most of the Guernsey women are born artists. We were constantly compelled to come to a compromise, each yielding some point; not without a secret misgiving on my part that the new house would have many an eyesore about it for me. But then it was Julia's money that was doing it, and after all she was more anxious to please me than I deserved.

That afternoon Pellet and I, like two assistants in a furnishing-house, unrolled carpets and stretched them along the floors before the critical gaze of my mother and Julia. We unpacked chairs and tables, scanning anxiously for damages on the polished wood, and setting them one after another in a row against the walls. I went about as in some dream. The house commanded a splendid view of the whole group of the Channel Islands, and the rocky islets innumerable strewed about the sea. The afternoon sun was shining full upon Sark, and whenever I looked through the window I could see the cliffs of the Havre Gosselin, purple in the distance, with a silver thread of foam at their foot. No wonder that my thoughts wandered, and the words my mother and Julia were speaking went in at one ear and out at the other. Certainly I was dreaming; but which part was the dream?

"I don't believe he cares a straw about the carpets!" exclaimed Julia, in a disappointed tone.

"I do indeed, dear Julia," I said, bringing myself back to the carpets. Here I had been obliged to give in to Julia's taste. She had set her mind upon having flowers in her drawing-room carpet, and there they were, large garlands of bright-colored blossoms, very gay, and, as I ventured to remark to myself, very gaudy.

"You like it better than you did in the pattern?" she asked, anxiously.

I did not like it one whit better, but I should have been a brute if I had said so. She was gazing at it and me with so troubled an expression, that I felt it necessary to set her mind at ease.

"It is certainly handsomer than the pattern?" I said, regarding it attentively; "very much handsomer."

"You like it better than the plain thing you chose at first?" pursued Julia.

I was about to be hunted into a corner, and forced into denying my own taste—a process almost more painful than denying one's faith—when my mother came to my rescue. She could read us both as an open book, and knew the precise moment to come between us.

"Julia, my love," she said, "remember that we wish to show Martin those patterns while it is daylight. To-morrow is Sunday, you know."

A little tinge of color crept over Julia's tintless face as she told Pellet he might go. I almost wished that I might be dismissed too; but it was only a vague, wordless wish. We then drew near to the window, from which we could see Sark so clearly, and Julia drew out of her pocket a very large envelope, which was bursting with its contents.

They were small scraps of white silk and white satin. I took them mechanically into my hand, and could not help admiring the pure, lustrous, glossy beauty of them. I passed my fingers over them softly. There was something in the sight of them that moved me, as if they were fragments of the shining garments of some vision, which in times gone by, when I was much younger, had now and then floated before my fancy. I did not know any one lovely enough to wear raiment of glistening white like these, unless— unless—. A passing glimpse of the pure white face, and glossy hair, and deep gray eyes of my Sark patient flashed across me.

"They are patterns for Julia's wedding-dress," said my mother, in a low, tender voice.

CHAPTER THE ELEVENTH

TRUE TO BOTH

"For Julia!" I repeated, the treacherous vision fading away instantaneously. "Oh, yes! I understand. They are very beautiful—very beautiful indeed."

"Which do you like most?" asked Julia, in a whisper, as she leaned against my shoulder.

"I like them all," I said. "There is scarcely any difference among them that I can see."

"No difference!" she exclaimed. "That is so like a man! Why, they are as different as can be. Look here, this one is only five shillings a yard, and that is twelve. Isn't that a difference?"

"A very great one," I replied. "But do you think you will look well in white, my dear Julia? You never do wear white."

"A bride cannot wear any thing but white," she said, angrily. "I declare, Martin, you would not mind if I looked a perfect fright."

"But I should mind very much," I urged, putting my arm around her; "for you will be my wife then, Julia."

She smiled almost for the first time that afternoon, for her mind had been full of the furniture, and too burdened for happiness. But now she looked happy.

"You can be as nice and good as any one, when you like," she said, gently.

"I shall always be nice and good when we are married," I answered, with a laugh. "You are not afraid of venturing, are you, Julia?"

"Not the least in the world," she said. "I know you, Martin, and I can trust you implicitly."

My heart ached at the words, so softly and warmly spoken. But I laughed again—at myself this time, not at her. Why should she not trust me? I would be as true as steel to her. I loved no one better, and I would take care not to love any one. My word, my honor, my troth, were all plighted to her. Only a scoundrel and a fool would be unfaithful to an engagement like ours.

We walked home together, we three, all contented and all happy. We had a good deal to talk of during the evening, and sat up late. Sundry small events had happened in Guernsey during my six-days' absence, and these were discussed with that charming minuteness with which women canvass family matters. It was midnight before I found myself alone in my own room.

I had half forgotten the crumpled paper in my waistcoat-pocket, but now I smoothed it out before me and pondered over every word. No, there could not be a doubt that it referred to Miss Ollivier. "Bright-brown hair, gray eyes, and delicate features." That exactly corresponded with her appearance. "Blue-silk dress, and seal-skin jacket and hat." It was precisely the dress which Tardif had described. "Fifty pounds reward." That was a large sum to offer, and the inference was that her friends were persons of good means, and anxious for her recovery.

Why should she have strayed from home? That was the question. What possible reason could there have been, strong enough to impel a young and delicately-nurtured girl to run all the risks and dangers of a flight alone and unprotected? Her friends evidently believed that she had not been run away with; there was not the ordinary element of an elopement in this case.

But Miss Ollivier had assured me she had no friends. What did she mean by the word? Here were persons evidently anxious to discover her place of concealment. Were they friends? or could they by any chance be enemies? This is not an age when enmity is very rampant. For my own part, I had not an enemy in the world. Why should this pretty, habitually-obedient, self-controlled girl have any? Most probably it was one of those instances of bitter misunderstanding which sometimes arise in families, and which had driven her to the desperate step of seeking peace and quietness by flight.

Then what ought I to do with this advertisement, thrust, as it would seem, purposely under my notice? If I had not wrapped up the parcel myself at Barbet's, I should have missed seeing it; or if Barbet had picked up any other piece of paper, it would not have come under my eye. A curious concatenation of very trivial circumstances had ended in putting into my hands a clew by which I could unravel all the mystery about my Sark patient. What was I to do with the clew?

I might communicate at once with Messrs. Scott and Brown, giving them the information they had advertised for six months before, and receive a reply, stating that it was no longer valuable to them, or containing an acknowledgment of my claim to the fifty pounds reward. I might sell my knowledge of Miss Ollivier for fifty pounds. In doing so I might render her a great service, by restoring her to her proper sphere in society. But the recollection of Tardif's description of her as looking terrified and hunted recurred vividly to me. The advertisement put her age as twenty-one. I should not have judged her so old myself, especially since her hair had been cut short. But if she was twenty-one, she was old enough to form plans and purposes for herself, and to choose, as far as she could, her own mode of living. I was not prepared to deliver her up, until I knew something more of both sides of the question.

Settled—that if I could see Messrs. Scot and Brown, and learn something about Miss Ollivier's friends, I might be then able to decide whether I would betray her to them but I would not write. Also, that I must see her again first, and once more urge her to have confidence in me. If she would trust me with her secret, I would be as true to her as a friend as I meant to be true to Julia.

Having come to these conclusions, I cut the advertisement carefully out of the crumpled paper, and placed it in my pocket-book with portraits of my mother and Julia, Here were mementos of the three women I cared most for in the world: my mother first, Julia second, and my mysterious patient third.

CHAPTER THE TWELFTH

STOLEN WATERS ARE SWEET

I was neither in good spirits nor in good temper during the next few days. My mother and Julia appeared astonished at this, for I was not ordinarily as touchy and fractious as I showed myself immediately after my sojourn in Sark.

I was ashamed of it myself. The new house, which occupied their time and thoughts so agreeably, worried me as it had not done before. I made every possible excuse not to be sent to it, or taken to it, several times a day.

The discussions over Julia's wedding-dress also, which had by no means been decided upon on Saturday afternoon, began to bore me beyond words. Whenever I could, I made my patients a pretext for getting away from them.

One of them, a cousin of my mother—as I have said, we were all cousins of one degree or another—Captain Carey, met me on the quay, a day or two after my return. He had been a commander in the Royal Navy, and, after cruising about in all manner of unhealthy latitudes, had returned to his native island for the recovery of his health. He and his sister lived together in a very pleasant house of their own, in the Vale, about two miles from St. Peter-Port.

He looked yellow enough to be on the verge of an attack of jaundice when he came across me.

"Hallo, Martin!" he cried, "I am delighted to see you, my boy. I've been a little out of sorts lately; but I would not let Johanna send for your father. He does very well to go dawdling after women, and playing with their pulses, but I don't want him dawdling after me. Tell me what you have to say about me, my lad."

He went on to tell me his symptoms, while a sudden idea struck me almost like a flash of genius.

I am nothing of a genius; but at that time new thoughts came into my mind with wonderful rapidity. It was positively necessary that I should run over to Sark this week—I had given my word to Miss Ollivier that I would do so—but I dared not mention such a project at home. My mother and Julia would be up in arms at the first syllable I uttered.

What if I could do two patients good at one stroke, kill two birds with one stone? Captain Carey had a pretty little yacht lying idle in St. Sampson's Harbor, and a day's cruising would do him all the good in the world. Why should he not carry me over to Sark, when I could visit my other patient, and nobody be made miserable by the trip?

"I will make you up some of your old medicine," I said, "but I strongly recommend you to have a day out on the water; seven or eight hours at any rate. If the weather keeps as fine as it is now, it will do you a world of good."

"It is so dreary alone," he objected, "and Johanna would not care to go out at this season, I know."

"If I could manage it," I said, deliberating, "I should be glad to have a day with you."

"Ah! if you could do that!" he replied, eagerly.

"I'll see about it," I said. "Should you mind where you sailed to?"

"Not at all, not at all, my boy," he answered, "so that I get your company. You shall be skipper, or helmsman, or both, if you like."

"Well, then," I replied, "you might take me over to the Havre Gosselin, to see how my patient's broken arm is going on. It's a bore there being no resident medical man there at this moment. The accident last autumn was a great loss to the island."

"Ah! poor fellow!" said Captain Carey, "he was a sad loss to them. But I'll take you over with pleasure, Martin; any day you fix upon."

"Get the yacht ship-shape, then," I said; "I think I can manage it on Thursday."

I did not say at home whither I was bound on Thursday. I informed them merely that Captain Carey and I were going out in his yacht for a few hours. This was simply to prevent them from worrying themselves.

It was as delicious a spring morning as ever I remember. As I rode along the flat shore between St. Peter-Port and St. Sampson's, the fresh air from the sea played about my face, as if to drive dull care away, and make me as buoyant and debonair as itself. The little waves were glittering and dancing in the sunshine, and chiming with the merry carols of the larks, outsinging one another in the blue sky overhead. The numerous wind-mills, like children's toys, which were pumping water out of the stone-quarries, whirled and spun busily in the brisk breeze. Every person I met saluted me with a blithe and cheery greeting. My dull spirits had been blown far away before I set foot on the deck of Captain Carey's little yacht.

The run over was all that we could wish. The cockle-shell of a boat, belonging to the yacht, bore me to the foot of the ladder hanging down the rock at Havre Gosselin. A very few minutes took me to the top of the cliff, and there lay the little thatched, nest-like home of my patient. I hastened forward eagerly.

The place seemed very solitary and deserted; and a sudden fear came across me. Was it possible that she should be dead? It was possible. I had left her six days ago only just over a terrible crisis. There might have been a relapse, a failure of vital force. I might be come to find those shining eyes hid beneath their lids forever, and the pale, suffering face motionless in death.

Certainly the rhythmic motion of my heart was disturbed. I felt it contract painfully, and its beating suspended for a moment or two. The farmstead was intensely quiet, with the ominous stillness of death. All the windows were shrouded with their check curtains. There was no clatter of Suzanne's wooden clogs about the fold or the kitchen. If it had been Sunday, this supernatural silence would have been easily accounted for; but it was Thursday. I scarcely dared go on and learn the cause of it.

All silent still as I crossed the stony causeway of the yard. Not a face looked out from door or window. Mam'zelle's casement stood a little way open, and the breeze played with the curtains, fluttering them like banners in a procession. I dared not try to look in. The house-door was ajar, and I approached it cautiously. "Thank God!" I cried within myself as I gazed eagerly into the cottage.

She was lying there upon the fern-bed, half asleep, her head fallen back upon the pillow, and the book she had been reading dropped from her hand. Her dress was of some coarse, dark-green stuff, which made a charming contrast to her delicate face and bright hair. The whole interior of the cottage formed a picture. The old furniture of oak, almost black with age, the neutral tints of the wall and ceiling, and the deep tone of her green dress, threw out into strong relief the graceful, shining head, and pale face.

I suppose she became subtly conscious, as women always are, that somebody's eyes were fixed upon her, for she awoke fully, and looked up as I lingered on the door-sill.

"O Dr. Martin!" she cried, "I am so glad!"

She looked pleased enough to be upon the point of trying to raise herself up in order to welcome me, but I interposed quickly. It was more difficult than I had expected to assume a grave, professional tone, but by an effort I did so. I bade her lie still, and took a chair at some little distance.

"Tardif is gone out fishing," she said, "and his mother is gone away too, to a christening-feast somewhere; but Mrs. Renouf is to be here in an hour or two. I told them I could manage very well as long as that."

"They ought not to have left you alone," I replied.

"And I shall not be left alone," she said, smiling, "for you are come, you see. I am rather glad they are away; for I wanted to tell you how much I felt your goodness to me all through that dreadful week. You are the first doctor I ever had about me, the very first. Perhaps you thought I did not know what care you were taking of me; but, somehow or other, I knew every thing. My mind did not quite go. You were very, very good to me."

"Never mind that," I said; "I am come to see how my work is going on. How is the arm, first of all?"

I almost wished that Mother Renouf or Suzanne Tardif had been at hand. But Miss Ollivier seemed perfectly composed, as much so as a child. She looked like one with her cropped head of hair, and frank, open face. My own momentary embarrassment passed away. The arm was going on all right, and so was Mother Renouf's charge, the sprained ankle.

"We must take care you are not lame," I said, while I was feeling carefully the complicated joint of her ankle.

"Lame!" she repeated, in an alarmed voice, "is there any fear of that?"

"Not much," I answered, "but we must be careful, mam'zelle. You must promise me not to set your foot on the ground, or in any way rest your weight upon it, till I give you leave."

"That means that you will have to come to see me again," she said; "is it not very difficult to come over from Guernsey?"

"Not at all," I answered, "it is quite a treat to me."

Her face grew very grave, as if she was thinking of some unpleasant topic. She looked at me earnestly and questioningly.

"May I speak to you with great plainness, Dr. Martin?" she asked.

"Speak precisely what is in your mind at this moment," I replied.

"You are very, very good to me," she said, holding out her hand to me, "but I do not want you to come more often than is quite necessary, because I am very poor. If I were rich," she went on hurriedly, "I should like you to come every day—it is so pleasant—but I can never pay you sufficiently for that long week you were here. So please do not visit me oftener than is quite necessary."

My face felt hot, but I scarcely knew what to say. I bungled out an answer:

"I would not take any money from you, and I shall come to see you as often as I can."

I bound up her little foot again without another word, and then sat down, pushing my chair farther from her.

"You are not offended with me, Dr. Martin?" she asked, in a pleading tone.

"No," I answered; "but you are mistaken in supposing that a medical man has no love for his profession apart from its profits. To see that your arm gets properly well is part of my duty, and I shall fulfil it without any thought of whether I shall get paid for it or no."

"Now," she said, "I must let you know how poor I am. Will you please to fetch me my box out of my room?"

I was only too glad to obey her. This seemed to be an opening to a complete confidence between us. Now I came to think of it, Fortune had favored me in thus throwing us together alone.

I lifted the small, light box very easily—there could not be many treasures in it—and carried it back to her. She took a key out of her pocket and unlocked it with some difficulty, but she could not raise the lid without my help. I took care not to offer any assistance until she asked it.

Yes, there were very few possessions in that light trunk, but the first glance showed me a blue-silk dress, and seal-skin jacket and hat. I lifted them out for her, and after them a pair of velvet slippers, soiled, as if they had been through muddy roads. I did not utter a remark. Beneath these lay a handsome watch and chain, a fine diamond ring, and five sovereigns lying loose in the box.

"That is all the money I have in the world," she said, sadly.

I laid the five sovereigns in her small, white hand, and she turned them over, one after another, with a pitiful look on her face. I felt foolish enough to cry over them myself.

"Dr. Martin," was her unexpected question after a long pause, "do you know what became of my hair?"

"Why?" I asked, looking at her fingers running through the short curls we had left her.

"Because that ought to be sold for something," she said. "I am almost glad you had it cut off. My hair-dresser told me once he would give five guineas for a head of hair like mine, it was so long and the color was uncommon. Five guineas would not be half enough to pay you though, I know."

She spoke so simply and quietly, that I did not attempt to remonstrate with her about her anxiety to pay me.

"Tardif has it," I said; "but of course he will give it you back again. Shall I sell it for you, mam'zelle?"

"Oh, that is just what I could not ask you!" she exclaimed. "You see there is no one to buy it here, and I hope it may be a long time before I go away. I don't know, though; that depends upon whether I can dispose of my things. There is my seal-skin, it cost twenty-five guineas last year, and it ought to be worth something. And my watch—see what a nice one it is. I should like to sell them all, every one. Then I could stay here as long as the money lasted."

"How much do you pay here?" I inquired, for she had taken me so far into counsel that I felt justified in asking that question.

"A pound a week," she answered.

"A pound a week!" I repeated, in amazement. "Does Tardif know that?"

"I don't think he does," she said. "When I had been here a week I gave Mrs. Tardif a sovereign, thinking perhaps she would give me a little out of it. I am not used to being poor, and I did not know how much I ought to pay. But she kept it all, and came to me every week for more. Was it too much to pay?"

"Too much!" I said. "You should have spoken to Tardif about it, my poor child."

"I could not talk to Tardif about his mother," she answered. "Besides, it would not have been too much if I had only had plenty. But it has made me so anxious. I did not know whatever I should do when it was all gone. I do not know now."

Here was a capital opening for a question about her friends.

"You will be compelled to communicate with your family," I said. "You have told me how poor you are; cannot you trust me about your friends?"

"I have no friends," she answered, sorrowfully. "If I had any, do you suppose I should be here?"

"I am one," I said, "and Tardif is another."

"Ah, new friends," she replied; "but I mean real old friends who have known you all your life, like your mother, Dr. Martin, or your cousin Julia. I want somebody to go to who knows all about me, and say to them, after telling them every thing, keeping nothing back at all, 'Have I done right? What else ought I to have done?' No new friend could answer questions like those."

Was there any reason I could bring forward to increase her confidence in me? I thought there was, and her friendlessness and helplessness touched me to the core of my heart. Yet it was with an indefinable reluctance that I brought forward my argument.

"Miss Ollivier," I said, "I have no claim of old acquaintance or friendship, yet it is possible I might answer those questions, if you could prevail upon yourself to tell me the circumstances of your former life. In a few weeks I shall be in a position to show you more friendship than I can do now. I shall have a home of my own, and a wife who will be your friend more fittingly, perhaps, than myself."

"I knew it," she answered, half shyly. "Tardif told me you were going to marry your cousin Julia."

Just then we heard the fold-yard gate swing to behind some one who was coming to the house.

CHAPTER THE THIRTEENTH

ONE IN A THOUSAND

I had altogether forgotten that Captain Carey's yacht was waiting for me off the little bay below; and I sprang quickly to the door in the dread that he had followed me.

It was an immense relief to see only Tardif's tall figure bending under his creel and nets, and crossing the yard slowly. I hailed him and he quickened his pace, his honest features lighting up at the sight of me.

"How do you find mam'zelle, doctor?" were his first eager words.

"All right," I said; "going on famously. Sark is enough to cure any one and any thing of itself, Tardif. There is no air like it. I should not mind being a little ill here myself."

"Captain Carey is impatient to be gone," he continued. "He sent word by me that you might be visiting every house in the island, you had been away so long."

"Not so very long," I said, testily; "but I will just run in and say good-by, and then I want you to walk with me to the cliff."

I turned back for a last look and a last word. No chance of learning her secret now. The picture was as perfect as when I had had the first glimpse of it, only her face had grown, if possible, more charming after my renewed scrutiny of it.

There are faces that grow upon you the longer and the oftener you look upon them; faces that seem to have a veil over them, which melts away like the thin, fine mist of the morning upon the cliffs, until they flash out in their full color and beauty. The last glance was eminently satisfactory, and so was the last word.

"Shall I send you the hair?" asked Miss Ollivier, returning practically to a matter of business.

"To be sure," I answered. "I shall dispose of it to advantage, but I have not time to wait for it now."

"And may I write a letter to you?"

"Yes," was my reply: I was too pleased to express myself more eloquently.

"Good-by," she said; "you are a very good doctor to me."

"And friend?" I added.

"And friend," she repeated.

That was the last word, for I was compelled to hurry away. Tardif accompanied me to the cliff, and I took the opportunity to tell him as pleasantly as I could the extravagant charge his mother had made upon her lodger, and the girl's anxiety about the future. A more grieved look never came across a man's face.

"Dr. Martin," he said, "I would have cut off my hand rather than it had been so. Poor little mam'zelle! Poor old mother! She is growing old, sir, and old people are greedy. The fall of the year is dark and cold, and gives nothing, but takes away all it can, and hoards it for the young new spring that is to follow. It seems almost the nature of old age. Poor old mother! I am very grieved for her. And I am troubled, troubled about mam'zelle. To think she has been fretting all the winter about this, when I was trying to find out how to cheer her! Only five pounds left, poor little soul! Why! all I have is at her service. It is enough to have her only in the house, with her pretty ways and sweet voice. I'll put it all right with mam'zelle, sir, and with my poor old mother too. I am very sorry for her."

"Miss Ollivier has been asking me to sell her hair," I said.

"No, no," he answered hastily, "not a single hair! I cannot say yes to that. The pretty bright curls! If anybody is to buy them, I will. Yes, doctor! that is famous. She wishes you to sell her hair? Very good; I will buy it; it must be mine. I have more money than you think, perhaps. I will buy mam'zelle's pretty curls; and she shall have the money, and then there will be more than five pounds in her little purse. Tell me how much they will be. Ten pounds? Fifteen? Twenty?"

"Nonsense, Tardif!" I answered; "keep one of them, if you like; but I must have the rest. We will settle it between us."

"No, doctor," he said; "your cousin will not like that. You are going to be married soon; it would not do for you to keep mam'zelle's curls."

It was said with so much simplicity and good-heartedness that I felt ashamed of a rising feeling of resentment, and parted with him cordially. In a few minutes afterward I was on board the yacht, and laughing at Captain Carey's reproaches. Tardif was still visible on the edge of the cliff, watching our departure.

"That is as good a fellow as ever breathed," said Captain Carey, waving his cap to him.

"I know it better than you do," I replied.

"And how is the young woman?" he asked.

"Going on as well as a broken arm and a sprained ankle can do," I answered.

"You will want to come again, Martin," he said; "when are we to have another day?"

"Well, I shall hear how she is every now and then," I answered; "it takes too long a time to come more often than is necessary. But you will bring me if it is necessary?"

"With all my heart," said Captain Carey.

For the next few days I waited with some impatience for Miss Ollivier's promised letter. It came at last, and I put it into my pocket to read when I was alone—why, I could scarcely have explained to myself.

"Dear Dr. Martin," it began, "I have no little commission to trouble you with. Tardif tells me it was quite a mistake, his mother taking a sovereign from me each week. She does not understand English money; and he says I have paid quite sufficient to stay with them a whole year longer without paying any more. I am quite content about that now. Tardif says, too, that he has a friend in Southampton who will buy my hair, and give more than anybody in Guernsey. So I need not trouble you about it, though I am sure you would have done it for me.

"I have not put my foot to the ground yet; but yesterday Tardif carried me all the way down to his boat, and took me out for a little sail under the beautiful cliffs, where we could look up and see all those strange carvings upon the rocks. I thought that perhaps there were real things written there that we should like to read. Sometimes in the sky there are fine faint lines across the blue which look like written sentences, if one could only make them out. Here they are on the rocks, but every tide washes them away, leaving fresh ones. Perhaps they are messages to me, answers to those questions that I cannot answer myself.

"Good-by, my good doctor. I am trying to do every thing you told me exactly; and I am getting well again fast. I do not believe I shall be lame; you are too clever for that. Your patient,

"OLIVIA."

Olivia! I looked at the word again to make sure of it. Then it was not her surname that was Ollivier, and I was still ignorant of that. I saw in a moment how the mistake had arisen, and how innocent she was of any deception in the matter. She would tell Tardif that her name was Olivia, and he thought only of the Olliviers he knew. It was a mistake that had been of use in checking curiosity, and I did not feel bound to put it right. My mother and Julia appeared to have forgotten my patient in Sark altogether.

Olivia! I thought it a very pretty name, and repeated it to myself with its abbreviations, Olive, Livy. It was difficult to abbreviate Julia; Ju I had called her in my rudest school-boy days. I wondered how high Olivia would stand beside me; for I had never seen her on her feet. Julia was not two inches shorter than myself; a tall, stiff figure, neither slender enough to be lissome, nor well-proportioned enough to be majestic. But she was very good, and her price was far above rubies.

According to the wise man, it was a difficult task to find a virtuous woman.

It was a quiet time in the afternoon, and in order to verify my recollection of the wise man's saying, which was a little cloudy in my memory, I searched through Julia's Bible for it. I came across a passage which made me pause and consider. "Behold, this have I found, saith the preacher, counting one by one, to find out the account: which yet my soul seeketh, but I find not; one man among a thousand have I found; but a woman among all those have I not found."

"Tardif is the man," I said to myself, "but is Julia the woman? Have I had better luck than Solomon?"

"What are you reading, Martin?" asked my father, who had just come in, and was painfully fitting on a pair of new and very tight kid gloves. I read the passage aloud, without comment.

"Very good," he remarked, chuckling, "upon my word! I did not know there was any thing as rich as that in the old book! Who says it, Martin? A very wise preacher he was, and knew what he was talking about. Had seen life, eh? It's as true as—as—as the gospel."

I could not help laughing at the comparison he was forced to; yet I felt angry with him and myself.

"What do you say about my mother and Julia, sir?" I asked.

He chuckled again cynically, examining with care a spot on the palm of one of his gloves. "Ha! ha! my son"—I hated to hear him say "my son"—"I will answer you in the words of another wise man: 'Most virtuous women, like hidden treasures, are secure because nobody seeks after them.'"

So saying, he turned out of the room, swinging his gold-headed cane jauntily between his fingers.

I visited Sark again in about ten days, to set Olivia free from my embargo upon her walking. I allowed her to walk a little way along a smooth meadow-path, leaning on my arm; and I found that she was a head lower than myself—a beautiful height for a woman. That time Captain Carey had set me down at the Havre Gosselin, appointing me to meet him at the Creux Harbor, which was exactly on the opposite side of the island. In crossing over to it—a distance of rather more than a mile—I encountered Julia's friends, Emma and Maria Brouard.

"You here again, Martin!" exclaimed Emma.

"Yes," I answered; "Captain Carey set me down at the Havre Gosselin, and is gone round to meet me at the Creux."

"You have been to see that young person?" asked Maria.

"Yes," I replied.

"She is a very singular young woman," she continued; "we think her stupid. We cannot make anything of her. But there is no doubt poor Tardif means to marry her."

"Nonsense!" I ejaculated, hotly; "I beg your pardon, Maria, but I give Tardif credit for sense enough to know his own position."

"So did we," said Emma, "but it looks odd. He married an Englishwoman before. It's old Mère Renouf who says he worships the ground she treads upon. You know he holds a very good position in the island, and he is a great favorite with the seigneur. There are dozens of girls of his own class in Guernsey and Alderney, to say nothing of Sark, who would be only too glad to have him. He is a very handsome man, Martin."

"Tardif is a fine fellow," I admitted.

"I shall be very sorry for him to be taken in again," continued Emma; "nobody knows who that young person may be; it looks odd on the face of it. Are you in a hurry? Well, good-by. Give our best love to dear Julia. We are busy at work on a wedding-present for her; but you must not tell her that, you know."

I went on in a hot rage, shapeless and wordless, but smouldering like a fire within me. The cool, green lane, deep between hedge-rows, the banks of which were gemmed with primroses, had no effect upon me just then. Tardif marry Olivia! That was an absurd, preposterous notion indeed. It required all my knowledge of the influence of dress on the average human mind, to convince myself that Olivia, in her coarse green serge dress, had impressed the people of Sark with the notion that she would be no unsuitable mate for their rough, though good and handsome fisherman.

Was it possible that they thought her stupid? Reserved and silent she might be, as she wished to remain unmolested and concealed; but not stupid! That any one should dream so wildly as to think of Olivia marrying Tardif, was the utmost folly I could imagine.

I had half an hour to wait in the little harbor, its great cliffs rising all about me, with only a tunnel bored through them to form an entrance to the green island within. My rage had partly fumed itself away before the yacht came in sight.

CHAPTER THE FOURTEENTH

OVERHEAD IN LOVE

Awfully fast the time sped away. It was the second week in March I passed in Sark; the second week in May came upon me as if borne by a whirlwind. It was only a month to the day so long fixed upon for our marriage. My mother began to fidget about my going over to London to pay my farewell bachelor visit to Jack Senior, and to fit myself out with wedding toggery. Julia's was going on fast to completion. Our trip to Switzerland was distinctly planned out, almost from day to day. Go I must to London; order my wedding-suit I must.

But first there could be no harm in running over to Sark to see Olivia once more. As soon as I was married I would tell Julia all about her. But if either arm or ankle went wrong for want of attention, I should never forgive myself.

"When shall we have another run together, Captain Carey?" I asked.

"Any day you like, my boy," he answered; "your days of liberty are growing few and short now, eh? I've never had a chance of trying it myself, Martin, but they are nervous times, I should think. Cruising in doubtful channels, eh? with uncertain breezes? How does Julia keep up?"

"I can spare to-morrow," I replied, ignoring his remarks; "on Saturday I shall cross over to England to see Jack Senior."

"And bid him adieu?" he said, laughing, "or give him an invitation to your own house? I shall be glad to see you in a house of your own. Your father is too young a man for you."

"Can you take me to Sark to-morrow?" I asked.

"To be sure I can," he answered.

It was the last time I could see Olivia before my marriage. Afterward I should see much of her; for Julia would invite her to our house, and be a friend to her. I spent a wretchedly sleepless night; and whenever I dozed by fits and starts, I saw Olivia before me, weeping bitterly, and refusing to be comforted.

From St. Sampson's we set sail straight for the Havre Gosselin, without a word upon my part; and the wind being in our favor, we were not long in crossing the channel. To my extreme surprise and chagrin, Captain Carey announced his intention of landing with me, and leaving the yacht in charge of his men to await our return.

"The ladder is excessively awkward," I objected, "and some of the rungs are loose. You don't mind running the risk of a plunge into the water?"

"Not in the least," he answered, cheerily; "for the matter of that, I plunge into it every morning at L'Ancresse. I want to see Tardif. He is one in a thousand, as you say; and one cannot see such a man every day of one's life."

There was no help for it, and I gave in, hoping some good luck awaited me. I led the way up the zigzag path, and just as we reached the top I saw the slight, erect figure of Olivia seated upon the brow of a little grassy knoll at a short distance from us. Her back was toward us, so she was not aware of our vicinity; and I pointed toward her with an assumed air of indifference.

"I believe that is my patient yonder," I said; "I will just run across and speak to her, and then follow you to the farm."

"Ah!" he exclaimed, "there is a lovely view from that spot. I recollect it well. I will go with you, Martin. There will be time enough to see Tardif."

Did Captain Carey suspect any thing? Or what reason could he have for wishing to see Olivia? Could it be merely that he wanted to see the view from that particular spot? I could not forbid him accompanying me, but I wished him at Jericho.

What is more stupid than to have an elderly man dogging one's footsteps?

I trusted devoutly that we should see or hear Tardif before reaching the knoll; but no such good fortune befell me. Olivia did not hear our footsteps upon the soft turf, though we approached her very nearly. The sun shone upon her glossy hair, every thread of which seemed to shine back again. She was reading aloud, apparently to herself, and the sounds of her sweet voice were wafted by the air toward us. Captain Carey's face became very thoughtful.

A few steps nearer brought us in view of Tardif, who had spread his nets on the grass, and was examining them narrowly for rents. Just at this moment he was down on his knees, not far from Olivia, gathering some broken meshes together, but listening to her, with an expression of huge contentment upon his handsome face. A bitter pang shot through me. Could it be true by any possibility—that lie I had heard the last time I was in Sark?

"Good-day, Tardif," shouted Captain Carey; and both Tardif and Olivia started. But both of their faces grew brighter at seeing us, and both sprang up to give us welcome. Olivia's color had come back to her cheeks, and a sweeter face no man ever looked upon.

"I am very glad you are come once more," she said, putting her hand in mine; "you told me in your last letter you were going to England, and might not come over to Sark before next autumn. How glad I am to see you again!"

I glanced from the corner of my eye at Captain Carey. He looked very grave, but his eyes could not rest upon Olivia without admiring her, as she stood before us, bright-faced, slender, erect, with the heavy folds of her coarse dress falling about her as gracefully as if they were of the richest material.

"This is my friend, Captain Carey, Miss Olivia," I said, "in whose yacht I have come over to visit you."

"I am very glad to see any friend of Dr. Martin's," she answered, as she hold out her hand to him with a smile; "my doctor and I are great friends, Captain Carey."

"So I suppose," he said, significantly—or at least his tone and look seemed fraught with significance to me.

"We were talking of you only a few minutes ago, Dr. Martin," she continued; "I was telling Tardif how you sang the 'Three Fishers' to me the last time you were here, and how it rings in my ears still, especially when he is away fishing. I repeated the three last lines to him:

'For men must work, and women must weep; And the sooner it's over, the sooner to sleep. So good-by to the bar, with its moaning.'"

"I do not like it, doctor," said Tardif: "there's no hope in it. Yet to sleep out yonder at last, on the great plain under the sea, would be no bad thing."

"You must sing it for Tardif," added Olivia, with a pretty imperiousness, "and then he will like it."

My throat felt dry, and my tongue parched. I could not utter a word in reply.

"This would be the very place for such a song," said Captain Carey. "Come, Martin, let us have it."

"No; I can sing nothing to-day," I answered, harshly.

The very sight of her made me feel miserable beyond words; the sound of her voice maddened me. I felt as if I was angry with her almost to hatred for her grace and sweetness; yet I could have knelt down at her feet, and been happy only to lay my hand on a fold of her dress. No feeling had ever stirred me so before, and it made me irritable. Olivia's clear gray eyes looked at me wonderingly.

"Is there anything the matter with you, Dr. Martin?" she inquired.

"No," I replied, turning away from her abruptly. Every one of them felt my rudeness; and there was a dead silence among us for half a minute, which seemed an age to me. Then I heard Captain Carey speaking in his suavest tones.

"Are you quite well again, Miss Ollivier?" he asked.

"Yes, quite well, I think," she said, in a very subdued voice. "I cannot walk far yet, and my arm is still weak: but I think I am quite well. I have given Dr. Martin a great deal of trouble and anxiety."

She spoke in the low, quiet tones of a child who has been chidden unreasonably. I was asking myself what Captain Carey meant by not leaving me alone with my patient. When a medical man makes a call, the intrusion of any unprofessional, indifferent person is unpardonable. If it had been Suzanne, Tardif, or Mother Renouf, who was keeping so close beside us, I could have made no reasonable objection. But Captain Carey!

"Tardif," I said, "Captain Carey came ashore on purpose to visit you and your farm."

I knew he was excessively proud of his farm, which consisted of about four or five acres. He caught at the words with alacrity, and led the way toward his house with tremendous strides. There was no means of evading a tour of inspection, though Captain Carey appeared to follow him reluctantly. Olivia and I were left alone, but she was moving after them slowly, when I ran to her, and offered her my arm on the plea that her ankle was still too weak to bear her weight unsupported.

"Olivia!" I exclaimed, after we had gone a few yards, bringing her and myself to a sudden halt. Then I was struck dumb. I had nothing special to say to her. How was it I had called her so familiarly Olivia?

"Well, Dr. Martin?" she said, looking into my face again with eager, inquiring eyes, as if she was wishful to understand my varying moods if she could.

"What a lovely place this is!" I ejaculated.

More lovely than any words I ever heard could describe. It was a perfect day, and a perfect view. The sea was like an opal, changing every minute with the passing shadows of snow-white clouds which floated lazily across the bright blue of the sky. The cliffs, Sark Cliffs, which have not their equal in the world, stretched below us, with every hue of gold and bronze, and hoary white, and soft gray; and here and there a black rock, with livid shades of purple, and a bloom upon it like a raven's wing. Rocky islets, never trodden by human foot, over which the foam poured ceaselessly, were dotted all about the changeful surface of the water. And just beneath the level of my eyes was Olivia's face—the loveliest thing there, though there was so much beauty lying around us.

"Yes, it is a lovely place," she assented, a mischievous smile playing about her lips.

"Olivia," I said, taking my courage by both hands, "it is only a month now till my wedding-day."

Was I deceiving myself, or did she really grow paler? It was but for a moment if it were so. But how cold the air felt all in an instant! The shock was like that of a first plunge into chilly waters, and I was shivering through every fibre.

"I hope you will be happy," said Olivia, "very happy. It is a great risk to run. Marriage will make you either very happy or very wretched."

"Not at all," I answered, trying to speak gayly; "I do not look forward to any vast amount of rapture. Julia and I will get along very well together, I have no doubt, for we have known one another all our lives. I do not expect to be any happier than other men; and the married people I have known have not exactly dwelt in paradise. Perhaps your experience has been different?"

"Oh, no!" she said, her hand trembling on my arm, and her face very downcast; "but I should have liked you to be very, very happy."

So softly spoken, with such a low, faltering voice! I could not trust myself to speak again. A stern sense of duty toward Julia kept me silent; and we moved on, though very slowly and lingeringly.

"You love her very much?" said the quiet voice at my side, not much louder than the voice of conscience, which was speaking imperiously just then.

"I esteem her more highly than any other woman, except my mother," I said. "I believe she would die sooner than do any thing she considered wrong. I do not deserve her, and she loves me, I am sure, very truly and faithfully."

"Do you think she will like me?" asked Olivia, anxiously.

"No; she must love you," I said, with warmth; "and I, too, can be a more useful friend to you after my marriage than I am now. Perhaps then you will feel free to place perfect confidence in us."

She smiled faintly, without speaking—a smile which said plainly she could keep her own secret closely. It provoked me to do a thing I had had no intention of doing, and which I regretted very much afterward. I opened my pocket-book, and drew out the little slip of paper containing the advertisement.

"Read that," I said.

But I do not think she saw more than the first line, for her face went deadly white, and her eyes turned upon me with a wild, beseeching look—as Tardif described it, the look of a creature hunted and terrified. I thought she would have fallen, and I put my arm round her. She fastened both her hands about mine, and her lips moved, though I could not catch a word she was saying.

"Olivia!" I cried, "Olivia! do you suppose I could do any thing to hurt you? Do not be so frightened! Why, I am your friend truly. I wish to Heaven I had not shown you the thing. Have more faith in me, and more courage."

"But they will find me, and force me away from here," she muttered.

"No," I said; "that advertisement was printed in the Times directly after your flight last October. They have not found you out yet; and the longer you are hidden, the less likely they are to find you. Good Heavens! what a fool I was to show it to you!"

"Never mind," she answered, recovering herself a little, but still clinging to my arm; "I was only frightened for the time. You would not give me up to them if you knew all."

"Give you up to them!" I repeated, bitterly. "Am I a Judas?"

But she could not talk to me any more. She was trembling like an aspen-leaf, and her breath came sobbingly. All I could do was to take her home, blaming myself for my cursed folly.

Captain Carey and Tardif met us at the farm-yard gate, but Olivia could not speak to them; and we passed them in silence, challenged by their inquisitive looks. She could only bid me good-by in a tremulous voice; and I watched her go on into her own little room, and close the door between us. That was the last I should see of her before my marriage.

Tardif walked with us to the top of the cliff, and made me a formal, congratulatory speech before quitting us. When he was gone, Captain Carey stood still until he was quite out of hearing, and then stretched out his hand toward the thatched roof, yellow with stone-crop and lichens.

"This is a serious business, Martin," he said, looking sternly at me; "you are in love with that girl."

"I love her with all my heart and soul!" I cried.

CHAPTER THE FIFTEENTH

IN A FIX

Yes, I loved Olivia with all my heart and soul.

I had not known it myself till that moment; and now I acknowledged it boldly, almost defiantly, with a strange mingling of delight and pain in the confession.

Yet the words startled me as I uttered them. They had involved in them so many unpleasant consequences, so much chagrin and bitterness as their practical result, that I stood aghast—even while my pulses throbbed, and my heart beat high, with the novel rapture of loving any woman as I loved Olivia. If I followed out my avowal to its just issue, I should be a traitor to Julia; and all my life up to the present moment would be lost to me. I had scarcely spoken it before I dropped my head on my hands with a groan.

"Come, come, my poor fellow!" said Captain Carey, who could never see a dog with his tail between his legs without whistling to him and patting him, "we must see what can be done."

It was neither a time nor a place for the indulgence of emotion of any kind. It was impossible for me to remain on the cliffs, bemoaning my unhappy fate. I strode on doggedly down the path, kicking the loose stones into the water as they came in my way. Captain Carey followed, whistling softly to himself, and, of all the tunes in the world, he chose the one to the "Three Fishers," which I had sung to Olivia. He continued doing so after we were aboard the yacht, and I saw the boatmen exchange apprehensive glances.

"We shall have wind enough, without whistling for it, before we reach Guernsey," said one of them, after a while; and Captain Carey relapsed into silence. We scarcely spoke again, except about the shifting of the sails, in our passage across. A pretty stiff breeze was blowing, and we found plenty of occupation.

"I cannot leave you like this, Martin, my boy," said Captain Carey, when we went ashore at St. Sampson's; and he put his arm through mine affectionately.

"You will keep my secret?" I said—my voice a key or two lower than usual.

"Martin," answered the good-hearted, clear-sighted old bachelor, "you must not do Julia the wrong of keeping this secret from her."

"I must," I urged. "Olivia knows nothing of it; nobody guesses it but you. I must conquer it. Things have gone too far with poor Julia, for me to back out of our marriage now. You know that as well as I do. Think of it, Captain Carey!"

"But shall you conquer it?" asked Captain Carey, seriously.

I could not answer yes frankly and freely. It seemed a sheer impossibility for me to root out this new love, which I found in my heart below all the old loves and friendships of my whole life. Mad as I was with myself at the thought of my folly, the folly was so sweet to me, that I would as soon have parted with life itself. Nothing in the least resembling this feeling had been a matter of experience with me before. I had read of it in poetry and novels, and laughed a little at it; but now it had come upon me like a strong man armed. I quailed and flinched before the painful conflict necessary to cast out the precious guest.

"Martin," urged Captain Carey, "come up to Johanna, and tell her all about it."

Johanna Carey was one of the powers in the island. Everybody knew her; and everybody went to her for comfort and counsel. She was, of course, related to us all; and knew the exact degree of relationship among us, having the genealogy of each family at her fingers' ends. But, besides these family histories, which were common property, she was also intrusted with the inmost secrets of every household— those secrets which were the most carefully and jealously guarded. I had always been a favorite with her, and nothing could be more natural than this proposal of her brother's, that I should go and tell her all my dilemma.

The house stood on the border of L'Ancresse Common, with no view of the sea, but with the soft, undulating brows and hollows of the common lying before it, and a broken battlement of rocks rising beyond them.

There was always a low, solemn murmur of the invisible sea, singing like a lullaby about the peaceful dwelling, and hushing it into a more profound quiet than even utter silence; for utter silence is irksome and fretting to the ear, which needs some slight reverberation to keep the brain behind it still. A perfume of violets, and the more dainty scent of primroses, pervaded the garden. It seemed incredible that any man should be allowed to live in such a spot; but then Captain Carey was almost as gentle and fastidious as a woman.

Johanna was not unlike her home. There was a repose about her similar to the calm of a judge, which gave additional weight to her counsels. The moment we entered through the gates, a certainty of comfort and help appeared to be wafted upon the pure breeze, floating across the common from the sea.

Johanna was standing at one of the windows in a Quakerish dress of some gray stuff, and with a plain white cap over her white hair. She came down to the door as soon as she saw me, and received me with a motherly kiss, which I returned with more than usual warmth, as one does in any new kind of trouble. I think she was instantly aware that something was amiss with me.

"Is dinner ready, Johanna?" asked her brother; "we are as hungry as hunters."

That was not true as far as I was concerned. For the first time within my recollection my appetite quite failed me, and I merely played with my knife and fork.

Captain Carey regarded me pitifully, and said, "Come, come, Martin, my boy!" several times.

Johanna made no remark; but her quiet, searching eyes looked me through and through, till I almost longed for the time when she would begin to question and cross-question me. After she was gone, Captain Carey gave me two or three glasses of his choicest wine, to cheer me up, as he said; but we were not long before we followed his sister.

"Johanna," said Captain Carey, "we have something to tell you."

"Come and sit here by me," she said, making room for me beside her on her sofa; for long experience had taught her how much more difficult it is to make a confession face to face with one's confessor, under the fire of his eyes, as it were, than when one is partially concealed from him.

"Well," she said, in her calm, inviting voice.

"Johanna," I replied, "I am in a terrible fix!"

"Awful!" cried Captain Carey, sympathetically; but a glance from his sister put him to silence.

"What is it, my dear Martin?" asked her inviting voice again.

"I will tell you frankly," I said, feeling I must have it out at once, like an aching tooth. "I love, with all my heart and soul, that girl in Sark; the one who has been my patient there."

"Martin!" she cried, in a tone full of surprise and agitation—"Martin!"

"Yes; I know all you would urge—my honor; my affection for Julia; the claims she has upon me, the strongest claims possible; how good and worthy she is; what an impossibility it is even to look back now. I know it all, and feel how miserably binding it is upon me. Yet I love Olivia; and I shall never love Julia."

"Martin!" she cried again.

"Listen to me, Johanna," I said, for now the ice was broken, my frozen words were flowing as rapidly as a runnel of water; "I used to dream of a feeling something like this years ago, but no girl I saw could kindle it into reality. I have always esteemed Julia, and when my youth was over, and I had never felt any devouring passion, I began to think love was more of a word than a fact, or to believe that it had become only a word in these cold late times. At any rate, I concluded I was past the age for falling in love. There was my cousin Julia certainly dearer to me than any other woman, except my mother. I knew all her little ways; and they were not annoying to me, or were so in a very small degree. Besides, my father had had a grand passion for my mother, and what had that come to? There would be no such white ashes of a spent fire for Julia to shiver over. That was how I argued the matter out with myself. At eight-and-twenty I had never lost a quarter of an hour's sleep, or missed a meal, for the sake of any girl. Surely I was safe. It was quite fair for me to propose to Julia, and she would be satisfied with the affection I could offer her. Then there was my mother; it was the greatest happiness I could give her, and her life has not been a happy one, God knows. So I proposed to Julia, and she accepted me last Christmas."

"And you are to be married next month?" said Johanna, in an exceedingly troubled tone.

"Yes," I answered, "and now every word Julia speaks, and every thing she does, grates upon me. I love her as much as ever as my cousin, but as my wife! Good Heavens! Johanna, I cannot tell you how I dread it."

"What can be done?" she exclaimed, looking from me to Captain Carey, whose face was as full of dismay as her own. But he only shook his head despondingly.

"Done!" I repeated, "nothing, absolutely nothing. It is utterly impossible to draw back. Our house is nearly ready for us, and even Julia's wedding-dress and veil are bought."

"There is not a house you enter," said Johanna, solemnly, "where they are not preparing a wedding-present for Julia and you. There has not been a marriage in your district, among ourselves, for nine years. It is as public as a royal marriage."

"It must go on," I answered, with the calmness of despair. "I am the most good-for-nothing scoundrel in Guernsey to fall in love with my patient. You need not tell me so, Johanna. And yet, if I could think that Olivia loved me, I would not change with the happiest man alive."

"What is her name?" asked Johanna.

"One of the Olliviers," answered Captain Carey; "but what Olliviers she belongs to, I don't know. She is one of the prettiest creatures I ever saw."

"An Ollivier!" exclaimed Johanna, in her severest accents. "Martin, what are you thinking of?"

"Her Christian name is Olivia," I said, hastily; "she does not belong to the Olliviers at all. It was Tardif's mistake, and very natural. She was born in Australia, I believe."

"Of a good family, I hope?" asked Johanna. "There are some persons it would be a disgrace to you to love. What is her other name?"

"I don't know," I answered, reluctantly but distinctly.

Johanna turned her face full upon me now—a face more agitated than I had ever seen it. There was no use in trying to keep back any part of my serious delinquency, so I resolved to make a clean breast of it.

"I know very little about her," I said—"that is, about her history; as for herself, she is the sweetest, dearest, loveliest girl in the whole world to me. If I were free, and she loved me, I should not know what else to wish for. All I know is, that she has run away from her people; why, I have no more idea than you have, or who they are, or where they live; and she has been living in Tardif's cottage since last October. It is an infatuation, do you say? So it is, I dare say. It is an infatuation; and I don't know that I shall ever shake it off."

"What is she like?" asked Johanna. "Is she very merry and bright?"

"I never saw her laugh," I said.

"Very melancholy and sad, then?"

"I never saw her weep," I said.

"What is it then, Martin?" she asked, earnestly.

"I cannot tell what it is," I answered. "Everything she does and says has a charm for me that I could never describe. With her for my wife I should be more happy than I ever was; with any one else I shall be wretched. That is all I know."

I had left my seat by Johanna, and was pacing to and fro in the room, too restless and miserable to keep still. The low moan of the sea sighed all about the house. I could have cast myself on the floor had I been alone, and wept and sobbed like a woman. I could see no loop-hole of escape from the mesh of circumstances which caught me in their net.

A long, dreary, colorless, wretched life stretched before me, with Julia my inseparable companion, and Olivia altogether lost to me. Captain Carey and Johanna, neither of whom had tasted the sweets and bitters of marriage, looked sorrowfully at me and shook their heads.

"You must tell Julia," said Johanna, after a long pause.

"Tell Julia!" I echoed. "I would not tell her for worlds!"

"You must tell her," she repeated; "it is your clear duty. I know it will be most painful to you both, but you have no right to marry her with this secret on your mind."

"I should be true to her," I interrupted, somewhat angrily.

"What do you call being true, Martin Dobrée?" she asked, more calmly than she had spoken before. "Is it being true to a woman to let her believe you choose and love her above all other women when that is absolutely false? No; you are too honorable for that. I tell you it is your plain duty to let Julia know this, and know it at once."

"It will break her heart," I said, with a sharp twinge of conscience and a cowardly shrinking from the unpleasant duty urged upon me.

"It will not break Julia's heart," said Johanna, very sadly; "it may break your mother's."

I reeled as if a sharp blow had struck me. I had been thinking far less of my mother than of Julia; but I saw, as with a flash of lightning, what a complete uprooting of all her old habits and long-cherished hopes this would prove to my mother, whose heart was so set upon this marriage. Would Julia marry me if she once heard of my unfortunate love for Olivia? And, if not, what would become of our home? My mother would have to give up one of us, for it was not to be supposed she would consent to live under the same roof with me, now the happy tie of cousinship was broken, and none dearer to be formed.

Which could my mother part with best? Julia was almost as much her daughter as I was her son; yet me she pined after if ever I was absent long. No; I could not resolve to run the risk of breaking that gentle, faithful heart, which loved me so fully. I went back to Johanna, and took her hand in both of mine.

"Keep my secret," I said, earnestly, "you two. I will make Julia and my mother happy. Do not mistrust me. This infatuation overpowered me unawares. I will conquer it; at the worst I can conceal it. I promise you Julia shall never regret being my wife."

"Martin," answered Johanna, determinedly, "if you do not tell Julia I must tell her myself. You say you love this other girl with all your heart and soul."

"Yes, and that is true," I said.

"Then Julia must know before she marries you."

Nothing could move Johanna from that position, and in my heart I recognized its righteousness. She argued with me that it was Julia's due to hear it from myself. I knew afterward that she believed the sight of her distress and firm love for myself would dissipate the infatuation of my love for Olivia. But she did not read Julia's character as well as my mother did.

Before she let me leave her I had promised to have my confession and subsequent explanation with Julia all over the following day; and to make this the more inevitable, she told me she should drive into St. Peter-Port the next afternoon about five o'clock, when she should expect to find this troublesome matter settled, either by a renewal of my affection for my betrothed, or the suspension of the betrothal. In the latter case she promised to carry Julia home with her until the first bitterness was over.

CHAPTER THE SIXTEENTH

A MIDNIGHT RIDE

I took care not to reach home before the hour when Julia usually went to bed. She had been out in the country all day, visiting the south cliffs of our island, with some acquaintances from England who were staying for a few days in St. Peter-Port. In all probability she would be too tired to sit up till my return if I were late.

I had calculated aright. It was after eleven o'clock when I entered, and my mother only was waiting for me. I wished to avoid any confidential chat that evening, and, after answering briefly her fond inquiries as to what could have kept me out so late, I took myself off to my own room.

But it was quite vain to think of sleep that night. I had soon worked myself up into that state of nervous, restless agitation; when one cannot remain quietly in one; room. I attempted to conquer it, but I could not.

The moon, which was at the full, was shining out of a cloudless field of sky upon my window. I longed for fresh air, and freedom, and motion; for a distance between myself and my dear old home—that home which I was about to plunge into troubled waters. The peacefulness oppressed me.

About one o'clock I opened my door as softly as possible, and stole silently downstairs—but not so silently that my mother's quick ear did not catch the slight jarring of my door.

The night-bell hung in my room, and occasionally I was summoned away at hours like this to visit a patient. She called to me as I crept down the stairs.

"Martin, what is the matter?" she whispered, over the banisters.

"Nothing, mother; nothing much," I answered. "I shall be home again in an hour or two. Go to bed, and go to sleep. Whatever makes you so thin-eared?"

"Are you going to take Madam?" she asked, seeing my whip in my hand. "Shall I ring up Pellet?"

"No, no!" I said; "I can manage well enough. Good-night again, my darling old mother."

Her pale, worn face smiled down upon me very tenderly as she kissed her hand to me. I stood, as if spellbound, watching her, and she watching me, until we both laughed, though somewhat falteringly.

"How romantic you are, my boy!" she said, in a tremulous voice.

"I shall not stir till you go back to bed," I answered, peremptorily; and as just then we heard my father calling out fretfully to ask why the door was open, and what was going on in the house, she disappeared, and I went on my way to the stables.

Madam was my favorite mare, first-rate at a gallop when she was in good temper, but apt to turn vicious now and then. She was in good temper to-night, and pricked up her ears and whinnied when I unlocked the stable-door. In a few minutes we were going up the Grange Road at a moderate pace till we reached the open country, and the long, white, dusty roads stretched before us, glimmering in the moonlight. I turned for St. Martin's, and Madam, at the first touch of my whip on her flanks, started off at a long and steady gallop.

It was a cool, quiet night in May. A few of the larger fixed stars twinkled palely in the sky, but the smaller ones were drowned in the full moonlight. The largest of them shone solemnly and brightly in afield of golden green just above the spot where the sun had set hours before. The trees, standing out with a blackness and distinctness never seen by day, appeared to watch for me and look after me as I rode along, forming an avenue of silent but very stately spectators; and to my fancy, for my fancy was highly excited that night, the rustling of the young leaves upon them whispered the name of Olivia. The hoof-beats of my mare's feet upon the hard roads echoed the name Olivia, Olivia!

By-and-by I turned off the road to got nearer the sea, and rode along sandy lanes with banks of turf instead of hedge-rows, which were covered thickly with pale primroses, shining with the same hue as the moon above them. As I passed the scattered cottages, here and there a dog yapped a shrill, snarling hark, and woke the birds, till they gave a sleepy twitter in their new nests.

Now and then I came in full sight of the sea, glittering in the silvery light. I crossed the head of a gorge, and stopped for a while to gaze down it, till my flesh crept. It was not more than a few yards in breadth, but it was of unknown depth, and the rocks stood above it with a thick, heavy blackness. The tide was rushing into its narrow channel with a thunder which throbbed like a pulse; yet in the intervals of its pulsation I could catch the thin, prattling tinkle of a brook running merrily down the gorge to plunge headlong into the sea. Round every spar of the crags, and over every islet of rock, the foam played ceaselessly, breaking over them like drifts of snow, forever melting, and forever forming again.

I kept on my way, as near the sea as I l could, past the sleeping cottages and hamlets, round through St. Pierre du Bois and Torteval, with the gleaming light-houses out on the Hanways, and by Rocquaine Bay, and Vazon Bay, and through the vale to Captain Carey's peaceful house, where, perhaps, to-morrow night—nay, this day's night—Julia might be weeping and wailing broken-hearted.

I had made the circuit of our island—a place so dear to me that it seemed scarcely possible to live elsewhere; yet I should be forced to live elsewhere. I knew that with a clear distinctness. There could be no home for me in Guernsey when my conduct toward Julia should become known.

But now Sark, which had been behind me all my ride, lay full in sight, and the eastern sky behind it began to quicken with new light. The gulls were rousing themselves, and flying out to sea, with their plaintive cries; and the larks were singing their first sleepy notes to the coming day.

As the sun rose, Sark looked very near, and the sea, a plain of silvery blue, seemed solid and firm enough to afford me a road across to it. A white mist lay like a huge snow-drift in hazy, broad curves over the Havre Gosselin, with sharp peaks of cliffs piercing through.

Olivia was sleeping yonder behind that veil of shining mist; and, dear as Guernsey was to me, she was a hundredfold dearer.

But my night's ride bad not made my day's task any easier for me. No new light had dawned upon my difficulty. There was no loop-hole for me to escape from the most painful and perplexing strait I had ever been in. How was I to break it to Julia? and when? It was quite plain to me that the sooner it was over the better it would be for myself, and perhaps the better for her. How was I to go through my morning's calls, in the state of nervous anxiety I found myself in?

I resolved to have it over as soon as breakfast was finished, and my father had gone to make his professional toilet, a lengthy and important duty with him. Yet when breakfast came I was listening intently for some summons, which would give me an hour's grace from fulfilling my own determination. I prolonged my meal, keeping my mother in her place at the table; for she had never given up her office of pouring out my tea and coffee.

I finished at List, and still no urgent message had come for me. My mother left us together alone, as her custom was, for what time I had to spare—a variable quantity always with me.

Now was the dreaded moment. But how was I to begin? Julia was so calm and unsuspecting. In what words could I convey my fatal meaning most gently to her? My head throbbed, and I could not raise my eyes to her face. Yet it must be done.

"Dear Julia," I said, in as firm a voice as I could command.

"Yes, Martin."

But just then Grace, the housemaid, knocked emphatically at the door, and after a due pause entered with a smiling, significant face, yet with an apologetic courtesy.

"If you please, Dr. Martin," she said, "I'm very sorry, but Mrs. Lihou's baby is taken with convulsion-fits; and they want you to go as fast as ever you can, please, sir."

"Was I sorry or glad? I could not tell. It was a reprieve; but then I knew positively it was nothing more than a reprieve. The sentence must be executed. Julia came to me, bent her cheek toward me, and I kissed it. That was our usual salutation when our morning's interview was ended.

"I am going down to the new house," she said. "I lost a good deal of time yesterday, and I must make up for it to-day. Shall you be passing by at any time, Martin?"

"Yes—no—I cannot tell exactly," I stammered.

"If you are passing, come in for a few minutes," she answered; "I have a thousand things to speak to you about."

"Shall you come in to lunch?" I asked.

"No, I shall take something with me," she replied; "it hinders so; coming back here."

I was not overworked that morning. The convulsions of Mrs. Lihou's baby were not at all serious; and, as I have before stated, the practice which my father and I shared between us was a very limited one. My part of it naturally fell among our poorer patients, who did not expect me to waste their time and my own, by making numerous or prolonged visits. So I had plenty of time to call upon Julia at the new house; but I could not summon sufficient courage. The morning slipped away while I was loitering about Fort George, and chatting carelessly with the officers quartered there.

I went to lunch, pretty sure of finding no one but my mother at home. There was no fear of losing her love, if every other friend turned me the cold shoulder, as I was morally certain they would, with no blame to themselves. But the very depth and constancy of her affection made it the more difficult and the more terrible for me to wound her. She had endured so much, poor mother! and was looking so wan and pale. If it had not been for Johanna's threat, I should have resolved to say nothing about Olivia, and to run my chance of matrimonial happiness.

What a cruel turn Fate had done me when it sent me across the sea to Sark ten weeks ago!

My mother was full of melancholy merriment that morning, making pathetic little jokes about Julia and me, and laughing at them heartily herself—short bursts of laughter which left her paler than she had been before.

I tried to laugh myself, in order to encourage her brief playfulness, though the effort almost choked me. Before I went out again, I sat beside her for a few minutes, with my head, which ached awfully by this time, resting on her dear shoulder.

"Mother," I said, "you are very fond of Julia?"

"I love her just the same as if she were my daughter, Martin—as she will be soon," she answered.

"Do you love her as much as me?" I asked.

"Jealous boy!" she said, laying her hand on my hot forehead, "no, not half as much; not a quarter, not a tenth part as much! Does that content you?"

"Suppose something should prevent our marriage?" I suggested.

"But nothing can," she interrupted; "and, O Martin! I am sure you will be very happy with Julia."

I said no more, for I did not dare to tell her yet; but I wished I had spoken to her about Olivia, instead of hiding her name, and all belonging to her, in my inmost heart. My mother would know all quite soon enough, unless Julia and I agreed to keep it secret, and let things go on as they were.

If Julia said she would marry me, knowing that I was heart and soul in love with another woman, why, then I would go through with it, and my mother need never hear a word about my dilemma.

Julia must decide my lot. My honor was pledged to her; and if she insisted upon the fulfilment of my engagement to her, well, of course, I would fulfil it.

I went down reluctantly at length to the new house; but it was at almost the last hour. The church-clocks had already struck four; and I knew Johanna would be true to her time, and drive up the Grange at five. I left a message with my mother for her, telling her where she would find Julia and me. Then doggedly, but sick at heart with myself and all the world, I went down to meet my doom.

It was getting into nice order, this new house of ours. We had had six months to prepare it in, and to fit it up exactly to our minds; and it was as near my ideal of a pleasant home as our conflicting tastes permitted. Perhaps this was the last time I should cross its threshold. There was a pang in the thought.

This was my position. If Julia listened to my avowal angrily, and renounced me indignantly, passionately, I lost fortune, position, profession; my home and friends, with the sole exception of my mother. I should be regarded alternately as a dupe and a scoundrel. Guernsey would become too hot to hold me, and I should be forced to follow my luck in some foreign land. If, on the other hand, Julia clung to me, and would not give me up, trusting to time to change my feelings, then I lost Olivia; and to lose her seemed the worse fate of the two.

Julia was sitting alone in the drawing-room, which overlooked the harbor and the group of islands across the channel. There was no fear of interruption; no callers to ring the bell and break in upon our tête-à-tête. It was an understood thing that at present only Julia's most intimate friends had been admitted into our new house, and then by special invitation alone.

There was a very happy, very placid expression on her face. Every harsh line seemed softened, and a pleased smile played about her lips. Her dress was one of those simple, fresh, clean muslin gowns, with knots of ribbon about it, which make a plain woman almost pretty, and a pretty woman bewitching. Her dark hair looked less prim and neat than usual. She pretended not to hear me open the door; but as I stood still at the threshold gazing at her, she lifted up her head, with a very pleasant smile.

"I am very glad you are come, my dear Martin," she said, softly.

CHAPTER THE SEVENTEENTH

A LONG HALF-HOUR

I dared not dally another moment. I must take my plunge at once into the icy-cold waters.

"I have something of importance to say to you, dear cousin," I began.

"So have I," she said, gayly; "a thousand things, as I told you this morning, sir, though you are so late in coming to hear them. See, I have been making a list of a few commissions for you to do in London. They are such as I can trust to you; but for plate, and glass, and china, I think we had better wait till we return from Switzerland. We are sure to come home through London."

Her eyes ran over a paper she was holding in her hand; while I stood opposite to her, not knowing what to do with myself, and feeling the guiltiest wretch alive.

"Cannot you find a seat?" she asked, after a short silence.

I sat down on the broad window-sill instead of on the chair close to hers. She looked up at that, and fixed her eyes upon me keenly. I had often quailed before Julia's gaze as a boy, but never as I did now.

"Well! what is it?" she asked, curtly. The incisiveness of her tone brought life into me, as a probe sometimes brings a patient out of stupor.

"Julia," I said, "are you quite sure you love me enough to be happy with me as my wife?"

She opened her eyes very widely, and arched her eyebrows at the question, laughed a little, and then drooped her head over the work in her hands.

"Think of it well, Julia," I urged.

"I know you well enough to be as happy as the day is long with you," she replied, the color rushing to her face. "I have no vocation for a single life, such as so many of the girls here have to make up their minds to. I should hate to have nothing to do and nobody to care for. Every night and morning I thank God that he has ordained another life for me. He knows how I love you, Martin."

"What was I to say to this? How was I to set my foot down to crush this blooming happiness of hers?

"You do not often look as if you loved me," I said at last.

"That is only my way," she answered. "I can't be soft and purring like many women. I don't care to be always kissing and hanging about anybody. But if you are afraid I don't love you enough—well! I will ask you what you think in ten years' time."

"What would you say if I told you I had once loved a girl better than I do you?" I asked.

"That's not true," she said, sharply. "I've known you all your life, and you could not hide such a thing from your mother and me. You are only laughing at me, Martin."

"Heaven knows I'm not laughing," I answered, solemnly; "it's no laughing matter. Julia, there is a girl I love better than you, even now."

The color and the smile faded out of her face, leaving it ashy pale. Her lips parted once or twice, but her voice failed her. Then she broke out into a short, hysterical laugh.

"You are talking nonsense, dear Martin!" she gasped; "you ought not! I am not very strong. Get me a glass of water."

I fetched a glass of water from the kitchen; for the servant, who had been at work, had gone home, and we were quite alone in the house. When I returned, her face was still working with nervous twitchings.

"Martin, you ought not!" she repeated, after she had swallowed some water. "Tell me it is a joke directly."

"I cannot," I replied, painfully and sorrowfully; "it is the truth, though I would almost rather face death than own it. I love you dearly, Julia; but I love another woman better. God help us both!"

There was dead silence in the room after those words. I could not hear Julia breathe or move, and I could not look at her. My eyes were turned toward the window and the islands across the sea, purple and hazy in the distance.

"Leave me!" she said, after a very long stillness; "go away, Martin."

"I cannot leave you alone," I exclaimed; "no, I will not, Julia. Let me tell you more; let me explain it all. You ought to know every thing now."

"Go away!" she repeated, in a slow, mechanical tone.

I hesitated still, seeing her white and trembling, with her eyes glassy and fixed. But she motioned me from her toward the door, and her pale lips parted again to reiterate her command.

How I crossed that room I do not know; but the moment after I had closed the door I heard the key turn in the lock. I dared not quit the house and leave her alone in such a state; and I longed ardently to hear the clocks chime five, and the sound of Johanna's wheels on the roughly-paved street. She could not be here yet for a full half-hour, for she had to go up to our house in the Grange Road and come back again. What if Julia should have fainted, or be dead!

That was one of the longest half-hours in my life. I stood at the street-door watching and waiting, and nodding to people who passed by, and who simpered at me in the most inane fashion.

"The fools!" I called them to myself. At length Johanna turned the corner, and her pony-carriage came rattling cheerfully over the large round stones. I ran to meet her.

"For Heaven's sake, go to Julia!" I cried. "I have told her."

"And what does she say?" asked Johanna.

"Not a word, not a syllable," I replied, "except to bid me go away. She has locked herself into the drawing-room."

"Then you had better go away altogether," she said, "and leave me to deal with her. Don't come in, and then I can say you are not here."

A friend of mine lived in the opposite house, and, though I knew he was not at home, I knocked at his door and asked permission to sit for a while in his parlor.

The windows looked into the street, and there I sat watching the doors of our new house, for Johanna and Julia to come out. No man likes to be ordered out of sight, as if he were a vagabond or a criminal, and I felt myself aggrieved and miserable.

At length the door opposite opened, and Julia appeared, her face completely hidden behind a veil. Johanna helped her into the low carriage, as if she had been an invalid, and paid her those minute trivial attentions which one woman showers upon another when she is in great grief. Then they drove off, and were soon out of my sight.

By this time our dinner-hour was near, and I knew my mother would be looking out for us both. I was thankful to find at the table a visitor, who had dropped in unexpectedly: one of my father's patients—a widow, with a high color, a loud voice, and boisterous spirits, who kept up a rattle of conversation with Dr. Dobrée. My mother glanced anxiously at me very often, but she could say little.

"Where is Julia?" she had inquired, as we sat down to dinner without her.

"Julia?" I said, quite absently; "oh! she is gone to the Vale, with Johanna Carey."

"Will she come back to-night?" asked my mother.

"Not to-night," I said, aloud; but to myself I added, "nor for many nights to come; never, most probably, while I am under this roof. We have been building our house upon the sand, and the floods have come, and the winds have blown, and the house has fallen; but my mother knows nothing of the catastrophe yet."

If it were possible to keep her ignorant of it! But that could not be. She read trouble in my face, as clearly as one sees a thunder-cloud in the sky, and she could not rest till she had fathomed it. After she and our guest had left us, my father lingered only a few minutes. He was not a man that cared for drinking much wine, with no companion but me, and he soon pushed the decanters from him.

"You are as dull as a beetle to-night, Martin," he said. "I think I will go and see how your mother and Mrs. Murray get along together."

He went his way, and I went mine—up into my own room, where I should be alone to think over things. It was a pleasant room, and had been mine from my boyhood. There were some ugly old pictures still hanging against the walls, which I could not find in my heart to take down. The model of a ship I had carved with my penknife, the sails of which had been made by Julia, occupied the top shelf over my books. The first pistol I had ever possessed lay on the same shelf. It was my own den, my nest, my sanctuary, my home within the home. I could not think of myself being quite at home anywhere else.

Of late I had been awakened in the night two or three times, and found my mother standing at my bedside, with her thin, transparent fingers shading the light from my eyes. When I remonstrated with her she had kissed me, smoothed the clothes about me, and promised meekly to go back to bed. Did she visit me every night? and would there come a time when she could not visit me?

CHAPTER THE EIGHTEENTH

BROKEN OFF

As I asked myself this question, with an unerring premonition that the time would soon come when my mother and I would be separated, I heard her tapping lightly at the door. She was not in the habit of leaving her guests, and I was surprised and perplexed at seeing her.

"Your father and Mrs. Murray are having a game of chess," she said, answering my look of astonishment. "We can be alone together half an hour. And now tell me what is the matter? There is something going wrong with you."

She sank down weariedly into a chair, and I knelt down beside her. It was almost harder to tell her than to tell Julia; but it was worse than useless to put off the evil moment. Better for her to hear all from me before a whisper reached her from any one else.

"Johanna came here," she continued, "with a face as grave as a judge, and asked for Julia in a melancholy voice. Has there been any quarrel between you two?"

She was accustomed to our small quarrels, and to setting them right again; for we were prone to quarrel in a cousinly fashion, without much real bitterness on either side, but with such an intimate and irritating knowledge of each other's weak points, that we needed a peace-maker at hand.

"Mother, I am not going to marry my cousin Julia," I said.

"So I have heard before," she answered, with a faint smile. "Come, come, Martin! it is too late to talk boyish nonsense like this."

"But I love somebody else," I said, warmly, for my heart throbbed at the thought of Olivia; "and I told Julia so this afternoon. It is broken off for good now, mother."

She gave me no answer, and I looked up into her dear face in alarm. It had grown rigid, and a peculiar blue tinge of pallor was spreading over it. Her head had fallen back against the chair. I had never seen her look so death-like in any of her illnesses, and I sprang to my feet in terror. She stopped me by a slight convulsive pressure of her hand, as I was about to unfasten her brooch and open her dress to give her air.

"No, Martin," she whispered, "I shall be better in a moment."

But it was several minutes before she breathed freely and naturally, or could lift up her head. Then she did not look at me, but lifted up her eyes to the pale evening sky, and her lips quivered with agitation.

"Martin, it will be the death of me," she said; and a few tears stole down her cheeks, which I wiped away.

"It shall not be the death of you," I exclaimed. "If Julia is willing to marry me, knowing the whole truth, I am ready to marry her for your sake, mother. I would do any thing for your sake. But Johanna said she ought to be told, and I think it was right myself."

"Who is it, who can it be that you love?" she asked.

"Mother," I said, "I wish I had told you before, but I did not know that I loved the girl as I do, till I saw her yesterday in Sark, and Captain Carey charged me with it."

"That girl!" she cried. "One of the Olliviers! O Martin, you must marry in your own class."

"That was a mistake," I answered. "Her Christian name is Olivia; I do not know what her surname is."

"Not know even her name!" she exclaimed.

"Listen, mother," I said; and then I told her all I knew about Olivia, and drew such a picture of her as I had seen her, as made my mother smile and sigh deeply in turns.

"But she may be an adventuress; you know nothing about her," she objected. "Surely, you cannot love a woman you do not esteem?"

"Esteem!" I repeated. "I never thought whether I esteemed Olivia, but I am satisfied I love her. You may be quite sure she is no adventuress. An adventuress would not hide herself in Tardif's out-of-the-world cottage."

"A girl without friends and without a name!" she sighed; "a runaway from her family and home! It does not look well, Martin."

I could answer nothing, and it would be of little use to try. I saw when my mother's prejudices could blind her. To love any one not of our own caste was a fatal error in her eyes.

"Does Julia know all this?" she asked.

"She has not heard a word about Olivia," I answered. "As soon as I told her I loved some one else better than her, she bade me begone out of her sight. She has not an amiable temper."

"But she is an upright, conscientious, religious woman," she said, somewhat angrily. "She would never have run away from her friends; and we know all about her. I cannot think what your father will say, Martin. It has given him more pleasure and satisfaction than any thing that has happened for years. If this marriage is broken off, it upsets every thing."

Of course it would upset every thing; there was the mischief of it. The convulsion would be so great, that I felt ready to marry Julia in order to avoid it, supposing she would marry me. That was the question, and it rested solely with her. I would almost rather face the long, slow weariness of an unsuitable marriage than encounter the immediate results of the breaking off of our engagement just on the eve of its consummation. I was a coward, no doubt, but events had hurried me on too rapidly for me to stand still and consider the cost.

"O Martin, Martin!" wailed my poor mother, breaking down again suddenly. "I had so set my heart upon this! I did so long to see you in a home of your own! And Julia was so generous, never looking as if all the money was hers, and you without a penny! What is to become of you now, my boy? I wish I had been dead and in my grave before this had happened!"

"Hush, mother!" I said, kneeling down again beside her and kissing her tenderly; "it is still in Julia's hands. If she will marry me, I shall marry her."

"But then you will not be happy?" she said, with fresh sobs.

It was impossible for me to contradict that. I felt that no misery would be equal to that of losing Olivia. But I did my best to comfort my mother, by promising to see Julia the next day and renew my engagement, if possible.

"Pray, may I be informed as to what is the matter now?" broke in a satirical, cutting voice—the voice of my father. It roused us both—my mother to her usual mood of gentle submission, and me to the chronic state of irritation which his presence always provoked in me.

"Not much, sir," I answered, coldly; "only my marriage with my cousin Julia is broken off."

"Broken off!" he ejaculated—"broken off!"

CHAPTER THE NINETEENTH

My father's florid face looked almost as rigid and white as my mother's had done. He stood in the doorway, with a lamp in his hand (for it had grown quite dark while my mother and I were talking), and the light shone full upon his changed face. His hand shook violently, so I took the lamp from him and set it down on the table.

"Go down to Mrs. Murray," he said, turning savagely upon my mother. "How could you be so rude as to leave her? She talks of going away. Let her go as soon as she likes. I shall stay here with Martin."

"I did not know I had been away so long," she answered, meekly, and looking deprecatingly from the one to the other of us—"You will not quarrel with your father, Martin, if I leave you, will you?" This she whispered in my ear, in a beseeching tone.

"Not if I can help it, mother," I replied, also in a whisper.

"Now, confound it!" cried Dr. Dobrée, after she had gone, slowly and reluctantly, and looking back at the door to me—"now just tell me shortly all about this nonsense of yours. I thought some quarrel was up, when Julia did not come home to dinner. Out with it, Martin."

"As I said before, there is not much to tell," I answered. "I was compelled in honor to tell Julia I loved another woman more than herself; and I presume, though I am not sure, she will decline to become my wife."

"In love with another woman!" repeated my father, with a long whistle, partly of sympathy, and partly of perplexity. "Who is it, my son?"

"That is of little moment," I said, having no desire whatever to confide the story to him. "The main point is that it's true, and I told Julia so, this afternoon."

"Good gracious, Martin!" he cried, "what accursed folly! What need was there to tell her of any little peccadillo, if you could conceal it? Why did you not come to me for advice? Julia is a prude, like your mother. It will not be easy for her to overlook this."

"There is nothing to overlook," I said. "As soon as I knew my own mind, I told her honestly about it."

At that moment it did not occur to me that my honesty was due to Johanna's insistent advice. I believed just then that I had acted from the impulse of my own sense of honor, and the belief gave my words and tone more spirit than they would have had otherwise. My father's face grew paler and graver as he listened; he looked older, by ten years, than he had done an hour ago in the dining-room.

"I don't understand it," he muttered; "do you mean that this is a serious thing? Are you in love with some girl of our own class? Not a mere passing fancy, that no one would think seriously of for an instant? Just a trifling faux pas, that it is no use telling women about, eh? I could make allowance for that, Martin, and get Julia to do the same. Come, it cannot be any thing more."

I did not reply to him. Here we had come, he and I, to the very barrier that had been growing up between us ever since I had first discovered my mother's secret and wasting grief. He was on one side of it and I on the other—a wall of separation which neither of us could leap over.

"Why don't you speak, Martin?" he asked, testily.

"Because I hate the subject," I answered. "When I told Julia I loved another woman, I meant that some one else occupied that place in my affection which belonged rightfully to my wife; and so Julia understood it."

"Then," he cried with a gesture of despair, "I am a ruined man!"

His consternation and dismay were so real that they startled me; yet, knowing what a consummate actor he was, I restrained both my fear and my sympathy, and waited for him to enlighten me further. He sat with his head bowed, and his hands hanging down, in an attitude of profound despondency, so different from his usual jaunty air, that every moment increased my anxiety.

"What can it have to do with you?" I asked, after a long pause.

"I am a ruined and disgraced man." he reiterated, without looking up; "if you have broken off your marriage with Julia, I shall never raise my head again."

"But why?" I asked, uneasily.

"Come down into my consulting-room," he said, after another pause of deliberation. I went on before him, carrying the lamp, and, turning round once or twice, saw his face look gray, and the expression of it vacant and troubled. His consulting-room was a luxurious room, elegantly furnished; and with several pictures on the walls, including a painted photograph of himself, taken recently by the first photographer in Guernsey. There were book-cases containing a number of the best medical works; behind which lay, out of sight, a numerous selection of French novels, more thumbed than the ponderous volumes in front. He sank down into an easy-chair, shivering as if we were in the depth of winter.

"Martin, I am a ruined man!" he said, for the third time.

"But how?" I asked again, impatiently; for my fears were growing strong. Certainly he was not acting a part this time.

"I dare not tell you," he cried, leaning his head upon his desk, and sobbing. How white his hair was! and how aged he looked! I recollected how he used to play with me when I was a boy, and carry me before him on horseback, as long back as I could remember. My heart softened and warmed to him as it had not done for years.

"Father!" I said, "if you can trust any one, you can trust me. If you are ruined and disgraced I shall be the same, as your son."

"That's true," he answered, "that's true! It will bring disgrace on you and your mother. We shall be forced to leave Guernsey, where she has lived all her life; and it will be the death of her. Martin, you must save us all by making it up with Julia."

"But why?" I demanded, once more. "I must know what you mean."

"Mean?" he said, turning upon me angrily, "you blockhead! I mean that unless you marry Julia I shall have to give an account of her property; and I could not make all square, not if I sold every stick and stone I possess."

I sat silent for a time, trying to take in this piece of information. He had been Julia's guardian ever since she was left an orphan, ten years old; but I had never known that there had not been a formal and legal settlement of her affairs when she was of age. Our family name had no blot upon it; it was one of the most honored names in the island. But if this came to light, then the disgrace would be dark indeed.

"Can you tell me all about it?" I asked.

My father, after making his confession, settled himself in his chair comfortably; appearing to feel that he had begun to make reparation for the wrong. His temperament was more buoyant than mine. Selfish natures are often buoyant.

"It would take a long time," he said, "and it would be a deuse of a nuisance. You make it up with Julia, and marry her, as you're bound to do. Of course, you will manage all her money when you are her husband, as you will be. Now you know all."

"But I don't know all," I replied; "and I insist upon doing so, before I make up my mind what to do."

I believe he expected this opposition from me, for otherwise all he had said could have been said in my room. But after feebly giving battle on various points, and staving off sundry inquiries, he opened a drawer in one of his cabinets, and produced a number of deeds, scrip, etc., belonging to Julia.

For two hours I was busy with his accounts. Once or twice he tried to slink out of the room; but that I would not suffer. At length the ornamental clock on his chimney-piece struck eleven, and he made another effort to beat a retreat.

"Do not go away till every thing is clear," I said; "is this all?"

"All?" he repeated; "isn't it enough?"

"Between three and four thousand pounds deficient!" I answered; "it is quite enough."

"Enough to make me a felon," he said, "if Julia chooses to prosecute me."

"I think it is highly probable," I replied; "though I know nothing of the law."

"Then you see clearly, Martin, there is no alternative, but for you to marry her, and keep our secret. I have reckoned upon this for years, and your mother and I have been of one mind in bringing it about. If you marry Julia, her affairs go direct from my hands to yours, and we are all safe. If you break with her she will leave us, and demand an account of my guardianship; and your name and mine will be branded in our own island."

"That is very clear," I said, sullenly.

"Your mother would not survive it!" he continued, with a solemn accent.

"Oh! I have been threatened with that already," I exclaimed, very bitterly. "Pray does my mother know of this disgraceful business?"

"Heaven forbid!" he cried. "Your mother is a good woman, Martin; as simple as a dove. You ought to think of her before you consign us all to shame. I can quit Guernsey. I am an old man, and it signifies very little where I lie down to die. I have not been as good a husband as I might have been; but I could not face her after she knows this. Poor Mary! My poor, poor love! I believe she cares enough for me still to break her heart over it."

"Then I am to be your scape-goat," I said.

"You are my son," he answered; "and religion itself teaches us that the sins of the fathers are visited on the children. I leave the matter in your hands. But only answer one question: Could you show your face among your own friends if this were known?"

I knew very well I could not. My father a fraudulent steward of Julia's property! Then farewell forever to all that had made my life happy! We were a proud family—proud of our rank, and of our pure blood; above all, of our honor, which had never been tarnished by a breath. I could not yet bear to believe that my father was a rogue. He himself was not so lost to shame that he could meet my eye. I saw there was no escape from it—I must marry Julia.

"Well," I said, at last, "as you say, the matter is in my hands now; and I must make the best of it. Good-night, sir."

Without a light I went up to my own room, where the moon that had shone upon me in my last night's ride, was gleaming brightly through the window. I intended to reflect and deliberate, but I was worn out. I flung myself down on the bed, but could not have remained awake for a single moment. I fell into a deep sleep which lasted till morning.

CHAPTER THE TWENTIETH

TWO LETTERS

When I awoke, my poor mother was sitting beside me, looking very ill and sorrowful. She had slipped a pillow under my head, and thrown a shawl across me. I got up with a bewildered brain, and a general sense of calamity, which I could not clearly define.

"Martin," she said, "your father has gone by this morning's boat to Jersey. He says you know why; but he has left this note for you. Why have you not been in bed last night?"

"Never mind, mother," I answered, as I tore open the note, which was carefully sealed with my father's private seal. He had written it immediately after I left him.

"11.30 P.M.

"MY SON: To-morrow morning, I shall run over to Jersey for a few days until this sad business of yours is settled. I cannot bear to meet your changed face. You make no allowances for your father. Half my expenses have been incurred in educating you; you ought to consider this, and that you owe more to me, as your father, than to any one else. But in these days parents receive little honor from their children. When all is settled, write to me at Prince's Hotel. It rests upon you whether I ever see Guernsey again. Your wretched father,

"RICHARD DOBRÉE."

"Can I see it?" asked my mother, holding out her hand.

"No, never mind seeing it," I answered, "it is about Julia, you know. It would only trouble you."

"Captain Carey's man brought a letter from Julia just now," she said, taking it from her pocket; "he said there was no answer."

Her eyelids were still red from weeping, and her voice faltered as if she might break out into sobs any moment. I took the letter from her, but I did not open it.

"You want to be alone to read it?" she said. "O Martin! if you can change your mind, and save us all from this trouble, do it, for my sake?"

"If I can I will," I answered; "but every thing is very hard upon me, mother."

She could not guess how hard, and, if I could help it, she should never know. Now I was fully awake, the enormity of my father's dishonesty and his extreme egotism weighed heavily upon me. I could not view his conduct in a fairer light than I had done in my amazement the night before. It grew blacker as I dwelt upon it. And now he was off to Jersey, shirking the disagreeable consequences of his own delinquency. I knew how he would spend his time there. Jersey is no retreat for the penitent.

As soon as my mother was gone I opened Julia's letter. It began:

"MY DEAR MARTIN: I know all now. Johanna has told me. When you spoke to me so hurriedly and unexpectedly, this afternoon, I could not bear to hear another word. But now I am calm, and I can think it all over quite quietly.

"It is an infatuation, Martin. Johanna says so as well as I, and she is never wrong. It is a sheer impossibility that you, in your sober senses, should love a strange person, whose very name you do not know, better than you do me, your cousin, your sister, your fiancée, whom you have known all your life, and loved. I am quite sure of that, with a very true affection.

"It vexes me to write about that person in any connection with yourself. Emma spoke of her in her last letter from Sark; not at all in reference to you, however. She is so completely of a lower class, that it would never enter Emma's head that you could see any thing in her. She said there was a rumor afloat that Tardif was about to marry the girl you had been attending, and that everybody in the island regretted it. She said it would be a mésalliance for him, Tardif! What then would it be for you, a Dobrée? No; it is a delusion, an infatuation, which will quickly pass away. I cannot believe you are so weak as to be taken in by mere prettiness without character; and this person—I do not say so harshly, Martin—has no character, no name. Were you free you could not marry her. There is a mystery about her, and mystery usually means shame. A Dobrée could not make an adventuress his wife. Then you have seen so little of her. Three times, since the week you were there in March! What is that compared to the years we have spent together? It is impossible that in your heart of hearts you should love her more than me.

"I have been trying to think what you would do if all is broken off between us. We could not keep this a secret in Guernsey, and everybody would blame you. I will not ask you to think of my mortification at being jilted, for people would call it that. I could outlive that. But what are you to do? We cannot go on again as we used to do. I must speak plainly about it. Your practice is not sufficient to maintain the family in a proper position for the Dobrées; and if I go to live alone at the new house, as I must do, what is to become of my uncle and aunt? I have often considered this, and have been glad the difficulty was settled by our marriage. Now every thing will be unsettled again.

"I did not intend to say any thing about myself; but, O Martin! you do not know the blank that it will be to me. I have been so happy since you asked me to be your wife. It was so pleasant to think that I should live all my life in Guernsey, and yet not be doomed to the empty, vacant lot of an unmarried woman. You think that perhaps Johanna is happy single? She is content—good women ought to be content; but, I tell you, I would gladly exchange her contentment for Aunt Dobrée's troubles, with her pride and happiness in you. I have seen her troubles clearly; and I say, Martin, I would give all Johanna's calm, colorless peace for her delight in her son.

"Then I cannot give up the thought of our home, just finished and so pretty. It was so pleasant this afternoon before you came in with your dreadful thunder-bolt. I was thinking what a good wife I would be to you; and how, in my own house, I should never be tempted into those tiresome tempers you have seen in me sometimes. It was your father often who made me angry, and I visited it upon you, because you are so good-tempered. That was foolish of me. You could not know how much I love you, how my life is bound up in you, or you would have been proof against that person in Sark.

"I think it right to tell you all this now, though it is not in my nature to make professions and demonstrations of my love. Think of me, of yourself, of your poor mother. You were never selfish, and you can do noble things. I do not say it would be noble to marry me; but it would be a noble thing to conquer an ignoble passion. How could Martin Dobrée fall in love with an unknown adventuress?

"I shall remain in the house all day to-morrow, and if you can come to see me, feeling that this has been a dream of folly from which you have awakened, I will not ask you to own it. That you come at all will be a sign to me that you wish it forgotten and blotted out between us, as if it had never been.

"With true, deep love for you, Martin, believe me still

"Your affectionate JULIA."

I pondered over Julia's letter as I dressed. There was not a word of resentment in it. It was full of affectionate thought for us all. But what reasoning! I had not known Olivia so long as I had known her, therefore I could not love her as truly!

A strange therefore!

I had scarcely had leisure to think of Olivia in the hurry and anxiety of the last twenty-four hours. But now "that person in Sark," the "unknown adventuress," presented itself very vividly to my mind. Know her! I felt as if I knew every tone of her voice and every expression of her face; yet I longed to know them more intimately. The note she had written to me a few weeks ago I could repeat word for word, and the handwriting seemed far more familiar to me even than Julia's. There was no doubt my love for her was very different from my affection for Julia; and if it was an infatuation, it was the sweetest, most exquisite infatuation that could ever possess me.

Yet there was no longer any hesitation in my mind as to what I must do. Julia knew all now. I had told her distinctly of my love for Olivia, and she would not believe it. She appeared wishful to hold me to my engagement in spite of it; at any rate, so I interpreted her letter. I did not suppose that I should not live it down, this infatuation, as they chose to call it. I might hunger and thirst, and be on the point of perishing; then my nature would turn to other nutriment, and assimilate it to its contracted and stultified capacities.

After all there was some reason in the objections urged against Olivia. The dislike of all insulated people against foreigners is natural enough; and in her case there was a mystery which I must solve before I could think of asking her to become my wife. Ask her to become my wife! That was impossible now. I had chosen my wife months before I saw her.

I went mechanically through the routine of my morning's work, and it was late in the afternoon before I could get away to ride to the Vale. My mother knew where I was going, and gazed wistfully into my face, but without otherwise asking me any questions. At the last moment, as I touched Madam's bridle, I looked down at her standing on the door-step. "Cheer up, mother!" I said, almost gayly, "it will all come right."

CHAPTER THE TWENTY-FIRST

ALL WRONG

By this time you know that I could not ride along the flat, open shore between St. Peter-Port and the Vale without having a good sight of Sark, though it lay just a little behind me. It was not in human nature to turn my back doggedly upon it. I had never seen it look nearer; the channel between us scarcely seemed a mile across. The old windmill above the Havre Gosselin stood out plainly. I almost fancied that but for Breckhou I could have seen Tardif's house, where my darling was living. My heart leaped at the mere thought of it. Then I shook Madam's bridle about her neck, and she carried me on at a sharp canter toward Captain Carey's residence.

I saw Julia standing at a window up-stairs, gazing down the long white road, which runs as straight as an arrow through the Braye du Valle to L'Ancresse Common.

She must have seen Madam and me half a mile away; but she kept her post motionless as a sentinel, until I jumped down to open the gate. Then she vanished.

The servant-man was at the door by the time I reached it, and Johanna herself was on the threshold, with her hands outstretched and her face radiant. I was as welcome as the prodigal son, and she was ready to fall on my neck and kiss me.

"I felt sure of you," she said, in a low voice. "I trusted to your good sense and honor, and they have not failed you. Thank God you are come! Julia has neither ate nor slept since I brought her here."

She led me to her own private sitting-room, where I found Julia standing by the fireplace, and leaning against it, as if she could not stand alone. When I went up to her and took her hand, she flung her arms round my neck, and clung to me, in a passion of tears. It was some minutes before she could recover her self-command. I had never seen her abandon herself to such a paroxysm before.

"Julia, my poor girl!" I said, "I did not think you would take it so much to heart as this."

"I shall come all right directly," she sobbed, sitting down, and trembling from head to foot. "Johanna said you would come, but I was not sure."

"Yes, I am here," I answered, with a very dreary feeling about me.

"That is enough," said Julia; "you need not say a word more. Let us forget it, both of us. You will only give me your promise never to see her, or speak to her again."

It might be a fair thing for her to ask, but it was not a fair thing for me to promise. Olivia had told me she had no friends at all except Tardif and me; and if the gossip of the Sark people drove her from the shelter of his roof, I should be her only resource; and I believed she would come frankly to me for help.

"Olivia quite understands about my engagement to you," I said. "I told her at once that we were going to be married, and that I hoped she would find a friend in you.'"

"A friend in me, Martin!" she exclaimed, in a tone of indignant surprise; "you could not ask me to be that!"

"Not now, I suppose," I replied; "the girl is as innocent and blameless as any girl living; but I dare say you would sooner befriend the most good-for-nothing Jezebel in the Channel Islands."

"Yes, I would," she said. "An innocent girl indeed! I only wish she had been killed when she fell from the cliff."

"Hush!" I cried, shuddering at the bare mention of Olivia's death; "you do not know what you say. It is worse than useless to talk about her. I came to ask you to think no more of what passed between us yesterday."

"But you are going to persist in your infatuation," said Julia; "you can never deceive me. I know you too well. Oh, I see that you still think the same of her'"

"You know nothing about her," I replied.

"And I shall take care I never do," she interrupted, spitefully.

"So it is of no use to go on quarrelling about her," I continued, taking no notice of the interruption. "I made up my mind before I came here that I must see as little as possible of her for the future. You must understand, Julia, she has never given me a particle of reason to suppose she loves me."

"But you are still in love with her?" she asked.

I stood biting my nails to the quick, a trick I had while a boy, but one that had been broken off by my mother's and Julia's combined vigilance. Now the habit came back upon me in full force, as my only resource from speaking.

"Martin," she said, with flashing eyes, and a rising tone in her voice, which, like the first shrill moan of the wind, presaged a storm, "I will never marry you until you can say, on your word of honor, that you love that person no longer, and are ready to promise to hold no further communication with her. Oh! I know what my poor aunt has had to endure, and I will not put up with it."

"Very well, Julia," I answered, controlling myself as well as I could, "I have only one more word to say on this subject. I love Olivia, and, as far as I know myself, I shall love her as long as I live. I did not come here to give you any reason for supposing my mind is changed as to her. If you consent to be my wife, I will do my best, God helping me, to be most true, most faithful to you; and God forbid I should injure Olivia in thought by supposing she could care for me other than as a friend. But my motive for coming now is to tell you some particulars about your property, which my father made known to me only last night."

It was a miserable task for me; but I told her simply the painful discovery I had made. She sat listening with a dark and sullen face, but betraying not a spark of resentment, so far as her loss of fortune was concerned.

"Yes," she said, bitterly, when I had finished, "robbed by the father and jilted by the son."

"I would give my life to cancel the wrong," I said.

"It is so easy to talk," she replied, with a deadly coldness of tone and manner.

"I am ready to do whatever you choose," I urged. "It is true my father has robbed you; but it is not true that I have jilted you. I did not know my own heart till a word from Captain Carey revealed it to me; and I told you frankly, partly because Johanna insisted upon it, and partly because I believed it right to do so. If you demand it, I will even promise not to see Olivia again, or to hold direct communication with her. Surely that is all you ought to require from me."

"No," she replied, vehemently; "do you suppose I could become your wife while you maintain that you love another woman better than me? You must have a very low opinion of me."

"Would you have me tell you a falsehood?" I rejoined, with vehemence equal to hers.

"You had better leave me," she said, "before we hate one another. I tell you I have been robbed by the father and jilted by the son. Good-by, Martin."

"Good-by, Julia," I replied; but I still lingered, hoping she would speak to me again. I was anxious to hear what she would do against my father. She looked at me fully and angrily, and, as I did not move, she swept out of the room, with a dignity which I had never seen in her before. I retreated toward the house-door, but could not make good my escape without encountering Johanna.

"Well, Martin?" she said.

"It is all wrong," I answered. "Julia persists in it that I am jilting her."

"All the world will think you have behaved very badly," she said.

"I suppose so," I replied; "but don't you think so, Johanna."

She shook her head in silence, and closed the hall-door after me. Many a door in Guernsey would be shut against me as soon as this was known.

I had to go round to the stables to find Madam. The man had evidently expected me to stay a long while, for her saddle-girths were loosened, and the bit out of her mouth, that she might enjoy a liberal feed of oats. Captain Carey came up to me as I was buckling the girths.

"Well, Martin?" he asked, exactly as Johanna had done before him.

"All wrong," I repeated.

"Dear! dear!" he said, in his mildest tones, and with his hand resting affectionately on my shoulder; "I wish I had lost the use of my eyes or tongue the other day, I am vexed to death that I found out your secret."

"Perhaps I should not have found it out myself," I said, "and it is better now than after."

"So it is, my boy; so it is," he rejoined. "Between ourselves, Julia is a little too old for you. Cheer up! she is a good girl, and will get over it, and be friends again with you by-and-by. I will do all I can to bring that about. If Olivia is only as good as she is handsome, you'll be happier with her than with poor Julia."

He patted my back with a friendliness that cheered me, while his last words sent the blood bounding through my veins. I rode home again, Sark lying in full view before me; and, in spite of the darkness of my prospects, I felt intensely glad to be free to win my Olivia.

Four days passed without any sign from either Julia or my father. I wrote to him detailing my interview with her, but no reply came. My mother and I had the house to ourselves; and, in spite of her frettings, we enjoyed considerable pleasure during the temporary lull. There were, however, sundry warnings out-of-doors which foretold tempest. I met cold glances and sharp inquiries from old friends, among whom some rumors of our separation were floating. There was sufficient to justify suspicion: my father's absence, Julia's prolonged sojourn with the Careys at the Vale, and the postponement of my voyage to England. I began to fancy that even the women-servants flouted at me.

DEAD TO HONOR

The mail from Jersey on Monday morning brought us no letter from my father. But during the afternoon, as I was passing along the Canichers, I came suddenly upon Captain Carey and Julia, who wore a thick veil over her face. The Canichers is a very narrow, winding street, where no conveyances are allowed to run, and all of us had chosen it in preference to the broad road along the quay, where we were liable to meet many acquaintances. There was no escape for any of us. An enormously high, strong wall, such as abound in St. Peter-Port, was on one side of us, and some locked-up stables on the other. Julia turned away her head, and appeared absorbed in the contemplation of a very small placard, which did not cover one stone of the wall, though it was the only one there. I shook hands with Captain Carey, who regarded us with a comical expression of distress, and waited to see if she would recognize me; but she did not.

"Julia has had a letter from your father," he said.

"Yes?" I replied, in a tone of inquiry.

"Or rather from Dr. Collas," he pursued. "Prepare yourself for bad news, Martin. Your father is very ill; dangerously so, he thinks."

The news did not startle me. I had been long aware that my father was one of those medical men who are excessively nervous about their own health, and are astonished that so delicate and complicated an organization as the human frame should ever survive for sixty years the ills it is exposed to. But at this time it was possible that distress of mind and anxiety for the future might have made him really ill. There was no chance of crossing to Jersey before the next morning.

"He wished Dr. Collas to write to Julia, so as not to alarm your mother," continued Captain Carey, as I stood silent.

"I will go to-morrow," I said; "but we must not frighten my mother if we can help it."

"Dr. Dobrée begs that you will go," he answered—"you and Julia."

"Julia!" I exclaimed. "Oh, impossible!"

"I don't see that it is impossible," said Julia, speaking for the first time. "He is my own uncle, and has acted as my father. I intend to go to see him; but Captain Carey has promised to go with me."

"Thank you a thousand times, dear Julia," I answered, gratefully. A heavy load was lifted off my spirits, for I came to this conclusion—that she had said nothing, and would say nothing, to the Careys about his defalcations. She would not make her uncle's shame public.

I told my mother that Julia and I were going over to Jersey the next morning, and she was more than satisfied. We went on board together as arranged—Julia, Captain Carey, and I. But Julia did not stay on deck, and I saw nothing of her during our two-hours' sail.

Captain Carey told me feelingly how terribly she was fretting, notwithstanding all their efforts to console her. He was full of this topic, and could think and speak of nothing else, worrying me with the most minute particulars of her deep dejection, until I felt myself one of the most worthless scoundrels in existence. I was in this humiliated state of mind when we landed in Jersey, and drove in separate cars to the hotel where my father was lying ill.

The landlady received us with a portentous face. Dr. Collas had spoken very seriously indeed of his patient, and, as for herself, she had not the smallest hope. I heard Julia sob, and saw her lift her handkerchief to her eyes behind her veil.

Captain Carey looked very much frightened. He was a man of quick sympathies, and nervous about his own life into the bargain, so that any serious illness alarmed him. As for myself, I was in the miserable condition of mind I have described above.

We were not admitted into my father's room for half an hour, as he sent word he must get up his strength for the interview. Julia and myself alone were allowed to see him. He was propped up in bed with a number of pillows; with the room darkened by Venetian blinds, and a dim green twilight prevailing, which cast a sickly hue over his really pallid face. His abundant white hair fell lankly about his head, instead of being in crisp curls as usual. I was about to feel his pulse for him, but he waved me off.

"No, my son," he said, "my recovery is not to be desired. I feel that I have nothing now to do but to die. It is the only reparation in my power. I would far rather die than recover."

I had nothing to say to that; indeed, I had really no answer ready, so amazed was I at the tone he had taken. But Julia began to sob again, and pressed past me, sinking down on the chair by his side, and laying her hand upon one of his pillows.

"Julia, my love," he continued, feebly, "you know how I have wronged you; but you are a true Christian. You will forgive your uncle when he is dead and gone. I should like to be buried in Guernsey with the other Dobrées."

Neither did Julia answer, save by sobs. I stepped toward the window to draw up the blinds, but he stopped me, speaking in a much stronger voice than before.

"Leave them alone," he said. "I have no wish to see the light of day. A dishonored man does not care to show his face. I have seen no one since I left Guernsey, except Collas."

"I think you are alarming yourself needlessly," I answered. "You know you are fidgety about your own health. Let me prescribe for you. Surely I know as much as Collas."

"No, no, let me die," he said, plaintively; "then you can all be happy. I have robbed my only brother's only child, who was dear to me as my own daughter. I cannot hold up my head after that. I should die gladly if you two were but reconciled to one another."

By this time Julia's hand had reached his, and was resting in it fondly. I never knew a man gifted with such power over women and their susceptibilities as he had. My mother herself would appear to forget all her unhappiness, if he only smiled upon her.

"My poor dear Julia!" he murmured; "my poor child!"

"Uncle," she said, checking her sobs by a great effort, "if you imagine I should tell any one—Johanna Carey even—what you have done, you wrong me. The name of Dobrée is as dear to me as to Martin, and he was willing to marry a woman he detested in order to shield it. No, you are quite safe from disgrace as far as I am concerned."

"God in heaven bless you, my own Julia!" he ejaculated, fervently. "I knew your noble nature; but it grieves me the more deeply that I have so thoughtlessly wronged you. If I should live to get over this illness, I will explain it all to you. It is not so bad as it seems. But will you not be equally generous to Martin? Cannot you forgive him as you do me?"

"Uncle," she cried, "I could never, never marry a man who says he loves some one else more than me."

Her face was hidden in the pillows, and my father stroked her head, glancing at me contemptuously at the same time.

"I should think not, my girl!" he said, in a soothing tone; "but Martin will very soon repent. He is a fool just now, but he will be wise again presently. He has known you too long not to know your worth."

"Julia," I said, "I do know how good you are. You have always been generous, and you are so now. I owe you as much gratitude as my father does, and any thing I can do to prove it I am ready to do this day."

"Will you marry her before we leave Jersey?" asked my father.

"Yes," I answered.

The word slipped from me almost unawares, yet I did not wish to retract it. She was behaving so nobly and generously toward us both, that I was willing to do any thing to make her happy.

"Then, my love," he said, "you hear what Martin promises. All's well that ends well. Only make up your mind to put your proper pride away, and we shall all be as happy as we were before."

"Never!" she cried, indignantly. "I would not marry Martin here, hurriedly and furtively; no, not if you were dying, uncle!"

"But, Julia, if I were dying, and wished to see you united before my death!" he insinuated. A sudden light broke upon me. It was an ingenious plot—one at which I could not help laughing, mad as I was. Julia's pride was to be saved, and an immediate marriage between us effected, under cover of my father's dangerous illness. I did smile, in spite of my anger, and he caught it, and smiled back again. I think Julia became suspicious too.

"Martin," she said, sharpening her voice to address me, "do you think your father is in any danger?"

"No, I do not," I answered, notwithstanding his gestures and frowns.

"Then that is at an end," she said. "I was almost foolish enough to think that I would yield. You don't know what this disappointment is to me. Everybody will be talking of it, and some of them will pity me, and the rest laugh at me. I am ashamed of going out-of-doors anywhere. Oh, it is too bad! I cannot bear it."

She was positively writhing with agitation; and tears, real tears I am sure, started into my father's eyes.

"My poor little Julia!" he said; "my darling! But what can be done if you will not marry Martin?"

"He ought to go away from Guernsey," she sobbed. "I should feel better if I was quite sure I should never see him, or hear of other people seeing him."

"I will go," I said. "Guernsey will be too hot for me when all this is known."

"And, uncle," she pursued, speaking to him, not me, "he ought to promise me to give up that girl. I cannot set him free to go and marry her—a stranger and adventuress. She will be his ruin. I think, for my sake, he ought to give her up."

"So he ought, and so he will, my love," answered my father. "When he thinks of all we owe to you, he will promise you that."

I pondered over what our family owed to Julia for some minutes. It was truly a very great debt. Though I had brought her into perhaps the most painful position a woman could be placed in, she was generously sacrificing her just resentment and revenge against my father's dishonesty, in order to secure our name from blot.

On the other hand, I had no reason to suppose Olivia loved me, and I should do her no wrong. I felt that, whatever it might cost me, I must consent to Julia's stipulation.

"It is the hardest thing you could ask me," I said, "but I will give her up. On one condition, however; for I must not leave her without friends. I shall tell Tardif, if he ever needs help for Olivia, he must apply to me through my mother."

"There could be no harm in that," observed my father.

"How soon shall I leave Guernsey?" I asked.

"He cannot go until you are well again, uncle," she answered. "I will stay here to nurse you, and Martin must take care of your patients. We will send him word a day or two before we return, and I should like him to be gone before we reach home."

That was my sentence of banishment. She had only addressed me once during the conversation. It was curious to see how there was no resentment in her manner toward my father, who had systematically robbed her, while she treated me with profound wrath and bitterness.

She allowed him to hold her hand and stroke her hair; she would not have suffered me to approach her. No doubt it was harder for her to give up a lover than to lose the whole of her property.

She left us, to make the necessary arrangements for staying with my father, whose illness appeared to have lost suddenly its worst symptoms. As soon as she was gone he regarded me with a look half angry, half contemptuous.

"What a fool you are!" he said. "You have no tact whatever in the management of women. Julia would fly back to you, if you only held up your finger."

"I have no wish to hold up my finger to her," I answered. "I don't think life with her would be so highly desirable."

"You thought so a few weeks ago," he said, "and you'll be a pauper without her."

"I was not going to marry her for her money," I replied. "A few weeks ago I cared more for her than for any other woman, except my mother, and she knew it. All that is changed now."

"Well well!" he said, peevishly, "do as you like. I wash my hands of the whole business. Julia will not forsake me if she renounces you, and I shall have need of her and her money. I shall cling to Julia."

"She will be a kind nurse to you," I remarked.

"Excellent!" he answered, settling himself languidly down among his pillows. "She may come in now and watch beside me; it will be the sort of occupation to suit her in her present state of feeling. You had better go out and amuse yourself in your own way. Of course you will go home to-morrow morning."

I would have gone back to Guernsey at once, but I found neither cutter nor yacht sailing that afternoon, so I was obliged to wait for the steamer next morning. I did not see Julia again, but Captain Carey told me she had consented that he should remain at hand for a day or two, to see if he could be of any use to her.

The report of my father's illness had spread before I reached home, and sufficiently accounted for our visit to Jersey, and the temporary postponement of my last trip to England before our marriage. My mother, Johanna, and I, kept our own counsel, and answered the many questions asked us as vaguely as the Delphic oracle.

Still an uneasy suspicion and suspense hung about our circle. The atmosphere was heavily charged with electricity, which foreboded storms. It would be well for me to quit Guernsey before all the truth came out. I wrote to Tardif, telling him I was going for an indefinite period to London, and that if any difficulty or danger threatened Olivia, I begged of him to communicate with my mother, who had promised me to befriend her as far as it lay in her power. My poor mother thought of her without bitterness, though with deep regret. To Olivia herself I wrote a line or two, finding myself too weak to resist the temptation. I said:

"MY DEAR OLIVIA: I told you I was about to be married to my cousin Julia Dobrée; that engagement is at an end. I am obliged to leave Guernsey, and seek my fortune elsewhere. It will be a long time before I can see you again, if I ever have that great happiness. Whenever you feel the want of a true and tender friend, my mother is prepared to love you as if you were her own daughter. Think of me also as your friend. MARTIN DOBRÉE."

CHAPTER THE TWENTY-THIRD

IN EXILE

I left Guernsey the day before my father and Julia returned from Jersey.

My immediate future was not as black as it might have been. I was going direct to the house of my friend Jack Senior, who had been my chum both at Elizabeth College and at Guy's. He, like myself, had been hitherto a sort of partner to his father, the well-known physician, Dr. Senior of Brook Street. They lived together in a highly-respectable but gloomy residence, kept bachelor fashion, for they had no woman-kind at all belonging to them. The father and son lived a good deal apart, though they were deeply attached to one another. Jack had his own apartments, and his own guests, in the spacious house, and Dr. Senior had his.

The first night, as Jack and I sat up together in the long summer twilight, till the dim, not really dark, midnight came over us, I told him every thing; as one tells a friend a hundred things one cannot put into words to any person who dwells under the same roof, and is witness of every circumstance of one's career.

As I was talking to him, every emotion and perception of my brain, which had been in a wild state of confusion and conflict, appeared to fall into its proper rank. I was no longer doubtful as to whether I had been the fool my father called me. My love for Olivia acquired force and decision. My judgment that it would have been a folly and a crime to marry Julia became confirmed.

"Old fellow," said Jack, when I had finished, "you are in no end of a mess."

"Well, I am," I admitted; "but what am I to do?"

"First of all, how much money have you?" he asked.

"I'd rather not say," I answered.

"Come, old friend," he said, in his most persuasive tones, "have you fifty pounds in hand?"

"No," I replied.

"Thirty?"

I shook my head, but I would not answer him further.

"That's bad!" he said; "but it might be worse. I've lots of tin, and we always went shares."

"I must look out for something to do to-morrow," I remarked.

"Ay, yes!" he answered, dryly; "you might go as assistant to a parish doctor, or get a berth on board an emigrant-ship. There are lots of chances for a young fellow."

He sat smoking his cigar—a dusky outline of a human figure, with a bright speck of red about the centre of the face. For a few minutes he was lost in thought.

"I tell you what," he said, "I've a good mind to marry Julia myself. I've always liked her, and we want a woman in the house. That would put things straighter, wouldn't it?"

"She would never consent to leave Guernsey," I answered, laughing. "That was one reason why she was so glad to marry me."

"Well, then," he said, "would you mind me having Olivia?"

"Don't jest about such a thing," I replied; "it is too serious a question with me."

"You are really in love!" he answered. "I will not jest at it. But I am ready to do any thing to help you, old boy."

So it proved, for he and Dr. Senior did their best during the next few weeks to find a suitable opening for me. I made their house my home, and was treated as a most welcome guest in it. Still the time was irksome—more irksome than I ever could have imagined. They were busy while I was unoccupied.

Occasionally I went out to obey some urgent summons, when either of them was absent; but that was a rare circumstance. The hours hung heavily upon me; and the close, sultry air of London, so different from the fresh sea-breezes of my native place, made me feel languid and irritable.

My mother's letters did not tend to raise my spirits. The tone of them was uniformly sad. She told me the flood of sympathy for Julia had risen very high indeed: from which I concluded that the public indignation against myself must have risen to the same tide-mark, though my poor mother said nothing about it. Julia had resumed her old occupations, but her spirit was quite broken. Johanna Carey had offered to go abroad with her, but she had declined it, because it would too painfully remind her of our projected trip to Switzerland.

A friend of Julia's, said my mother in another letter, had come to stay with her, and to try to rouse her.

It was evident she did not like this Kate Daltrey, herself, for the dislike crept out unawares through all the gentleness of her phrases. "She says she is the same age as Julia," she wrote, "but she is probably some years older; for, as she does not belong to Guernsey, we have no opportunity of knowing." I laughed when I read that. "Your father admires her very much," she added.

No, my mother felt no affection for her new guest.

There was not a word about Olivia. Sark itself was never mentioned, and it might have sunk into the sea. My eye ran over every letter first, with the hope of catching that name, but I could not find it. This persistent silence on my mother's part was very trying.

I had been away from Guernsey two months, and Jack was making arrangements for a long absence from London as soon as the season was over, leaving me in charge, when I received the following letter from Johanna Carey:

"DEAR MARTIN: Your father and Julia have been here this afternoon, and have confided to me a very sad and very painful secret, which they ask me to break gently to you. I am afraid no shadow of a suspicion of it has ever fallen upon your mind, and, I warn you, you will need all your courage and strength as a man to bear it. I was myself so overwhelmed that I could not write to you until now, in the dead of the night, having prayed with all my heart to our merciful God to sustain and comfort you, who will feel this sorrow more than any of us. My dearest Martin, my poor boy, how can I tell it to you? You must come home again for a season. Even Julia wishes it, though she cannot stay in the same house with you, and will go to her own with her friend Kate Daltrey. Your father cried like a child. He takes it more to heart than I should have expected. Yet there is no immediate danger; she may live for some months yet. My poor Martin, you will have a mother only a few months longer. Three weeks ago she and I went to Sark, at her own urgent wish, to see your Olivia. I did not then know why. She had a great longing to see the unfortunate girl who had been the cause of so much sorrow to us all, but especially to her, for she has pined sorely after you. We did not find her in Tardif's house, but Suzanne directed us to the little graveyard half a mile away. We followed her there, and recognized her, of course, at the first glance. She is a charming creature, that I allow, though I wish none of us had ever seen her. Your mother told her who she was, and the sweetest flush and smile came across her face! They sat down side by side on one of the graves, and I strolled away, so I do not know what they said to one another. Olivia walked down with us to the Havre Gosselin, and your mother held her in her arms and kissed her tenderly. Even I could not help kissing her.

"Now I understand why your mother longed to see Olivia. She knew then—she has known for months—that her days are numbered. When she was in London last November, she saw the most skilful physicians, and they all agreed that her disease was incurable and fatal. Why did she conceal it from you? Ah, Martin, you must know a woman's heart, a mother's heart, before you can comprehend that. Your father knew, but no one else. What a martyrdom of silent agony she has passed through! She has a clear calculation, based upon the opinion of the medical men, as to how long she might have lived had her mind been kept calm and happy. How far that has not been the case we all know too well.

"If your marriage with Julia had taken place, you would now have been on your way home, not to be parted from her again till the final separation. We all ask you to return to Guernsey, and devote a few more weeks to one who has loved you so passionately and fondly. Even Julia asks it. Her resentment gives way before this terrible sorrow. We have not told your mother what we are about to do, lest any thing should prevent your return. She is as patient and gentle as a lamb, and is ready with a quiet smile for every one. O Martin, what a loss she will be to us all! My heart is bleeding for you.

"Do not come before you have answered this letter, that we may prepare her for your return. Write by the next boat, and come by the one after. Julia will have to move down to the new house, and that will be excitement enough for one day.

"Good-by, my dearest Martin. I have forgiven every thing; so will all our friends as soon as they know this dreadful secret.

"Your faithful, loving cousin, JOHANNA CAREY."

I read this letter twice, with a singing in my ears and a whirling of my brain, before I could realize the meaning. Then I refused to believe it. No one knows better than a doctor how the most skilful head among us may be at fault.

My mother dying of an incurable disease! Impossible! I would go over at once and save her. She ought to have told me first. Who could have attended her so skilfully and devotedly as her only son?

Yet the numbing, deadly chill of dread rested upon my heart. I felt keenly how slight my power was, as I had done once before when I thought Olivia would die. But then I had no resources, no appliances. Now I would take home with me every remedy the experience and researches of man had discovered.

CHAPTER THE TWENTY-FOURTH

OVERMATCHED

My mother had consulted Dr. Senior himself when she had been in London. He did not positively cut off all hope from me, though I knew well he was giving me encouragement in spite of his own carefully-formed opinion. He asserted emphatically that it was possible to alleviate her sufferings and prolong her life, especially if her mind was kept at rest. There was not a question as to the necessity for my immediate return to her. But there was still a day for me to tarry in London.

"Martin," said Jack, "why have you never followed up the clew about your Olivia—the advertisement, you know? Shall we go to those folks in Gray's-Inn Road this afternoon?"

It had been in my mind all along to do so, but the listless procrastination of idleness had caused me to put it off from time to time. Besides, while I was absent from the Channel Islands my curiosity appeared to sleep. It was enough to picture Olivia in her lowly home in Sark. Now that I was returning to Guernsey, and the opportunity was about to slip by, I felt more anxious to seize it. I would learn all I could about Olivia's family and friends, without betraying any part of her secret.

At the nearest cab-stand we found a cabman patronized by Jack—a red-faced, good-tempered, and good-humored man, who was as fond and proud of Jack's notice as if he had been one of the royal princes.

Of course there was not the smallest difficulty in finding the office of Messrs. Scott and Brown. It was on the second floor of an ordinary building, and, bidding the cabman wait for us, we proceeded at once up the staircase.

There did not seem much business going on, and our appearance was hailed with undisguised satisfaction. The solicitors, if they were solicitors, were two inferior, common-looking men, but sharp enough to be a match for either of us. We both felt it, as if we had detected a snake in the grass by its rattle. I grew wary by instinct, though I had not come with any intention to tell them what I knew of Olivia. My sole idea had been to learn something myself, not to impart any information. But, when I was face to face with these men, my business, and the management of it, did not seem quite so simple as it had done until then.

"Do you wish to consult my partner or me?" asked the keenest-looking man. "I am Mr. Scott."

"Either will do," I answered. "My business will be soon dispatched. Some months ago you inserted an advertisement in the Times."

"To what purport?" inquired Mr. Scott.

"You offered fifty pounds reward," I replied, "for information concerning a young lady."

A gleam of intelligence and gratification flickered upon both their faces, but quickly faded away into a sober and blank gravity. Mr. Scott waited for me to speak again, and bowed silently, as if to intimate he was all attention.

"I came," I added, "to ask you for the name and address of that young lady's friends, as I should prefer communicating directly with them, with a view to cooperation in the discovery of her hiding-place. I need scarcely say I have no wish to receive any reward. I entirely waive any claim to that, if you will oblige me by putting me into connection with the family."

"Have you no information you can impart to us?" asked Mr. Scott.

"None," I answered, decisively. "It is some months since I saw the advertisement, and it must be nine months since you put it into the Times. I believe it is nine months since the young lady was missing."

"About that time," he said.

"Her friends must have suffered great anxiety," I remarked.

"Very great indeed," he admitted.

"If I could render them any service, it would be a great pleasure to me," I continued; "cannot you tell me where to find them?"

"We are authorized to receive any information," he replied. "You must allow me to ask if you know any thing about the young lady in question?"

"My object is to combine with her friends in seeking her," I said, evasively. "I really cannot give you any information; but if you will put me into communication with them, I may be useful to them."

"Well," he said, with an air of candor, "of course the young lady's friends are anxious to keep in the background. It is not a pleasant circumstance to occur in a family; and if possible they would wish her to be restored without any éclat. Of course, if you could give us any definite information it would be quite another thing. The young lady's family is highly connected. Have you seen any one answering to the description?"

"It is a very common one," I answered. "I have seen scores of young ladies who might answer to it. I am surprised that in London you could not trace her. Did you apply to the police?"

"The police are blockheads," replied Mr. Scott—"Will you be so good as to see if there is any one in the outer office, Mr. Brown, or on the stairs? I believe I heard a noise outside."

Mr. Brown disappeared for a few minutes; but his absence did not interrupt our conversation. There was not much to be made out of it on either side, for we were only fencing with one another. I learned nothing about Olivia's friends, and I was satisfied he had learned nothing about her.

At last we parted with mutual dissatisfaction; and I went moodily downstairs, followed by Jack. We drove back to Brook Street, to spend the few hours that remained before the train started for Southampton.

"Doctor," said Simmons, as Jack paid him his fare, with a small coin added to it, "I'm half afeard I've done some mischief. I've been turning it over and over in my head, and can't exactly see the rights of it. A gent, with a pen behind his ear, comes down, at that orfice in Gray's Inn Road, and takes my number. But after that he says a civil thing or two. 'Fine young gents,' he says, pointing up the staircase. 'Very much so,' says I. 'Young doctors?' he says. 'You're right,' I says. 'I guessed so,' he says; 'and pretty well up the tree, eh?' 'Ay,' I says; 'the light-haired gent is son to Dr. Senior, the great pheeseecian; and the other he comes from Guernsey, which is an island in the sea.' 'Just so,' he says; 'I've heard as much.' I hope I've done no mischief, doctor?"

"I hope not, Simmons," answered Jack; "but your tongue hangs too loose, my man—Look out for a squall on the Olivia coast, Martin," he added.

My anxiety would have been very great if I had not been returning immediately to Guernsey. But once there, and in communication with Tardif, I could not believe any danger would threaten Olivia from which I could not protect or rescue her. She was of age, and had a right to act for herself. With two such friends as Tardif and me, no one could force her away from her chosen home.

CHAPTER THE TWENTY-FIFTH

HOME AGAIN

My mother was looking out for me when I reached home the next morning. I had taken a car from the pier-head to avoid meeting any acquaintances; and hers was almost the first familiar face I saw. It was pallid with the sickly hue of a confirmed disease, and her eyes were much sunken; but she ran across the room to meet me. I was afraid to touch her, knowing how a careless movement might cause her excruciating pain; but she was oblivious of every thing save my return, and pressed me closer and closer in her arms, with all her failing strength, while I leaned my face down upon her dear head, unable to utter a word.

"God is very good to me," sobbed my mother.

"Is He?" I said, my voice sounding strange to my own ears, so forced and altered it was.

"Very, very good," she repeated. "He has brought you back to me."

"Never to leave you again, mother," I said—"never again!"

"No; you will never leave me alone again here," she whispered. "Oh, how I have missed you, my boy!"

I made her sit down on the sofa, and sat beside her, while she caressed my hand with her thin and wasted fingers.

I must put an end to this, if I was to maintain my self-control.

"Mother," I said, "you forget that I have been on the sea all night, and have not had my breakfast yet."

"The old cry, Martin," she answered, smiling. "Well, you shall have your breakfast here, and I will wait upon you once more."

I watched her furtively as she moved about, not with her usual quick and light movements, but with a slow and cautious tread. It was part of my anguish to know, as only a medical man can know, how every step was a fresh pang to her. She sat down with me at the table, though I would not suffer her to pour out my coffee, as she wished to do. There was a divine smile upon her face; yet beneath it there was an indication of constant and terrible pain, in the sunken eyes and drawn lips. It was useless to attempt to eat with that smiling face opposite me. I drank thirstily, but I could not swallow a crumb. She knew what it meant, and her eyes were fastened upon me with a heart-breaking expression.

That mockery of a meal over, she permitted me to lay her down on the sofa, almost as submissively as a tired child, and to cover her with an eider-down quilt; for her malady made her shiver with its deadly coldness, while she could not bear any weight upon her. My father was gone out, and would not be back before evening. The whole day lay before us; I should have my mother entirely to myself.

We had very much to say to one another; but it could only be said at intervals, when her strength allowed of it. We talked together, more calmly than I could have believed possible, of her approaching death; and, in a stupor of despair, I owned to myself and her that there was not a hope of her being spared to me much longer.

"I have longed so," she murmured, "to see my boy in a home of his own before I died. Perhaps I was wrong, but that was why I urged on your marriage with Julia. You will have no real home after I am gone, Martin; and I feel as if I could die so much more quietly if I had some knowledge of your future life. Now I shall know nothing. I think that is the sting of death to me."

"I wish it had been as you wanted it to be," I said, never feeling so bitterly the disappointment I had caused her, and almost grieved that I had ever seen Olivia.

"I suppose it is all for the best," she answered, feebly. "O Martin! I have seen your Olivia."

"Well?" I said.

"I did so want to see her," she continued—"though she has brought us all into such trouble. I loved her because you love her. Johanna went with me, because she is such a good judge, you know, and I did not like to rely upon my own feelings. Appearances are very much against her; but she is very engaging, and I believe she is a good girl. I am sure she is good."

"I know she is," I said.

"We talked of you," she went on—"how good you were to her that week in the spring. She had never been quite unconscious, she thought; but she had seen and heard you all the time, and knew you were doing your utmost to save her. I believe we talked more of you than of any thing else."

That was very likely, I knew, as far as my mother was concerned. But I was anxious to hear whether Olivia had not confided to her more of her secret than I had yet been able to learn from other sources. To a woman like my mother she might have intrusted all her history.

"Did you find any thing out about her friends and family?" I asked.

"Not much," she answered. "She told me her own mother had died when she was quite a child; and she had a step-mother living, who has been the ruin of her life. That was her expression. 'She has been the ruin of my life!' she said; and she cried a little, Martin, with her head upon my lap. If I could only have offered her a home here, and promised to be a mother to her!"

"God bless you, my darling mother!" I said.

"She intends to stay where she is as long as it is possible," she continued; "but she told me she wanted work to do—any kind of work by which she could earn a little money. She has a diamond ring, and a watch and chain, worth a hundred pounds; so she must have been used to affluence. Yet she spoke as if she might have to live in Sark for years. It is a very strange position for a young girl."

"Mother," I said, "you do not know how all this weighs upon me. I promised Julia to give her up, and never to see her again; but it is almost more than I can bear, especially now. I shall be as friendless and homeless as Olivia by-and-by."

I had knelt down beside her, and she pressed my face to hers, murmuring those soft, fondling words, which a man only hears from his mother's lips. I knew that the anguish of her soul was even greater than my own. The agitation was growing too much for her, and would end in an access of her disease. I must put an end to it at once.

"I suppose Julia is gone to the new house now," I said, in a calm voice.

"Yes," she answered, but she could say no more.

"And Miss Daltrey with her?" I pursued.

The mention of that name certainly roused my mother more effectually than any thing else I could have said. She released me from her clinging hands, and looked up with a decided expression of dislike on her face.

"Yes," she replied. "Julia is just wrapped up in her, though why I cannot imagine. So is your father. But I don't think you will like her, Martin. I don't want you to be taken with her."

"I won't, mother," I said. "I am ready to hate her, if that is any satisfaction to you."

"Oh, you must not say that," she answered, in a tone of alarm. "I do not wish to set you against her, not in the least, my boy. Only she has so much influence over Julia and your father; and I do not want you to go over to her side. I know I am very silly; but she always makes my flesh creep when she is in the room."

"Then she shall not come into the room," I said.

"Martin," she went on, "why does it rouse one up more to speak evil of people than to speak good of them? Speaking of Kate Daltrey makes me feel stronger than talking of Olivia."

I laughed a little. It had been an observation of mine, made some years ago, that the surest method of consolation in cases of excessive grief, was the introduction of some family or neighborly gossip, seasoned slightly with scandal. The most vehement mourning had been turned into another current of thought by the lifting of this sluice.

"It restores the balance of the emotions," I answered. "Anything soft, and tender, and touching, makes you more sensitive. A person like Miss Daltrey acts as a tonic; bitter, perhaps, but invigorating."

The morning passed without any interruption; but in the afternoon Grace came in, with a face full of grave importance, to announce that Miss Dobrée had called, and desired to see Mrs. Dobrée alone. "Quite alone," repeated Grace, emphatically.

"I'll go up-stairs to my own room," I said to my mother.

"I am afraid you cannot, Martin," she answered, hesitatingly. "Miss Daltrey has taken possession of it, and she has not removed all her things yet. She and Julia did not leave till late last night. You must go to the spare room."

"I thought you would have kept my room for me, mother," I said, reproachfully.

"So I would," she replied, her lips quivering, "but Miss Daltrey took a fancy to it, and your father and Julia made a point of indulging her. I really think Julia would have had every thing belonging to you swept into the streets. It was very hard for me, Martin. I was ten times more vexed than you are to give up your room to Miss Daltrey. It was my only comfort to go and sit there, and think of my dear boy." "Never mind, never mind," I answered. "I am at home now, and you will never be left alone with them again—nevermore, mother."

I retreated to the spare room, fully satisfied that I should dislike Miss Daltrey quite as much as my mother could wish. Finding that Julia prolonged her visit downstairs, I went out after a while for a stroll in the old garden, where the trees and shrubs had grown with my growth, and were as familiar as human friends to me. I visited Madam in her stall, and had a talk with old Pellet; and generally established my footing once more as the only son of the house; not at all either as if I were a prodigal son, come home repentant. I was resolved not to play that rôle, for had I not been more sinned against than sinning?

My father came in to dinner; but, like a true man of the world, he received me back on civil and equal terms, not alluding beyond a word or two to my long absence. We began again as friends; and our mutual knowledge of my mother's fatal malady softened our hearts and manners toward one another. Whenever he was in-doors he waited upon her with sedulous attention. But, for the certainty that death was lurking very near to us, I should have been happier in my home than I had ever been since that momentous week in Sark. But I was also nearer to Olivia, and every throb of my pulse was quickened by the mere thought of that.

CHAPTER THE TWENTY-SIXTH

A NEW PATIENT

In one sense, time seemed to be standing still with me, so like were the days that followed the one to the other. But in another sense those days fled with awful swiftness, for they were hurrying us both, my mother and me, to a great gulf which would soon, far too soon, lie between us.

Every afternoon Julia came to spend an hour or two with my mother; but her arrival was always formally announced, and it was an understood thing that I should immediately quit the room, to avoid meeting her. There was an etiquette in her resentment which I was bound to observe.

What our circle of friends thought, had become a matter of very secondary consideration to me; but there seemed a general disposition to condone my offences, in view of the calamity that was hanging by a mere thread above me. I discovered from their significant remarks that it had been quite the fashion to visit Sark during the summer, by the Queen of the Isles, which made the passage every Monday; and that Tardif's cottage had been an object of attraction to many of my relatives of every degree. Few of them had caught even a glimpse of Olivia; and I suspected that she had kept herself well out of sight on those days when the weekly steamer flooded the island with visitors.

I had not taken up any of my old patients again, for I was determined that everybody should feel that my residence at home was only temporary. But, about ten days after my return, the following note was brought to me, directed in full to Dr. Martin Dobrée:

"A lady from England, who is only a visitor in Guernsey, will be much obliged by Dr. Martin Dobrée calling upon her, at Rose Villa, Vauvert Road. She is suffering from a slight indisposition; and, knowing Dr. Senior by name and reputation, she would feel great confidence in the skill of Dr. Senior's friend."

I wondered for an instant who the stranger could be, and how she knew the Seniors; but, as there could be no answer to these queries without visiting the lady, I resolved to go. Rose Villa was a house where the rooms were let to visitors during the season, and the Vauvert Road was scarcely five minutes' walk from our house. Julia was paying her daily visit to my mother, and I was at a loss for something to do, so I went at once.

I found a very handsome, fine-looking woman; dark, with hair and eyes as black as a gypsy's, and a clear olive complexion to match. Her forehead was low, but smooth and well-shaped; and the lower part of her face, handsome as it was, was far more developed than the upper. There was not a trace of refinement about her features; yet the coarseness of them was but slightly apparent as yet. She did not strike me as having more than a very slight ailment indeed, though she dilated fluently about her symptoms, and affected to be afraid of fever. It is not always possible to deny that a woman has a violent headache; but, where the pulse is all right, and the tongue clean, it is clear enough that there is not any thing very serious threatening her. My new patient did not inspire me with much sympathy; but she attracted my curiosity, and interested me by the bold style of her beauty.

"You Guernsey people are very stiff with strangers," she remarked, as I sat opposite to her, regarding her with that close observation which is permitted to a doctor.

"So the world says," I answered. "Of course I am no good judge, for we Guernsey people believe ourselves as perfect as any class of the human family. Certainly, we pride ourselves on being a little more difficult of approach than the Jersey people. Strangers are more freely welcome there than here, unless they bring introductions with them. If you have any introductions, you will find Guernsey as hospitable a spot as any in the world."

"I have been here a week," she replied, pouting her full crimson lips, "and have not had a chance of speaking a word, except to strangers like myself who don't know a soul."

That, then, was the cause of the little indisposition which had obtained me the honor of attending her. I indulged myself in a mild sarcasm to that effect, but it was lost upon her. She gazed at me solemnly with her large black eyes, which shone like beads.

"I am really ill," she said, "but it has nothing to do with not seeing anybody, though that's dull. There's nothing for me to do but take a bath in the morning, and a drive in the afternoon, and go to bed very early. Good gracious! it's enough to drive me mad!"

"Try Jersey," I suggested.

"No, I'll not try Jersey," she said. "I mean to make my way here. Don't you know anybody, doctor, that would take pity on a poor stranger?"

"I am sorry to say no," I answered.

She frowned at that, and looked disappointed. I was about to ask her how she knew the Seniors, when she spoke again.

"Do you have many visitors come to Guernsey late in the autumn, as late as October?" she inquired.

"Not many," I answered; "a few may arrive who intend to winter here."

"A dear young friend of mine came here last autumn," she said, "alone, as I am, and I've been wondering, ever since I've been here, however she would get along among such a set of stiff, formal, stand-offish folks. She had not money enough for a dash, or that would make a difference, I suppose."

"Not the least," I replied, "if your friend came without any introductions."

"What a dreary winter she'd have!" pursued my patient, with a tone of exultation. "She was quite young, and as pretty as a picture. All the young men would know her, I'll be bound, and you among them, Dr. Martin. Any woman who isn't a fright gets stared at enough to be known again."

Could this woman know any thing of Olivia? I looked at her more earnestly and critically. She was not a person I should like Olivia to have any thing to do with. A coarse, ill-bred, bold woman, whose eyes met mine unabashed, and did not blink under my scrutiny. Could she be Olivia's step-mother, who had been the ruin of her life?

"I'd bet a hundred to one you know her," she said, laughing and showing all her white teeth. "A girl like her couldn't go about a little poky place like this without all the young men knowing her. Perhaps she left the island in the spring. I have asked at all the drapers' shops, but nobody recollects her. I've very good news for her if I could find her—a slim, middle-sized girl, with a clear, fair skin, and gray eyes, and hair of a bright brown. Stay, I can show you her photograph."

She put into my hands an exquisite portrait of Olivia, taken in Florence. There was an expression of quiet mournfulness in the face, which touched me to the core of my heart. I could not put it down and speak indifferently about it. My heart beat wildly, and I felt tempted to run off with the treasure and return no more to this woman.

"Ah! you recognize her!" she exclaimed triumphantly.

"I never saw such a person in Guernsey," I answered, looking steadily into her face. A sullen and gloomy expression came across it, and she snatched the portrait out of my hand.

"You want to keep it a secret," she said, "but I defy you to do it. I am come here to find her, and find her I will. She hasn't drowned herself, and the earth hasn't swallowed her up. I've traced her as far as here, and that I tell you. She crossed in the Southampton boat one dreadfully stormy night last October—the only lady passenger—and the stewardess recollects her well. She landed here. You must know something about her."

"I assure you I never saw that girl here," I replied, evasively. "What inquiries have you made after her?"

"I've inquired here, and there, and everywhere," she said. "I've done nothing else ever since I came. It is of great importance to her, as well as to me, that I should find her. It's a very anxious thing when a girl like that disappears and is never heard of again, all because she has a little difference with her friends. If you could help me to find her you would do her family a very great service."

"Why do you fix upon me?" I inquired. "Why did you not send for one of the resident doctors? I left Guernsey some time ago."

"You were here last winter," she said; "and you're a young man, and would notice her more."

"There are other young doctors in Guernsey," I remarked.

"Ah! but you've been in London," she answered, "and I know something of Dr. Senior. When you are in a strange place you catch at any chance of an acquaintance."

"Come, be candid with me," I said. "Did not Messrs. Scott and Brown send you here?"

The suddenness of my question took her off her guard and startled her. She hesitated, stammered, and finally denied it with more than natural emphasis.

"I could take my oath I don't know any such persons," she answered. "I don't know whom you mean, or what you mean. All I want is quite honest. There is a fortune waiting for that poor girl, and I want to take her back to those who love her, and are ready to forgive and forget every thing. I feel sure you know something of her. But no body except me and her other friends have any thing to do with it."

"Well," I said, rising to take my leave, "all the information I can give you is, that I never saw such a person here, either last winter or since. It is quite possible she went on to Jersey, or to Granville, when the storm was over. That she did not stay in Guernsey, I am quite sure."

I went away in a fever of anxiety. The woman, who was certainly not a lady, had inspired me with a repugnance that I could not describe. There was an ingrain coarseness about her—a vulgarity excessively distasteful to me as in any way connected with Olivia. The mystery which surrounded her was made the deeper by it. Surely, this person could not be related to Olivia! I tried to guess in what relationship to her she could possibly stand. There was the indefinable delicacy and refinement of a lady, altogether independent of her surroundings, so apparent in Olivia, that I could not imagine her as connected by blood with this woman. Yet why and how should such a person have any right to pursue her? I felt more chafed than I had ever done about Olivia's secret.

I tried to satisfy myself with the reflection that I had put Tardif on his guard, and that he would protect her. But that did not set my mind at ease. I never knew a mother yet who believed that any other woman could nurse her sick child as well as herself; and I could not be persuaded that even Tardif would shield Olivia from danger and trouble as I could, if I were only allowed the privilege. Yet my promise to Julia bound me to hold no communication with her. Besides, this was surely no time to occupy myself with any other woman in the world than my mother. She herself, good, and amiable, and self-forgetting, as she was, might feel a pang of jealousy, and I ought not to be the one to add a single drop of bitterness to the cup she was drinking.

On the other hand, I was distracted at the thought that this stranger might discover the place of Olivia's retreat, from which there was no chance of escape if it were once discovered. A hiding-place like Sark becomes a trap as soon as it is traced out. Should this woman catch the echo of those rumors which had circulated so widely through Guernsey less than three months ago—and any chance conversation with one of our own people might bring them to her ears—then farewell to Olivia's safety and concealment. Here was the squall which had been foretold by Jack. I cursed the idle curiosity of mine which had exposed her to this danger.

I had strolled down some of the quieter streets of the town while I was turning this affair over in my mind, and now, as I crossed the end of Rue Haute, I caught sight of Kate Daltrey turning into a milliner's shop. There was every reasonable probability that she would not come out again soon, for I saw a bonnet reached out of the window. If she were gone to buy a bonnet, she was safe for half an hour, and Julia would be alone. I had felt a strong desire to see Julia ever since I returned home. My mind was made up on the spot. I knew her so well as to be certain that, if I found her in a gentle mood, she would, at any rate, release me from the promise she had extorted from me when she was in the first heat of her anger and disappointment. It was a chance worth trying. If I were free to declare to Olivia my love for her, I should establish a claim upon her full confidence, and we could laugh at further difficulties. She was of age, and, therefore, mistress of herself. Her friends, represented by this odious woman, could have no legal authority over her.

I turned shortly up a side-street, and walked as fast as I could toward the house which was to have been our home. By a bold stroke I might reach Julia's presence. I rang, and the maid who answered the bell opened wide eyes of astonishment at seeing me there. I passed by quickly.

"I wish to speak to Miss Dobrée," I said. "Is she in the drawing-room?"

"Yes, sir," she answered, in a hesitating tone.

I waited for nothing more, but knocked at the drawing-room door for myself, and heard Julia call, "Come in."

CHAPTER THE TWENTY-SEVENTH

SET FREE

Julia looked very much the same as she had done that evening when I came reluctantly to tell her that my heart was not in her keeping, but belonged to another. She wore the same kind of fresh, light muslin dress, with ribbons and lace about it, and she sat near the window, with a piece of needle-work in her hands; yet she was not sewing, and her hands lay listlessly on her lap. But, for this attitude of dejection, I could have imagined that it was the same day and the same hour, and that she was still ignorant of the change in my feelings toward her. If it had not been for our perverse fate, we should now be returning from our wedding-trip, and receiving the congratulations of our friends. A mingled feeling of sorrow, pity, and shame, prevented me from advancing into the room. She looked up to see who was standing in the doorway, and my appearance there evidently alarmed and distressed her.

"Martin!" she cried.

"May I come in and speak to you, Julia?" I asked.

"Is my aunt worse?" she inquired, hurriedly. "Are you come to fetch me to her?"

"No, no, Julia," I said; "my mother is as well as usual, I hope. But surely you will let me speak to you after all this time?"

"It is not a long time," she answered.

"Has it not been long to you?" I asked. "It seems years to me. All life has changed for me. I had no idea then of my mother's illness."

"Nor I," she said, sighing deeply.

"If I had known it," I continued, "all this might not have happened. Surely, the troubles I shall have to bear must plead with you for me!"

"Yes, Martin," she answered; "yes, I am very sorry for you."

She came forward and offered me her hand, but without looking into my face. I saw that she had been crying, for her eyes were red. In a tone of formal politeness she asked me if I would not sit down. I considered it best to remain standing, as an intimation that I should not trouble her with my presence for long.

"My mother loves you very dearly, Julia," I ventured to say, after a long pause, which she did not seem inclined to break. I had no time to lose, lest Kate Daltrey should come in, and it was a very difficult subject to approach.

"Not more than I love her," she said, warmly. "Aunt Dobrée has been as good to me as any mother could have been. I love her as dearly as my mother. Have you seen her since I was with her this afternoon?"

"No. I have just come from visiting a very curious patient, and have not been home yet."

I hoped Julia would catch at the word curious, and make some inquiries which would open a way for me; but she seemed not to hear it, and another silence fell upon us both. For the life of me I could not utter a syllable of what I had come to say.

"We were talking of you," she said at length, in a harried and thick voice. "Aunt is in great sorrow about you. It preys upon her day and night that you will be dreadfully alone when she is gone, and—and—Martin, she wishes to know before she dies that the girl in Sark will become your wife."

The word struck like a shot upon my ear and brain. What! had Julia and my mother been arranging between them my happiness and Olivia's safety that very afternoon? Such generosity was incredible. I could not believe I had heard aright.

"She has seen the girl," continued Julia, in the same husky tone, which she could not compel to be clear and calm; "and she is convinced she is no adventuress. Johanna says the same. They tell me it is unreasonable and selfish in me to doom you to the dreadful loneliness I feel. If Aunt Dobrée asked me to pluck out my right eye just now, I could not refuse. It is something like that, but I have promised to do it. I release you from every promise you ever made to me, Martin."

"Julia!" I cried, crossing to her and bending over her with more love and admiration than I had ever felt before; "this is very noble, very generous."

"No," she said, bursting into tears; "I am neither noble nor generous. I do it because I cannot help myself, with aunt's white face looking so imploringly at me. I do not give you up willingly to that girl in Sark. I hope I shall never see her or you for many, many years. Aunt says you will have no chance of marrying her till you are settled in a practice somewhere; but you are free to ask her to be your wife. Aunt wants you to have somebody to love you and care for you after she is gone, as I should have done."

"But you are generous to consent to it," I said again.

"So," she answered, wiping her eyes, and lifting up her head; "I thought I was generous; I thought I was a Christian, but it is not easy to be a Christian when one is mortified, and humbled, and wounded. I am a great disappointment to myself; quite as great as you are to me. I fancied myself very superior to what I am. I hope you may not be disappointed in that girl in Sark."

The latter words were not spoken in an amiable tone, but this was no time for criticising Julia. She had made a tremendous sacrifice, that was evident; and a whole sacrifice without any blemish is very rarely offered up nowadays, however it may have been in olden times. I could not look at her dejected face and gloomy expression without a keen sense of self-reproach.

"Julia," I said, "I shall never be quite happy—no, not with Olivia as my wife—unless you and I are friends. We have grown up together too much as brother and sister, for me to have you taken right out of my life without a feeling of great loss. It is I who would lose a right hand or a right eye in losing you. Some day we must be friends again as we used to be."

"It is not very likely," she answered; "but you had better go now, Martin. It is very painful to me for you to be here."

I could not stay any longer after that dismissal. Her hand was lying on her lap, and I stooped down and kissed it, seeing on it still the ring I had given her when we were first engaged. She did not look at me or bid me good-by; and I went out of the house, my veins tingling with shame and gladness. I met Captain Carey coming up the street, with a basket of fine grapes in his hand. He appeared very much amazed.

"Why, Martin!" he exclaimed; "can you have been to see Julia?"

"Yes," I answered.

"Reconciled?" he said, arching his eyebrows, which were still dark and bushy though his hair was grizzled.

"Not exactly," I replied, with a stiff smile, exceedingly difficult to force; "nothing of the sort indeed. Captain, when will you take me across to Sark?"

"Come, come! none of that, Martin," he said; "you're on honor, you know. You are pledged to poor Julia not to visit Sark again."

"She has just set me free," I answered; and out of the fulness of my heart I told him all that had just passed between us. His eyes glistened, though a film came across them which he had to wipe away.

"She is a noble girl," he ejaculated; "a fine, generous, noble girl. I really thought she'd break her heart over you at first, but she will come round again now. We will have a run over to Sark to-morrow."

I felt myself lifted into a third heaven of delight all that evening. My mother and I talked of no one but Olivia. The present rapture so completely eclipsed the coming sorrow, that I forgot how soon it would be upon me. I remember now that my mother neither by word nor sign suffered me to be reminded of her illness. She listened to my rhapsodies, smiling with her divine, pathetic smile. There is no love, no love at all, like that of a mother!

CHAPTER THE TWENTY-EIGHTH

Not the next day, which was wet and windy, but the day following, did Captain Carey take me over to Sark. I had had time to talk over all my plans for the future with my mother, and I bore with me many messages from her to the girl I was about to ask to become my wife.

Coxcomb as I was, there was no doubt in my mind that I could win Olivia.

To explain my coxcombry is not a very easy task. I do not suppose I had a much higher sense of my own merits than such as is common to man. I admit I was neither shy nor nervous on the one hand, but on the other I was not blatantly self-conceited. It is possible that my course through life hitherto—first as an only son adored by his mother, and secondly as an exceedingly eligible party in a circle where there were very few young men of my rank and family, and where there were twenty or more marriageable women to one unmarried man—had a great deal to do with my feeling of security with regard to this unknown, poor, and friendless stranger. But, added to this, there was Olivia's own frank, unconcealed pleasure in seeing me, whenever I had had a chance of visiting her, and the freedom with which she had always conversed with me upon any topic except that of her own mysterious position. I was sure I had made a favorable impression upon her. In fact, when I had been talking with her, I had given utterance to brighter and clearer thoughts than I had ever been conscious of before. A word from her, a simple question, seemed to touch the spring of some hidden treasure of my brain, and I had surprised myself by what I had been enabled to say to her. It was this, probably more than her beauty, which had drawn me to her and made me happy in her companionship. No, I had never shown myself contemptible, but quite the reverse, in her presence. No doubt or misgiving assailed me as the yacht carried us out of St. Sampson's Harbor.

Swiftly we ran across, with a soft wind drifting over the sea and playing upon our faces, and a long furrow lying in the wake of our boat. It was almost low tide when we reached the island—the best time for seeing the cliffs. They were standing well out of the water, scarred and chiselled with strange devices, and glowing in the August sunlight with tints of the most gorgeous coloring, while their feet, swathed with brown seaweed, were glistening with the dashing of the waves. I had seen nothing like them since I had been there last, and the view of these wild, rugged crags, with their regal robes of amber and gold and silver, almost oppressed me with delight. If I could but see Olivia on this summit!

The currents and the wind had been in favor of our running through the channel between Sark and Jethou, and so landing at the Creux Harbor, on the opposite coast of the island to the Havre Gosselin. I crossed in headlong haste, for I was afraid of meeting with Julia's friends, or some of my own acquaintances who were spending the summer months there. I found Tardif's house completely deserted. The only sign of life was a family of hens clucking about the fold.

The door was not fastened, and I entered, but there was nobody there. I stood in the middle of the kitchen and called, but there was no answer. Olivia's door was ajar, and I pushed it a little more open. There lay books I had lent her on the table, and her velvet slippers were on the floor, as if they had only just been taken off. Very worn and brown were the little slippers, but they reassured me she had been wearing them a short time ago.

I returned through the fold and mounted the bank that sheltered the house, to see if I could discover any trace of her, or Tardif, or his mother. All the place seemed left to itself. Tardif's sheep were browsing along the cliffs, and his cows were tethered here and there, but nobody appeared to be tending them.

At last I caught sight of a head rising from behind a crag, the rough shock head of a boy, and I shouted to him, making a trumpet with my hands.

"Where is neighbor Tardif?" I called.

"Down below there," he shouted back again, pointing downward to the Havre Gosselin. I did not wait for any further information, but darted off down the long, steep gulley to the little strand, where the pebbles were being lapped lazily by the ripple of the lowering tide. Tardif's boat was within a stone's throw, and I saw Olivia sitting in the stern of it. I shouted again with a vehemence which made them both start.

"Come back, Tardif," I cried, "and take me with you."

The boat was too far off for me to see how my sudden appearance affected Olivia. Did she turn white or red at the sound of my voice? By the time it neared the shore, and I plunged in knee-deep to meet it, her face was bright with smiles, and her hands were stretched out to help me over the boat's side.

If Tardif had not been there, I should have kissed them both. As it was, I tucked up my wet legs out of reach of her dress, and took an oar, unable to utter a word of the gladness I felt.

I recovered myself in a few seconds, and touched her hand, and grasped Tardif's with almost as much force as he gripped mine.

"Where are you going to?" I asked, addressing neither of them in particular.

"Tardif was going to row me past the entrance to the Gouliot Caves," answered Olivia, "but we will put it off now. We will return to the shore, and hear all your adventures, Dr. Martin. You come upon us like a phantom, and take an oar in ghostly silence. Are you really, truly there?"

"I am no phantom," I said, touching her hand again. "No, we will not go back to the shore. Tardif shall row us to the caves, and I will take you into them, and then we two will return along the cliffs. Would you like that, mam'zelle?"

"Very much," she answered, the smile still playing about her face. It was brown and freckled with exposure to the sun, but so full of health and life as to be doubly beautiful to me, who saw so many wan and sickly faces. There was a bloom and freshness about her, telling of pure air, and peaceful hours and days spent in the sunshine. I was seated on the bench before Tardif, with my back to him, and Olivia was in front of me—she, and the gorgeous cliffs, and the glistening sea, and the cloudless sky overhead. No, there is no language on earth that could paint the rapture of that moment.

"Doctor," said Tardif's deep, grave voice behind me, "your mother, is she better?"

It was like the sharp prick of a poniard, which presently you knew must pierce your heart.

The one moment of rapture had fled. The paradise, that had been about me for an instant, with no hint of pain, faded out of my sight. But Olivia remained, and her face grew sad, and her voice low and sorrowful, as she leaned forward to speak to me.

"I have been so grieved for you," she said. "Your mother came to see me once, and promised to be my friend. Is it true? Is she so very ill?" "Quite true," I answered, in a choking voice.

We said no more for some minutes, and the splash of the oars in the water was the only sound. Olivia's air continued sad, and her eyes were downcast, as if she shrank from looking me in the face.

"Pardon me, doctor," said Tardif in our own dialect, which Olivia could not understand, "I have made you sorry when you were having a little gladness. Is your mother very ill?"

"There is no hope, Tardif," I answered, looking round at his honest and handsome face, full of concern for me.

"May I speak to you as an old friend?" he asked. "You love mam'zelle, and you are come to tell her so?"

"What makes you think that?" I said.

"I see it in your face," he answered, lowering his voice, though he knew Olivia could not tell what we were saying. "Your marriage with mademoiselle your cousin was broken off—why? Do you suppose I did not guess? I knew it from the first-week you stayed with us. Nobody could see mam'zelle as we see her, without loving her."

"The Sark folks say you are in love with her yourself, Tardif," I said, almost against my will, and certainly without any intention beforehand of giving expression to such a rumor.

His lips contracted and his face saddened, but he met my eyes frankly.

"It is true," he answered; "but what then? If it had only pleased God to make me like you, or that she should be of my class, I would have done my utmost to win her. But that is impossible! See, I am nothing else than a servant in her eyes. I do not know how to be any thing else, and I am content. She is as far above my reach as one of the white clouds up yonder. To think of myself as any thing but her servant would be irreligious."

"You are a good fellow, Tardif," I exclaimed.

"God is the judge, of that," he said, with a sigh. "Mam'zelle thinks of me only as her servant. 'My good Tardif, do this, or do that.' I like it. I do not know any happier moment than when I hold her little boots in my hand and brush them. You see she is as helpless and tender as my little wife was; but she is very much higher than my poor little wife. Yes, I love her as I love the blue sky, and the white clouds and the stars shining in the night. But it will be quite different between her and you."

"I hope so," I thought to myself.

"You do not feel like a servant," he continued, his oars dipping a little too deeply and setting the boat a-rocking. "By-and-by, when you are married, she will look up to you and obey you. I do not understand altogether why the good God has made this difference between us two; but I see it and feel it. It would be fitting for you to be her husband; it would be a shame to her to become my wife."

"Are you grieved about it, Tardif?" I asked.

"No, no," he answered; "we have always been good friends, you and I, doctor. No, you shall marry her, and I will be happy. I will come to visit you sometimes, and she will call me her good Tardif. That is enough for me."

"What are you talking about?" asked Olivia. It was impossible to tell her, or to continue the conversation. Moreover, the narrow channel between Breckhou and Sark is so strong in its current, that it required both caution and skill to steer the boat amid the needle-like points of the rocks. At last we gained one of the entrances to the caves, but we could not pull the boat quite up to the strand. A few paces of shallow water, clear as glass, with pebbles sparkling like gems beneath it, lay between us and the caves.

"Tardif," I said, "you need not wait for us. We will return by the cliffs."

"You know the Gouliot Caves as well as I do?" he replied, though in a doubtful tone.

"All right!" I said, as I swung over the side of the boat into the water, when I found myself knee-deep. Olivia looked from me to Tardif with a flushed face—an augury that made my pulses leap. Why should her face never change when he carried her in his arms? Why should she shrink from me?

"Are you as strong as Tardif?" she asked, lingering and hesitating before she would trust herself to me.

"Almost, if not altogether," I answered gayly. "I'm strong enough to undertake to carry you without wetting the soles of your feet. Come, it is not more than half a dozen yards."

She was standing on the bench I had just left, looking down at me with the same vivid flush upon her cheeks and forehead, and with an uneasy expression in her eyes. Before she could speak again I put my arms round her, and lifted her down.

"You are quite as light as a feather," I said, laughing, as I carried her to the strip of moist and humid strand under the archway in the rocks. As I put her down I looked back to Tardif, and saw him regarding us with grave and sorrowful eyes.

"Adieu!" he cried; "I am going to look after my lobster-pots. God bless you both!"

He spoke the last words heartily; and we stood watching him as long as he was in sight. Then we went on into the caves.

CHAPTER THE TWENTY-NINTH

THE GOULIOT CAVES

Olivia was very silent.

The coast of Sark shows some of the most fantastic workmanship of the sea, but the Gouliot Caves are its wildest and maddest freak. A strong, swift current sets in from the southwest, and being lashed into a giddy fury by the lightest southwest wind, it has hewn out of the rock a series of cells, and grottos, and alcoves, some of them running far inland, in long, vaulted passages and corridors, with now and then a shaft or funnel in the rocky roof, through which the light streams down into recesses far from the low porches, which open from the sea. Here and there a crooked, twisted tunnel forms a skylight overhead, and the blue heavens look down through it like a far-off eye. You cannot number the caverns and niches. Everywhere the sea has bored alleys and galleries, or hewn out solemn aisles, with arches intersecting each other, and running off into capricious furrows and mouldings. There are innumerable refts, and channels, and crescents, and cupolas, half-finished or only hinted at. There are chambers of every height and shape, leading into one another by irregular portals, but all rough and rude, as though there might have been an original plan, from which, while the general arrangement is kept, every separate stroke perversely diverged.

But another, and not a secondary, curiosity of this ocean-labyrinth is, that it is the habitat of a multitude of marine creatures, not to be seen at home in many other places. Except twice a month, at the neaptides, the lower chambers are filled with the sea; and here live and flourish thousands, upon thousands of those mollusks and zoophytes which can exist only in its salt waters. The sides of the caves, as far as the highest tides swept, were studded with crimson and purple and amber mollusca, glistening like jewels in the light pouring down upon them from the eyelet-openings overhead. Not the space of a finger-tip was clear. Above them in the clefts of the rock hung fringes of delicate ferns of the most vivid green, while here and there were nooks and crevices of profound darkness, black with perpetual, unbroken shadow.

I had known the caves well when I was a boy, but it was many years since I had been there. Now I was alone in them with Olivia, no other human being in sight or sound of us. I had scarcely eyes for any sight but that of her face, which had grown shy and downcast, and was generally turned away from me. She would be frightened, I thought, if I spoke to her in that lonesome place, I would wait till we were on the cliffs, in the open eye of day.

She left my side for one moment while I was poking under a stone for a young pieuvre, which had darkened the little pool of water round it with its inky fluid. I heard her utter an exclamation of delight, and I gave up my pursuit instantly to learn what was giving her pleasure. She was stooping down to look beneath a low arch, not more than two feet high, and I knelt down beside her. Beyond lay a straight narrow channel of transparent water, blue from a faint reflected light, with smooth, sculptured walls of rock, clear from mollusca, rising on each side of it. Level lines of mimic waves rippled monotonously upon it, as if it was stirred by some soft wind which we could not feel. You could have peopled it with tiny boats flitting across it, or skimming lightly down it. Tears shone in Olivia's eyes.

"It reminds me so of a canal in Venice," she said, in a tremulous voice.

"Do you know Venice?" I asked; and the recollection of her portrait taken in Florence came to my mind. Well, by-and-by I should have a right to hear about all her wanderings.

"Oh, yes!" she answered; "I spent three months there once, and this place is like it."

"Was it a happy time?" I inquired, jealous of those tears.

"It was a hateful time," she said, vehemently. "Don't let us talk of it. I hate to remember it. Why cannot we forget things, Dr. Martin? You, who are so clever, can tell me that."

"That is simple enough," I said, smiling. "Every circumstance of our life makes a change in the substance of the brain, and, while that remains sound and in vigor, we cannot forget. To-day is being written on our brain now. You will have to remember this, Olivia."

"I know I shall remember it," she answered, in a low tone.

"You have travelled a great deal, then?" I pursued, wishing her to talk about herself, for I could scarcely trust my resolution to wait till we were out of the caves. "I love you with all my heart and soul" was on my tongue's end.

"We travelled nearly all over Europe," she replied.

I wondered whom she meant by "we." She had never used the plural pronoun before, and I thought of that odious woman in Guernsey—an unpleasant recollection.

We had wandered back to the opening where Tardif had left us. The rapid current between us and Breckhou was running in swift eddies, which showed the more plainly because the day was calm, and the open sea smooth. Olivia stood near me; but a sort of chilly diffidence had crept over me, and I could not have ventured to press too closely to her, or to touch her with my hand.

"How have you been content to live here?" I asked.

"This year in Sark has saved me," she answered, softly.

"What has it saved you from?" I inquired, with intense eagerness. She turned her face full upon me, with a world of reproach in her gray eyes.

"Dr. Martin," she said, "why will you persist in asking me about my former life? Tardif never does. He never implies by a word or look that he wishes to know more than I choose to tell. I cannot tell you any thing about it."

I felt uncomfortably that she was drawing a comparison unfavorable to me between Tardif and myself— the gentleman, who could not conquer or conceal his desire to fathom a mystery, and the fisherman, who acted as if there were no mystery at all. Yet Olivia appeared more grieved than offended; and when she knew how I loved her she would admit that my curiosity was natural. She should know, too, that I was willing to take her as she was, with all the secrets of her former life kept from me. Some day I would make her own I was as generous as Tardif.

Just then my ear caught for the first time a low boom-boom, which had probably been sounding through the caves for some minutes.

"Good Heavens!" I ejaculated.

Yet a moment's thought convinced me that, though there might be a little risk, there was no paralyzing danger. I had forgotten the narrowness of the gully through which alone we could gain the cliffs. From the open span of beach where we were now standing, there was no chance of leaving the caves except as we had come to them, by a boat; for on each side a crag ran like a spur into the water. The comparatively open space permitted the tide to lap in quietly, and steal imperceptibly higher upon its pebbles. But the low boom I heard was the sea rushing in through the throat of the narrow outlet through which lay our only means of escape. There was not a moment to lose. Without a word, I snatched up Olivia in my arms, and ran back into the caves, making as rapidly as I could for the long, straight passage.

Neither did Olivia speak a word or utter a cry. We found ourselves in a low tunnel, where the water was beginning to flow in pretty strongly. I set her down for an instant, and tore off my coat and waistcoat. Then I caught her up again, and strode along over the slippery, slimy masses of rock which lay under my feet, covered with seaweed.

"Olivia," I said, "I must have my right hand free to steady myself with. Put both your arms round my neck, and cling to me so. Don't touch my arms or shoulders."

Yet the clinging of her arms about my neck, and her cheek close to mine, almost unnerved me. I held her fast with my left arm, and steadied myself with my right. We gained in a minute or two the mouth of the tunnel. The drift was pouring into it with a force almost too great for me, burdened as I was. But there was the pause of the tide, when the waves rushed out again in white floods, leaving the water comparatively shallow. There were still six or eight yards to traverse before we could reach an archway in the cliffs, which would land us in safety in the outer caves. Across this small space the tide came in strongly, beating against the foot of the rocks, and rebounding with great force. There was some peril; but we had no alternative. I lifted Olivia a little higher against my shoulder, for her long serge dress wrapped dangerously around us both; and then, waiting for the pause in the throbbing of the tide, I dashed hastily across.

One swirl of the water coiled about us, washing up nearly to my throat, and giving me almost a choking sensation of dread; but before a second could swoop down upon us I had staggered half-blinded to the arch, and put down Olivia in the small, secure cave within it. She had not spoken once. She did not seem able to speak now. Her large, terrified eyes looked up at me dumbly, and her face was white to the lips. I clasped her in my arms once more, and kissed her forehead and lips again and again in a paroxysm of passionate love and gladness.

"Thank God!" I cried. "How I love you, Olivia!"

I had told her only a few minutes before that the brain is ineffaceably stamped with the impress of every event in our lives. But how much more deeply do some events burn themselves there than others' I see it all now—more clearly, it seems to me, than my eyes saw it then. There is the huge, high entrance to the outer caves where we are standing, with a massive lintel of rocks overhead, all black but for a few purple and gray tints scattered across the blackness. Behind us the sea is glistening, and prismatic colors play upon the cliffs. Shadows fall from rocks we cannot see. Olivia stands before me, pale and terrified, the water running from her heavy dress, which clings about her slender figure. She shrinks away from me a pace or two.

"Hush!" she cries, in a tone of mingled pain and dread—"hush!"

There was something so positive, so prohibitory in her voice and gesture, that my heart contracted, and a sudden chill of despondency ran through me. But I could not be silent now. It was impossible for me to hold my peace, even at her bidding.

"Why do you say hush?" I asked, peremptorily. "I love you, Olivia. Is there any reason why I should not love you?"

"Yes," she said, very slowly and with quivering lips. "I was married four years ago, and my husband is living still!"

A GLOOMY ENDING

Olivia's answer struck me like an electric shock. For some moments I was simply stunned, and knew neither what she had said, nor where we were.

I suppose half a minute had elapsed before I fairly received the meaning of her words into my bewildered brain. It seemed as if they were thundering in my ears, though she had uttered them in a low, frightened voice. I scarcely understood them when I looked up and saw her leaning against the rock, with her hands covering her face.

"Olivia!" I cried, stretching out my arms toward her, as though she would flutter back to them and lay her head again where it had been resting upon my shoulder, with her face against my neck.

But she did not see my gesture, and the next moment I knew that she could never let me hold her in my arms again. I dared not even take one step nearer to her.

"Olivia," I said again, after another minute or two of troubled silence, with no sound but the thunders of the sea reverberating through the perilous strait where we had almost confronted death together— "Olivia, is it true?"

She bowed her head still lower upon her hands, in speechless confirmation. A stricken, helpless, cowering child she seemed to me, standing there in her drenched clothing. An unutterable tenderness, altogether different from the feverish passion of a few minutes ago, filled my heart as I looked at her.

"Come," I said, as calmly as I could speak, "I am at any rate your doctor, and I am bound to take care of you. You must not stay here wet and cold. Let us make haste back to Tardif's, Olivia."

I drew her hand down from her face and through my arm, for we had still to re-enter the outer cave, and to return through a higher gallery, before we could reach the cliffs above. I did not glance at her. The road was very rough, strewed with huge bowlders, and she was compelled to receive my help. But we did not speak again till we were on the cliffs, in the eye of day, with our faces and our steps turned toward Tardif's farm.

"Oh!" she cried, suddenly, in a tone that made my heart ache the keener, "how sorry I am!"

"Sorry that I love you?" I asked, feeling that my love was growing every moment in spite of myself. The sun shone on her face, which was just below my eyes. There was an expression of sad perplexity and questioning upon it, which kept away every other sign of emotion. She lifted her eyes to me frankly, and no flush of color came over her pale cheeks.

"Yes," she answered; "it is such a miserable, unfortunate thing for you. But how could I have helped it?"

"You could not help it," I said.

"I did not mean to deceive you," she continued—"neither you nor any one. When I fled away from him I had no plan of any kind. I was just like a leaf driven about by the wind, and it tossed me here. I did not think I ought to tell any one I was married. I wish I could have foreseen this. Why did God let me have that accident in the spring? Why did he let you come over to see me?"

"Are you surprised that I love you?" I asked.

Now I saw a subtle flush steal across her face, and her eyes fell to the ground.

"I never thought of it till this afternoon," she murmured. "I knew you were going to marry your cousin Julia, and I knew I was married, and that there could be no release from that. All my life is ruined, but you and Tardif made it more bearable. I did not think you loved me till I saw your face this afternoon."

"I shall always love you," I cried, passionately, looking down on the shining, drooping head beside me, and the sad face and listless arms hanging down in an attitude of dejection. She seemed so forlorn a creature that I wished I could take her to my heart again; but that was impossible now.

"No," she answered in her calm, sorrowful voice. "When you see clearly that it is an evil thing, you will conquer it. There will be no hope whatever in your love for me, and it will pass away. Not soon, perhaps; I can scarcely wish you to forget me soon. Yet it would be wrong for you to love me now. Why was I driven to marry him so long ago?"

A sharp, bitter tone rang through her quiet voice, and for a moment she hid her face in her hands.

"Olivia," I said, "it is harder upon me than you can think, or I can tell."

She had not the faintest notion of how hard this trial was. I had sacrificed every plan and purpose of my life in the hope of winning her. I had cast away, almost as a worthless thing, the substantial prosperity which had been within my grasp, and now that I stretched out my hand for the prize, I found it nothing but an empty shadow. Deeper even than this lay the thought of my mother's bitter disappointment.

"Your husband must have treated you very badly, before you would take such a desperate step as this," I said again, after a long silence, scarcely knowing what I said.

"He treated me so ill," said Olivia, with the same hard tone in her voice, "that when I had a chance of escape it seemed as if God Himself opened the door for me. He treated me so ill that, if I thought there was any fear of him finding me out here, I would rather a thousand times you had left me to die in the caves."

That brought to my mind what I had almost forgotten—the woman whom my imprudent curiosity had brought into pursuit; of her. I felt ready to curse my folly aloud, as I did in my heart, for having gone to Messrs. Scott and Brown.

"Olivia," I said, "there is a woman in Guernsey who has some clew to you—"

But I could say no more, for I thought she would have fallen to the ground in her terror. I drew her hand through my arm, and hastened to reassure her.

"No harm can come to you," I continued, "while Tardif and I are here to protect you. Do not frighten yourself; we will defend you from every danger."

"Martin," she whispered—and the pleasant familiarity of my name spoken by her gave me a sharp pang, almost of gladness—"no one can help me or defend me. The law would compel me to go back to him. A woman's heart may be broken without the law being broken. I could prove nothing that would give me a right to be free—nothing. So I took it into my own hands. I tell you I would rather have been drowned this afternoon. Why did you save me?"

I did not answer, except by pressing her hand against my side. I hurried her on silently toward the cottage. She was shivering in her cold, wet dress, and trembling with fear. It was plain to me that even her fine health should not be trifled with, and I loved her too tenderly, her poor, shivering, trembling frame, to let her suffer if I could help it. When we reached the fold-yard gate, I stopped her for a moment to speak only a few words.

"Go in." I said, "and change, every one of your wet clothes. I will see you again, once again, when we can talk with one another calmly. God bless and take care of you, my darling!"

She smiled faintly, and laid her hand in mine.

"You forgive me?" she said.

"Forgive you!" I repeated, kissing the small brown hand lingeringly; "I have nothing to forgive."

She went on across the little fold and into the house, without looking back toward me. I could see her pass through the kitchen into her own room, where I had watched her through the struggle between life and death, which had first made her dear to me. Then I made my way, blind and deaf, to the edge of the cliff, seeing nothing, hearing-nothing. I flung myself down on the turf with my face to the ground, to hide my eyes from the staring light of the summer sun.

Already it seemed a long time since I had known that Olivia was married. The knowledge had lost its freshness and novelty, and the sting of it had become a rooted sorrow. There was no mystery about her now. I almost laughed, with a resentful bitterness, at the poor guesses I had made. This was the solution, and it placed her forever out of my reach. As with Tardif, so she could be nothing for me now, but as the blue sky, and the white clouds, and the stars shining in the night. My poor Olivia! whom I loved a hundredfold more than I had done even this morning. This morning I had been full of my own triumph and gladness. Now I had nothing in my heart but a vast pity and reverential tenderness for her.

Married? That was what she had said. It shut out all hope for the future. She must have been a mere child four years ago; she looked very young and girlish still. And her husband treated her ill—my Olivia, for whom I had given up all I had to give. She said the law would compel her to return to him, and I could do nothing. I could not interfere even to save her from a life which was worse to her than death.

My heart was caught in a vice, and there was no escape from the torture of its relentless grip. Whichever way I looked there was sorrow and despair. I wished, with a faint-heartedness I had never felt before, that Olivia and I had indeed perished together down in the caves where the tide was now sweeping below me.

"Martin!" said a clear, low, tender tone in my ear, which could never be deaf to that voice. I looked up at Olivia without moving. My head was at her feet, and I laid my hand upon the hem of her dress.

"Martin," she said again, "see, I have brought you Tardifs coat in place of your own. You must not lie here in this way. Captain Carey's yacht is waiting for you below."

I staggered giddily when I stood on my feet, and only Olivia's look of pain steadied me. She had been weeping bitterly. I could not trust myself to look in her face again. At any rate my next duty was to go away without adding to her distress, if that were possible. Tardif was standing behind her, regarding us both with great concern.

"Doctor," he said, "when I came in from my lobster-pots, the captain sent a message by me to say the sun would be gone down before you reach Guernsey. He has come round to the Havre Gosselin. I'll walk down the cliff with you."

I should have said no, but Olivia caught at his words eagerly.

"Yes, go, my good Tardif," she cried, "and bring me word that Dr. Martin is safe on board—Good-by!"

Her hand in mine again for a moment, with its slight pressure. Then she was gone, Tardif was tramping down the stony path before me, speaking to me over his shoulder.

"It has not gone well, then, doctor?" he said.

"She will tell you," I answered, briefly, not knowing how much Olivia might wish him to know.

"Take care of mam'zelle," I said, when we had reached the top of the ladder, and the little boat from the yacht was dancing at the foot of it. "There is some danger ahead, and you can protect her better than I."

"Yes, yes," he replied; "you may trust her with me. But God knows I should have been glad if it had gone well with you."

CHAPTER THE THIRTY-FIRST

A STORY IN DETAIL

"Well?" said Captain Carey, as I set my foot on the deck. His face was all excitement; and he put his arm affectionately through mine.

"It is all wrong," I answered, gloomily.

"You don't mean that she will not have you?" he exclaimed.

I nodded, for I had no spirit to explain the matter just then.

"By George!" he cried; "and you've thrown over Julia, and offended all our Guernsey folks, and half broken your poor mother's heart, all for nothing!"

The last consideration was the one that stung me to the quick. It had half broken my mother's heart. No one knew better than I that it had without doubt tended to shorten her fleeting term of life. At this moment she was waiting for me to bring her good news—perhaps the promise that Olivia had consented to become my wife before her own last hour arrived; for my mother and I had even talked of that. I had thought it a romantic scheme when my mother spoke of it, but my passion had fastened eagerly upon it, in spite of my better judgment. These were the tidings she was waiting to hear from my lips.

When I reached home I found her full of dangerous excitement. It was impossible to allay it without telling her either an untruth or the whole story. I could not deceive her, and with a desperate calmness I related the history of the day. I tried to make light of my disappointment, but she broke down into tears and wailings.

"Oh, my boy!" she lamented; "and I did so want to see you happy before I died: I wanted to leave some one who could comfort you; and Olivia would have comforted you and loved you when I am gone! You had set your heart upon her. Are you sure it is true? My poor, poor Martin, you must forget her now. It becomes a sin for you to love her."

"I cannot forget her," I said; "I cannot cease to love her. There can be no sin in it as long as I think of her as I do now."

"And there is poor Julia!" moaned my mother.

Yes, there was Julia; and she would have to be told all, though she would rejoice over it. Of course, she would rejoice; it was not in human nature, at least in Julia's human nature, to do otherwise. She had warned me against Olivia; had only set me free reluctantly. But how was I to tell her? I must not leave to my mother the agitation of imparting such tidings. I couldn't think of deputing the task to my father. There was no one to do it but myself.

My mother passed a restless and agitated night, and I, who sat up with her, was compelled to listen to all her lamentation. But toward the morning she fell into a heavy sleep, likely to last for some hours. I could leave her in perfect security; and at an early hour I went down to Julia's house, strung up to bear the worst, and intending to have it all out with her, and put her on her guard before she paid her daily visit to our house. She must have some hours for her excitement and rejoicing to bubble over, before she came to talk about it to my mother.

"I wish to see Miss Dobrée," I said to the girl who quickly answered my noisy peal of the house-bell.

"Please, sir,'" was her reply, "she and Miss Daltrey are gone to Sark with Captain Carey."

"Gone to Sark!" I repeated, in utter amazement.

"Yes, Dr. Martin. They started quite early because of the tide, and Captain Carey's man brought the carriage to take them to St. Sampson's. I don't look for them back before evening. Miss Dobrée said I was to come, with her love, and ask how Mrs. Dobrée is to-day, and if she's home in time she'll come this evening; but if she's late she'll come to-morrow morning."

"When did they make up their minds to go to Sark?" I inquired, anxiously.

"Only late last night, sir," she answered. "Cook had settled with Miss Dobrée to dine early to-day; but then Captain Carey came in, and after he was gone she said breakfast must be ready at seven this morning in their own rooms while they were dressing; so they must have settled it with Captain Carey last night."

I turned away very much surprised and bewildered, and in an irritable state which made the least thing jar upon me. Curiosity, which had slept yesterday, or was numbed by the shock of my disappointment, was feverishly awake to-day. How little I knew, after all, of the mystery which surrounded Olivia! The bitter core of it I knew, but nothing of the many sheaths and envelops which wrapped it about. There might be some hope, some consolation to be found wrapped up with it. I must go again to Sark in the steamer on Monday, and hear Olivia tell me all she could tell of her history.

Then, why were Julia and Kate Daltrey gone to Sark? What could they have to do with Olivia? It made me almost wild with anger to think of them finding Olivia, and talking to her perhaps of me and my love—questioning her, arguing with her, tormenting her! The bare thought of those two badgering my Olivia was enough to drive me frantic.

In the cool twilight, Julia and Kate Daltrey were announced. I was about to withdraw from my mother's room, in conformity with the etiquette established among us, when Julia recalled me in a gentler voice than she had used toward me since the day of my fatal confession.

"Stay, Martin," she said; "what we have to tell concerns you more than any one."

I sat down again by my mother's sofa, and she took my hand between both her own, fondling it in the dusk.

"It is about Olivia," I said, in as cool a tone as I could command.

"Yes," answered Julia; "we have seen her, and we have found out why she has refused you. She is married already."

"She told me so yesterday," I replied.

"Told you so yesterday!" repeated Julia, in an accent of chagrin. "If we had only known that, we might have saved ourselves the passage across to Sark."

"My dear Julia," exclaimed my mother, feverishly, "do tell us all about it, and begin at the beginning."

There was nothing Julia liked so much, or could do so well, as to give a circumstantial account of any thing she had done. She could relate minute details with so much accuracy, without being exactly tedious, that when one was lazy or unoccupied it was pleasant to listen. My mother enjoyed, with all the delight of a woman, the small touches by which Julia embellished her sketches. I resigned myself to hearing a long history, when I was burning to ask one or two questions and have done with the topic.

"To begin at the beginning, then," said Julia, "dear Captain Carey came into town very late last night to talk to us about Martin, and how the girl in Sark had refused him. I was very much astonished, very much indeed! Captain Carey said that he and dear Johanna had come to the conclusion that the girl felt some delicacy, perhaps, because of Martin's engagement to me. We talked it over as friends, and thought of you, dear aunt, and your grief and disappointment, till all at once I made up my mind in a moment. 'I will go over to Sark and see the girl myself,' I said. 'Will you?' said Captain Carey. 'Oh, no, Julia, it will be too much for you.' 'It would have been a few weeks ago,' I said; 'but now I could do any thing to give Aunt Dobrée a moment's happiness.'"

"God bless you, Julia!" I interrupted, going across to her and kissing her cheek impetuously.

"There, don't stop me, Martin," she said, earnestly. "So it was arranged off-hand that Captain Carey should send for us at St. Sampson's this morning, and take us over to Sark. You know Kate has never been yet. We had a splendid passage, and landed at the Creux, where the yacht was to wait till we returned. Kate was in raptures with the landing-place, and the lovely lane leading up into the island. We went on past Vaudin's Inn and the mill, and turned down the nearest way to Tardifs. Kate said she never felt any air like the air of Sark. Well, you know that brown pool, a very brown pool, in the lane leading to the Havre Gosselin? Just there, where there are some low, weather-beaten trees meeting overhead and making a long green isle, with the sun shining down through the knotted branches, we saw all in a moment a slim, erect, very young-looking girl coming toward us. She was carrying her bonnet in her hand, and her hair curled in short, bright curls all over her head. I knew in an instant that it was Miss Ollivier."

She paused for a minute. How plainly I could see the picture! The arching trees, and the sunbeams playing fondly with her shining golden hair! I held my breath to listen.

"What completely startled me," said Julia, "was that Kate suddenly darted forward and ran to meet her, crying 'Olivia!'"

"How does she know her?" I exclaimed.

"Hush. Martin! Don't interrupt me. The girl went so deadly pale, I thought she was going to faint, but she did not. She stood for a minute looking at us, and then she burst into the most dreadful fit of crying!

"I ran to her, and made her sit down on a little bank of turf close by, and gave her my smelling-bottle, and did all I could to comfort her. By-and-by, as soon as she could speak, she said to Kate, 'How did you find me out?' and Kate told her she had not the slightest idea of finding her there. 'Dr. Martin Dobrée, of Guernsey, told me you were looking for me, only yesterday,' she said.

"That took us by surprise, for Kate had not the faintest idea of seeing her. I have always thought her name was Ollivier, and so did Kate. 'For pity's sake,' said the girl, 'if you have any pity, leave me here in peace. For God's sake do not betray me!'

"I could hardly believe it was not a dream. There was Kate standing over us, looking very stern and severe, and the girl was clinging to me—to me, as if I were her dearest friend. Then all of a sudden up came old Mother Renouf, looking half crazed, and began to harangue us for frightening mam'zelle. Tardif, she said, would be at hand in a minute or two, and he would take care of her from us and everybody else. 'Take me away!' cried the girl, running to her; and the old woman tucked her hand under her arm, and walked off with her in triumph, leaving us by ourselves in the lane."

"But what does it all mean?" asked my mother, while I paced to and fro in the dim room, scarcely able to control my impatience, yet afraid to question Julia too eagerly.

"I can tell you," said Kate Daltrey, in her cold, deliberate tones; "she is the wife of my half-brother, Richard Foster, who married her more than four years ago in Melbourne; and she ran away from him last October, and has not been heard of since."

"Then you know her whole history," I said, approaching her and pausing before her. "Are you at liberty to tell it to us?"

"Certainly," she answered; "it is no secret. Her father was a wealthy colonist, and he died when she was fifteen, leaving her in the charge of her step-mother, Richard Foster's aunt. The match was one of the stepmother's making, for Olivia was little better than a child. Richard was glad enough to get her fortune, or rather the income from it, for of course she did not come into full possession of it till she was of age. One-third of it was settled upon her absolutely; the other two-thirds came to her for her to do what she pleased with it. Richard was looking forward eagerly to her being one-and-twenty, for he had made ducks and drakes of his own property, and tried to do the same with mine. He would have done so with his wife's; but a few weeks before Olivia's twenty-first birthday, she disappeared mysteriously. There her fortune lies, and Richard has no more power than I have to touch it. He cannot even claim the money lying in the Bank of Australia, which has been remitted by her trustees; nor can Olivia claim it without making herself known to him. It is accumulating there, while both of them are on the verge of poverty."

"But he must have been very cruel to her before she would run away!" said my mother in a very pitiful voice. Poor mother! she had borne her own sorrows dumbly, and to leave her husband had probably never occurred to her.

"Cruel!" repeated Kate Daltrey. "Well, there are many kinds of cruelty. I do not suppose Richard would ever transgress the limits of the law. But Olivia was one of those girls who can suffer great torture—mental torture I mean. Even I could not live in the same house with him, and she was a dreamy, sensitive, romantic child, with as much knowledge of the world as a baby. I was astonished to hear she had had daring enough to leave him."

"But there must be some protection for her from the law," I said, thinking of the bold, coarse woman, no doubt his associate, who was in pursuit of Olivia. "She might sue for a judicial separation, at the least, if not a divorce."

"I am quite sure nothing could be brought against him in a court of law," she answered. "He is very wary and cunning, and knows very well what he may do and what he may not do. A few months before Olivia's flight, he introduced a woman as her companion—a disreputable woman probably; but he calls her his cousin, and I do not know how Olivia could prove her an unfit person to be with her. Our suspicions may be very strong, but suspicion is not enough for an English judge and jury. Since I saw her this morning I have been thinking of her position in every light, and I really do not see any thing she could have done, except running away as she did, or making up her mind to be deaf and blind and dumb. There was no other alternative."

"But could he not be induced to leave her in peace if she gave up a portion of her property?" I asked.

"Why should he?" she retorted. "If she was in his hands the whole of the property would be his. He will never release her—never. No, her only chance is to hide herself from him. The law cannot deal with wrongs like hers, because they are as light as air apparently, though they are as all-pervading as air is, and as poisonous as air can be. They are like choke-damp, only not quite fatal. He is as crafty and cunning as a serpent. He could prove himself the kindest, most considerate of husbands, and Olivia next thing to an idiot. Oh, it is ridiculous to think of pitting a girl like her against him!"

"If she had been older, or if she had had a child, she would never have left him," said my mother's gentle and sorrowful voice.

"But what can be done for her?" I asked, vehemently and passionately. "My poor Olivia! what can I do to protect her?"

"Nothing!" answered Kate Daltrey, coldly. "Her only chance is concealment, and what a poor chance that is! I went over to Sark, never thinking that your Miss Ollivier whom I had heard so much of was Olivia Foster. It is an out-of-the-world place; but so much the more readily they will find her, if they once get a clew. A fox is soon caught when it cannot double; and how could Olivia escape if they only traced her to Sark?"

My dread of the woman into whose hands my imbecile curiosity had put the clew was growing greater every minute. It seemed as if Olivia could not be safe now, day or night; yet what protection could I or Tardif give to her?

"You will not betray her?" I said to Kate Daltrey, though feeling all the time that I could not trust her in the smallest degree.

"I have promised dear Julia that," she answered.

I should fail to give you any clear idea of my state of mind should I attempt to analyze it. The most bitter thought in it was that my own imprudence had betrayed Olivia. But for me she might have remained for years, in peace and perfect seclusion, in the home to which she had drifted. Richard Foster and his accomplice must have lost all hope of finding her during the many months that had elapsed between her disappearance and my visit to their solicitors. That had put them on the track again. If the law forced her back to her husband, it was I who had helped him to find her. That was a maddening thought. My love for her was hopeless; but what then? I discovered to my own amazement that I had loved her for her sake, not my own. I had loved the woman in herself, not the woman as my wife. She could never become that, but she was dearer to me than ever. She was as far removed from me as from Tardif.

Could I not serve her with as deep a devotion and as true a chivalry as his? She belonged to both of us by as unselfish and noble a bond as ever knights of old were pledged to.

It became my duty to keep a strict watch over the woman who had come to Guernsey to find Olivia. If possible I must decoy her away from the lowly nest where my helpless bird was sheltered. She had not sent for me again, but I called upon her the next morning professionally, and stayed some time talking with her. But nothing resulted from the visit beyond the assurance that she had not yet made any progress toward the discovery of my secret. I almost marvelled at this, so universal had been the gossip about my visits to Sark in connection with the breaking-off of my engagement to Julia. But that had occurred in the spring, and the nine-days' wonder had ceased before my patient came to the island. Still, any accidental conversation might give her the information, and open up a favorable chance for her. I must not let her go across to Sark unknown to myself.

Neither did I feel quite safe about Kate Daltrey. She gave me the impression of being as crafty and cunning as she described her half-brother. Did she know this woman by sight? That was a question I could not answer. There was another question hanging upon it. If she saw her, would she not in some way contrive to give her a sufficient hint, without positively breaking her promise to Julia? Kate Daltrey's name did not appear in the newspapers among the list of visitors, as she was staying in a private house; but she and this woman might meet any day in the streets or on the pier.

Then the whole story had been confided by Julia at once to Captain Carey and Johanna. That was quite natural; but it was equally natural for them to confide it again to some one or two of their intimate friends. The secret was already an open one among six persons. Could it be considered a secret any longer? The tendency of such a singular story, whispered from one to another, is to become in the long-run more widely circulated than if it were openly proclaimed. I had a strong affection for my circle of cousins, which widened as the circle round a stone cast into water; but I knew I might as well try to arrest the eddying of such waters as stop the spread of a story like Olivia's.

I had resolved, in the first access of my curiosity, to cross over to Sark the next week, alone and independent of Captain Carey. Every Monday the Queen of the Isles made her accustomed trip to the island, to convey visitors there for the day.

I had not been on deck two minutes the following Monday when I saw my patient step on after me. The last clew was in her fingers now, that was evident.

CHAPTER THE THIRTY-SECOND

OLIVIA GONE

She did not see me at first; but her air was exultant and satisfied. There was no face on board so elated and flushed. I kept out of her way as long as I could without consigning myself to the black hole of the cabin; but at last she caught sight of me, and came down to the forecastle to claim me as an acquaintance.

"Ha! ha! Dr. Dobrée!" she exclaimed; "so you are going to visit Sark too?"

"Yes," I answered, more curtly than courteously.

"You are looking rather low," she said, triumphantly—"rather blue, I might say. Is there any thing the matter with you? Your face is as long as a fiddle. Perhaps it is the sea that makes you melancholy."

"Not at all," I answered, trying to speak briskly; "I am an old sailor. Perhaps you will feel melancholy by-and-by."

Luckily for me, my prophecy was fulfilled shortly after, for the day was rough enough to produce uncomfortable sensations in those who were not old sailors like myself. My tormentor was prostrate to the last moment.

When we anchored at the entrance of the Creux, and the small boats came out to carry us ashore, I managed easily to secure a place in the first, and to lose sight of her in the bustle of landing. As soon as my feet touched the shore I started off at my swiftest pace for the Havre Gosselin.

But I had not far to go, for at Vaudin's Inn, which stands at the top of the steep lane running from the Creux Harbor, I saw Tardif at the door. Now and then he acted as guide when young Vaudin could not fill that office, or had more parties than he could manage; and Tardif was now waiting the arrival of the weekly stream of tourists. He came to me instantly, and we sat down on a low stone wall on the roadside, but well out of hearing of any ears but each other's.

"Tardif," I said, "has mam'zelle told you her secret?"

"Yes, yes," he answered; "poor little soul! and she is a hundredfold dearer to me now than before."

He looked as if he meant it, for his eyes moistened and his face quivered.

"She is in great danger at this moment," I continued. "A woman sent by her husband has been lurking about in Guernsey to get news of her, and she has come across in the steamer to-day. She will be in sight of us in a few minutes. There is no chance of her not learning where she is living. But could we not hide Olivia somewhere? There are caves strangers know nothing of. We might take her over to Breckhou. Be quick, Tardif! we must decide at once what to do."

"But mam'zelle is not here. She is gone!" he answered.

"Gone!" I ejaculated. I could not utter another word; but I stared at him as if my eyes could tear further information from him.

"Yes," he said; "that lady came last week with Miss Dobrée, your cousin. Then mam'zelle told me all, and we took counsel together. It was not safe for her to stay any longer, though I would have died for her gladly. But what could be done? We knew she must go elsewhere, and the next morning I rowed her over to Peter-Port in time for the steamer to England. Poor little thing! poor little hunted soul!"

His voice faltered as he spoke, and he drew his fisherman's cap close down over his eyes. I did not speak again for a minute or two.

"Tardif," I said at last, as the foremost among the tourists came in sight, "did she leave no message for me?"

"She wrote a letter for you," he said, "the very last thing. She did not go to bed that night, neither did I. I was going to lose her, doctor, and she had been like the light of the sun to me. But what could I do? She was terrified to death at the thought of her husband claiming her. I promised to give the letter into your own hands; but we settled I must not show myself in Peter-Port the day she left. Here it is."

It had been lying in his breast-pocket, and the edges were worn already. He gave it to me lingeringly, as if loath to part with it. The tourists were coming up in greater numbers, and I made a retreat hastily toward a quiet and remote part of the cliffs seldom visited in Little Sark.

There, with the sea, which had carried her away from me, playing buoyantly among the rocks, I read her farewell letter. It ran thus:

"My dear Friend: I am glad I can call you my friend, though nothing can ever come of our friendship—nothing, for we may not see one another as other friends do. My life was ruined four years ago, and every now and then I see afresh how complete and terrible the ruin is. Yet if I had known beforehand how your life would be linked with mine, I would have done any thing in my power to save you from sharing in my ruin. Ought I to have told you at once that I was married? But just that was my secret, and it seemed so much safer while no one knew it but myself. I did not see, as I do now, that I was acting a falsehood. I do not see how I can help doing that. It is as shocking to me as to you. Do not judge me harshly.

"I do not like to speak to you about my marriage. I was very young and very miserable; any change seemed better than living with my step-mother. I did not know what I was doing. The Saviour said, 'Father, forgive them, for they know not what they do.' I hope I shall be forgiven by you, and your mother, and God, for indeed I did not know what I was doing.

"Last October when I escaped from them, it was partly because I felt I should soon be as wicked as they. I do not think any one ought to remain where there is no chance of being good. If I am wrong, remember I am not old yet. I may learn what my duty is, and then I will do it. I am only waiting to find out exactly what I ought to do, and then I will do it, whatever it may be.

"Now I am compelled to flee away again from this quiet, peaceful home where you and Tardif have been so good to me. I began to feel perfectly safe here, and all at once the refuge fails me. It breaks my heart, but I must go, and my only gladness is that it will be good for you. By-and-by you will forget me, and return to your cousin Julia, and be happy just as you once thought you should be—as you would have been but for me. You must think of me as one dead. I am quite dead—lost to you.

"Yet I know you will sometimes wish to hear what has become of me. Tardif will. And I owe you both more than I can ever repay. But it would not be well for me to write often. I have promised Tardif that I will write to him once a year, that you and he may know that I am still alive. When there comes no letter, say, 'Olivia is dead!' Do not be grieved for that; it will be the greatest, best release God can give me. Say, 'Thank God, Olivia is dead!'

"Good-by, my dear friend; good-by, good-by!

"OLIVIA."

The last line was written in a shaken, irregular hand, and her name was half blotted out, as if a tear had fallen upon it. I remained there alone on the wild and solitary cliffs until it was time to return to the steamer.

Tardif was waiting for me at the entrance of the little tunnel through which the road passes down to the harbor. He did not speak at first, but he drew out of his pocket an old leather pouch filled with yellow papers. Among them lay a long curling tress of shining hair. He touched it gently with his finger, as if it had feeling and consciousness.

"You would like to have it, doctor?" he said.

"Ay," I answered, and that only. I could not venture upon another word.

CHAPTER THE THIRTY-THIRD

THE EBB OF LIFE

There was nothing now for me to do but to devote myself wholly to my mother.

I made the malady under which she was slowly sinking my special study. There remained a spark of hope yet in my heart that I might by diligent, intense, unflagging search, discover some remedy yet untried, or perhaps unthought of. I succeeded only in alleviating her sufferings. I pored over every work which treated of the same class of diseases. At last in an old, almost-forgotten book, I came upon a simple medicament, which, united with appliances made available by modern science, gave her sensible relief, and without doubt tended to prolong her shortening days. The agonizing thought haunted me that, had I come upon this discovery at an earlier stage of her illness, her life might have been spared for many years.

But it was too late now. She suffered less, and her spirits grew calm and even. We even ventured, at her own wish, to spend a week together in Sark, she and I—a week never to be forgotten, full of exquisite pain and exquisite enjoyment to us both. We revisited almost every place where we had been many years before, while I was but a child and she was still young and strong. Tardif rowed us out in his boat under the cliffs. Then we came home again, and she sank rapidly, as if the flame of life had been burning too quickly in the breath of those innocent pleasures.

Now she began to be troubled again with the dread of leaving me alone and comfortless. There is no passage in Christ's farewell to His disciples which, touches me so much as those words, "I will not leave you comfortless; I will come unto you." My mother could not promise to come back to me, and her dying vision looked sorrowfully into the future for me. Sometimes she put her fear into words—faltering and foreboding words; but it was always in her eyes, as they followed me wherever I went with a mute, pathetic anxiety. No assurances of mine, no assumed cheerfulness and fortitude could remove it. I even tried to laugh at it, but my laugh only brought the tears into her eyes. Neither reason nor ridicule could root it out—a root of bitterness indeed.

"Martin," she said, in her failing, plaintive voice, one evening when Julia and I were both sitting with her, for we met now without any regard to etiquette—"Martin, Julia and I have been talking about your future life while you were away."

Julia's face flushed a little. She was seated on a footstool by my mother's sofa, and looked softer and gentler than I had ever seen her look. She had been nursing my mother with a single-hearted, self-forgetful devotion that had often touched me, and had knit us to one another by the common bond of an absorbing interest. Certainly I had never leaned upon or loved Julia as I was doing now.

"There is no chance of your ever marrying Olivia now," continued my mother, faintly, "and it is a sin for you to cherish your love for her. That is a very plain duty, Martin."

"Such love as I cherish for Olivia will hurt neither her nor myself," I answered. "I would not wrong her by a thought."

"But she can never be your wife," she said.

"I never think of her as my wife," I replied; "but I can no more cease to love her than I can cease to breathe. She has become part of my life, mother."

"Still, time and change must make a difference," she said. "You will realize your loneliness when I am gone, though you cannot before. I want to have some idea of what you will be doing in the years to come, before we meet again. If I think at all, I shall be thinking of you, and I do long to have some little notion. You will not mind me forming one poor little plan for you once more, my boy?"

"No," I answered, smiling to keep back the tears that were ready to start to my eyes.

"I scarcely know how to tell you," she said. "You must not be angry or offended with us. But my dear Julia has promised me, out of pure love and pity for me, you know, that if ever—how can I express it?— if you ever wish you could return to the old plans—it may be a long time first, but if you conquered your love for Olivia, and could go back, and wished to go back to the time before you knew her—Julia will forget all that has come between. Julia would consent to marry you if you asked her to be your wife. O Martin, I should die so much happier if I thought you would ever marry Julia, and go to live in the house I helped to get ready for you!"

Julia's head had dropped upon my mother's shoulder, and her face was hidden, while my mother's eyes sought mine beseechingly. I was irresistibly overcome by this new proof of her love for both of us, for I knew well what a struggle it must have been to her to gain the mastery over her proper pride and just resentment. I knelt down beside her, clasping her hand and my mother's in my own.

"Mother, Julia," I said, "I promise that if ever I can be true in heart and soul to a wife, I will ask Julia to become mine. But it may be many years hence; I dare not say how long. God alone knows how dear Olivia is to me. And Julia is too good to waste herself upon so foolish a fellow. She may change, and see some one she can love better."

"That is nonsense, Martin," answered Julia, with a ring of the old sharpness in her tone; "at my age I am not likely to fall in love again—Don't be afraid, aunt; I shall not change, and I will take care of Martin. His home is ready, and he will come back to me some day, and it will all be as you wish."

I know that promise of ours comforted her, for she never lamented over my coming solitude again.

I have very little more I can say about her. When I look back and try to write more fully of those last, lingering days, my heart fails me. The darkened room, the muffled sounds, the loitering, creeping, yet too rapid hours! I had no time to think of Julia, of Olivia, or of myself; I was wrapped up in her.

One evening—we were quite alone—she called me to come closer to her, in that faint, far-off voice of hers, which seemed already to be speaking from another world. I was sitting so near to her that I could touch her with my hand, but she wanted me nearer—with my arm across her, and my cheek against hers.

"My boy," she whispered, "I am going."

"Not yet, mother," I cried; "not yet! I have so much to say. Stay with me a day or two longer."

"If I could," she murmured, every word broken with her panting breath, "I would stay with you forever! Be patient with your father, Martin. Say good-by for me to him and Julia. Don't stir. Let me die so!"

"You shall not die, mother," I said, passionately.

"There is no pain," she whispered—"no pain at all; it is taken away. I am only sorry for my boy. What will he do when I am gone? Where are you, Martin?"

"I am here, mother!" I answered—"close to you. O God! I would go with you if I could."

Then she lay still for a time, pressing my arm about her with her feeble fingers. Would she speak to me no more? Had the dearest voice in the world gone away altogether into that far-off, and, to us, silent country whither the dying go? Dumb, blind, deaf to me? She was breathing yet, and her heart fluttered faintly against my arm. Would not my mother know me again?

"O Martin!" she murmured, "there is great love in store for us all! I did not know how great the love was till now!"

There had been a quicker, more irregular throbbing of her heart as she spoke. Then—I waited, but there came no other pulsation. Suddenly I felt as if I also must be dying, for I passed into a state of utter darkness and unconsciousness.

CHAPTER THE THIRTY-FOURTH

A DISCONSOLATE WIDOWER

My senses returned painfully, with a dull and blunted perception that some great calamity had overtaken me. I was in my mother's dressing-room, and Julia was holding to my nostrils some sharp essence, which had penetrated to the brain and brought back consciousness. My father was sitting by the empty grate, sobbing and weeping vehemently. The door into my mother's bedroom was closed. I knew instantly what was going on there.

I suppose no man ever fainted without being ashamed of it. Even in the agony of my awakening consciousness I felt the inevitable sting of shame at my weakness and womanishness. I pushed away Julia's hand, and raised myself. I got up on my feet and walked unsteadily and blindly toward the shut door.

"Martin," said Julia, "you must not go back there. It is all over."

I heard my father calling me in a broken voice, and I turned to him. His frame was shaken by the violence of his sobs, and he could not lift up his head from his hands. There was no effort at self-control about him. At times his cries grew loud enough to be heard all over the house.

"Oh, my son!" he said, "we shall never see any one like your poor mother again! She was the best wife any man ever had! Oh, what a loss she is to me!"

I could not speak of her just then, nor could I say a word to comfort him. She had bidden me be patient with him, but already I found the task almost beyond me. I told Julia I was going up to my own room for the rest of the night, if there were nothing for me to do. She put her arms round my neck and kissed me as if she had been my sister, telling me I could leave every thing to her. Then I went away into the solitude that had indeed begun to close around me.

When the heart of a man is solitary, there is no society for him even among a crowd of friends. All deep love and close companionship seemed stricken out of my life.

We laid her in the cemetery, in a grave where the wide-spreading branches of some beech-trees threw a pleasant shadow over it during the day. At times the moan of the sea could be heard there, when the surf rolled in strongly upon the shore of Cobo Bay. The white crest of the waves could be seen from it, tossing over the sunken reefs at sea; yet it lay in the heart of our island. She had chosen the spot for herself, not very long ago, when we had been there together. Now I went there alone.

I counted my father and his loud grief as nothing. There was neither sympathy nor companionship between us. He was very vehement in his lamentations, repeating to every one who came to condole with us that there never had lived such a wife, and his loss was the greatest that man could bear. His loss was nothing to mine.

Yet I did draw a little nearer to him in the first few weeks of our bereavement. Almost insensibly I fell into our old plan of sharing the practice, for he was often unfit to go out and see our patients. The house was very desolate now, and soon lost those little delicate traces of feminine occupancy which constitute the charm of a home, and to which we had been all our lives accustomed. Julia could not leave her own household, even if it had been possible for her to return to her place in our deserted dwelling. The flowers faded and died unchanged in the vases, and there was no dainty woman's work lying about— that litter of white and colored shreds of silk and muslin, which give to a room an inhabited appearance. These were so familiar to me, that the total absence of them was like the barrenness of a garden without flowers in bloom.

My father did not feel this as I did, for he was not often at home after the first violence of his grief had spent itself. Julia's house was open to him in a manner it could not be open to me. I was made welcome there, it is true; but Julia was not unembarrassed and at home with me. The half-engagement renewed between us rendered it difficult to us both to meet on the simple ground of friendship and relationship. Moreover, I shrank from setting gossips' tongues going again on the subject of my chances of marrying my cousin; so I remained at home, alone, evening after evening, unless I was called out professionally, declining all invitations, and brooding unwholesomely over my grief. There is no more cowardly a way of meeting a sorrow. But I was out of heart, and no words could better express the morbid melancholy I was sinking into.

There was some tedious legal business to go through, for my mother's small property, bringing in a hundred a year, came to me on her death. I could not alienate it, but I wished Julia to receive the income as part payment of my father's defalcations. She would not listen to such a proposal, and she showed me that she had a shrewd notion of the true state of our finances. They were in such a state that if I left Guernsey with my little income my father would positively find some difficulty in making both ends meet; the more so as I was becoming decidedly the favorite with our patients, who began to call him slightingly the "old doctor." No path opened up for me in any other direction. It appeared as if I were to be bound to the place which was no longer a home to me.

I wrote to this effect to Jack Senior, who was urging my return to England. I could not bring myself to believe that this dreary, monotonous routine of professional duties, of very little interest or importance, was all that life should offer to me. Yet for the present my duty was plain. There was no help for it.

I made some inquiries at the lodging-house in Vauvert Road, and learned that the person who had been in search of Olivia had left Guernsey about the time when I was so fully engrossed with my mother as to have but little thought for any one else. Of Olivia there was neither trace nor tidings. Tardif came up to see me whenever he crossed over from Sark, but he had no information to give to me. The chances were that she was in London; but she was as much lost to me as if she had been lying beside my mother under the green turf of Foulon Cemetery.

In this manner three months passed slowly away after my mother's death. Dr. Dobrée, who was utterly inconsolable the first few weeks, fell into all his old maundering, philandering ways again, spending hours upon his toilet, and paying devoted attentions to every passable woman who came across his path. My temper grew like touch-wood; the least spark would set it in a blaze. I could not take such things in good part.

We had been at daggers-drawn for a day or two, he and I, when one morning I was astonished by the appearance of Julia in our consulting-room, soon after my father, having dressed himself elaborately, had quitted the house. Julia's face was ominous, the upper lip very straight, and a frown upon her brow. I wondered what could be the matter, but I held my tongue. My knowledge of Julia was intimate enough for me to hit upon the right moment for speech or silence—a rare advantage. It was the time to refrain from speaking. Julia was no termagant—simply a woman who had had her own way all her life, and was so sure it was the best way that she could not understand why other people should wish to have theirs.

"Martin," she began in a low key, but one that might run up to shrillness if advisable, "I am come to tell you something that fills me with shame and anger. I do not know how to contain myself. I could never have believed that I could have been so blind and foolish. But it seems as if I were doomed to be deceived and disappointed on every hand—I who would not deceive or disappoint anybody in the world. I declare it makes me quite ill to think of it. Just look at my hands, how they tremble."

"Your nervous system is out of order," I remarked.

"It is the world that is out of order," she said, petulantly; "I am well enough. Oh, I do not know how ever I am to tell you. There are some things it is a shame to speak of."

"Must you speak of them?" I asked.

"Yes; you must know, you will have to know all, sooner or later. If there was any hope of it coming to nothing, I should try to spare you this; but they are both so bent upon disgracing themselves, so deaf to reason! If my poor, dear aunt knew of it, she could not rest in her grave. Martin, cannot you guess? Are men born so dull that they cannot see what is going on under their own eyes?"

"I have not the least idea of what you are driving at," I answered. "Sit down, my dear Julia, and calm yourself. Shall I give you a glass of wine?"

"No, no," she said, with a gesture of impatience. "How long is it since my poor, dear aunt died?"

"You know as well as I do," I replied, wondering that she should touch the wound so roughly. "Three months next Sunday."

"And Dr. Dobrée," she said, in a bitter accent—then stopped, looking me full in the face. I had never heard her call my father Dr. Dobrée in my life. She was very fond of him, and attracted by him, as most women were, and as few women are attracted by me. Even now, with all the difference in our age, the advantage being on my side, it was seldom I succeeded in pleasing as much as he did. I gazed back in amazement at Julia's dark and moody face.

"What now?" I asked. "What has my unlucky father been doing now?"

"Why," she exclaimed, stamping her foot, while the blood mantled to her forehead, "Dr. Dobrée is in haste to take a second wife! He is indeed, my poor Martin. He wishes to be married immediately to that viper, Kate Daltrey."

"Impossible!" I cried, stung to the quick by these words. I remembered my mother's mild, instinctive dislike to Kate Daltrey, and her harmless hope that I would not go over to her side. Go over to her side! No. If she set her foot into this house as my mother's successor, I would never dwell under the same roof. As soon as my father made her his wife I would cut myself adrift from them both. But he knew that; he would never venture to outrage my mother's memory or my feelings in such a flagrant manner.

"It is possible, for it is true," said Julia. She had not let her voice rise above its low, angry key, and now it sank nearly to a whisper, as she glanced round at the door. "They have understood each other these four weeks. You may call it an engagement, for it is one; and I never suspected them, not for a moment! He came down to my house to be comforted, he said: his house was so dreary now. And I was as blind as a mole. I shall never forgive myself, dear Martin. I knew he was given to all that kind of thing, but then he seemed to mourn for my poor aunt so deeply, and was so heart-broken. He made ten times more show of it than you did. I have heard people say you bore it very well, and were quite unmoved, but I knew better. Everybody said he could never get over it. Couldn't you take out a commission of lunacy against him? He must be mad to think of such a thing."

"How did you find it out?" I inquired.

"Oh, I was so ashamed!" she said. "You see I had not the faintest shadow of a suspicion. I had left them in the drawing-room to go up-stairs, and I thought of something I wanted, and went back suddenly, and there they were—his arm around her waist, and her head on his shoulder—he with his gray hairs too! She says she is the same age as me, but she is forty if she is a day. The simpletons! I did not know what to say, or how to look. I could not get out of the room again as if I had not seen, for I cried 'Oh!' at the first sight of them. Then I stood staring at them; but I think they felt as uncomfortable as I did."

"What did they say?" I asked, sternly.

"Oh, he came up to me quite in his dramatic way, you know, trying to carry it off by looking grand and majestic; and he was going to take my hand and lead me to her, but I would not stir a step. 'My love,' he said, 'I am about to steal your friend from you.' 'She is no friend of mine,' I said, 'if she is going to be what all this intimates, I suppose. I will never speak to her or you again, Dr. Dobrée.' Upon that he began to weep, and protest, and declaim, while she sat still and glared at me. I never thought her eyes could look like that. 'When do you mean to be married?' I asked, for he made no secret of his intention to make her his wife. 'What is the good of waiting?' he said, 'My home is miserable with no woman in it.' 'Uncle,' I said, 'if you will promise me to give up the idea of a second marriage, which is ridiculous at your age, I will come back to you, in spite of all the awkwardness of my position with regard to Martin. For my aunt's sake I will come back.' Even an arrangement like this would be better than his marriage with that woman—don't you think so?"

"A hundred times better," I said, warmly. "It was very good of you, Julia. But he would not agree to that, would he?"

"He wouldn't hear of it. He swore that Kate was as dear to him as ever my poor aunt was. He vowed he could not live without her and her companionship. He maintained that his age did not make it ridiculous. Kate hid her brazen face in her hands, and sobbed aloud.

"That made him ten times worse an idiot. He knelt down before her, and implored her to look at him. I reminded him how all the island would rise against him—worse than it did against you, Martin—and he declared he did not care a fig for the island! I asked him how he would face the Careys, and the Brocks, and the De Saumarez, and all the rest of them, and he snapped his fingers at them all. Oh, he must be going out of his mind."

I shook my head. Knowing him as thoroughly as a long and close study could help me to know any man, I was less surprised than Julia, who had only seen him from a woman's point of view, and had always been lenient to his faults. Unfortunately, I knew my father too well.

"Then I talked to him about the duty he owed to our family name," she resumed, "and I went so far as to remind him of what I had done to shield him and it from disgrace, and he mocked at it—positively mocked at it! He said there was no sort of parallel. It would be no dishonor to our house to receive Kate into it, even if they were married at once. What did it signify to the world that only three months had elapsed? Besides, he did not mean to marry her for a month to come, as the house would need beautifying for her—beautifying for her! Neither had he spoken of it to you; but he had no doubt you would be willing to go on as you have done."

"Never!" I said.

"I was sure not," continued Julia. "I told him I was convinced you would leave Guernsey again, but he pooh-poohed that. I asked him how he was to live without any practice, and he said his old patients might turn him off for a while, but they would be glad to send for him again. I never saw a man so obstinately bent upon his own ruin."

"Julia," I said, "I shall leave Guernsey before this marriage can come off. I would rather break stones on the highway than stay to see that woman in my mother's place. My mother disliked her from the first."

"I know it," she replied, with tears in her eyes, "and I thought it was nothing but prejudice. It was my fault, bringing her to Guernsey. But I could not bear the idea of her coming as mistress here. I said so distinctly. 'Dr. Dobrée,' I said, 'you must let me remind you that the house is mine, though you have paid me no rent for years. If you ever take Kate Daltrey into it, I will put my affairs into a notary's hands. I will, upon my word, and Julia Dobrée never broke her word yet.' That brought him to his senses better than any thing. He turned very pale, and sat down beside Kate, hardly knowing what to say. Then she began. She said if I was cruel, she would be cruel too. Whatever grieved you, Martin, would grieve me, and she would let her brother Richard Foster know where Olivia was."

"Does she know where she is?" I asked, eagerly, in a tumult of surprise and hope.

"Why, in Sark, of course," she replied.

"What! Did you never know that Olivia left Sark before my mother's death?" I said, with a chill of disappointment. "Did I never tell you she was gone, nobody knows where?"

"You have never spoken of her in my hearing, except once—you recollect when, Martin? We have supposed she was still living in Tardif's house. Then there is nothing to prevent me from carrying out my threat. Kate Daltrey shall never enter this house as mistress."

"Would you have given it up for Olivia's sake?" I asked, marvelling at her generosity.

"I should have done it for your sake," she answered, frankly.

"But," I said, reverting to our original topic, "if my father has set his mind upon marrying Kate Daltrey, he will brave any thing."

"He is a dotard," replied Julia. "He positively makes me dread growing old. Who knows what follies one may be guilty of in old age! I never felt afraid of it before. Kate says she has two hundred a year of her own, and they will go and live on that in Jersey, if Guernsey becomes unpleasant to them. Martin, she is a viper—she is indeed. And I have made such a friend of her! Now I shall have no one but you and the Careys. Why wasn't I satisfied with Johanna as my friend?"

She stayed an hour longer, turning over this unwelcome subject till we had thoroughly discussed every point of it. In the evening, after dinner, I spoke to my father briefly but decisively upon the same topic. After a very short and very sharp conversation, there remained no alternative for me but to make up my mind to try my fortune once more out of Guernsey. I wrote by the next mail to Jack Senior, telling him my purpose, and the cause of it, and by return of post I received his reply:

"Dear old boy: Why shouldn't you come, and go halves with me? Dad says so. He is giving up shop, and going to live in the country at Fulham. House and practice are miles too big for me. 'Senior and Dobrée,' or 'Dobrée and Senior,' whichever you please. If you come I can pay dutiful attention to Dad without losing my customers. That is his chief reason. Mine is that I only feel half myself without you at hand. Don't think of saying no.

"JACK."

It was a splendid opening, without question. Dr. Senior had been in good practice for more than thirty years, and he had quietly introduced Jack to the position he was about to resign. Yet I pondered over the proposal for a whole week before agreeing to it. I knew Jack well enough to be sure he would never regret his generosity; but if I went I would go as junior partner, and with a much smaller proportion of the profits than that proffered by Jack. Finally I resolved to accept the offer, and wrote to him as to the terms upon which alone I would join him.

CHAPTER THE THIRTY-SIXTH

FINAL ARRANGEMENTS

I did not wait for my father to commit the irreparable folly of his second marriage. Guernsey had become hateful to me. In spite of my exceeding love for my native island, more beautiful in the eyes of its people than any other spot on earth, I could no longer be happy or at peace there. A few persons urged me to stay and live down my chagrin and grief, but most of my friends congratulated me on the change in my prospects, and bade me God-speed. Julia could not conceal her regret, but I left her in the charge of Captain Carey and Johanna. She promised to be my faithful correspondent, and I engaged to write to her regularly. There existed between us the half-betrothal to which we had pledged ourselves at my mother's urgent request. She would wait for the time when Olivia was no longer the first in my heart; then she would be willing to become my wife. But if ever that day came, she would require me to give up my position in England, and settle down for life in Guernsey.

Fairly, then, I was launched upon the career of a physician in the great city. The completeness of the change suited me. Nothing here, in scenery, atmosphere, or society, could remind me of the fretted past. The troubled waters subsided into a dull calm, as far as emotional life went. Intellectual life, on the contrary, was quickened in its current, and day after day drifted me farther away from painful memories. To be sure, the idea crossed me often that Olivia might be in London—even in the same street with me. I never caught sight of a faded green dress but my steps were hurried, and I followed till I was sure that the wearer was not Olivia. But I was aware that the chances of our meeting were so small that I could not count upon them. Even if I found her, what then? She was as far away from me as though the Atlantic rolled between us. If I only knew that she was safe, and as happy as her sad destiny could let her be, I would be content. For this assurance I looked forward through the long months that must intervene before her promised communication would come to Tardif.

Thus I was thrown entirely upon my profession for interest and occupation. I gave myself up to it with an energy that amazed Jack, and sometimes surprised myself. Dr. Senior, who was an old veteran, loved it with ardor for its own sake, was delighted with my enthusiasm. He prophesied great things for me.

So passed my first winter in London.

CHAPTER THE THIRTY-SEVENTH

THE TABLES TURNED

A dreary season was that first winter in London.

It happened quite naturally that here, as in Guernsey, my share of the practice fell among the lower and least important class of patients. Jack Senior had been on the field some years sooner, and he was London-born and London-bred. All the surroundings of his life fitted him without a wrinkle. He was at home everywhere, and would have counted the pulse of a duchess with as little emotion as that of a dairy-maid. On the other hand, I could not accommodate myself altogether to haughty and aristocratic strangers—though I am somewhat ante-dating later experiences, for during the winter our fashionable clients were all out of town, and our time comparatively unoccupied. To be at ease anywhere, it was, at that time, essential to me to know something of the people with whom I was associating—an insular trait, common to all those who are brought up in a contracted and isolated circle.

Besides this rustic embarrassment which hung like a clog about me out-of-doors, within-doors I missed wofully the dainty feminine ways I had been used to. There was a trusty female servant, half cook, half house-keeper, who lived in the front-kitchen and superintended our household; but she was not at all the angel in the house whom I needed. It was a well-appointed, handsome dwelling, but it was terribly gloomy. The heavy, substantial leather chairs always remained undisturbed in level rows against the wall, and the crimson cloth upon the table was as bare as a billiard-table. A thimble lying upon it, or fallen on the carpet and almost crushed by my careless tread, would have been as welcome a sight to me as a blade of grass or a spring of water in some sandy desert. The sound of a light foot and rustling dress, and low, soft voice, would have been the sweetest music in my ears. If a young fellow of eight-and-twenty, with an excellent appetite and in good health, could be said to pine, I was pining for the pretty, fondling woman's ways which had quite vanished out of my life.

At times my thoughts dwelt upon my semi-engagement to Julia. As soon as I could dethrone the image of Olivia from its pre-eminence in my heart, she was willing to welcome me back again—a prodigal suitor, who had spent all his living in a far country. We corresponded regularly and frequently, and

Julia's letters were always good, sensible, and affectionate. If our marriage, and all the sequel to it, could have been conducted by epistles, nothing could have been more satisfactory. But I felt a little doubtful about the termination of this Platonic friendship, with its half-betrothal. It did not appear to me that Olivia's image was fading in the slightest degree; no, though I knew her to be married, though I was ignorant where she was, though there was not the faintest hope within me that she would ever become mine.

During the quiet, solitary evenings, while Jack was away at some ball or concert, to which I had no heart to go, my thoughts were pretty equally divided between my lost mother and my lost Olivia—lost in such different ways! It would have grieved Julia in her very soul if she could have known how rarely, in comparison, I thought of her.

Yet, on the whole, there was a certain sweetness in feeling myself not altogether cut off from womanly love and sympathy. There was a home always open to me—a home, and a wife devotedly attached to me, whenever I chose to claim them. That was not unpleasant as a prospect. As soon as this low fever of the spirit was over, there was a convalescent hospital to go to, where it might recover its original tone and vigor. At present the fever had too firm and strong a hold for me to pronounce myself convalescent; but if I were to believe all that sages had said, there would come a time when I should rejoice over my own recovery.

Early in the spring I received a letter from Julia, desiring me to look out for apartments, somewhere in my neighborhood, for herself, and Johanna and Captain Carey. They were coming to London to spend two or three months of the season. I had not had any task so agreeable since I left Guernsey. Jack was hospitably anxious for them to come to our own house, but I knew they would not listen to such a proposal. I found some suitable rooms for them, however, in Hanover Street, where I could be with them at any time in five minutes.

On the appointed day I met them at Waterloo Station, and installed them in their new apartments.

It struck me that, notwithstanding the fatigue of the journey, Julia was looking better and happier than I had seen her look for a long time. Her black dress suited her, and gave her a style which she never had in colors. Her complexion looked dark, but not sallow; and her brown hair was certainly more becomingly arranged. Her appearance was that of a well-bred, cultivated, almost elegant woman, of whom no man need be ashamed. Johanna was simply herself, without the least perceptible change. But Captain Carey again looked ten years younger, and was evidently taking pains with his appearance. That suit of his had never been made in Guernsey; it must have come out of a London establishment. His hair was not so gray, and his face was less hypochondriac. He assured me that his health had been wonderfully good all the winter. I was more than satisfied, I was proud of all my friends.

"We want you to come and have a long talk with us to-morrow," said Johanna; "it is too late to-night. We shall be busy shopping in the morning, but can you come in the evening?"

"Oh, yes," I answered; "I am at leisure most evenings, and I count upon spending them with you. I can escort you to as many places of amusement as you wish to visit."

"To-morrow, then," she said, "we shall take tea at eight o'clock."

I bade them good-night with a lighter heart than I had felt for a long while. I held Julia's hand the longest, looking into her face earnestly, till it flushed and glowed a little under my scrutiny.

"True heart!" I said to myself, "true and constant! and I have nothing, and shall have nothing, to offer it but the ashes of a dead passion. Would to Heaven," I thought as I paced along Brook Street, "I had never been fated to see Olivia!"

I was punctual to my time the next day. The dull, stiff drawing-room was already invested with those tokens of feminine occupancy which I missed so greatly in our much handsomer house. There were flowers blooming in the centre of the tea-table, and little knick-knacks lay strewed about. Julia's work-basket stood on a little stand near the window. There was the rustle and movement of their dresses, the noiseless footsteps, the subdued voices caressing my ear. I sat among them quiet and silent, but revelling in this partial return of olden times. When Julia poured out my tea, and passed it to me with her white hand, I felt inclined to kiss her jewelled fingers. If Captain Carey had not been present I think I should have done so.

We lingered over the pleasant meal as if time were made expressly for that purpose, instead of hurrying over it, as Jack and I were wont to do. At the close Captain Carey announced that he was about to leave us alone together for an hour or two. I went down to the door with him, for he had made me a mysterious signal to follow him. In the hall he laid his hand upon my shoulder, and whispered a few incomprehensible sentences into my ear.

"Don't think any thing of me, my boy. Don't sacrifice yourself for me. I'm an old fellow compared to you, though I'm not fifty yet; everybody in Guernsey knows that. So put me out of the question, Martin. 'There's many a slip 'twixt the cup and the lip.' That I know quite well, my dear fellow."

He was gone before I could ask for an explanation, and I saw him tearing off toward Regent Street. I returned to the drawing-room, pondering over his words. Johanna and Julia were sitting side by side on a sofa, in the darkest corner of the room—though the light was by no means brilliant anywhere, for the three gas-jets were set in such a manner as not to turn on much gas.

"Come here, Martin," said Johanna; "we wish to consult you on a subject of great importance to us all."

I drew up a chair opposite to them, and sat down, much as if it was about to be a medical consultation. I felt almost as if I must feel somebody's pulse, and look at somebody's tongue.

"It is nearly eight months since your poor dear mother died," remarked Johanna.

Eight months! Yes; and no one knew what those eight months had been to me—how desolate! how empty!

"You recollect," continued Johanna, "how her heart was set on your marriage with Julia, and the promise you both made to her on her death-bed?"

"Yes," I answered, bending forward and pressing Julia's hand, "I remember every word."

There was a minute's silence after this; and I waited in some wonder as to what this prelude was leading to.

"Martin," asked Johanna, in a solemn tone, "are you forgetting Olivia?"

"No," I said, dropping Julia's hand as the image of Olivia flashed across me reproachfully, "not at all. What would you have me say? She is as dear to me at this moment as she ever was."

"I thought you would say so," she replied; "I did not think yours was a love that would quickly pass away, if it ever does. There are men who can love with the constancy of a woman. Do you know any thing of her?"

"Nothing!" I said, despondently; "I have no clew as to where she may be now."

"Nor has Tardif," she continued; "my brother and I went across to Sark last week to ask him."

"That was very good of you," I interrupted.

"It was partly for our own sakes," she said, blushing faintly. "Martin, Tardif says that if you have once loved Olivia, it is once for all. You would never conquer it. Do you think that this is true? Be candid with us."

"Yes," I answered, "it is true. I could never love again as I love Olivia."

"Then, my dear Martin," said Johanna, very softly, "do you wish to keep Julia to her promise?"

I started violently. What! Did Julia wish to be released from that semi-engagement, and be free? Was it possible that any one else coveted my place in her affections, and in the new house which we had fitted up for ourselves? I felt like the dog in the manger. It seemed an unheard-of encroachment for any person to come between my cousin Julia and me.

"Do you ask me to set you free from your promise, Julia?" I asked, somewhat sternly.

"Why, Martin," she said, averting her face from me, "you know I should never consent to marry you, with the idea of your caring most for that girl. No, I could never do that. If I believed you would ever think of me as you used to do before you saw her, well, I would keep true to you. But is there any hope of that?"

"Let us be frank with one another," I answered; "tell me, is there any one else whom you would marry if I release you from this promise, which was only given, perhaps, to soothe my mothers last hours?"

Julia hung her head, and did not speak. Her lips trembled. I saw her take Johanna's hand and squeeze it, as if to urge her to answer the question.

"Martin," said Johanna, "your happiness is dear to every one of us. If we had believed there was any hope of your learning to love Julia as she deserves, and as a man ought to love his wife, not a word of this would have been spoken. But we all feel there is no such hope. Only say there is, and we will not utter another word."

"No," I said, "you must tell me all now. I cannot let the question rest here. Is there any one else whom Julia would marry if she felt quite free?"

"Yes," answered Johanna, while Julia hid her face in her hands, "she would marry my brother."

Captain Carey! I fairly gasped for breath. Such an idea had never once occurred to me; though I knew she had been spending most of her time with the Careys at the Vale. Captain Carey to marry! and to marry Julia! To go and live in our house! I was struck dumb, and fancied that I had heard wrongly. All the pleasant, distant vision of a possible marriage with Julia, when my passion had died out, and I could be content in my affection and esteem for her—all this vanished away, and left my whole future a blank. If Julia wished for revenge—and when is not revenge sweet to a jilted woman?—she had it now. I was as crestfallen, as amazed, almost as miserable, as she had been. Yet I had no one to blame, as she had. How could I blame her for preferring Captain Carey's love to my réchauffé affections?

"Julia," I said, after a long silence, and speaking as calmly as I could, "do you love Captain Carey?"

"That is not a fair question to ask," answered Johanna. "We have not been treacherous to you. I scarcely know how it has all come about. But my brother has never asked Julia if she loves him; for we wished to see you first, and hear how you felt about Olivia. You say you shall never love again as you love her. Set Julia free then, quite free, to accept my brother or reject him. Be generous, be yourself, Martin."

"I will," I said—"My dear Julia, you are as free as air from all obligation to me. You have been very good and very true to me. If Captain Carey is as good and true to you, as I believe he will be, you will be a very happy woman—happier than you would ever be with me."

"And you will not make yourself unhappy about it?" asked Julia, looking up.

"No," I answered, cheerfully, "I shall be a merry old bachelor, and visit you and Captain Carey, when we are all old folks. Never mind me, Julia; I never was good enough for you. I shall be very glad to know that you are happy."

Yet when I found myself in the street—for I made my escape as soon as I could get away from them—I felt as if every thing worth living for were slipping away from me. My mother and Olivia were gone, and here was Julia forsaking me. I did not grudge her her new happiness. There was neither jealousy nor envy in my feelings toward my supplanter. But in some way I felt that I had lost a great deal since I entered their drawing-room two hours ago.

CHAPTER THE THIRTY-EIGHTH

OLIVIA'S HUSBAND

I did not go straight home to our dull, gloomy, bachelor dwelling-place; for I was not in the mood for an hour's soliloquy. Jack and I had undertaken between us the charge of the patients belonging to a friend of ours, who had been called out of town for a few days. I was passing by the house, chewing the bitter cud of my reflections, and, recalling this, I turned in to see if any messages were waiting there for us.

Lowry's footman told me a person had been with an urgent request that he would go as soon as possible to No. 19 Bellringer Street. I did not know the street, or what sort of a locality it was in.

"What kind of a person called?" I asked.

"A woman, sir; not a lady. On foot—poorly dressed. She's been here before, and Dr. Lowry has visited the case twice. No. 19 Bellringer Street. Perhaps you will find him in the case-book, sir."

I went in to consult the case-book. Half a dozen words contained the diagnosis. It was the same disease, in an incipient form, of which my poor mother died. I resolved to go and see this sufferer at once, late as the hour was.

"Did the person expect some one to go to-night?" I asked, as I passed through the hall.

"I couldn't promise her that, sir," was the answer. "I did say I'd send on the message to you, and I was just coming with it, sir. She said she'd sit up till twelve o'clock."

"Very good," I said.

Upon inquiry I found that the place was two miles away; and, as our old friend Simmons was still on the cab-stand, I jumped into his cab, and bade him drive me as fast as he could to No. 19 Bellringer Street. I wanted a sense of motion, and a chance of scene. If I had been in Guernsey, I should have mounted Madam, and had another midnight ride round the island. This was a poor substitute for that; but the visit would serve to turn my thoughts from Julia. If any one in London could do the man good, I believed it was I; for I had studied that one malady with my soul thrown into it.

"We turned at last into a shabby street, recognizable even in the twilight of the scattered lamps as being a place for cheap lodging-houses. There was a light burning in the second-floor windows of No. 19; but all the rest of the front was in darkness. I paid Simmons and dismissed him, saying I would walk home. By the time I turned to knock at the door, it was opened quietly from within. A woman stood in the doorway; I could not see her face, for the candle she had brought with her was on the table behind her; neither was there light enough for her to distinguish mine.

"Are you come from Dr. Lowry's?" she asked.

The voice sounded a familiar one, but I could not for the life of me recall whose it was.

"Yes," I answered, "but I do not know the name of my patient here."

"Dr. Martin Dobrée!" she exclaimed, in an accent almost of terror.

I recollected her then as the person who had been in search of Olivia. She had fallen back a few paces, and I could now see her face. It was startled and doubtful, as if she hesitated to admit me. Was it possible I had come to attend Olivia's husband?

"I don't know whatever to do!" she ejaculated; "he is very ill to-night, but I don't think he ought to see you—I don't think he would."

"Listen to me," I said; "I do not think there is another man in London as well qualified to do him good."

"Why?" she asked, eagerly.

"Because I have made this disease my special study," I answered. "Mind, I am not anxious to attend him. I came here simply because my friend is out of town. If he wishes to see me, I will see him, and do my best for him. It rests entirely with himself."

"Will you wait here a few minutes?" she asked, "while I see what he will do?"

She left me in the dimly-lighted hall, pervaded by a musty smell of unventilated rooms, and a damp, dirty underground floor. The place was altogether sordid, and dingy, and miserable. At last I heard her step coming down the two flights of stairs, and I went to meet her.

"He will see you," she said, eying me herself with a steady gaze of curiosity.

Her curiosity was not greater than mine. I was anxious to see Olivia's husband, partly from the intense aversion I felt instinctively toward him. He was lying back in an old, worn-out easy-chair, with a woman's shawl thrown across his shoulders, for the night was chilly. His face had the first sickly hue and emaciation of the disease, and was probably refined by it. It was a handsome, regular, well-cut face, narrow across the brows, with thin, firm lips, and eyes perfect in shape, but cold and glittering as steel. I knew afterward that he was fifteen years older than Olivia. Across his knees lay a shaggy, starved-looking cat, which he held fast by the fore-paws, and from time to time entertained himself by teasing and tormenting it. He scrutinized me as keenly as I did him.

"I believe we are in some sort connected. Dr. Martin Dobrée," he said, smiling coldly; "my half-sister, Kate Daltrey, is married to your father, Dr. Dobrée."

"Yes," I answered, shortly. The subject was eminently disagreeable to me, and I had no wish to pursue it with him.

"Ay! she will make him a happy man," he continued, mockingly; "you are not yourself married, I believe, Dr. Martin Dobrée?"

I took no notice whatever of his question, or the preceding remark, but passed on to formal inquiries concerning his health. My close study of his malady helped me here. I could assist him to describe and localize his symptoms, and I soon discovered that the disease was as yet in a very early stage.

"You have a better grip of it than Lowry," he said, sighing with satisfaction. "I feel as if I were made of glass, and you could look through me. Can you cure me?"

"I will do my best," I answered.

"So you all say," he muttered, "and the best is generally good for nothing. You see I care less about getting over it than my wife does. She is very anxious for my recovery."

"Your wife!" I repeated, in utter surprise; "you are Richard Foster, I believe?"

"Certainly," he replied.

"Does your wife know of your present illness?" I inquired.

"To be sure," he answered; "let me introduce you to Mrs. Richard Foster."

The woman looked at me with flashing eyes and a mocking smile, while Mr. Foster indulged himself with extorting a long and plaintive mew from the poor cat on his knees.

"I cannot understand," I said. I did not know how to continue my speech. Though they might choose to pass as husband and wife among strangers, they could hardly expect to impose upon me.

"Ah! I see you do not," said Mr. Foster, with a visible sneer. "Olivia is dead."

"Olivia dead!" I exclaimed.

I repeated the words mechanically, as if I could not make any meaning out of them. Yet they had been spoken with such perfect deliberation and certainty that there seemed to be no question about the fact. Mr. Foster's glittering eyes dwelt delightedly upon my face.

"You were not aware of it?" he said, "I am afraid I have been too sudden. Kate tells us you were in love with my first wife, and sacrificed a most eligible match for her. Would it be too late to open fresh negotiations with your cousin? You see I know all your family history."

"When did Olivia die?" I inquired, though my tongue felt dry and parched, and the room, with his fiendish face, was swimming giddily before my eyes.

"When was it, Carry?" he asked, turning to his wife.

"We heard she was dead on the first of October," she answered. "You married me the next day."

"Ah, yes!" he said; "Olivia had been dead to me for more than twelve months and the moment I was free I married her, Dr. Martin. We could not be married before, and there was no reason to wait longer. It was quite legal."

"But what proof have you?" I asked, still incredulous, yet with a heart so heavy that it could hardly rouse itself to hope.

"Carry, have you those letters?" said Richard Foster.

She was away for a few minutes, while he leaned back again in his chair, regarding nic with his half-closed, cruel eyes. I said nothing, and resolved to betray no emotion. Olivia dead! my Olivia! I could not believe it.

"Here are the proofs," said Mrs. Foster, reentering the room. She put into my hand an ordinary certificate of death, signed by J. Jones, M.D. It stated that the deceased, Olivia Foster, had died on September the 27th, of acute inflammation of the lungs. Accompanying this was a letter written in a good handwriting, purporting to be from a clergyman or minister, of what denomination it was not stated, who had attended Olivia in her fatal illness. He said that she had desired him to keep the place of her death and burial a secret, and to forward no more than the official certificate of the former event. This letter was signed E. Jones. No clew was given by either document as to the place where they were written.

"Are you not satisfied?" asked Foster.

"No," I replied; "how is it, if Olivia is dead, that you have not taken possession of her property?"

"A shrewd question," he said, jeeringly. "Why am I in these cursed poor lodgings? Why am I as poor as Job, when there are twenty thousand pounds of my wife's estate lying unclaimed? My sweet, angelic Olivia left no will, or none in my favor, you may be sure; and by her father's will, if she dies intestate or without children, his property goes to build almshouses, or some confounded nonsense, in Melbourne. All she bequeaths to me is this ring, which I gave to her on our wedding-day, curse her!"

He held out his hand, on the little finger of which shone a diamond, which might, as far as I knew, be the one I had once seen in Olivia's possession.

"Perhaps you do not know," he continued, "that it was on this very point, the making of her will, or securing her property to me in some way, that my wife took offence and ran away from me. Carry was just a little too hard upon her, and I was away in Paris. But consider, I expected to be left penniless, just as you see me left, and Carry was determined to prevent it."

"Then you are sure of her death?" I said.

"So sure," he replied, calmly, "that we were married the next day. Olivia's letter to me, as well as those papers, was conclusive of her identity. Will you like to see it?"

Mrs. Foster gave me a slip of paper, on which were written a few lines. The words looked faint, and grew paler as I read them. They were without doubt Olivia's writing:

"I know that, you are poor, and I send you all I can spare—the ring you once gave to me. I am even poorer than yourself, but I have just enough for my last necessities. I forgive you, as I trust that God forgives me."

There was no more to be said or done. Conviction had been brought home to me. I rose to take my leave, and Foster held out his hand to me, perhaps with a kindly intention. Olivia's ring was glittering on it, and I could not take it into mine.

"Well, well," he said, "I understand; I am sorry for you. Come again, Dr. Martin Dobrée. If you know of any remedy for my ease, you are no true man if you do not try it."

I went down the narrow staircase, closely followed by Mrs. Foster. Her face had lost its gayety and boldness, and looked womanly and careworn, as she laid her hand upon my arm before opening the house-door.

"For God's sake, come again," she said, "if you can do any thing for him! We have money left yet, and I am earning more every day. We can pay you well. Promise me you will come again."

"I can promise nothing to-night," I answered.

"You shall not go till you promise," she said, emphatically.

"Well, then, I promise," I answered, and she unfastened the chain almost noiselessly, and opened the door into the street.

CHAPTER THE THIRTY-NINTH

SAD SEWS

A fine, drizzling rain was falling; I was just conscious of it as an element of discomfort, but it did not make me quicken my steps. I wanted no rapidity of motion now. There was nothing to be done, nothing to look forward to, nothing to flee away from. Olivia was dead!

I had said the same thing again and again to myself, that Olivia was dead to me; but at this moment I learned how great a difference there was between the words as a figure of speech and as a terrible reality. I could no longer think of her as treading the same earth—the same streets, perhaps; speaking the same language; seeing the same daylight as myself. I recalled her image, as I had seen her last in Sark; and then I tried to picture her white face, with lips and eyes closed forever, and the awful chill of death resting upon her. It seemed impossible; yet the cuckoo-cry went on in my brain, "Olivia is dead—is dead!"

I reached home just as Jack was coming in from his evening amusement. He let me in with his latch-key, giving me a cheery greeting; but as soon as we had entered the dining-room, and he saw my face, he exclaimed. "Good Heavens! Martin, what has happened to you?"

"Olivia is dead," I answered.

His arm was about my neck in a moment, for we were like boys together still, when we were alone. He knew all about Olivia, and he waited patiently till I could put my tidings into words.

"It must be true," he said, though in a doubtful tone; "the scoundrel would not have married again if he had not sufficient proof."

"She must have died very soon after my mother," I answered, "and I never knew it!"

"It's strange!" he said. "I wonder she never got anybody to write to you or Tardif."

There was no way of accounting for that strange silence toward us. We sat talking in short, broken sentences, while Jack smoked a cigar; but we could come to no conclusion about it. It was late when we parted, and I went to bed, but not to sleep.

For as soon as the room was quite dark, visions of Olivia haunted me. Phantasms of her followed one another rapidly through my brain. She had died, so said the certificate, of inflammation of the lungs, after an illness of ten days. I felt myself bound to go through every stage of her illness, dwelling upon all her sufferings, and thinking of her as under careless or unskilled attendance, with no friend at hand to take care of her. She ought not to have died, with her perfect constitution. If I had been there she should not have died.

About four o'clock Jack tapped softly upon the wall between our bedrooms—it was a signal we had used when we were boys—as though to inquire if I was all right; but it was quiet enough not to wake me if I were asleep. It seemed like the friendly "Ahoy!" from a boat floating on the same dark sea. Jack was lying awake, thinking of me as I was thinking of Olivia. There was something so consolatory in this sympathy that I fell asleep while dwelling upon it.

Upon going downstairs in the morning I found that Jack was already off, having left a short note for me, saying he would visit my patients that day. I had scarcely begun breakfast when the servant announced "a lady," and as the lady followed close upon his heels, I saw behind his shoulder the familiar face of Johanna, looking extremely grave. She was soon seated beside me, watching me with something of the tender, wistful gaze of my mother. Her eyes were of the same shape and color, and I could hardly command myself to speak calmly.

"Your friend Dr. John Senior called upon us a short time since," she said; "and told us this sad, sad news."

I nodded silently.

"If we had only known it yesterday," she continued, "you would never have heard what we then said. This makes so vast a difference. Julia could not have become your wife while there was another woman living whom you loved more. You understand her feeling?"

"Yes," I said; "Julia is right."

"My brother and I have been talking about the change this will make," she resumed. "He would not rob you of any consolation or of any future happiness; not for worlds. He relinquishes all claim to or hope of Julia's affection—"

"That would be unjust to Julia," I interrupted. "She must not be sacrificed to me any longer. I do not suppose I shall ever marry—"

"You must marry, Martin," she interrupted in her turn, and speaking emphatically; "you are altogether unfitted for a bachelor's life. It is all very well for Dr. John Senior, who has never known a woman's companionship, and who can do without it. But it is misery to you—this cold, colorless life. No. Of all the men I ever knew, you are the least fitted for a single life."

"Perhaps I am," I admitted, as I recalled my longing for some sign of womanhood about our bachelor dwelling.

"I am certain of it," she said. "Now, but for our precipitation last night, you would have gone naturally to Julia for comfort. So my brother sends word that he is going back to Guernsey to-night, leaving us in Hanover Street, where we are close to you. We have said nothing to Julia yet. She is crying over this sad news—mourning for your sorrow. You know that my brother has not spoken directly to Julia of his love;

and now all that is in the past, and is to be as if it had never been, and we go on exactly as if we had not had that conversation yesterday."

"But that cannot be," I remonstrated. "I cannot consent to Julia wasting her love and time upon me. I assure you most solemnly I shall never marry my cousin now."

"You love her?" said Johanna.

"Certainly," I answered, "as my sister."

"Better than any woman now living?" she pursued.

"Yes," I replied.

"That is all Julia requires," she continued; "so let us say no more at present, Martin. Only understand that all idea of marriage between her and my brother is quite put away. Don't argue with me, don't contradict me. Come to see us as you would have done but for that unfortunate conversation last night. All will come right by-and-by."

"But Captain Carey—" I began.

"There! not a word!" she interrupted imperatively. "Tell me all about that wretch, Richard Foster. How did you come across him? Is he likely to die? Is he any thing like Kate Daltrey?—I will never call her Kate Dobrée as long as the world lasts. Come, Martin, tell me every thing about him."

She sat with me most of the morning, talking with animated perseverance, and at last prevailed upon me to take her a walk in Hyde Park. Her pertinacity did me good in spite of the irritation it caused me. When her dinner-hour was at hand I felt bound to attend her to her house in Hanover Street; and I could not get away from her without first speaking to Julia. Her face was very sorrowful, and her manner sympathetic. We said only a few words to one another, but I went away with the impression that her heart was still with me.

CHAPTER THE FORTIETH

A TORMENTING DOUBT

At dinner Jack announced his intention of paying a visit to Richard Foster.

"You are not fit to deal with the fellow," he said; "you may be sharp enough upon your own black sheep in Guernsey, but you know nothing of the breed here. Now, if I see him, I will squeeze out of him every mortal thing he knows about Olivia. Where did those papers come from?"

"There was no place given," I answered.

"But there would be a post-mark on the envelop," he replied; "I will make him show me the envelop they were in."

"Jack," I said, "you do not suppose he has any doubt of her death?"

"I can't say," he answered. "You see he has married again, and if she were not dead that would be bigamy—an ugly sort of crime. But are you sure they are married?"

"How can I be sure?" I asked fretfully, for grief as often makes men fretful as illness. "I did not ask for their marriage-certificate."

"Well, well! I will go," he answered.

I awaited his return with impatience. With this doubt insinuated by Jack, it began to seem almost incredible that Olivia's exquisitely healthy frame should have succumbed suddenly under a malady to which she had no predisposition whatever. Moreover, her original soundness of constitution had been strengthened by ten months' residence in the pure, bracing air of Sark. Yet what was I to think in face of those undated documents, and of her own short letter to her husband? The one I knew was genuine; why should I suppose the others to be forged? And if forgeries, who had been guilty of such a cruel and crafty artifice, and for what purpose?

I had not found any satisfactory answer to these queries before Jack returned, his face kindled with excitement. He caught my hand, and grasped it heartily.

"I no more believe she is dead than I am," were his first words. "You recollect me telling you of a drunken brawl in a street off the Strand, where a fellow, as drunk as a lord, was for claiming a pretty girl as his wife; only I had followed her out of Ridley's agency-office, and was just in time to protect her from him—a girl I could have fallen in love with myself. You recollect?"

"Yes, yes," I said, almost breathless.

"He was the man, and Olivia was the girl!" exclaimed Jack.

"No!" I cried.

"Yes!" continued Jack, with an affectionate lunge at me; "at any rate I can swear he is the man; and I would bet a thousand to one that the girl was Olivia."

"But when was it?" I asked.

"Since he married again," he answered; "they were married on the 2d of October, and this was early in November. I had gone to Ridley's after a place for a poor fellow as an assistant to a druggist; and I saw the girl distinctly. She gave the name of Ellen Martineau. Those letters about her death are all forgeries."

"Olivia's is not," I said; "I know her handwriting too well."

"Well, then," observed Jack, "there is only one explanation. She has sent them herself to throw Foster off the scent; she thinks she will be safe if he believes her dead."

"No," I answered, hotly, "she would never have done such a thing as that."

"Who else is benefited by it?" he asked, gravely. "It does not put Foster into possession of any of her property; or that would have been a motive for him to do it. But he gains nothing by it; and he is so convinced of her death that he has married a second wife."

It was difficult to hit upon any other explanation; yet I could not credit this one. I felt firmly convinced that Olivia could not be guilty of an artifice so cunning. I was deceived in her indeed if she would descend to any fraud so cruel. But I could not discuss the question even with Jack Senior. Tardif was the only person who knew Olivia well enough to make his opinion of any value. Besides, my mind was not as clear as Jack's that she was the girl he had seen in November. Yet the doubt of her death was full of hope; it made the earth more habitable, and life more endurable.

"What can I do now?" I said, speaking aloud, though I was thinking to myself.

"Martin," he replied, gravely, "isn't it wisest to leave the matter as it stands? If you find Olivia, what then? she is as much separated from you as she can be by death. So long as Foster lives, it is worse than useless to be thinking of her. There is no misery like that of hanging about a woman you have no right to love."

"I only wish to satisfy myself that she is alive," I answered. "Just think of it, Jack, not to know whether she is living or dead! You must help me to satisfy myself. Foster has got the only valuable thing she had in her possession, and if she is living she may be in absolute want. I cannot be contented with that dread on my mind. There can be no harm in my taking some care of her at a distance. This mystery would be intolerable to me."

"You're right, old fellow," he said, cordially; "we will go to Ridley's together to-morrow morning."

We were there soon after the doors were open. There were not many clients present, and the clerks were enjoying a slack time. Jack had recalled to his mind the exact date of his former visit; and thus the sole difficulty was overcome. The clerk found the name of Ellen Martineau entered under that date in his book.

"Yes," he said, "Miss Ellen Martineau, English teacher in a French school; premium to be paid, about 10 Pounds; no salary; reference, Mrs. Wilkinson, No. 19 Bellringer Street."

"No. 19 Bellringer Street!" we repeated in one breath.

"Yes, gentlemen, that is the address," said the clerk, closing the book. "Shall I write it down for you? Mrs. Wilkinson was the party who should have paid our commission; as you perceive, a premium was required instead of a salary given. We feel pretty sure the young lady went to the school, but Mrs. Wilkinson denies it, and it is not worth our while to pursue our claim in law."

"Can you describe the young lady?" I inquired.

"Well, no. We have such hosts of young ladies here. But she was pretty, decidedly pretty; she made that impression upon me, at least. We are too busy to take particular notice; but I should know her again if she came in. I think she would have been here again, before this, if she had not got that engagement."

"Do you know where the school is?" I asked.

"No. Mrs. Wilkinson was the party," he said. "We had nothing to do with it, except send any ladies to her who thought it worth their while. That was all."

As we could obtain no further information, we went away, and paced up and down the tolerably quiet street, deep in consultation. That we should have need for great caution, and as much craftiness as we both possessed, in pursuing our inquiries at No. 19 Bellringer Street, was quite evident. Who could be this unknown Mrs. Wilkinson? Was it possible that she might prove to be Mrs. Foster herself? At any rate, it would not do for either of us to present ourselves there in quest of Miss Ellen Martineau. It was finally settled between us that Johanna should be intrusted with the diplomatic enterprise. There was not much chance that Mrs. Foster would know her by sight, though she had been in Guernsey; and it would excite less notice for a lady to be inquiring after Olivia. We immediately turned our steps toward Hanover Street, where we found her and Julia seated at some fancy-work in their sombre drawing-room.

Julia received me with a little embarrassment, but conquered it sufficiently to give me a warm pressure of the hand, and to whisper in my ear that Johanna had told her every thing. Unluckily, Johanna herself knew nothing of our discovery the night before. I kept Julia's hand in mine, and looked steadily into her eyes.

"My dear Julia," I said, "we bring strange news. We have reason to believe that Olivia is not dead, but that something underhand is going on, which we cannot yet make out."

Julia's face grew crimson, but I would not let her draw her hand away from my clasp. I held it the more firmly; and, as Jack was busy talking to Johanna, I continued speaking to her in a lowered tone.

"My dear," I said, "you have been as true, and faithful, and generous a friend as any man ever had. But this must not go on, for your own sake. You fancied you loved me, because every one about us wished it to be so; but I cannot let you waste your life on me. Speak to me exactly as your brother. Do you believe you could be really happy with Captain Carey?"

"Arthur is so good," she murmured, "and he is so fond of me."

I had never heard her call him Arthur before. The elder members of our Guernsey circle called him by his Christian name, but to us younger ones he had always been Captain Carey. Julia's use of it was more eloquent than many phrases. She had grown into the habit of calling him familiarly by it.

"Then, Julia," I said, "what folly it would be for you to sacrifice yourself to a false notion of faithfulness! I could not accept such a sacrifice. Think no more of me or my happiness."

"But my poor aunt was so anxious for you to have a home of your own," she said, sobbing, "and I do love you dearly. Now you will never marry. I know you will not, if you can have neither Olivia nor me for your wife."

"Very likely," I answered, trying to laugh away her agitation; "I shall be in love with two married women instead. How shocking that will sound in Guernsey! But I'm not afraid that Captain Carey will forbid me his house."

"How little we thought!" exclaimed Julia. I knew very well what her mind had gone back to—the days when she and I and my mother were furnishing and settling the house that would now become Captain Carey's home.

"Then it is all settled," I said, "and I shall write to him by to-night's post, inviting him back again—that is, if he really left you last night."

"Yes," she replied; "he would not stay a day longer."

Her face had grown calm as we talked together. A scarcely perceptible smile was lurking about her lips, as if she rejoiced that her suspense was over. There was something very like a pang in the idea of some one else filling the place I had once fully occupied in her heart; but the pain was unworthy of me. I drove it away by throwing myself heart and soul into the mystery which hung over the fate of Olivia.

"We have hit upon a splendid plan," said Jack: "Miss Carey will take Simmons's cab to Bellringer Street, and reach the house about the same time as I visit Foster. That is for me to be at hand if she should need any protection, you know. I shall stay up-stairs with Foster till I hear the cab drive off again, and it will wait for me at the corner of Dawson Street. Then we will come direct here, and tell you every thing at once. Of course, Miss Dobrée will wish to hear it all."

"Cannot I go with Johanna?" she asked.

"No," I said, hastily; "it is very probable Mrs. Foster knows you by sight, though she is less likely to know Johanna. I fancy Mrs. Wilkinson will turn out to be Mrs. Foster herself. Yet why they should spirit Olivia away into a French school, and pretend that she is dead, I cannot see."

Nor could any one of the others see the reason. But as the morning was fast waning away, and both Jack and I were busy, we were compelled to close the discussion, and, with our minds preoccupied to a frightful extent, make those calls upon our patients which were supposed to be in each case full of anxious and particular thought for the ailments we were attempting to alleviate.

Upon meeting again for a few minutes at luncheon, we made a slight change in our plan; for we found a note from Foster awaiting me, in which he requested me to visit him in the future, instead of Dr. John Senior, as he felt more confidence in my knowledge of his malady.

CHAPTER THE FORTY-FIRST

MARTIN DOBRÉE'S PLEDGE

I followed Simmons's cab up Bellringer Street, and watched Johanna alight and enter the house. The door was scarcely closed upon her when I rang, and asked the slatternly drudge of a servant if I could see Mr. Foster. She asked me to go up to the parlor on the second floor, and I went alone, with little expectation of finding Mrs. Foster there, unless Johanna was there also, in which case I was to appear as a stranger to her.

The parlor looked poorer and shabbier by daylight than at night. There was not a single element of comfort in it. The curtains hung in rags about a window begrimed with soot and smoke. The only easy-chair was the one occupied by Foster, who himself looked as shabby and worn as the room. The cuffs and collar of his shirt were yellow and tattered; his hair hung long and lank; and his skin had a sallow, unwholesome tint. The diamond ring upon his finger was altogether out of keeping with his threadbare coat, buttoned up to the chin, as if there were no waistcoat beneath it. From head to foot he looked a broken-down, seedy fellow, yet still preserving some lingering traces of the gentleman. This was Olivia's husband!

A good deal to my surprise, I saw Mrs. Foster seated quietly at a table drawn close to the window, very busily writing—engrossing, as I could see, for some miserable pittance a page. She must have had some considerable practice in the work, for it was done well, and her pen ran quickly over the paper. A second chair left empty opposite to her showed that Foster had been engaged at the same task, before he heard my step on the stairs. He looked weary, and I could not help feeling something akin to pity for him. I did not know that they had come down as low as that.

"I did not expect you to come before night," he said, testily; "I like to have some idea when my medical attendant is coming."

"I was obliged to come now," I answered, offering no other apology. The man irritated me more than any other person that had ever come across me. There was something perverse and splenetic in every word he uttered, and every expression upon his face.

"I do not like your partner," he said; "don't send him again. He knows nothing about his business."

He spoke with all the haughtiness of a millionaire to a country practitioner. I could hardly refrain from smiling as I thought of Jack's disgust and indignation.

"As for that," I replied, "most probably neither of us will visit you again. Dr. Lowry will return to-morrow, and you will be in his hands once more."

"No!" he cried, with a passionate urgency in his tone—"no, Martin Dobrée; you said if any man in London could cure me, it was yourself. I cannot leave myself in any other hands. I demand from you the fulfilment of your words. If what you said is true, you can no more leave me to the care of another physician, than you could leave a fellow-creature to drown without doing your utmost to save him. I refuse to be given up to Dr. Lowry."

"But it is by no means a parallel ease," I argued; "you were under his treatment before, and I have no reason whatever to doubt his skill. Why should you feel safer in my hands than in his?"

"Well!" he said, with a sneer, "if Olivia were alive, I dare scarcely have trusted you, could I? But you have nothing to gain by my death, you know; and I have so much faith in you, in your skill, and your honor, and your conscientiousness—if there be any such qualities in the world—that I place myself unfalteringly under your professional care. Shake hands upon it, Martin Dobrée."

In spite of my repugnance, I could not resist taking his offered hand. His eyes were fastened upon me with something of the fabled fascination of a serpent's. I knew instinctively that he would have the power, and use it, of probing every wound he might suspect in me to the quick. Yet he interested me;

and there was something not entirely repellent to me about him. Above all for Olivia's sake, should we find her still living, I was anxious to study his character. It might happen, as it does sometimes, that my honor and straight-forwardness might prove a match for his crafty shrewdness.

"There," he said, exultantly, "Martin Dobrée pledges himself to cure me—Carry, you are the witness of it. If I die, he has been my assassin as surely as if he had plunged a stiletto into me."

"Nonsense!" I answered; "it is not in my power to heal or destroy. I simply pledge myself to use every means I know of for your recovery."

"Which comes to the same thing," he replied; "for, mark you, I will be the most careful patient you ever had. There should be no chance for you, even if Olivia were alive."

Always harping on that one string. Was it nothing more than a lore of torturing some one that made him reiterate those words? Or did he wish to drive home more deeply the conviction that she was indeed dead?

"Have you communicated the intelligence of her death to her trustee in Australia?" I asked.

"No; why should I?" he said, "no good would come of it to me. Why should I trouble myself about it?"

"Nor to your step-sister?" I added.

"To Mrs. Dobrée?" he rejoined; "no, it does not signify a straw to her either. She holds herself aloof from me now, confound her! You are not on very good terms with her yourself, I believe?"

"The cab was still standing at the door, and I could not leave before it drove away, or I should have made my visit a short one. Mrs. Foster was glancing through the window from time to time, evidently on the watch to see the visitor depart. Would she recognize Johanna? She had stayed some weeks in Guernsey; and Johanna was a fine, stately-looking woman, noticeable among strangers. I must do something to get her away from her post of observation.

"Mrs. Foster," I said, and her eyes sparkled at the sound of her name, "I should be exceedingly obliged to you if you will give me another sight of those papers you showed to me the last time I was here."

She was away for a few minutes, and I heard the cab drive off before she returned. That was the chief point gained. When the papers were in my hand, I just glanced at them, and that was all.

"Have you any idea where they came from?" I asked.

"There is the London post-mark on the envelop," answered Foster—"Show it to him, Carry. There is nothing to be learned from that."

"No," I said, comparing the handwriting on the envelop with the letter, and finding them the same. "Well, good-by! I cannot often pay you as long a visit as this."

I hurried off quickly to the corner of Dawson Street, where Johanna was waiting for me. She looked exceedingly contented when I took my seat beside her in the cab.

"Well, Martin," she said, "you need suffer no more anxiety. Olivia has gone as English teacher in an excellent French school, where the lady is thoroughly acquainted with English ways and comforts. This is the prospectus of the establishment. You see there are 'extensive grounds for recreation, and the comforts of a cheerfully happy home, the domestic arrangements being on a thoroughly liberal scale.' Here is also a photographic view of the place: a charming villa, you see, in the best French style. The lady's husband is an avocat; and every thing is taught by professors—cosmography and pedagogy, and other studies of which we never heard when I was a girl. Olivia is to stay there twelve months, and in return for her services will take lessons from any professors attending the establishment. Your mind may be quite at ease now."

"But where is the place?" I inquired.

"Oh! it is in Normandy—Noireau," she said—"quite out of the range of railways and tourists. There will be no danger of any one finding her out there; and you know she has changed her name altogether this time."

"Did you discover that Olivia and Ellen Martineau are the same persons?" I asked.

An expression of bewilderment and consternation came across her contented face.

"No, I did not," she answered; "I thought you were sure of that."

But I was not sure of it; neither could Jack be sure. He puzzled himself in trying to give a satisfactory description of his Ellen Martineau; but every answer he gave to my eager questions plunged us into greater uncertainty. He was not sure of the color either of her hair or eyes, and made blundering guesses at her height. The chief proof we had of Olivia's identity was the drunken claim made upon Ellen Martineau by Foster, a month after he had received convincing proof that she was dead. What was I to believe?

It was running too great a risk to make any further inquiries at No. 19 Bellringer Street. Mrs. Wilkinson was the landlady of the lodging-house, and she had told Johanna that Madame Perrier boarded with her when she was in London. But she might begin to talk to her other lodgers, if her own curiosity were excited; and once more my desire to fathom the mystery hanging about Olivia might plunge her into fresh difficulties, should they reach the ears of Foster or his wife.

"I must satisfy myself about her safety now," I said. "Only put yourself in my place, Jack. How can I rest till I know more about Olivia?"

"I do put myself in your place," he answered. "What do you say to having a run down to this place in Basse-Normandie, and seeing for yourself whether Miss Ellen Martineau is your Olivia?"

"How can I?" I asked, attempting to hang back from the suggestion. It was a busy time with us. The season was in full roll, and our most aristocratic patients were in town. The easterly winds were bringing in their usual harvest of bronchitis and diphtheria. If I went, Jack's hands would be more than full. Had these things come to perplex us only two months earlier, I could have taken a holiday with a clear conscience.

"Dad will jump at the chance of coming back for a week," replied Jack; "he is bored to death down at Fulham. Go you must, for my sake, old fellow. You are good for nothing as long as you're so down in the mouth. I shall be glad to be rid of you."

We shook hands upon that, as warmly as if he had paid me the most flattering compliments.

CHAPTER THE FORTY-SECOND

NOIREAU

In this way it came to pass that two evenings later I was crossing the Channel to Havre, and found myself about five o'clock in the afternoon of the next day at Falaise. It was the terminus of the railway in that direction; and a very ancient conveyance, bearing the name of La Petite Vitesse, was in waiting to carry on any travellers who were venturesome enough to explore the regions beyond. There was space inside for six passengers, but it smelt too musty, and was too full of the fumes of bad tobacco, for me; and I very much preferred sitting beside the driver, a red-faced, smooth-cheeked Norman, habited in a blue blouse, who could crack his long whip with almost the skill of a Parisian omnibus-driver. We were friends in a trice, for my patois was almost identical with his own, and he could not believe his own ears that he was talking with an Englishman.

"La Petite Vitesse" bore out its name admirably, if it were meant to indicate exceeding slowness. We never advanced beyond a slow trot, and at the slightest hint of rising ground the trot slackened into a walk, and eventually subsided into a crawl. By these means the distance we traversed was made to seem tremendous, and the drowsy jingle of the collar-bells, intimating that progress was being accomplished, added to the delusion. But the fresh, sweet air, blowing over leagues of fields and meadows, untainted with a breath of smoke, gave me a delicious tingling in the veins. I had not felt such a glow of exhilaration since that bright morning when I bad crossed the channel to Sark, to ask Olivia to become mine.

The sun sank below the distant horizon, with the trees showing clearly against it, for the atmosphere was as transparent as crystal; and the light of the stars that came out one by one almost cast a defined shadow upon our path, from the poplar-trees standing in long, straight rows in the hedges. If I found Olivia at the end of that starlit path my gladness in it would be completed. Yet if I found her, what then? I should see her for a few minutes in the dull salon of a school perhaps with some watchful, spying Frenchwoman present. I should simply satisfy myself that she was living. There could be nothing more between us. I dare not tell her how dear she was to me, or ask her if she ever thought of me in her loneliness and friendlessness. I began to wish that I had brought Johanna with me, who could have taken her in her arms, and kissed and comforted her. Why had I not thought of that before?

As we proceeded at our delusive pace along the last stage of our journey, I began to sound the driver, cautiously wheeling about the object of my excursion into those remote regions. I had tramped through Normandy and Brittany three or four times, but there had been no inducement to visit Noireau, which resembled a Lancashire cotton-town, and I had never been there.

"There are not many English at Noireau?" I remarked, suggestively.

"Not one," he replied—"not one at this moment. There was one little English mam'zelle—peste!—a very pretty little English girl, who was voyaging precisely like you, m'sieur, some months ago. There was a little child with her, and the two were quite alone. They are very intrepid, are the English mam'zelles. She did not know a word of our language. But that was droll, m'sieur! A French demoiselle would never voyage like that."

The little child puzzled me. Yet I could not help fancying that this young Englishwoman travelling alone, with no knowledge of French, must be my Olivia. At any rate it could be no other than Miss Ellen Martineau.

"Where was she going to?" I asked.

"She came to Noireau to be an instructress in an establishment," answered the driver, in a tone of great enjoyment—"an establishment founded by the wife of Monsieur Emile Perrier, the avocat! He! he! he! Mon Dieu! how droll that was, m'sieur! An avocat! So they believed that in England? Bah! Emile Perrier an avocat—mon Dieu!"

"But what is there to laugh at?" I asked, as the man's laughter rang through the quiet night.

"Am I an avocat?" he inquired derisively, "am I a proprietor? am I even a curé? Pardon, m'sieur, but I am just as much avocat, proprietor, curé, as Emile Perrier. He was an impostor. He became bankrupt; he and his wife ran away to save themselves; the establishment was broken up. It was a bubble, m'sieur, and it burst comme ça."

My driver clapped his hands together lightly, as though Monsieur Perrier's bubble needed very little pressure to disperse it.

"Good heavens!" I exclaimed, "but what became of Oli—of the young English lady, and the child?"

"Ah, m'sieur!" he said, "I do not know. I do not live in Noireau, but I pass to and fro from Falaise in La Petite Vitesse. She has not returned in my omnibus, that is all I know. But she could go to Granville, or to Caen. There are other omnibuses, you see. Somebody will tell you down there."

For three or four miles before us there lay a road as straight as a rule, ending in a small cluster of lights glimmering in the bottom of a valley, into which we were descending with great precaution on the part of the driver and his team. That was Noireau. But already my exhilaration was exchanged for profound anxiety. I extorted from the Norman all the information he possessed concerning the bankrupt; it was not much, and it only served to heighten my solicitude.

It was nearly eleven o'clock before we entered the town; but I learned a few more particulars from the middle-aged woman in the omnibus bureau. She recollected the name of Miss Ellen Martineau, and her arrival; and she described her with the accuracy and faithfulness of a woman. If she were not Olivia herself, she must be her very counterpart. But who was the child, a girl of nine or ten years of age, who had accompanied her? It was too late to learn any more about them. The landlady of the hotel confirmed all I had heard, and added several items of information. Monsieur Perrier and his wife had imposed upon several English families, and had succeeded in getting dozens of English pupils, so she assured me, who had been scattered over the country, Heaven only knew where, when the school was broken up, about a month ago.

I started out early the next morning to find the Rue de Grâce, where the inscription on my photographic view of the premises represented them as situated. The town was in the condition of a provincial town in England about a century ago. The streets were as dirty as the total absence of drains and scavengers could make them, and the cleanest path was up the kennel in the centre. The filth of the houses was washed down into them by pipes, with little cisterns at each story, and under almost every window. There were many improprieties, and some indecencies, shocking to English sensibilities. In the Rue de Grâce I saw two nuns in their hoods and veils, unloading a cart full of manure. A ladies' school for English people in a town like this seemed ridiculous.

There was no difficulty in finding the houses in my photographic view. There were two of them, one standing in the street, the other lying back beyond a very pleasant garden. A Frenchman was pacing up and down the broad gravel-path which connected them, smoking a cigar, and examining critically the vines growing against the walls. Two little children were gambolling about in close white caps, and with frocks down to their heels. Upon seeing me, he took his cigar from his lips with two fingers of one hand, and lifted his hat with the other. I returned the salutation with a politeness as ceremonious as his own.

"Monsieur is an Englishman?" he said, in a doubtful tone.

"From the Channel Islands," I replied.

"Ah! you belong to us," he said, "but you are hybrid, half English, half French; a fine race. I also have English blood in my veins."

I paid monsieur a compliment upon the result of the admixture of blood in his own instance, and then proceeded to unfold my object in visiting him.

"Ah!" he said, "yes, yes, yes; Perrier was an impostor. These houses are mine, monsieur. I live in the front, yonder; my daughter and son-in-law occupy the other. We had the photographs taken for our own pleasure, but Perrier must have bought them from the artist, no doubt. I have a small cottage at the back of my house; voilà, monsieur! there it is. Perrier rented it from me for two hundred francs a year. I permitted him to pass along this walk, and through our coach-house into a passage which leads to the street where madame had her school. Permit me, and I will show it to you."

He led me through a shed, and along a dirty, vaulted passage, into a mean street at the back. A small, miserable-looking house stood in it, shut up, with broken persiennes covering the windows. My heart sank at the idea of Olivia living here, in such discomfort, and neglect, and sordid poverty.

"Did you ever see a young English lady here, monsieur?" I asked; "she arrived about the beginning of last November."

"But yes, certainly, monsieur," he replied, "a charming English demoiselle! One must have been blind not to observe her. A face sweet and gracieuse; with hair of gold, but a little more sombre. Yes, yes! The ladies might not admire her, but we others—"

He laughed, and shrugged his shoulders in a detestable manner.

"What height was she, monsieur?" I inquired.

"A just height," he answered, "not tall like a camel, nor too short like a monkey. She would stand an inch or two above your shoulder, monsieur."

It could be no other than my Olivia! She had been living here, then, in this miserable place, only a month ago; but where could she be now? How was I to find any trace of her?

"I will make some inquiries from my daughter," said the Frenchman; "when the establishment was broken up I was ill with the fever, monsieur. We have fever often here. But she will know—I will ask her."

He returned to me after some time, with the information that the English demoiselle had been seen in the house of a woman who sold milk, Mademoiselle Rosalie by name; and he volunteered to accompany me to her dwelling.

It was a poor-looking house, of one room only, in the same street as the school; but we found no one there except an old woman, exceedingly deaf, who told us, after much difficulty in making her understand our object, that Mademoiselle Rosalie was gone somewhere to nurse a relative, who was dangerously ill. She had not had any cows of her own, and she had easily disposed of her small business to this old woman and her daughter. Did the messieurs want any milk for their families? No. Well, then, she could not tell us any thing more about Mam'zelle Rosalie; and she knew nothing of an Englishwoman and a little girl.

I turned away baffled and discouraged; but my new friend was not so quickly depressed. It was impossible, he maintained, that the English girl and the child could have left the town unnoticed. He went with me to all the omnibus bureaus, where we made urgent inquiries concerning the passengers who had quitted Noireau during the last month. No places had been taken for Miss Ellen Martineau and the child, for there was no such name in any of the books. But at each bureau I was recommended to see the drivers upon their return in the evening; and I was compelled to give up the pursuit for that day.

CHAPTER THE FORTY-THIRD

A SECOND PURSUER

No wonder there was fever in the town, I thought, as I picked my way among the heaps of garbage and refuse lying out in the streets. The most hideous old women I ever saw, wrinkled over every inch of their skin, blear-eyed, and with eyelids reddened by smoke, met me at each turn. Sallow weavers, in white caps, gazed out at me from their looms in almost every house. There was scarcely a child to be seen about. The whole district, undrained and unhealthy, bears the name of the "Manufactory of Little Angels," from the number of children who die there. And this was the place where Olivia had been spending a very hard and severe winter!

There was going to be a large cattle-fair the next day, and all the town was alive. Every inn in the place was crowded to overflowing. As I sat at the window of my café, watching the picturesque groups which formed in the street outside, I heard a vehement altercation going on in the archway, under which was the entrance to my hotel.

"Grands Dieux!" cried the already familiar voice of my landlady, shrill as the cackling of a hen—"grands Dieux! not a single soul from Ville-en-bois can rest here, neither man nor woman! They have the fever like a pest there. No, no, m'sieur, that is impossible; go away, you and your beast. There is room at the Lion d'or. But the gensdarmes should not let you enter the town. We have fever enough of our own."

"But my farm is a league from Ville-en-bois," was the answer, in the slow, rugged accents of a Norman peasant.

"But I tell you it is impossible,'" she retorted; "I have an Englishman here, very rich, a milor, and he will not hear of any person from Ville-en-bois resting in the house. Go away to the Lion d'or, my good friend, where there are no English. They are as afraid of the fever as of the devil."

I laughed to myself at my landlady's ingenious excuses; but after this the conversation fell into a lower key, and I heard no more of it.

I went out late in the evening to question each of the omnibus—drivers, but in vain. Whether they were too busy to give me proper attention, or too anxious to join the stir and mirth of the townspeople, they all declared they knew nothing of any Englishwoman. As I returned dejectedly to my inn, I heard a lamentable voice, evidently English, bemoaning in doubtful French. The omnibus from Falaise had just come in, and under the lamp in the entrance of the archway stood a lady before my hostess, who was volubly asserting that there was no room left in her house. I hastened to the assistance of my countrywoman, and the light of the lamp falling full upon her face revealed to me who she was.

"Mrs. Foster!" I exclaimed, almost shouting her name in my astonishment. She looked ready to faint with fatigue and dismay, and she laid her hand heavily on my arm, as if to save herself from sinking to the ground.

"Have you found her?" she asked, involuntarily.

"Not a trace of her," I answered.

Mrs. Foster broke into an hysterical laugh, which was very quickly followed by sobs. I had no great difficulty in persuading the landlady to find some accommodation for her, and then I retired to my own room to smoke in peace, and turn over the extraordinary meeting which had been the last incident of the day.

It required very little keenness to come to the conclusion that the Fosters had obtained their information concerning Miss Ellen Martineau, where we had got ours, from Mrs. Wilkinson. Also that Mrs. Foster had lost no time in following up the clew, for she was only twenty-four hours behind me. She had looked thoroughly astonished and dismayed when she saw me there; so she had had no idea that I was on the same track. But nothing could be more convincing than this journey of hers that neither she nor Foster really believed in Olivia's death. That was as clear as day. But what explanation could I give to myself of those letters, of Olivia's above all? Was it possible that she had caused them to be written, and sent to her husband? I could not even admit such a question, without a sharp sense of disappointment in her.

I saw Mrs. Foster early in the morning, somewhat as a truce-bearer may meet another on neutral ground. She was grateful to me for my interposition in her behalf the night before; and, as I knew Ellen Martineau to be safely out of the way, I was inclined to be tolerant toward her. I assured her, upon my honor, that I had failed in discovering any trace of Olivia in Noireau, and I told her all I had learned about the bankruptcy of Monsieur Perrier, and the scattering of the school.

"But why should you undertake such a chase?" I asked; "if you and Foster are satisfied that Olivia is dead, why should you be running after Ellen Martineau? You show me the papers which seem to prove her death, and now I find you in this remote part of Normandy, evidently in pursuit of her. What does this mean?"

"You are doing the same thing yourself," she answered.

"Yes," I replied, "because I am not satisfied. But you have proved your conviction by becoming Richard Foster's second wife."

"That is the very point," she said, shedding a few tears; "as soon as ever Mrs. Wilkinson described Ellen Martineau to me, when she was talking about her visitor who had come to inquire after her, in that cab which was standing at the door the last time you visited Mr. Foster—and I had no suspicion of it—I grew quite frightened lest he should ever be charged with marrying me while she was alive. So I persuaded him to let me come here and make sure of it, though the journey costs a great deal, and we have very little money to spare. We did not know what tricks Olivia might do, and it made me very miserable to think she might be still alive, and I in her place."

I could not but acknowledge to myself that there was some reason in Mrs. Foster's statement of the case.

"There is not the slightest chance of your finding her," I remarked.

"Isn't there?" she asked, with an evil gleam in her eyes, which I just caught before she hid her face again in her handkerchief.

"At any rate," I said, "you would have no power over her if you found her. You could not take her back with you by force. I do not know how the French laws would regard Foster's authority, but you can have none whatever, and he is quite unfit to take this long journey to claim her. Really I do not see what you can do; and I should think your wisest plan would be to go back and take care of him, leaving her alone. I am here to protect her, and I shall stay until I see you fairly out of the place."

She did not speak again for some minutes, but she was evidently reflecting upon what I had just said.

"But what are we to live upon?" she asked at last; "there is her money lying in the bank, and neither she nor Richard can touch it. It must be paid to her personally or to her order; and she cannot prove her identity herself without the papers Richard holds. It is aggravating. I am at my wits' end about it."

"Listen to me," I said. "Why cannot we come to some arrangement, supposing Ellen Martineau proves to be Olivia? It would be better for you all to make some division of her property by mutual agreement. You know best whether Olivia could insist upon a judicial separation. But in any other case why should not Foster agree to receive half her income, and leave her free, as free as she can be, with the other half? Surely some mutual agreement could be made."

"He would never do it!" she exclaimed, clasping her hands round her knees, and swaying to and fro passionately; "he never loses any power. She belongs to him, and he never gives up any thing. He would torment her almost to death, but he would never let her go free. No, no. You do not know him, Dr. Martin."

"Then we will try to get a divorce," I said, looking at her steadily.

"On what grounds?" she asked, looking at me as steadily.

I could not and would not enter into the question with her.

"There has been no personal cruelty on Richard's part toward her," she resumed, with a half-smile. "It's true I locked her up for a few days once, but he was in Paris, and had nothing to do with it. You could not prove a single act of cruelty toward her."

Still I did not answer, though she paused and regarded me keenly.

"We were not married till we had reason to believe her dead," she continued; "there is no harm in that. If she has forged those papers, she is to blame. We were married openly, in our parish church; what could be said against that?"

"Let us return to what I told you at first," I said; "if you find Olivia, you have no more authority over her than I have. You will be obliged to return to England alone; and I shall place her in some safe custody. I shall ascertain precisely how the law stands, both here and in England. Now I advise you, for Foster's sake, make as much haste home as you can; for he will be left without nurse or doctor while we two are away."

She sat gnawing her under lip for some minutes, and looking as vicious as Madam was wont to do in her worst tempers.

"You will let me make some inquiries to satisfy myself?" she said.

"Certainly," I replied; "you will only discover, as I have, that the school was broken up a month ago, and Ellen Martineau has disappeared."

I kept no very strict watch over her during the day, for I felt sure she would find no trace of Olivia in Noireau. At night I saw her again. She was worn out and despondent, and declared herself quite ready to return to Falaise by the omnibus at five o'clock in the morning. I saw her off, and gave the driver a fee, to bring me word for what town she took her ticket at the railway-station. When he returned in the evening, he told me he had himself bought her one for Honfleur, and started her fairly on her way home.

As for myself, I had spent the day in making inquiries at the offices of the octrois—those local custom-houses which stand at every entrance into a town or village in France, for the gathering of trifling, vexatious taxes upon articles of food and merchandise. At one of these I had learned, that, three or four weeks ago, a young Englishwoman with a little girl had passed by on foot, each carrying a small bundle, which had not been examined. It was the octroi on the road to Granville, which was between thirty and forty miles away. From Granville was the nearest route to the Channel Islands. Was it not possible that Olivia had resolved to seek refuge there again? Perhaps to seek me! My heart, bowed down by the sad picture of her and the little child leaving the town on foot, beat high again at the thought of Olivia in Guernsey.

I set off for Granville by the omnibus next morning, and made further inquiries at every village we passed through, whether any thing had been seen of a young Englishwoman and a little girl. At first the answer was yes; then it became a matter of doubt; at last everywhere they replied by a discouraging no. At one point of our journey we passed a dilapidated sign-post with a rude, black figure of the Virgin hanging below it. I could just decipher upon one finger of the post, in half-obliterated letters, "Ville-en-bois." It recurred to me that this was the place where fever was raging like the pest.

"It is a poor place," said the driver, disparagingly; "there is nothing there but the fever, and a good angel of a curé, who is the only doctor into the bargain. It is two leagues and a kilometre, and it is on the road to nowhere."

I could not stop in my quest to turn aside, and visit this village smitten with fever, though I felt a strong inclination to do so. At Granville I learned that a young lady and a child had made the voyage to Jersey a short time before; and I went on with stronger hope. But in Jersey I could obtain no further information about her; nor in Guernsey, whither I felt sure Olivia would certainly have proceeded. I took one day more to cross over to Sark, and consult Tardif; but he knew no more than I did. He absolutely refused to believe that Olivia was dead.

"In August," he said, "I shall hear from her. Take courage and comfort. She promised it, and she will keep her promise. If she had known herself to be dying, she would have sent me word."

"It is a long time to wait," I said, with an utter sinking of spirit.

"It is a long time to wait!" he echoed, lifting up his hands, and letting them fall again with a gesture of weariness; "but we must wait and hope."

To wait in impatience, and to hope at times, and despair at times, I returned to London.

CHAPTER THE FORTY-FOURTH

THE LAW OF MARRIAGE

One of my first proceedings, after my return, was to ascertain how the English law stood with regard to Olivia's position. Fortunately for me, one of Dr. Senior's oldest friends was a lawyer of great repute, and he discussed the question with me after a dinner at his house at Fulham.

"There seems to be no proof against the husband of any kind," he said, after I had told him all.

"Why!" I exclaimed, "here you have a girl, brought up in luxury and wealth, willing to brave any poverty rather than continue to live with him."

"A girl's whim," he said; "mania, perhaps. Is there insanity in her family?"

"She is as sane as I am," I answered. "Is there no law to protect a wife against the companionship of such a woman as this second Mrs. Foster?"

"The husband introduces her as his cousin," he rejoined, "and places her in some little authority on the plea that his wife is too young to be left alone safely in Continental hotels. There is no reasonable objection to be taken to that."

"Then Foster could compel her to return to him?" I said.

"As far as I see into the case, he certainly could," was the answer, which drove me nearly frantic.

"But there is this second marriage," I objected.

"There lies the kernel of the case," he said, daintily peeling his walnuts. "You tell me there are papers, which you believe to be forgeries, purporting to be the medical certificate, with corroborative proof of her death. Now, if the wife be guilty of framing these, the husband will bring them against her as the grounds on which he felt free to contract his second marriage. She has done a very foolish and a very wicked thing there."

"You think she did it?" I asked.

He smiled significantly, but without saying any thing.

"I cannot!" I cried.

"Ah! you are blind," he replied, with the same maddening smile; "but let me return. On the other hand, if the husband has forged these papers, it would go far with me as strong presumptive evidence against him, upon which we might go in for a divorce, not a separation merely. If the young lady had remained with him till she had collected proof of his unfaithfulness to her, this, with his subsequent marriage to the same person during her lifetime, would probably have set her absolutely free."

"Divorced from him?" I said.

"Divorce," he repeated.

"But what can be done now?" I asked.

"All you can do," he answered, "is to establish your influence over this fellow, and go cautiously to work with him. As long as the lady is in France, if she be alive, and he is too ill to go after her, she is safe. You may convince him by degrees that it is to his interest to come to some terms with her. A formal deed of separation might be agreed upon, and drawn up; but even that will not perfectly secure her in the future."

I was compelled to remain satisfied with this opinion. Yet how could I be satisfied, while Olivia, if she was still living, was wandering about homeless, and, as I feared, destitute, in a foreign country?

I made my first call upon Foster the next evening. Mrs. Foster had been to Brook Street every day since her return, to inquire for me, and to leave an urgent message that I should go to Bellringer Street as soon as I was again in town. The lodging-house looked almost as wretched as the forsaken dwelling down at Noireau, where Olivia had perhaps been living; and the stifling, musty air inside it almost made me gasp for breath.

"So you are come back!" was Foster's greeting, as I entered the dingy room.

"Yes." I replied.

"I need not ask what success you've had," he said, sneering, 'Why so pale and wan, fond lover?' Your trip has not agreed with you, that is plain enough. It did not agree with Carry, either, for she came back swearing she would never go on such a wild-goose chase again. You know I was quite opposed to her going?"

"No," I said, incredulously. The diamond ring had disappeared from his finger, and it was easy to guess how the funds had been raised for the journey.

"Altogether opposed," he repeated. "I believe Olivia is dead. I am quite sure she has never been under this roof with me, as Miss Ellen Martineau has been. I should have known it as surely as ever a tiger scented its prey. Do you suppose I have no sense keen enough to tell me she was in the very house where I was?"

"Nonsense!" I answered. His eyes glistened cruelly, and made me almost ready to spring upon him. I could have seized him by the throat and shaken him to death, in my sudden passion of loathing against him; but I sat quiet, and ejaculated "Nonsense!" Such power has the spirit of the nineteenth century among civilized classes.

"Olivia is dead," he said, in a solemn tone. "I am convinced of that from another reason: through all the misery of our marriage, I never knew her guilty of an untruth, not the smallest. She was as true as the Gospel. Do you think you or Carry could make me believe that she would trifle with such an awful subject as her own death? No. I would take my oath that Olivia would never have had that letter sent, or write to me those few lines of farewell, but to let me know that she was really dead."

His voice faltered a little, as though even he were moved by the thought of her early death. Mrs. Foster glanced at him jealously, and he looked back at her with a provoking curve about his lips. For the moment there was more hatred than love in the regards exchanged between them. I saw it was useless to pursue the subject.

"Well," I said, "I came to arrange a time for Dr. Lowry to visit you with me, for the purpose of a thorough examination. It is possible that Dr. Senior may be induced to join us, though he has retired from practice. I am anxious for his opinion as well as Lowry's." "You really wish to cure me?" he answered, raising his eyebrows.

"To be sure," I replied. "I can have no other object in undertaking your case. Do you imagine it is a pleasure to me? It is possible that your death would be a greater benefit to the world than your life, but that is no question for me to decide. Neither is it for me to consider whether you are my friend or my enemy. There is simply a life to be saved if possible; whose, is not my business. Do you understand me?"

"I think so," he said. "I am nothing except material for you to exercise your craft upon."

"Precisely," I answered; "that and nothing more. As some writer says, 'It is a mere matter of instinct with me. I attend you just as a Newfoundland dog saves a drowning man.'"

I went from him to Hanover Street, where I found Captain Carey, who met me with the embarrassment and shamefacedness of a young girl. I had not yet seen them since my return from Normandy. There was much to tell them, though they already knew that my expedition had failed, and that it was still doubtful whether Ellen Martineau and Olivia were the same person.

Captain Carey walked along the street with me toward home. He had taken my arm in his most confidential manner, but he did not open his lips till we reached Brook Street.

"Martin," he said, "I've turned it over in my own mind, and I agree with Tardif. Olivia is no more dead than you or me. We shall find out all about it in August, if not before. Cheer up, my boy! I tell you what: Julia and I will wait till we are sure about Olivia."

"No, no," I interrupted; "you and Julia have nothing to do with it. When is your wedding to be?"

"If you have no objection," he answered—"have you the least shadow of an objection?"

"Not a shadow of a shadow," I said.

"Well, then," he resumed, bashfully, "what do you think of August? It is a pleasant month, and would give us time for that trip to Switzerland, you know. Not any sooner, because of your poor mother; and later, if you like that better."

"Not a day later," I said; "my father has been married again these four months."

Yet I felt a little sore for my mother's memory. How quickly it was fading away from every heart but mine! If I could but go to her now, and pour out all my troubled thoughts into her listening, indulgent ear! Not even Olivia herself, who could never be to me more than she was at this moment, could fill her place.

CHAPTER THE FORTY-FIFTH

FULFILLING THE PLEDGE

We—that is, Dr. Senior, Lowry, and I—made our examination of Foster, and held our consultation, three days from that time.

There was no doubt whatever that he was suffering from the same disease as that which had been the death of my mother—a disease almost invariably fatal, sooner or later. A few cases of cure, under most favorable circumstances, had been reported during the last half-century; but the chances were dead against Foster's recovery. In all probability, a long and painful illness, terminating in inevitable death, lay before him. In the opinion of my two senior physicians, all that I could do would be to alleviate the worst pangs of it.

His case haunted me day and night. In that deep under-current of consciousness which lurks beneath our surface sensations and impressions, there was always present the image of Foster, with his pale, cynical face, and pitiless eyes. With this, was the perpetual remembrance that a subtile malady, beyond the reach of our skill, was slowly eating away his life. The man I abhorred; but the sufferer, mysteriously linked with the memories which clung about my mother, aroused her most urgent, instinctive compassion. Only once before had I watched the conflict between disease and its remedy with so intense an interest.

It was a day or two after our consultation that I came accidentally upon the little note-book which I had kept in Guernsey—a private note-book, accessible only to myself. It was night; Jack, as usual, was gone out, and I was alone. I turned over the leaves merely for listless want of occupation. All at once I came upon an entry, made in connection with my mother's illness, which recalled to me the discovery I believed I had made of a remedy for her disease, had it only been applied in its earlier stages. It had slipped out of my mind, but now my memory leaped upon it with irresistible force.

I must tell the whole truth, however terrible and humiliating it may be. Whether I had been true or false to myself up to that moment I cannot say. I had taken upon myself the care, and, if possible, the cure of this man, who was my enemy, if I had an enemy in the world. His life and mine could not run parallel without great grief and hurt to me, and to one dearer than myself. Now that a better chance was thrust upon me in his favor, I shrank from seizing it with unutterable reluctance. I turned heart-sick at the thought of it. I tried my utmost to shake off the grip of my memory. Was it possible that, in the core of my heart, I wished this man to die?

Yes, I wished him to die. Conscience flashed the answer across the inner depths of my soul, as a glare of lightning over the sharp crags and cruel waves of our island in a midnight storm. I saw with terrible distinctness that there had been lurking within a sure sense of satisfaction in the certainty that he must die. I had suspected nothing of it till that moment. When I told him it was the instinct of a physician to save his patient, I spoke the truth. But I found something within me deeper than instinct, that was wailing and watching for the fatal issue of his malady, with a tranquil security so profound that it never stirred the surface of my consciousness, or lifted up its ghostly face to the light of conscience.

I took up my note-book, and went away to my room, lest Jack should come in suddenly, and read my secret on my face. I thrust the book into a drawer in my desk, and locked it away out of my sight. What need had I to trouble myself with it or its contents? I found a book, one of Charles Dickens's most amusing stories, and set myself resolutely to read it; laughing aloud at its drolleries, and reading faster and faster; while all the time thoughts came crowding into my mind of my mother's pale, worn face, and the pains she suffered, and the remedy found out too late. These images grew so strong at last that my eyes ran over the sentences mechanically, but my brain refused to take in the meaning of them. I threw the book from me; and, leaning my head on my hands, I let all the waves of that sorrowful memory flow over me.

How strong they were! how persistent! I could hear the tones of her languid voice, and see the light lingering to the last in her dim eyes, whenever they met mine. A shudder crept through me as I recollected how she travelled that dolorous road, slowly, day by day, down to the grave. Other feet were beginning to tread the same painful journey; but there was yet time to stay them, and the power to do it was intrusted to me. What was I to do with my power?

It seemed cruel that this power should come to me from my mother's death. If she were living still, or if she had died from any other cause, the discovery of this remedy would never have been made by me. And I was to take it as a sort of miraculous gift, purchased by her pangs, and bestow it upon the only man I hated. For I hated him; I said so to myself, muttering the words between my teeth.

What was the value of his life, that I should ransom it by such a sacrifice? A mean, selfish, dissipated life—a life that would be Olivia's curse as long as it lasted. For an instant a vision stood out clear before me, and made my heart beat fast, of Olivia free, as she must be in the space of a few months, should I leave the disease to take its course; free and happy, disenthralled from the most galling of all bondage. Could I not win her then? She knew already that I loved her; would she not soon learn to love me in return? If Olivia were living, what an irreparable injury it would be to her for this man to recover!

That seemed to settle the question. I could not be the one to doom her to a continuation of the misery she was enduring. It was irrational and over-scrupulous of my conscience to demand such a thing from me. I would use all the means practised in the ordinary course of treatment to render the recovery of my patient possible, and so fulfil my duty. I would carefully follow all Dr. Senior's suggestions. He was an experienced and very skilful physician; I could not do better than submit my judgment to his.

Besides, how did I know that this fancied discovery of mine was of the least value? I had never had a chance of making experiment of it, and no doubt it was an idle chimera of my brain, when it was overwrought by anxiety for my mother's sake. I had not hitherto thought enough of it to ask the opinion of any of my medical friends and colleagues. Why should I attach any importance to it now? Let it rest. Not a soul knew of it but myself. I had a perfect right to keep or destroy my own notes. Suppose I destroyed that one at once?

I unlocked the desk, and took out my book again. The leaf on which these special notes were written was already loose, and might have been easily lost at any time, I thought. I burned it by the flame of the gas, and threw the brown ashes into the grate. For a few minutes I felt elated, as if set free from an oppressive burden; and I returned to the story I had been reading, and laughed more heartily than before at the grotesque turn of the incidents. But before long the tormenting question came up again. The notes were not lost. They seemed now to be burned in upon my brain.

The power has been put into your hands to save life, said my conscience, and you are resolving to let it perish. What have you to do with the fact that the nature is mean, selfish, cruel? It is the physical life simply that you have to deal with. What is beyond that rests in the hands of God. What He is about to do with this soul is no question for you. Your office pledges you to cure him if you can, and the fulfilment of this duty is required of you. If you let this man die, you are a murderer.

But, I said in answer to myself, consider what trivial chances the whole thing has hung upon. Besides the accident that this was my mother's malady, there was the chance of Lowry not being called from home. The man was his patient, not mine. After that there was the chance of Jack going to see him, instead of me; or of him refusing my attendance. If the chain had broken at one of these links, no responsibility could have fallen upon me. He would have died, and all the good results of his death would have followed naturally. Let it rest at that.

But it could not rest at that. I fought a battle with myself all through the quiet night, motionless and in silence, lest Jack should become aware that I was not sleeping. How should I ever face him, or grasp his hearty hand again, with such a secret weight upon my soul? Yet how could I resolve to save Foster at the cost of dooming Olivia to a life-long bondage should he discover where she was, or to life-long poverty should she remain concealed? If I were only sure that she was alive! But if she were dead—why, then all motive for keeping back this chance of saving him would be taken away. It was for her sake merely that I hesitated.

For her sake, but for my own as well, said my conscience; for the subtle hope, which had taken deeper root day by day, that by-and-by the only obstacle between us would be removed. Suppose then that he was dead, and Olivia was free to love me, to become my wife. Would not her very closeness to me be a reproving presence forever at my side? Could I ever recall the days before our marriage, as men recall them when they are growing gray and wrinkled, as a happy golden time? Would there not always be a haunting sense of perfidy, and disloyalty to duty, standing between me and her clear truth and singleness of heart? There could be no happiness for me, even with Olivia, my cherished and honored wife, if I had this weight and cloud resting upon my conscience.

The morning dawned before I could decide. The decision, when made, brought no feeling of relief or triumph to me. As soon as it was probable that Dr. Senior could see me; I was at his house at Fulham; and in rapid, almost incoherent words laid what I believed to be my important discovery before him. He sat thinking for some time, running over in his own mind such cases as had come under his own observation. After a while a gleam of pleasure passed over his face, and his eyes brightened as he looked at me.

"I congratulate you, Martin," he said, "though I wish Jack had hit upon this. I believe it will prove a real benefit to our science. Let me turn it over a little longer, and consult some of my colleagues about it. But I think you are right. You are about to try it on poor Foster?"

"Yes," I answered, with a chilly sensation in my veins, the natural reaction upon the excitement of the past night.

"It can do him no harm," he said, "and in my opinion it will prolong his life to old age, if he is careful of himself. I will write a paper on the subject for the Lancet, if you will allow me."

"With all my heart," I said sadly.

The old physician regarded me for a minute with his keen eyes, which had looked through the window of disease into many a human soul. I shrank from the scrutiny, but I need not have done so. He grasped my hand firmly and closely in his own.

"God bless you, Martin!" he said, "God bless you!"

CHAPTER THE FORTY-SIXTH

That keen, benevolent glance of Dr. Senior's was like a gleam of sunlight piercing through the deepest recesses of my troubled spirit. I felt that I was no longer fighting my fight out alone. A friendly eye was upon me; a friendly voice was cheering me on. "The dead shall look me through and through," says Tennyson. For my part I should wish for a good, wise man to look me through and through; feel the pulse of my soul from time to time, when it was ailing, and detect what was there contrary to reason and to right. Dr. Senior's hearty "God bless you!" brought strength and blessing with it.

I went straight from Fulham to Bellringer Street. A healthy impulse to fulfil all my duty, however difficult, was in its first fervid moment of action. Nevertheless there was a subtle hope within me founded upon one chance that was left—it was just possible that Foster might refuse to be made the subject of an experiment; for an experiment it was.

I found him not yet out of bed. Mrs. Foster was busy at her task of engrossing in the sitting-room—a task she performed so well that I could not believe but that she had been long accustomed to it. I followed her to Foster's bedroom, a small close attic at the back, with a cheerless view of chimneys and the roofs of houses. There was no means of ventilation, except by opening a window near the head of the bed, when the draught of cold air would blow full upon him. He looked exceedingly worn and wan. The doubt crossed me, whether the disease had not made more progress than we supposed. His face fell as he saw the expression upon mine.

"Worse, eh?" he said; "don't say I am worse."

I sat down beside him, and told him what I believed to be his chance of life; not concealing from him that I proposed to try, if he gave his consent, a mode of treatment which had never been practised before. His eye, keen and sharp as that of a lynx, seemed to read my thoughts as Dr. Senior's had done.

"Martin Dobrée," he said, in a voice so different from his ordinary caustic tone that it almost startled me, "I can trust you. I put myself with implicit confidence into your hands."

The last chance—dare I say the last hope?—was gone. I stood pledged on my honor as a physician, to employ this discovery, which had been laid open to me by my mother's fatal illness, for the benefit of the man whose life was most harmful to Olivia and myself. I felt suffocated, stifled. I opened the window for a minute or two, and leaned through it to catch the fresh breath of the outer air.

"I must tell you," I said, when I drew my head in again, "that you must not expect to regain your health and strength so completely as to be able to return to your old dissipations. You must make up your mind to lead a regular, quiet, abstemious life, avoiding all excitement. Nine months out of the twelve at least, if not the whole year, you must spend in the country for the sake of fresh air. A life in town would kill you in six months. But if you are careful of yourself you may live to sixty or seventy."

"Life at any price!" he answered, in his old accents, "yet you put it in a dreary light before me. It hardly seems worth while to buy such an existence, especially with that wife of mine downstairs, who cannot endure the country, and is only a companion for a town-life. Now, if it had been Olivia—you could imagine life in the country endurable with Olivia?"

What could I answer to such a question, which ran through me like an electric shock? A brilliant phantasmagoria flashed across my brain—a house in Guernsey with Olivia in it—sunshine—flowers—the singing of birds—the music of the sea—the pure, exhilarating atmosphere. It had vanished into a dead blank before I opened my mouth, though probably a moment's silence had not intervened. Foster's lips were curled into a mocking smile.

"There would be more chance for you now," I said, "if you could have better air than this."

"How can I?" he asked.

"Be frank with me," I answered, "and tell me what your means are. It would be worth your while to spend your last farthing upon this chance."

"Is it not enough to make a man mad," he said, "to know there are thousands lying in the bank in his wife's name, and he cannot touch a penny of it? It is life itself to me; yet I may die like a dog in this hole for the want of it. My death will lie at Olivia's door, curse her!"

He fell back upon his pillows, with a groan as heavy and deep as ever came from the heart of a wretch perishing from sheer want. I could not choose but feel some pity for him; but this was an opportunity I must not miss.

"It is of no use to curse her," I said; "come, Foster, let us talk over this matter quietly and reasonably. If Olivia be alive, as I cannot help hoping she is, your wisest course would be to come to some mutual agreement, which-would release you both from your present difficulties; for you must recollect she is as penniless as yourself. Let me speak to you as if I were her brother. Of this one thing you may be quite certain, she will never consent to return to you; and in that I will aid her to the utmost of my power. But there is no reason why you should not have a good share of the property, which she would gladly relinquish on condition that you left her alone. Now just listen carefully. I think there would be small difficulty, if we set about it, in proving that you were guilty against her with your present wife; and in that case she could claim a divorce absolutely, and her property would remain her own. Your second marriage with the same person would set her free from you altogether."

"You could prove nothing." he replied, fiercely, "and my second marriage is covered by the documents I could produce."

"Which are forged," I said, calmly; "we will find out by whom. You are in a net of your own making. But we do not wish to push this question to a legal issue. Let us come to some arrangement. Olivia will consent to any terms I agree to."

Unconsciously I was speaking as if I knew where Olivia was, and could communicate with her when I chose. I was merely anticipating the time when Tardif felt sure of hearing from her. Foster lay still, watching me with his cold, keen eyes.

"If those letters are forged," he said, uneasily, "it is Olivia who has forged them. But I must consult my lawyers. I will let you know the result in a few days."

But the same evening I received a note, desiring me to go and see him immediately. I was myself in a fever of impatience, and glad at the prospect of any settlement "of this subject, in the hope of setting

Olivia free, as far as she could be free during his lifetime. He was looking brighter and better than in the morning, and an odd smile played now and then about his face as he talked to me, after having desired Mrs. Foster to leave us alone together.

"Mark!" he said, "I have not the slightest reason to doubt Olivia's death, except your own opinion to the contrary, which is founded upon reasons of which I know nothing. But, acting on the supposition that she may be still alive, I am quite willing to enter into negotiations with her, I suppose it must be through you."

"It must," I answered, "and it cannot be at present. You will have to wait for some months, perhaps, while I pursue my search for her. I do not know where she is any more than you do."

A vivid gleam crossed his face at these words, but whether of incredulity or satisfaction I could not tell.

"But suppose I die in the mean time?" he objected.

That objection was a fair and obvious one. His malady would not pause in its insidious attack while I was seeking Olivia. I deliberated for a few minutes, endeavoring to look at a scheme which presented itself to me from every point of view.

"I do not know that I might not leave you in your present position," I said at last; "it may be I am acting from an over-strained sense of duty. But if you will give me a formal deed protecting her from yourself, I am willing to advance the funds necessary to remove you to purer air, and more open quarters than these. A deed of separation, which both of you must sign, can be drawn up, and receive your signature. There will be no doubt as to getting hers, when we find her. But that may be some months hence, as I said. Still I will run the risk."

"For her sake?" he said, with a sneer.

"For her sake, simply," I answered; "I will employ a lawyer to draw up the deed, and as soon as you sign it I will advance the money you require. My treatment of your disease I shall begin at once; that falls, under my duty as your doctor; but I warn you that fresh air and freedom from agitation are almost, if not positively, essential to its success. The sooner you secure these for yourself, the better your chance."

Some further conversation passed between us, as to the stipulations to be insisted upon, and the division of the yearly income from Olivia's property, for I would not agree to her alienating any portion of it. Foster wished to drive a hard bargain, still with that odd smile on his face; and it was after much discussion that we came to an agreement.

I had the deed drawn up by a lawyer, who warned me that, if Foster sued for a restitution of his rights, they would be enforced. But I hoped that when Olivia was found she would have some evidence in her own favor, which would deter him from carrying the case into court. The deed was signed by Foster, and left in my charge till Olivia's signature could be obtained.

As soon as the deed was secured, I had my patient removed from Bellringer Street to some apartments in Fulham, near to Dr. Senior, whose interest in the case was now almost equal to my own. Here, if I could not visit him every day, Dr. Senior did, while his great professional skill enabled him to detect symptoms which might have escaped my less experienced eye. Never had any sufferer, under the highest and wealthiest ranks, greater care and science expended upon him than Richard Foster.

The progress of his recovery was slow, but it was sure. I felt that it would be so from the first. Day by day I watched the pallid hue of sickness upon his face changing into a more natural tone. I saw his strength coming back by slight but steady degrees. The malady was forced to retreat into its most hidden citadel, where it might lurk as a prisoner, but not dwell as a destroyer, for many years to come, if Foster would yield himself to the régime of life we prescribed. But the malady lingered there, ready to break out again openly, if its dungeon-door were set ajar. I had given life to him, but it was his part to hold it fast.

There was no triumph to me in this, as there would have been had my patient been any one else. The cure aroused much interest among my colleagues, and made my name more known. But what was that to me? As long as this man lived, Olivia was doomed to a lonely and friendless life. I tried to look into the future for her, and saw it stretch out into long, dreary years. I wondered where she would find a home. Could I persuade Johanna to receive her into her pleasant dwelling, which would become so lonely to her when Captain Carey had moved into Julia's house in St. Peter-Port? That was the best plan I could form.

CHAPTER THE FORTY-SEVENTH

A FRIENDLY, CABMAN

Julia's marriage arrangements were going on speedily. There was something ironical to me in the chance that made me so often the witness of them. We were so merely cousins again, that she discussed her purchases, and displayed them before me, as if there had never been any notion between us of keeping house together. Once more I assisted in the choice of a wedding-dress, for the one made a year before was said to be yellow and old-fashioned. But this time Julia did not insist upon having white satin. A dainty tint of gray was considered more suitable, either to her own complexion or the age of the bridegroom. Captain Carey enjoyed the purchase with the rapture I had failed to experience.

The wedding was fixed to take place the last week in July, a fortnight earlier than the time proposed; it was also a fortnight earlier than the date I was looking forward to most anxiously, when, if ever, news would reach Tardif from Olivia. All my plans were most carefully made, in the event of her sending word where she was. The deed of separation, signed by Foster, was preserved by me most cautiously, for I had a sort of haunting dread that Mrs. Foster would endeavor to get possession of it. She was eminently sulky, and had been so ever since the signing of the deed. Now that Foster was very near convalescence, they might be trying some stratagem to recover it. But our servants were trustworthy, and the deed lay safe in the drawer of my desk.

At last Dr. Senior agreed with me that Foster was sufficiently advanced on the road to recovery to be removed from Fulham to the better air of the south coast. The month of May had been hotter than usual, and June was sultry. It was evidently to our patient's advantage to exchange the atmosphere of London for that of the sea-shore, even though he had to dispense with our watchful attendance. In fact he could not very well fall back now, with common prudence and self-denial. We impressed upon him the urgent necessity of these virtues, and required Mrs. Foster to write us fully, three times a week, every variation she might observe in his health. After that we started them off to a quiet village in Sussex. I breathed more freely when they were out of my daily sphere of duty.

But before they went a hint of treachery reached me, which put me doubly on my guard. One morning, when Jack and I were at breakfast, each deep in our papers, with an occasional comment to one another on their contents, Simmons, the cabby, was announced, as asking to speak to one or both of us immediately. He was a favorite with Jack, who bade the servant show him in; and Simmons appeared, stroking his hat round and round with his hand, as if hardly knowing what to do with his limbs off the box.

"Nothing amiss with your wife, or the brats. I hope?" said Jack.

"No, Dr. John, no," he answered, "there ain't any thing amiss with them, except being too many of 'em p'raps, and my old woman won't own to that. But there's some thing in the wind as concerns Dr. Dobry, so I thought I'd better come and give you a hint of it."

"Very good, Simmons," said Jack.

"You recollect taking my cab to Gray's-Inn Road about this time last year, when I showed up so green, don't you?" he asked.

"To be sure," I said, throwing down my paper, and listening eagerly.

"Well, doctors," he continued, addressing us both, "the very last Monday as ever was, a lady walks slowly along the stand, eying us all very hard, but taking no heed to any of 'em, till she catches sight of me. That's not a uncommon event, doctors. My wife says there's something about me as gives confidence to her sex. Anyhow, so it is, and I can't gainsay it. The lady comes along very slowly—she looks hard at me—she nods her head, as much as to say, 'You, and your cab, and your horse, are what I'm on the lookout for;' and I gets down, opens the door, and sees her in quite comfortable. Says she, 'Drive me to Messrs. Scott and Brown, in Gray's-Inn Road.'"

"No!" I ejaculated.

"Yes, doctors," replied Simmons. "'Drive me,' she says, 'to Messrs. Scott and Brown, Gray's-Inn Road.' Of course I knew the name again; I was vexed enough the last time I were there, at showing myself so green. I looks hard at her. A very fine make of a woman, with hair and eyes as black as coals, and a impudent look on her face somehow. I turned it over and over again in my head, driving her there—could there be any reason in it? or had it any thing to do with last time? and cetera. She told me to wait for her in the street; and directly after she goes in, there comes down the gent I had seen before, with a pen behind his ear. He looks very hard at me, and me at him. Says he, 'I think I have seen your face before, my man.' Very civil; as civil as a orange, as folks say. 'I think you have,' I says. 'Could you step up-stairs for a minute or two?' says he, very polite; 'I'll find a boy to take charge of your horse.' And he slips a arf-crown into my hand, quite pleasant."

"So you went in, of course?" said Jack.

"Doctors," he answered, solemnly, "I did go in. There's nothing to be said against that. The lady is sitting in a orfice up-stairs, talking to another gent, with hair and eyes like hers, as black as coals, and the same look of brass on his face. All three of 'em looked a little under the weather. 'What's your name, my man?' asked the black gent. 'Walker,' I says. 'And where do you live?' he says, taking me serious. 'In Queer Street,' I says, with a little wink to show 'em I were up to a trick or two. They all three larfed a little among themselves, but not in a pleasant sort of way. Then the gent begins again. 'My good fellow,' he says, 'we want you to give us a little information that 'ud be of use to us, and we are willing to pay you handsome for it. It can't do you any harm, nor nobody else, for it's only a matter of business. You're not above taking ten shillings for a bit of useful information?' 'Not by no manner of means.' I says."

"Go on," I said, impatiently, as Simmons paused to look as hard at us as he had done at these people.

"Jest so doctors," he continued, "but this time I was minding my P's and Q's. 'You know Dr. Senior, of Brook Street?' he says. 'The old doctor?' I says; 'he's retired out of town.' 'No,' he says, 'nor the young doctor neither; but there's another of 'em isn't there?' 'Dr. Dobry?' I says. 'Yes,' he says, 'he often takes your cab, my friend?' 'First one and then the other,' I says, 'sometimes Dr. John and sometimes Dr. Dobry. They're as thick as brothers, and thicker.' 'Good friends of yours?' he says. 'Well,' says I, 'they take my cab when they can have it; but there's not much friendship, as I see, in that. It's the best cab and horse on the stand, though I say it, as shouldn't. Dr. John's pretty fair, but the other's no great favorite of mine.' 'Ah!' he says."

Simmons's face was illuminated with delight, and he winked sportively at us.

"It were all flummery, doctors," he said; "I don't deny as Dr. John is a older friend, and a older favorite; but that is neither here nor there. I jest see them setting a trap, and I wanted to have a finger in it. 'Ah!' he says, 'all we want to know, but we do want to know that very particular, is where you drive Dr. Dobry to the oftenest. He's going to borrow money from us, and we'd like to find out something about his habits; specially where he spends his spare time, and all that sort of thing, you understand. You know where he goes in your cab.' 'Of course I do,' I says; 'I drove him and Dr. John here nigh a twelvemonth ago. The other gent took my number down, and knew where to look for me when you wanted me.' 'You're a clever fellow,' he says. 'So my old woman thinks,' I says. 'And you'd be glad to earn a little more for your old woman?' he says. 'Try me,' I says. 'Well then,' says he, 'here's a offer for you. If you'll bring us word where he spends his spare time, we'll give you ten shillings; and if it turns out of any use to us, well make it five pounds.' 'Very good,' I says. 'You've not got any information to tell us at once?' he says. 'Well, no,' I says, 'but I'll keep my eye upon him now.' 'Stop,' he says, as I were going away; 'they keep a carriage, of course?' 'Of course,' I says; 'what's the good of a doctor that hasn't a carriage and pair?' 'Do they use it at night?' says he. 'Not often,' says I; 'they take a cab; mine if it's on the stand.' 'Very good,' he says; 'good-morning, my friend.' So I come away, and drives back again to the stand."

"And you left the lady there?" I asked, with no doubt in my mind that it was Mrs. Foster.

"Yes, doctor," he answered, "talking away like a poll-parrot with the black-haired gent. That were last Monday; to-day's Friday, and this morning there comes this bit of a note to me at our house in Dawson Street. So my old woman says. 'Jim, you'd better go and show it to Dr. John.' That's what's brought me here at this time, doctors."

He gave the note into Jack's hands; and he, after glancing at it, passed it on to me. The contents were simply these words: "James Simmons is requested to call at No—Gray's-Inn Road, at 6.30 Friday evening." The handwriting struck me as one I had seen and noticed before. I scanned it more closely for a minute or two; then a glimmering of light began to dawn upon my memory. Could it be? I felt almost sure it was. In another minute I was persuaded that it was the same hand as that which had written the letter announcing Olivia's death. Probably if I could see the penmanship of the other partner, I should find it to be identical with that of the medical certificate which had accompanied the letter.

"Leave this note with me, Simmons," I said, giving him half a crown in exchange for it. I was satisfied now that the papers had been forged, but not with Olivia's connivance. Was Foster himself a party to it? Or had Mrs. Foster alone, with the aid of these friends or relatives of hers, plotted and carried out the scheme, leaving him in ignorance and doubt like my own?

CHAPTER THE FORTY-EIGHTH

JULIA'S WEDDING

Before the Careys and Julia returned to Guernsey, Captain Carey came to see me one evening, at our own house in Brook Street. He seemed suffering from some embarrassment and shyness; and I could not for some time lead him to the point he was longing to gain.

"You are quite reconciled to all this, Martin?" he said, stammering. I knew very well what he meant.

"More than reconciled," I answered, "I am heartily glad of it. Julia will make you an excellent wife."

"I am sure of that," he said, simply, "yet it makes me nervous a little at times to think I may be standing in your light. I never thought what it was coming to when I tried to comfort Julia about you, or I would have left Johanna to do it all. It is very difficult to console a person without seeming very fond of them; and then there's the danger of them growing fond of you. I love Julia now with all my heart: but I did not begin comforting her with that view, and I am sure you exonerate me, Martin?"

"Quite, quite," I said, almost laughing at his contrition; "I should never have married Julia, believe me; and I am delighted that she is going to be married, especially to an old friend like you. I shall make your house my home."

"Do, Martin," he answered, his face brightening; "and now I am come to ask you a great favor—a favor to us all."

"I'll do it, I promise that beforehand," I said.

"We have all set our hearts on your being my best man," he replied—"at the wedding, you know. Johanna says nothing will convince the Guernsey people that we are all good friends except that. It will have a queer look, but if you are there everybody will be satisfied that you do not blame either Julia or me. I know it will be hard for you, dear Martin, because of your poor mother, and your father being in Guernsey still; but if you can conquer that, for our sakes, you would make us every one perfectly happy."

I had not expected them to ask this; but, when I came to think of it, it seemed very natural and reasonable. There was no motive strong enough to make me refuse to go to Julia's wedding; so I arranged to be with them the last week in July.

About ten days before going, I ran down to the little village on the Sussex coast to visit Foster, from whom, or from his wife, I had received a letter regularly three times a week. I found him as near complete health as he could ever expect to be, and I told him so; but I impressed upon him the urgent necessity of keeping himself quiet and unexcited. He listened with that cool, taunting sneer which had always irritated me.

"Ah! you doctors are like mothers," he said, "who try to frighten their children with bogies. A doctor is a good crutch to lean upon when one is quite lame, but I shall be glad to dispense with my crutch as soon as my lameness is gone."

"Very good," I replied; "you know your life is of no value to me. I have simply done my duty by you."

"Your mother, Mrs. Dobrée, wrote to me this week." he remarked, smiling as I winced at the utterance of that name; "she tells me there is to be a grand wedding in Guernsey; that of your fiancée, Julia Dobrée, with Captain Carey. You are to be present, so she says."

"Yes," I replied.

"It will be a pleasure to you to revisit your native island," he said, "particularly under such circumstances."

I took no notice of the taunt. My conversation with this man invariably led to full stops. He said something to which silence was the best retort. I did not stay long with him, for the train by which I was to return passed through the village in less than an hour from my arrival. As I walked down the little street I turned round once by a sudden impulse, and saw Foster gazing after me with his pale face and glittering eyes. Ho waved his hand in farewell to me, and that was the last I saw of him.

Some days after this I crossed in the mail-steamer to Guernsey, on a Monday night, as the wedding was to take place at an early hour on Wednesday morning, in time for Captain Carey and Julia to catch the boat to England. The old gray town, built street above street on the rock facing the sea, rose before my eyes, bathed in the morning sunlight. But there was no home in it for me now. The old familiar house in the Grange Road was already occupied by strangers. I did not even know where I was to go. I did not like the idea of staying under Julia's roof, where every thing would remind me of that short spell of happiness in my mother's life, when she was preparing it for my future home. Luckily, before the steamer touched the pier, I caught sight of Captain Carey's welcome face looking out for my appearance. He stood at the end of the gangway, as I crossed over it with my portmanteau.

"Come along, Martin," he said; "you are to go with me to the Vale, as my groomsman, you know. Are all the people staring at us, do you think? I daren't look round. Just look about you for me, my boy."

"They are staring awfully," I answered, "and there are scores of them waiting to shake hands with us."

"Oh, they must not!" he said, earnestly; "look as if you did not see them, Martin. That's the worst of getting married; yet most of them are married themselves, and ought to know better. There's the dog-cart waiting for us a few yards off, if we could only get to it. I have kept my face seaward ever since I came on the pier, with my collar turned up, and my hat over my eyes. Are you sure they see who we are?"

"Sure!" I cried, "why, there's Carey Dobrée, and Dobrée Carey, and Brock de Jersey, and De Jersey le Cocq, and scores of others. They know us as well as their own brothers. We shall have to shake hands with every one of them."

"Why didn't you come in disguise?" asked Captain Carey, reproachfully; but before I could answer I was seized upon by the nearest of our cousins, and we were whirled into a very vortex of greetings and congratulations. It was fully a quarter of an hour before we were allowed to drive off in the dog-cart; and Captain Carey was almost breathless with exhaustion.

"They are good fellows," he said, after a time, "very good fellows, but it is trying, isn't it, Martin? It is as if no man was ever married before; though they have gone through it themselves, and ought to know how one feels. Now you take it quietly, my boy, and you do not know how deeply I feel obliged to you."

There was some reason for me to take it quietly. I could not help thinking how nearly I had been myself in Captain Carey's position. I knew that Julia and I would have led a tranquil, matter-of-fact, pleasant enough life together, but for the unlucky fate that had carried me across to Sark to fall in love with Olivia. There was something enviable in the tranquil prosperity I had forfeited. Guernsey was the dearest spot on earth to me, yet I was practically banished from it. Julia was, beyond all doubt, the woman I loved most, next to Olivia, but she was lost to me. There was no hope for me on the other hand. Foster was well again, and by my means. Probably I might secure peace and comparative freedom for Olivia, but that was all. She could never be more to me than she was now. My only prospect was that of a dreary bachelorhood; and Captain Carey's bashful exultation made the future seem less tolerable to me.

I felt it more still when, after dinner in the cool of the summer evening, we drove lack into town to see Julia for the last time before we met in church the next morning. There was an air of glad excitement pervading the house. Friends were running in, with gifts and pleasant words of congratulation. Julia herself had a peculiar modest stateliness and frank dignity, which suited her well. She was happy and content, and her face glowed. Captain Carey's manner was one of tender chivalry, somewhat old-fashioned. I found it a hard thing to "look at happiness through another man's eyes."

I drove Captain Carey and Johanna home along the low, level shore which I had so often traversed with my heart full of Olivia. It was dusk, the dusk of a summer's night; but the sea was luminous, and Sark lay upon it a bank of silent darkness, sleeping to the music of the waves. A strong yearning came over me, a longing to know immediately the fate of my Olivia. Would to Heaven she could return to Sark, and be cradled there in its silent and isolated dells! Would to Heaven this huge load of anxiety and care for her, which bowed me down, might be taken away altogether!

"A fortnight longer," I said to myself, "and Tardif will know where she is; then I can take measures for her tranquillity and safety in the future."

It was well for me that I had slept during my passage, for I had little sleep during that night. Twice I was aroused by the voice of Captain Carey at my door, inquiring what the London time was, and if I could rely upon my watch not having stopped. At four o'clock he insisted upon everybody in the house getting up. The ceremony was to be solemnized at seven, for the mail-steamer from Jersey to England was due in Guernsey at nine, and there were no other means of quitting the island later in the day. Under these circumstances there could be no formal wedding-breakfast, a matter not much to be regretted. There would not be too much time, so Johanna said, for the bride to change her wedding-dress at her own house for a suitable travelling-costume, and the rest of the day would be our own.

Captain Carey and I were standing at the altar of the old church some minutes before the bridal procession appeared. He looked pale, but wound up to a high pitch of resolute courage. The church was nearly full of eager spectators, all of whom I had known from my childhood—faces that would have crowded about me, had I been standing in the bridegroom's place. Far back, half sheltered by a pillar, I saw the white head and handsome face of my father, with Kate Daltrey by his side; but though the church was so full, nobody had entered the same pew. His name had not been once mentioned in my hearing. As far as his old circle in Guernsey was concerned, Dr. Dobrée was dead.

At length Julia appeared, pale like the bridegroom, but dignified and prepossessing. She did not glance at me; she evidently gave no thought to me. That was well, and as it should be. If any fancy had been lingering in my head that she still regretted somewhat the exchange she had made, that fancy vanished forever. Julia's expression, when Captain Carey drew her hand through his arm, and led her down the aisle to the vestry, was one of unmixed contentment.

Yet there was a pang in it—reason as I would, there was a pang in it for me. I should have liked her to glance once at me, with a troubled and dimmed eye. I should have liked a shade upon her face as I wrote my name below hers in the register. But there was nothing of the kind. She gave me the kiss, which I demanded as her cousin Martin, without embarrassment, and after that she put her hand again upon the bridegroom's arm, and marched off with him to the carriage.

A whole host of us accompanied the bridal pair to the pier, and saw them start off on their wedding-trip, with a pyramid of bouquets before them on the deck of the steamer. We ran round to the light-house, and waved out hats and handkerchiefs as long as they were in sight. That duty done, the rest of the day was our own.

CHAPTER THE FORTY-NINTH

A TELEGRAM IN PATOIS

What a long day it was! How the hours seemed to double themselves, and creep along at the slowest pace they could!

I had had some hope of running over to Sark to see Tardif, but that could not be. I was needed too much by the party that had been left behind by Captain Carey and Julia. We tried to while away the time by a drive round the island, and by visiting many of my old favorite haunts; but I could not be myself.

Everybody rallied me on my want of spirits, but I found it impossible to shake off my depression. I was glad when the day was over, and Johanna and I were left in the quiet secluded house in the Vale, where the moan of the sea sighed softly through the night air.

"This has been a trying day for you, Martin," said Johanna.

"Yes," I answered; "though I can hardly account for my own depression. Johanna, in another fortnight I shall learn where Olivia is. I want to find a home for her. Just think of her desolate position! She has no friends but Tardif and me; and you know how the world would talk if I were too openly her friend. Indeed, I do not wish her to come to live in London; the trial would be too great for me. I could not resist the desire to see her, to speak to her—and that would be fatal to her. Dearest Johanna, I want such a home as this for her."

Johanna made no reply, and I could not see her face in the dim moonlight which filled the room. I knelt down beside her, to urge my petition more earnestly.

"Your name would be such a protection to her." I went on, "this house such a refuge! If my mother were living, I would ask her to receive her. You have been almost as good to me as my mother. Save me, save Olivia from the difficulty I see before us."

"Will you never get over this unfortunate affair?"' she asked, half angrily.

"Never!" I said; "Olivia is so dear to me that I am afraid of harming her by my love. Save her from me, Johanna. You have it in your power. I should be happy if I knew she was here with you. I implore you, for my mother's sake, to receive Olivia into your home."

"She shall come to me," said Johanna, after a few minutes' silence. I was satisfied, though the consent was given with a sigh. I knew that, before long, Johanna would be profoundly attached to my Olivia.

It was almost midnight the next day when I reached Brook Street, where I found Jack expecting my return. He had bought, in honor of it, some cigars of special quality, over which I was to tell him all the story of Julia's wedding. But a letter was waiting for me, directed in queer, crabbed handwriting, and posted in Jersey a week before. It had been so long on the road in consequence of the bad penmanship of the address. I opened it carelessly as I answered Jack's first inquiries; but the instant I saw the signature I held up my hand to silence him. It was from Tardif. This is a translation:

"DEAR DOCTOR AND FRIEND: This day I received a letter from mam'zelle; quite a little letter with only a few lines in it. She says, 'Come to me. My husband has found me; he is here. I have no friends but you and one other, and I cannot send for him. You said you would come to me whenever I wanted you. I have not time to write more. I am in a little village called Ville-en-bois, between Granville and Noireau. Come to the house of the curé; I am there.'

"Behold, I am gone, dear monsieur. I write this in my boat, for we are crossing to Jersey to catch the steamboat to Granville. To-morrow evening I shall be in Ville-en-bois. Will you learn the law of France about this affair? They say the code binds a woman to follow her husband wherever he goes. At London you can learn any thing. Believe me, I will protect mam'zelle, or I should say madame, at the loss of my life. Write to me as soon as you receive this. There will be an inn at Ville-en-bois; direct to me there. Take courage, monsieur. Your devoted TARDIF."

"I must go!" I exclaimed, starting to my feet, about to rush out of the house.

"Where?" cried Jack, catching my arm between both his hands, and holding me fast.

"To Olivia," I answered; "that villain, that scoundrel has hunted her out in Normandy. Read that, Jack. Let me go."

"Stay!" he said; "there is no chance of going so late as this; it is after twelve o'clock. Let us think a few minutes, and look at Bradshaw."

But at that moment a furious peal of the bell rang through the house. We both ran into the hall. The servant had just opened the door, and a telegraph-clerk stood on the steps, with a telegram, which he thrust into his hands. It was directed to me. I tore it open. "From Jean Grimont, Granville, to Dr. Dobrée. Brook Street, London." I did not know any Jean Grimont, of Granville, it was the name of a stranger to me. A message was written underneath in Norman patois, but so mispelt and garbled in its transmission that I could not make out the sense of it. The only words I was sure about were "mam'zelle," "Foster," "Tardif," and "à l'agonie." Who was on the point of death I could not tell.

CHAPTER THE FIRST

OLIVIA'S JUSTIFICATION

I know that in the eyes of the world I was guilty of a great fault—a fault so grave that society condemns it bitterly. How shall I justify myself before those who believe a woman owes her whole self to her husband, whatever his conduct to her may be? That is impossible. To them I merely plead "guilty," and say nothing of extenuating circumstances.

But there are others who will listen, and be sorry for me. There are women like Johanna Carey, who will pity me, and lay the blame where it ought to lie.

I was little more than seventeen when I was married; as mere a child as any simple, innocent girl of seventeen among you. I knew nothing of what life was, or what possibilities of happiness or misery it contained. I married to set away from a home that had been happy, but which had become miserable. This was how it was:

My own mother died when I was too young a child to feel her loss. For many years after that, my father and I lived alone together on one of the great sheep-farms of Adelaide, which belonged to him, and where he made all the fortune that he left me. A very happy life, very free, with no trammels of society and no fetters of custom; a simple, rustic life, which gave me no preparation for the years that came after it.

When I was thirteen my father married again—for my sake, and mine only. I knew afterward that he was already foreseeing his death, and feared to leave me alone in the colony. He thought his second wife would be a mother to me, at the age when I most needed one. He died two years after, leaving me to her care. He died more peacefully than he could have done, because of that. This he said to me the very last day of his life. Ah! I trust the dead do not know the troubles that come to the living. It would have troubled my father—nay, it would have been anguish to him, even in heaven itself, if he could have seen my life after he was gone. It is no use talking or thinking about it. After two wretched years I was only too glad to be married, and get away from the woman who owed almost the duty of a mother to me.

Richard Foster was a nephew of my step-mother, the only man I was allowed to see. He was almost twice my age; but he had pleasant manners, and a smooth, smooth tongue. I believed he loved me, he swore it so often and so earnestly; and I was in sore need of love. I wanted some one to take care of me, and think of me, and comfort me, as my father had been used to do. So much alone, so desolate I had been since his death, no one caring whether I were happy or miserable, ill or well, that I felt grateful to Richard Foster when he said he loved me. He seemed to come in my father's stead, and my step-mother urged and hurried on our marriage, and I did not know what I was doing. The trustees who had charge of my property left me to the care of my father's widow. That was how I came to marry him when I was only a girl of seventeen, with no knowledge of the world but what I had learned on my father's sheep-run.

It was a horrible, shameful thing, if you will only think of it. There was I, an ignorant, unconscious, bewildered girl, with the film of childhood over my eyes still; and there was he, a crafty, unprincipled, double-tongued adventurer, who was in love with my fortune, not with me. As quickly as he could carry me off from my home, and return to his own haunts in Europe, he brought me away from the colony, where all whom I could ever call friends were living. I was utterly alone with him—at his mercy. There was not an ear that I could whisper a complaint to; not one face that would look at me in pity and compassion. My father had been a good man, single-hearted, high-minded, and chivalrous. This man laughed at all honor and conscience scornfully.

I cannot tell you the shock and horror of it. I had not known there were such places and such people in the world, until I was thrust suddenly into the midst of them; innocent at first, like the child I was, but the film soon passed away from my eyes. I grew to loathe myself as well as him. How would an angel feel, who was forced to go down to hell, and become like the lost creatures there, remembering all the time the undefiled heaven he was banished from? I was no angel, but I had been a simple, unsullied, clear-minded girl, and I found myself linked in association with men and women such as frequent the gambling-places on the Continent. For we lived upon the Continent, going from one gambling-place to another. How was a girl like me to possess her own soul, and keep it pure, when it belonged to a man like Richard Foster?

There was one more injury and degradation for me to suffer. I recollect the first moment I saw the woman who wrought me so much misery afterward. We were staying in Homburg for a few weeks at a hotel; and she was seated at a little table in a window, not far from the one where we were sitting. A handsome, bold-looking, arrogant woman. They had known one another years before, it seemed. He said she was his cousin. He left me to go and speak to her, and I watched them, though I did not know then that any thing more would come of it than a casual acquaintance. I saw his face grow animated, and his eyes look into hers, with an expression that stirred something like jealousy within me, if jealousy can exist without love. When he returned to me, he told me he had invited her to join us as my companion. She came to us that evening.

She never left us after that. I was too young, he said, to be left alone in foreign towns while he was attending to his business, and his cousin would be the most suitable person to take care of me. I hated the woman instinctively. She was civil to me just at first, but soon there was open war between us, at which he laughed only; finding amusement for himself in my fruitless efforts to get rid of her. After a while I discovered it could only be by setting myself free from him.

Now judge me. Tell me what I was bound to do. Three voices I hear speak.

One says: "You, a poor hasty girl, very weak yet innocent, ought to have remained in the slough, losing day by day your purity, your worth, your nobleness, till you grew like your companions. You had vowed ignorantly, with a profound ignorance it might be, to obey and honor this man till death parted you. You had no right to break that vow."

Another says: "You should have made of yourself a spy, you should have laid traps; you should have gathered up every scrap of evidence you could find against them, that might have freed you in a court of law."

A third says: "It was right for you, for the health of your soul, and the deliverance of your whole self from an Intolerable bondage, to break the ignorantly-taken vow, and take refuge in flight. No soul can be bound irrevocably to another for its own hurt and ruin."

I listened then, as I should listen now, to the third voice. The chance came to me just before I was one-and-twenty. They were bent upon extorting from me that portion of my father's property which would come to me, and be solely in my own power, when I came of age. It had been settled upon me in such a way, that if I were married my husband could not touch it without my consent.

I must make this quite clear. One-third, of my fortune was so settled that I myself could not take any portion of it save the interest; but the other two-thirds were absolutely mine, whether I was married or single. By locking up one-third, my father had sought to provide against the possibility of my ever being reduced to poverty. The rest was my own, to keep if I pleased; to give up to my husband if I pleased.

At first they tried what fair words and flattery would do with me. Then they changed their tactics. They brought me over to London, where not a creature knew me. They made me a prisoner in dull, dreary rooms, where I had no employment and no resources. That is, the woman did it. My husband, after settling us in a house in London, disappeared, and I saw no more of him. I know now he wished to keep himself irresponsible for my imprisonment. She would have been the scape-goat, had any legal difficulties arisen. He was anxious to retain all his rights over me.

I can see how subtle he was. Though my life was a daily torture, there was positively nothing I could put into words against him—nothing that would have authorized me to seek a legal separation. I did not know any thing of the laws, how should I? except the fact which he dinned into my ears that he could compel me to live with him. But I know now that the best friends in the world could not have saved me from him in any other way than the one I took. He kept within the letter of the law. He forfeited no atom of his claim upon me.

Then God took me by the hand, and led me into a peaceful and untroubled refuge, until I had gathered strength again.

CHAPTER THE SECOND

ON THE WING AGAIN

How should I see that Dr. Martin Dobrée was falling in love with me? I was blind to it; strangely blind those wise people will think, who say a woman always knows when a man loves her. I knew so well that all my life was shut out from the ordinary hopes and prospects of girlhood, that I never realized the fact that to him I was a young girl whom he might love honorably, were he once set free from his engagement to his cousin Julia.

I had not looked for any trouble of that kind. He had been as kind to me as any brother could have been—kind, and chivalrous, and considerate. The first time I saw him I was weak and worn out with great pain, and my mind seemed wandering. His face came suddenly and distinctly before me; a pleasant face, though neither handsome nor regular in features. It possessed great vivacity and movement, changing readily, and always full of expression. He looked at me so earnestly and compassionately, his dark eyes seeming to search for the pain I was suffering, that I felt perfect confidence in him at once. I was vaguely conscious of his close attendance, and unremitting care, during the whole week that I lay ill. All this placed us on very pleasant terms of familiarity and friendship.

How grieved I was when this friendship came to an end—when he confessed his unfortunate love to me—it is impossible for me to say. Such a thought had never crossed my mind. Not until I saw the expression on his face, when he called to us from the shore to wait for him, and waded eagerly through the water to us, and held my hands fast as I helped him into the boat—not till then did I suspect his secret. Poor Martin!

Then there came the moment when I was compelled to say to him. "I was married four years ago, and my husband is still living"—a very bitter moment to me; perhaps more bitter than to him. I knew we must see one another no more; and I who was so poor in friends, lost the dearest of them by those words. That was a great shock to me.

But the next day came the second shock of meeting Kate Daltrey, my husband's half-sister. Martin had told me that there was a person in Guernsey who had traced my flight so far; but in my trouble and sorrow for him, I had not thought much of this intelligence. I saw in an instant that I had lost all again, my safety, my home, my new friends. I must flee once more, alone and unaided, leaving no trace behind me. When old Mother Renouf, whom Tardif had set to watch me for very fear of this mischance, had led me away from Kate Daltrey to the cottage, I sought out Tardif at once.

He was down at the water's edge, mending his boat, which lay with its keel upward. He heard my footsteps among the pebbles, and turned round to greet me with one of his grave smiles, which had never failed me whenever I went to him.

"Mam'zelle is triste," he said; "is there any thing I can do for you?"

"I must go away from here, Tardif," I answered, with a choking voice.

A change swept quickly across his face, but he passed his hand for a moment over it, and then regarded me again with his grave smile.

"For what reason, mam'zelle?" he asked.

"Oh! I must tell you every thing!" I cried.

"Tell me every thing," he repeated; "it shall be buried here, in my heart, as if it was buried in the depths of the sea. I will try not to think of it even, if you bid me. I am your friend as well as your servant."

Then leaning against his boat, for I could not control my trembling, I told him almost all about my wretched life, from which God had delivered me, leading me to him for shelter and comfort. He listened with his eyes cast down, never once raising them to my face, and in perfect silence, except that once or twice he groaned within himself, and clinched his hard hands together. I know that I could never have told my history to any other man as I told it to him, a homely peasant and fisherman, but with as noble and gentle a heart as ever beat.

"You must go," he said, when I had finished. His voice was hollow and broken, but the words were spoken distinctly enough for me to hear them.

"Yes, there is no help for me," I answered; "there is no rest for me but death."

"It would be better to die," he said, solemnly, "than return to a life like that. I would sooner bury you up yonder, in our little graveyard, than give you up to your husband."

"You will help me to get away at once?" I asked.

"At once," he repeated, in the same broken voice. His face looked gray, and his mouth twitched. He leaned against his boat, as if he could hardly stand; as I was doing myself, for I felt utterly weak and shaken.

"How soon?" I asked.

"To-morrow I will row you to Guernsey in time for the packet to England," he answered. Mon Dieu! how little I thought what I was mending my boat for! Mam'zelle, is there nothing, nothing in the world I can do for you?"

"Nothing, Tardif," I said, sorrowfully.

"Nothing!" he assented, dropping his head down upon his hands. No, there was positively nothing he could do for me. There was no person on the face of the earth who could help me.

"My poor Tardif," I said, laying my hand on his shoulder, "I am a great trouble to you."

"I cannot bear to let you go in this way," he replied, without looking up. "If it had been to marry Dr. Martin—why, then—but you have to go alone, poor little child!"

"Yes," I said, "alone."

After that we were both silent for some minutes. We could hear the peaceful lapping of the water at our feet, and its boom against the rocks, and the shrieking of the sea-gulls; but there was utter silence between us two. I felt as if it would break my heart to leave this place, and go whither I knew not. Yet there was no alternative.

"Tardif," I said at last, "I will go first to London. It is so large a place, nobody will find me there. Besides, they would never think of me going back to London. When I am there I will try to get a situation as governess somewhere. I could teach little children; and if I go into a school there will be no one to fall in love with me, like Dr. Martin. I am very sorry for him."

"Sorry for him!" repeated Tardif.

"Yes, very sorry," I replied; "it is as if I must bring trouble everywhere. You are troubled, and I cannot help it."

"I have only had one trouble as great," he said, as if to himself, "and that was when my poor little wife died. I wish to God I could keep you here in safety, but that is impossible."

"Quite impossible," I answered.

Yet it seemed too bad to be true. What had I done, to be driven away from this quiet little home into the cold, wide world? Poor and friendless, after all my father's far-seeing plans and precautions to secure me from poverty and friendlessness! What was to be my lot in that dismal future, over the rough threshold of which I must cross to-morrow?

Tardif and I talked it all over that evening, sitting at the cottage-door until the last gleam of daylight had faded from the sky. He had some money in hand just then, which he had intended to invest the next time he went to Guernsey, and could see his notary. This money, thirty pounds, he urged me to accept as a gift; but I insisted upon leaving with him my watch and chain in pledge, until I could repay the money. It would be a long time before I could do that, I knew; for I was resolved never to return to Richard Foster, and to endure any privation rather than claim my property.

I left Tardif after a while, to pack up my very few possessions. We did not tell his mother that I was going, for he said it would be better not. In the morning he would simply let her know I was going over to Guernsey. No communication had ever passed between the old woman and me except by signs, yet I should miss even her in that cold, careless crowd in which I was about to be lost, in the streets of London.

We started at four in the morning, while the gray sky was dappled over with soft clouds, and the sea itself seemed waking up from sleep, as if it too had been slumbering through the night. The morning mist upon the cliffs made them look mysterious, as if they had some secrets to conceal. Untrodden tracks climbed the surface of the rocks, and were lost in the fine filmy haze. The water looked white and milky, with lines across it like the tracks on the cliffs, which no human foot could tread; and the tide was coming back to the shore with a low, tranquil, yet sad moan. The sea-gulls skimmed past us with their white wings, almost touching us; their plaintive wailing seeming to warn us of the treachery and sorrow of the sea. I was not afraid of the treachery of the sea, yet I could not bear to hear them, nor could Tardif.

We landed at one of the stone staircases running up the side of the pier at Guernsey; for we were only just in time for the steamer. The steps were slimy and wet with seaweed, but Tardif's hand grasped mine firmly. He pushed his way through the crowd of idlers who were watching the lading of the cargo, and took me down immediately into the cabin.

"Good-by, mam'zelle," he said; "I must leave you. Send for me, or come to me, if you are in trouble and I can do any thing for you. If it were to Australia, I would follow you. I know I am only fit to be your servant, but all the same I am your friend. You have a little regard for me, mam'zelle?"

"O Tardif!" I sobbed, "I love you very dearly."

"Now that makes me glad," he said, holding my hand between his, and looking down at me with tears in his eyes; "you said that from your good heart, mam'zelle. When I am out alone in my boat, I shall think of it, and in the long winter nights by the fire, when there is no little mam'zelle to come and talk to me, I shall say to myself, 'She loves you very dearly.' Good-by, mam'zelle. God be with you and protect you!"

"Good-by," I said, with a sore grief in my heart, "good-by, Tardif. It is very dreadful to be alone again."

There was no time to say more, for a bell rang loudly on deck, and we heard the cry, "All friends on shore!" Tardif put his lips to my hand, and left me. I was indeed alone.

CHAPTER THE THIRD

IN LONDON LODGINGS

Once more I found myself in London, a city so strange to me that I did not know the name of any street in it. I had more acquaintance with almost every great city on the Continent. Fortunately, Tardif had given me the address of a boarding-house, or rather a small family hotel, where he had stayed two or three times, and I drove there at once. It was in a quiet back street, within sound of St. Paul's clock. The hour was so late, nearly midnight, that I was looked upon with suspicion, as a young woman travelling alone, and with little luggage. It was only when I mentioned Tardif, whose island bearing had made him noticeable among the stream of strangers passing through the house, that the mistress of the place consented to take me in.

This was my first difficulty, but not the last. By the advice of the mistress of the boarding-house, I went to several governess agencies, which were advertising for teachers in the daily papers. At most of these they would not even enter my name, as soon as I confessed my inability to give one or two references to persons who would vouch for my general character, and my qualifications. This was a fatal impediment, and one that had never occurred to me; yet the request was a reasonable one, even essential. What could be more suspicious than a girl of my age without a friend to give a guarantee of her respectability? There seemed no hope whatever of my entering into the ill-paid ranks of governesses.

When a fortnight had passed with no opening for me, I felt it necessary to leave the boarding-house which had been my temporary home. I must economize my funds, for I did not know how long I must make them hold out. Wandering about the least fashionable suburbs, where lodgings would cost least, I found a bedroom in the third story of a house in a tolerably respectable street. The rent was six shillings a week, to be paid in advance. In this place, I entered upon a new phase of life, so different from that in Sark that, in the delusions which solitude often brings, I could not always believe myself the same person.

A dreamy, solitary, gloomy life; shut in upon myself, with no outlet for association with my fellow creatures. My window opened upon a back-yard, with a row of half-built houses standing opposite to it. These houses had been left half-finished, and were partly falling into ruin. A row of bare, empty window-frames faced me whenever I turned my wearied eyes to the scene without. Not a sound or sign of life was there about them. Within, my room was; small and scantily furnished, yet there was scarcely space enough for me to move about it. There was no table for me to take my meals at, except the top of the crazy chest of drawers, which served as my dressing-table. One chair, broken in the back, and tied together with a faded ribbon, was the only seat, except my box, which, set in a corner where I could lean against the wall, made me the most comfortable place for resting. There was a little rusty grate, but it was still summer-time, and there was no need of a fire. A fire indeed would have been insupportable, for the sultry, breathless atmosphere of August, with the fever-heat of its sun burning in the narrow streets and close yards, made the temperature as parching as an oven. I panted for the cool cliffs and sweet fresh air of Sark.

In this feverish solitude one day dragged itself after another with awful monotony. As they passed by, the only change they brought was that the sultry heat grew ever cooler, and the long days shorter. The winter seemed inclined to set in early, and with unusual rigor, for a month before the usual time fires became necessary. I put off lighting mine, for fear of the cost, until my sunless little room under the roof was almost like an ice-house. A severe cold, which made me afraid of having to call in a doctor, compelled me to have a fire; and the burning of it, and the necessity of tending it, made it like a second person and companion in the lonely place. Hour after hour I sat in front of it on my box, with my elbows on my knees and my chin in my hands, watching the changeful scenery of its embers, and the exquisite motion of the flames, and the upward rolling of the tiny columns of smoke, and the fiery, gorgeous colors that came and went with a breath. To see the tongues of fire lap round the dull, black coal, and run about it, and feel it, and kindle it with burning touches, and never quit it till it was glowing and fervid, and aflame like themselves—that was my sole occupation for hours together.

Think what a dreary life for a young girl! I was as fond of companionship, and needed love, as much as any girl. Was it strange that my thoughts dwelt somewhat dangerously upon the pleasant, peaceful days in Sark?

When I awoke in the morning to a voiceless, solitary, idle day, how could I help thinking of Martin Dobrée, of Tardif, even of old Mother Renouf, with her wrinkled face and her significant nods and becks? Martin Dobrée's pleasant face would come before me, with his eyes gleaming so kindly under his square forehead, and his lips moving tremulously with every change of feeling. Had he gone back to his cousin Julia again, and were they married? I ought not to feel any sorrow at that thought. His path had run side by side with mine for a little while, but always with a great barrier between us; and now they had diverged, and must grow farther and farther apart, never to touch again. Yet, how my father would have loved him had he known him! How securely he would have trusted to his care for me! But stop! There was folly and wickedness in thinking that way. Let me make an end of that.

There was no loneliness like that loneliness. Twice a day I exchanged a word or two with the overworked drudge of a servant in the house where I lived; but I had no other voice to speak to me. No wonder that my imagination sometimes ran in forbidden and dangerous channels.

When I was not thinking and dreaming thus, a host of anxieties crowded about me. My money was melting away again, though slowly, for I denied myself every thing but the bare necessaries of life. What was to become of me when it was all gone? It was the old question; but the answer was as difficult to find as ever. I was ready for any kind of work, but no chance of work came to me. With neither work nor money, what was I to do? What was to be the end of it?

CHAPTER THE FOURTH

RIDLEY'S AGENCY-OFFICE

Now and then, when I ventured out into the streets, a panic would seize me, a dread unutterably great, that I might meet my husband amid the crowd. I did not even know that he was in London; he had always spoken of it as a place he detested. His habits made the free, unconventional life upon the Continent more agreeable to him. How he was living now, what he was doing, where he was, were so many enigmas to me; and I did not care to run any risk in finding out the answers to them. Twice I passed the Bank of Australia, where very probably. I could have learned if he was in the same city as myself; but I dared not do it, and as soon as I knew how to avoid that street, I never passed along it.

I had been allowed to leave my address with the clerk of a large general agency in the city, when I had not been permitted to enter my name in the books for want of a reference. Toward the close of October I received a note from him, desiring me to call at the office at two o'clock the following afternoon, without fail.

No danger of my failing to keep such an appointment! I felt in better spirits that night than I had done since I had been driven from Sark. There was an opening for me, a chance of finding employment, and I resolved beforehand to take it, whatever it might be.

It was an agency for almost every branch of employment not actually menial, from curates to lady's-maids, and the place of business was a large one. There were two entrances, and two distinct compartments, at the opposite ends of the building; but a broad, long counter ran the whole length of it, and a person at one end could see the applicants at the other as they stood by the counter. The compartment into which I entered was filled with a crowd of women, waiting their turn to transact their business. Behind the counter were two or three private boxes, in which employers might see the candidates, and question them on the spot. A lady was at that moment examining a governess, in a loud, imperious voice which we could all hear distinctly. My heart sank at the idea of passing through such a cross-examination as to my age, my personal history, my friends, and a number of particulars foreign to the question of whether I was fit for the work I offered myself for.

At last I heard the imperious voice say, "You may go. I do not think you will suit me," and a girl of about my own age came away from the interview, pale and trembling, and with tears stealing down her cheeks. A second girl was summoned to go through the same ordeal.

What was I to do if this person, unseen in her chamber of torture, was the lady I had been summoned to meet?

It was a miserable sight, this crowd of poor women seeking work, and my spirits sank like lead. A set of mournful, depressed, broken-down women! There was not one I would have chosen to be a governess for my girls. Those who were not dispirited were vulgar and self-asserting; a class that wished to rise above the position they were fitted for by becoming teachers. These were laughing loudly among themselves at the cross-questioning going on so calmly within their hearing. I shrank away into a corner, until my turn to speak to the busy clerk should come.

I had a long time to wart. The office clock pointed to half-past three before I caught the clerk's eye, and saw him beckon me up to the counter. I had thrown back my veil, for here I was perfectly safe from recognition. At the other end of the counter, in the compartment devoted to curates, doctors' assistants, and others, there stood a young man in earnest consultation with another clerk. He looked earnestly at me, but I was sure he could not know me.

"Miss Ellen Martineau?" said the clerk. That was my mother's name, and I had adopted it for my own, feeling as if I had some right to it.

"Yes," I answered.

"Would you object to go into a French school as governess?" he inquired.

"Not in the least," I said, eagerly.

"And pay a small premium?" he added. "How much?" I asked, my spirits falling again.

"A mere trifle," he said; "about ten pounds or so for twelve months. You would perfect yourself in French, you know; and you would gain a referee for the future."

"I must think about it," I replied.

"Well, there is the address of a lady who can give you all the particulars," he said, handing me a written paper.

I left the office heavy-hearted. Ten pounds would be more than the half of the little store left to me. Yet, would it not be wiser to secure a refuge and shelter for twelve months than run the risk of hearing of some other situation? I walked slowly along the street toward the busier thoroughfares, with my head bent down and my mind busy, when suddenly a heavy hand was laid upon my arm, grasping it with crushing force, and a harsh, thick voice shouted triumphantly in my ear:

"The devil! I've caught you at last!"

It was like the bitterness of death, that chill and terror sweeping over me. My husband's hot breath was upon my cheek, and his eyes were looking closely into mine. But before I could speak his grasp was torn away from me, and he was sent whirling into the middle of the road. I turned, almost in equal terror, to see who had thrust himself between us. It was the stranger whom I had seen in the agency-office. But his face was now dark with passion, and as my husband staggered back again toward us, his hand was ready to thrust him away a second time.

"She's my wife," he stammered, trying to get past the stranger to me. By this time a knot of spectators had formed about us, and a policeman had come up. The stranger drew my arm through his, and faced them defiantly.

"He's a drunken vagabond!" he said; "he has just come out of those spirit-vaults. This young lady is no more his wife than she is mine, and I know no more of her than that she has just come away from Ridley's office, where she has been looking after a situation. Good Heavens! cannot a lady walk through the streets of London without being insulted by a drunken scoundrel like that"?"

"Will you give him in charge, sir?" asked the policeman, while Richard Foster was making vain efforts to speak coherently, and explain his claim upon me. I clung to the friendly arm that had come to my aid, sick and almost speechless with fear.

"Shall I give him in charge?" he asked me.

"I have only just heard of a situation," I whispered, unable to speak aloud.

"And you are afraid of losing it?" he said; "I understand—Take the fellow away, policeman, and lock him up if you can for being drunk and disorderly in the streets; but the lady won't give him in charge. I've a good mind to make him go down on his knees and beg her pardon."

"Do, do!" said two or three voices in the crowd.

"Don't," I whispered again, "oh! take me away quickly."

He cleared a passage for us both with a vigor and decision that there was no resisting. I glanced back for an instant, and saw my husband struggling with the policeman, the centre of the knot of bystanders from which I was escaping. He looked utterly unlike a gay, prosperous, wealthy man, with a well-filled purse, such as he had used to appear. He was shabby and poor enough now for the policeman to be very hard upon him, and to prevent him from following me. The stranger kept my hand firmly on his arm, and almost carried me into Fleet Street, where, in a minute or two we were quite lost in the throng, and I was safe from all pursuit.

"You are not fit to go on," he said, kindly; "come out of the noise a little."

He led me down a covered passage between two shops, into a quiet cluster of squares and gardens, where only a subdued murmur of the uproar of the streets reached us. There were a sufficient number of passers-by to prevent it seeming lonely, but we could hear our own voices, and those of others, even in whispers.

"This is the Temple," he said, smiling, "a fit place for a sanctuary."

"I do not know how to thank you," I answered falteringly.

"You are trembling still!" he replied; "how lucky it was that I followed you directly out of Ridley's! If I ever come across that scoundrel again, I shall know him, you may be sure. I wish we were a little nearer home, you should go in to rest; but our house is in Brook Street, and we have no women-kind belonging to us. My name is John Senior. Perhaps you have heard of my father, Dr. Senior, of Brook Street?"

"No." I replied, "I know nobody in London."

"That's bad," he said. "I wish I was Jane Senior instead of John Senior; I do indeed. Do you feel better now, Miss Martineau?"

"How do you know my name?" I asked.

"The clerk at Ridley's called you Miss Ellen Martineau," he answered. "My hearing is very good, and I was not deeply engrossed in my business. I heard and saw a good deal while I was there, and I am very glad I heard and saw you. Do you feel well enough now for me to see you home?"

"Oh! I cannot let you see me home," I said, hurriedly.

"I will do just what you like best." he replied. "I have no more right to annoy you than that drunken vagabond had. If I did, I should be more blamable than he was. Tell me what I shall do for you then. Shall I call a cab?"

I hesitated, for my funds were low, and would be almost spent by the time I had paid the premium of ten pounds, and my travelling expenses; yet I dared not trust myself either in the streets or in an omnibus. I saw my new friend regard me keenly; my dress, so worn and faded, and my old-fashioned bonnet. A smile flickered across his face. He led me back into Fleet Street, and called an empty cab that was passing by. We shook hands warmly. There was no time for loitering; and I told him the name of the suburb where I was living, and he repeated it to the cabman.

"All right," he said, speaking through the window, "the fare is paid, and I've taken cabby's number. If he tries to cheat you, let me know; Dr. John Senior, Brook Street. I hope that situation will be a good one, and very pleasant. Good-by."

"Good-by," I cried, leaning forward and looking at his face till the crowd came between us, and I lost sight of it. It was a handsomer face than Dr. Martin Dobrée's, and had something of the same genial, vivacious light about it. I knew it well afterward, but I had not leisure to think much of it then.

CHAPTER THE FIFTH

BELLRINGER STREET

I was still trembling with the terror that my meeting with Richard Foster had aroused. A painful shuddering agitated me, and my heart fluttered with an excess of fear which I could not conquer. I could still feel his grasp upon my arm, where the skin was black with the mark; and there was before my eyes the sight of his haggard and enraged face, as he struggled to get free from the policeman. When he was sober would he recollect all that had taken place, and go to make inquiries after me at Ridley's agency-office? Dr. John Senior had said he had followed me from there. I scarcely believed he would. Yet there was a chance of it, a deadly chance to me. If so, the sooner I could fly from London and England the better.

I felt safer when the cabman set me down at the house where I lodged, and I ran up-stairs to my little room. I kindled the fire, which had gone out during my absence, and set my little tin tea-kettle upon the first clear flame which burned up amid the coal. Then I sat down on my box before it, thinking.

Yes; I must leave London. I must take this situation, the only one open to me, in a school in France. I should at least be assured of a home for twelve months; and, as the clerk had said, I should perfect myself in French and gain a referee. I should be earning a character, in fact. At present I had none, and so was poorer than the poorest servant-maid. No character, no name, no money; who could be poorer than the daughter of the wealthy colonist, who had owned thousands of acres in Adelaide? I almost laughed and cried hysterically at the thought of my father's vain care and provision for my future.

But the sooner I fled from London again the better, now that I knew my husband was somewhere in it and might be upon my track. I unfolded the paper on which was written the name of the lady to whom I was to apply. Mrs. Wilkinson. 19 Bellringer Street. I ran down to the sitting-room, to ask my landlady where it was, and told her, in my new hopefulness, that I had heard of a situation in France. Bellringer Street was less than a mile away, she said. I could be there before seven o'clock, not too late perhaps for Mrs. Wilkinson to give me an interview.

A thick yellow fog had come in with nightfall—a fog that could almost be tasted and smelt—but it did not deter me from my object. I inquired my way of every policeman I met, and at length entered the street. The fog hid the houses from my view, but I could see that some of the lower windows were filled with articles for sale, as if they were shops struggling into existence. It was not a fashionable street, and Mrs. Wilkinson could not be a very aristocratic person.

No. 19 was not difficult to find, and I pulled the bell-handle with a gentle and quiet pull, befitting my errand. I repeated this several times without being admitted, when it struck me that the wire might be broken. Upon that I knocked as loudly as I could upon the panels of the broad old door; a handsome, heavy door, such as are to be found in the old streets of London, from which the tide of fashion has ebbed away. A slight, thin child in rusty mourning opened it, with the chain across, and asked who I was in a timid voice.

"Does Mrs. Wilkinson live here?" I asked.

"Yes," said the child.

"Who is there?" I heard a voice calling shrilly from within; not an English voice, I felt sure, for each word was uttered distinctly and slowly.

"I am come about a school in France," I said to the child.

"Oh! I'll let you in," she answered, eagerly; "she will see you about that, I'm sure. I'm to go with you, if you go."

She let down the chain, and opened the door. There was a dim light burning in the hall, which looked shabby and poverty-stricken. There was no carpet upon the broad staircase, and nothing but worn-out oil-cloth on the floor. I had only time to take in a vague general impression, before the little girl conducted me to a room on the ground-floor. That too was uncarpeted and barely furnished; but the light was low, and I could see nothing distinctly, except the face of the child looking wistfully at me with shy curiosity.

"I'm to go if you go," she said again; "and, oh! I do so hope you will agree to go."

"I think I shall," I answered.

"I daren't be sure," she replied, nodding her head with an air of sagacity; "there have been four or five governesses here, and none of them would go. You'd have to take me with you; and, oh! it is such a lovely, beautiful place. See! here is a picture of it."

She ran eagerly to a side-table, on which lay a book or two, one of which she opened, and reached out a photograph, which had been laid there for security. When she brought it to me, she stood leaning lightly against me as we both looked at the same picture. It was a clear, sharply-defined photograph, with shadows so dark yet distinct as to show the clearness of the atmosphere in which it had been taken. At the left hand stood a handsome house, with windows covered with lace curtains, and provided with outer Venetian shutters. In the centre stood a large square garden, with fountains, and arbors, and statues, in the French style of gardening, evidently well kept; and behind this stood a long building of two stories, and a steep roof with dormer windows, every casement of which was provided, like the house in the front, with rich lace curtains and Venetian shutters. The whole place was clearly in good order and good taste, and looked like a very pleasant home. It would probably be my home for a time, and I scrutinized it the more closely. Which of those sunny casements would be mine? What nook in that garden would become my favorite? If I could only get there undetected, how secure and happy I might be!

Above the photograph was written in ornamental characters, "Pensionnat de Demoiselles, à Noireau, Calvados." Underneath it were the words, "Fondé par M. Emile Perrier, avocat, et par son épouse." Though I knew very little of French, I could make out the meaning of these sentences. Monsieur Perrier was an avocat. Tardif had happened to speak to me about the notaries in Guernsey, who appeared to me to be of the same rank as our solicitors, while the avocats were on a par with our barristers. A barrister founding a boarding-school for young ladies might be somewhat opposed to English customs, but it was clear that he must be a man of education and position; a gentleman, in fact.

"Isn't it a lovely place?" asked the child beside me, with a deep sigh of longing.

"Yes," I said; "I should like to go."

I had had time to make all these observations before the owner of the foreign voice, which I had heard at the door, came in. At the first glance I knew her to be a Frenchwoman, with the peculiar yellow tone in her skin which seems inevitable in middle-aged Frenchwomen. Her black eyes were steady and cold, and her general expression one of watchfulness. She had wrapped tightly about her a China crape shawl, which had once been white, but had now the same yellow tint as her complexion. The light was low, but she turned it a little higher, and scrutinized me with a keen and steady gaze.

"I have not the honor of knowing you," she said politely.

"I come from Ridley's agency-office," I answered, "about a situation as English teacher in a school in France."

"Be seated, miss," she said, pointing me to a stiff, high-backed chair, whither the little girl followed me, stroking with her hand the soft seal-skin jacket I was wearing.

"It is a great chance," she continued; "my friend Madame Perrier is very good, very amiable for her teachers. She is like a sister for them. The terms are very high, very high for France; but there is absolutely every comfort. The arrangements are precisely like England. She has lived in England for two years, and knows what English young ladies look for; and the house is positively English. I suppose you could introduce a few English pupils."

"No," I answered, "I am afraid I could not. I am sure I could not."

"That of course must be considered in the premium," she continued; "if you could have introduced, say, six pupils, the premium would be low. I do not think my friend would take one penny less than twenty pounds for the first year, and ten for the second."

The tears started to my eyes. I had felt so sure of going if I would pay ten pounds, that I was quite unprepared for this disappointment. There was still my diamond ring left; but how to dispose of it, for any thing like its value, I did not know. It was in my purse now, with all my small store of money, which I dared not leave behind me in my lodgings.

"What were you prepared to give?" asked Mrs. Wilkinson, while I hesitated.

"The clerk at Ridley's office told me the premium would be ten pounds," I answered;

"I do not see how I can give more."

"Well," she said, after musing a little, while I watched her face anxiously, "it is time this child went. She has been here a month, waiting for somebody to take her down to Noireau. I will agree with you, and will explain it to Madame Perrier. How soon could you go?"

"I should like to go to-morrow," I replied, feeling that the sooner I quitted London the better. Mrs. Wilkinson's steady eyes fastened upon me again with sharp curiosity.

"Have you references, miss?" she asked.

"No," I faltered, my hope sinking again before this old difficulty.

"It will be necessary then," she said, "for you to give the money to me, and I will forward it to Madame Perrier. Pardon, miss, but you perceive I could not send a teacher to them unless I knew that she could pay the money down. There is my commission to receive the money for my friend."

She gave me a paper written in French, of which I could read enough to see that it was a sort of official warrant to receive accounts for Monsieur Perrier, avocat, and his wife. I did not waver any longer. The prospect seemed too promising for me to lose it by any irresolution. I drew out my purse, and laid down two out of the three five-pound notes left me. She gave me a formal receipt in the names of Emile and Louise Perrier, and her sober face wore an expression of satisfaction.

"There! it is done," she said, wiping her pen carefully. "You will take lessons, any lessons you please, from the professors who attend the school. It is a grand chance, miss, a grand chance. Let us say you go the day after to-morrow; the child will be quite ready. She is going for four years to that splendid place, a place for ladies of the highest degree."

At that moment an imperious knock sounded upon the outer door, and the little girl ran to answer it, leaving the door of our room open. A voice which I knew well, a voice which made my heart stand still and my veins curdle, spoke in sharp loud tones in the hall.

"Is Mr. Foster come home yet?" were the words the terrible voice uttered, quite close to me it seemed; so close that I shrank back shivering as if every syllable struck a separate blow. All my senses were awake: I could hear every sound in the hall, each step that came nearer and nearer. Was she about to enter the room where I was sitting? She stood still for half a minute as if uncertain what to do.

"He is up stairs," said the child's voice. "He told me he was ill when I opened the door for him."

"Where is Mrs. Wilkinson?" she asked.

"She is here," said the child, "but there's a lady with her."

Then the woman's footsteps went on up the staircase. I listened to them climbing up one step after another, my brain throbbing with each sound, and I heard a door opened and closed. Mrs. Wilkinson had gone to the door, and looked out into the hall, as if expecting some other questions to be asked. She had not seen my panic of despair. I must get away before I lost the use of my senses, for I felt giddy and faint.

"I will send the child to you in a cab on Wednesday," she said, as I stood up and made my way toward the hall; "you have not told me your address."

I paused for a moment. Dared I tell her my address? Yet my money was paid, and if I did not I should lose both it and the refuge I had bought with it. Besides, I should awaken suspicion and inquiry by silence. It was a fearful risk to run; yet it seemed safer than a precipitous retreat. I gave her my address, and saw her write it down on a slip of paper.

As I returned to my lodgings I grew calmer and more hopeful. It was not likely that my husband would see the address, or even hear that any one like me had been at the house. I did not suppose he would know the name of Martineau as my mother's maiden name. As far as I recollected, I had never spoken of her to him. Moreover he was not a man to make himself at all pleasant and familiar with persons whom he looked upon as inferiors. It was highly improbable that he would enter into any conversation with his landlady. If that woman did so, all she would learn would be that a young lady, whose name was Martineau, had taken a situation as English teacher in a French school. What could there be in that to make her think of me?

I tried to soothe and reassure myself with these reasonings, but I could not be quiet or at peace. I watched all through the next day, listening to every sound in the house below; but no new terror assailed me. The second night I was tranquil enough to sleep.

CHAPTER THE SIXTH

LEAVING ENGLAND

I was on the rack all the next day. It was the last day I should be in England, and I had a nervous dread of being detained. If I should once more succeed in quitting the country undetected, it seemed as though I might hope to be in safety in Calvados. Of Calvados I knew even less than of the Channel Islands; I had never heard the name before. But Mrs. Wilkinson had given me the route by which we were to reach Noireau: by steamer to Havre, across the mouth of the Seine to Honfleur, to Falaise by train, and finally from Falaise to Noireau by omnibus. It was an utterly unknown region to me; and I had no reason to imagine that Richard Foster was better acquainted with it than I. My anxiety was simply to get clear away.

In the afternoon the little girl arrived quite alone, except that a man had been hired to carry a small box for her, and to deliver her into my charge. This was a great relief to me, and I paid the shilling he demanded gladly. The child was thinly and shabbily dressed for our long journey, and there was a forlorn loneliness about her position, left thus with a stranger, which touched me to the heart. We were alike poor, helpless, friendless—I was about to say childish, and in truth I was in many things little more than a child still. The small elf, with her sharp, large eyes, which were too big for her thin face, crept up to me, as the man slammed the door after him and clattered noisily downstairs.

"I'm so glad!" she said, with a deep-drawn sigh of relief; "I was afraid I should never go, and school is such a heavenly place!"

The words amused yet troubled me; they were so different from a child's ordinary opinion.

"It's such a hateful place at Mrs. Wilkinson's," she went on, "everybody calling me at once, and scolding me; and there are such a many people to run errands for. You don't know what it is to run errands when you are tired to death. And it's such a beautiful, splendid place where we're going to!"

"What is your name, my dear?" I asked, sitting down on my box and taking her on my lap. Such a thin, stunted little woman, precociously learned in trouble! Yet she nestled in my arms like a true child, and a tear or two rolled down her cheeks, as if from very contentment.

"Nobody has nursed me like this since mother died," she said. "I'm Mary; but father always called me Minima, because I was the least in the house. He kept a boys' school out of London, in Epping Forest, you know; and it was so heavenly! All the boys were good to me, and we used to call father Dominie. Then he died, and mother died just before him; and he said, 'Courage, Minima! God will take care of my little girl.' So the boys' fathers and mothers made a subscription for me, and they got a great deal of money, a hundred pounds; and somebody told them about this school, where I can stay four years for a hundred pounds, and they all said that was the best thing they could do with me. But I've had to stay with Mrs. Wilkinson nearly two months, because she could not find a governess to go with me. I hate her; I detest her; I should like to spit at her!"

The little face was all aflame, and the large eyes burning.

"Hush! hush!" I said, drawing her head down upon my shoulder again.

"Then there is Mr. Foster," she continued, almost sobbing; "he torments me so. He likes to make fun of me, and tease me, till I can't bear to go into his room. Father used to say it was wicked to hate anybody, and I didn't hate anybody then. I was so happy. But you'd hate Mr. Foster, and Mrs. Foster, if you only knew them."

"Why?" I asked in a whisper. My voice sounded husky to me, and my throat felt parched. The child's impotent rage and hatred struck a slumbering chord within me.

"Oh! they are horrid in every way," she said, with emphasis; "they frighten me. He is fond of tormenting any thing because he's cruel. We had a cruel boy in our school once, so I know. But they are very poor—poor as Job, Mrs. Wilkinson says, and I'm glad. Aren't you glad?"

The question jarred in my memory against a passionate craving after revenge, which had died away in the quiet and tranquillity of Sark. A year ago I should have rejoiced in any measure of punishment or retribution, which had overtaken those who had destroyed my happiness. But it was not so now; or perhaps I should rather own that it was only faintly so. It had never occurred to me that my flight would plunge him into poverty similar to my own. But now that the idea was thrust upon me. I wondered how I could have overlooked this necessary consequence of my conduct. Ought I to do any thing for him? Was there any thing I could do to help him?"

"He is ill, too," pursued the child; "I heard him say once to Mrs. Foster, he knew he should die like a dog. I was a little tiny bit sorry for him then; for nobody would like to die like a dog, and not go to heaven, you know. But I don't care now, I shall never see them again—never, never! I could jump out of my skin for joy. I sha'n't even know when he is dead, if he does die like a dog."

Ill! dead! My heart beat faster and faster as I pondered over these words. Then I should be free indeed; his death would release me from bondage, from terror, from poverty—those three evils which dogged my steps. I had never ventured to let my thoughts run that way, but this child's prattling had forced them into it. Richard Foster ill—dying! O God! what ought I to do?

I could not make myself known to him; that was impossible. I would ten thousand times sooner die myself than return to him. He was not alone either. But yet there came back to my mind the first days when I knew him, when he was all tenderness and devotion to me, declaring that he could find no fault in his girl-wife. How happy I had been for a little while, exchanging my stepmother's harshness for his indulgence! He might have won my love; he had almost won it. But that happy, golden time was gone, and could never come back to me. Yet my heart was softened toward him, as I thought of him ill, perhaps dying. What could I do for him, without placing myself in his power?

There was one thing only that I could do, only one little sacrifice I could make for him whom I had vowed, in childish ignorance, to love, honor, and cherish in sickness and in health, until death parted us. A home was secured to me for twelve months, and at the end of that time I should have a better career open to me. I had enough money still to last me until then. My diamond ring, which had been his own gift to me on our wedding-day, would be valuable to him. Sixty pounds would be a help to him, if he were as poor as this child said. He must be poor, or he would never have gone to live in that mean street and neighborhood.

Perhaps—if he had been alone—I do not know, but possibly if he had been quite alone, ill, dying in that poor lodging of his, I might have gone to him. I ask myself again, could you have done this thing? But I cannot answer it even to myself. Poor and ill he was, but he was not alone.

It was enough for me, then, that I could do something, some little service for him. The old flame of vengeance had no spark of heat left in it. I was free from hatred of him. I set the child gently away from me, and wrote my last letter to my husband. Both the letter and the ring I enclosed in a little box. These are the words I wrote, and I put neither date nor name of place:

"I know that you are poor, and I send you all I can spare—the ring you once gave to me. I am even poorer than yourself, but I have just enough for my immediate wants. I forgive you, as I trust God forgives me."

I sat looking at it, thinking of it for some time. There was a vague doubt somewhere in my mind that this might work some mischief. But at last I decided that it should go. I must register the packet at a post-office on our way to the station, and it could not fail to reach him.

This business settled, I returned to the child, who was sitting, as I had so often, done, gazing pensively into the fire. Was she to be a sort of miniature copy of myself?

"Come, Minima," I said, "we must be thinking of tea. Which would you like best, buns, or cake, or bread-and-butter? We must go out and buy them, and you shall choose."

"Which would cost the most?" she asked, looking at me with the careworn expression of a woman. The question sounded so oddly, coming from lips so young, that it grieved me. How bitterly and heavily must the burden of poverty have already fallen upon this child! I was almost afraid to think what it must mean. I put my arm round her, pressing my cheek against hers, while childish visions, more childish than any in this little head, flitted before me, of pantomimes, and toys, and sweetmeats, and the thousand things that children love. If I had been as rich as my father had planned for me to be, how I would have lavished them upon this anxious little creature!

We were discussing this question with befitting gravity, when a great thump against the door brought a host of fears upon me. But before I could stir the insecure handle gave way, and no one more formidable appeared than the landlady of the house, carrying before her a tray on which was set out a sumptuous tea, consisting of buttered crumpets and shrimps. She put it down on my dressing-table, and stood surveying it and us with an expression of benign exultation, until she had recovered her breath sufficiently to speak.

"Those as are going into foring parts," she said, "ought to get a good English meal afore they start. If you was going to stay in England, miss, it would be quite a differing thing; but me and my master don't know what they may give you to eat where you're going to. Therefore we beg you'll accept of the crumpets, and the shrimps, and the bread-and-butter, and the tea, and every thing; and we mean no offence by it. You've been a very quiet, regular lodger, and give no trouble; and we're sorry to lose you. And this, my master says, is a testimonial to you."

I could hardly control my laughter, and I could not keep back my tears. It was a long time now since any one had shown me so much kindness and sympathy as this. The dull face of the good woman was brightened by her kind-hearted feeling, and instead of thanking her I put my lips to her cheek.

"Lor!" she exclaimed, "why! God bless you, my dear! I didn't mean any offence, you know. Lor! I never thought you'd pay me like that. It's very pretty of you, it is; for I'm sure you're a lady to the backbone, as often and often I've said to my master. Be good enough to eat it all, you and the little miss, for you've a long journey before you. God bless you both, my dears, and give you a good appetite!"

She backed out of the room as she was speaking, her face beaming upon us to the last.

There was a pleasant drollery about her conduct, and about the intense delight of the child, and her hearty enjoyment of the feast, which for the time effectually dissipated my fears and my melancholy thoughts. It was the last hour I should spend in my solitary room; my lonely days were past. This little elf, with her large sharp eyes, and sagacious womanly face, was to be my companion for the future. I felt closely drawn to her. Even the hungry appetite with which she ate spoke of the hard times she had gone through. When she had eaten all she could eat, I heard her say softly to herself, "Courage, Minima!"

CHAPTER THE SEVENTH

A LONG JOURNEY

It as little more than twelve months since I had started from the same station on the same route; but there was no Tardif at hand now. As I went into the ticket-office, Minima caught me by the dress and whispered earnestly into my ear.

"We're not to travel first-class," she said; "it costs too much. Mrs. Wilkinson said we ought to go third, if we could; and you're to pay for me, please, only half-price, and they'll pay you again when we reach the school. I'll come with you, and then they'll see I'm only half-price. I don't look too old, do I?"

"You look very old," I answered, smiling at her anxious face.

"Oh, dear, dear!" she said; "but I sit very small. Perhaps I'd better not come to the ticket-office; the porters are sure to think me only a little girl."

She was uneasy until we had fairly started from the station, her right to a half-ticket unchallenged.

The November night was cold and foggy, and there was little difference between the darkness of the suburbs and the darkness of the open country.

Once again the black hulls and masts of two steamers stood before us, at the end of our journey, and hurrying voices shouted, "This way for Jersey and Guernsey," "This way to Havre." What would I not have given to return to Sark, to my quiet room under Tardif's roof, with his true heart and steadfast friendship to rest upon! But that could not be. My feet were setting out upon a new track, and I did not know where the hidden path would lead me.

The next morning found us in France. It was a soft, sunny day, with a mellow light, which seemed to dwell fondly on the many-tinted leaves of the trees which covered the banks of the Seine. From Honfleur to Falaise the same warm, genial sunshine filled the air. The slowly-moving train carried us through woods where the autumn seemed but a few days old, and where the slender leaflets of the acacias still fluttered in the caressing breath of the wind. We passed through miles upon miles of orchards, where a few red leaves were hanging yet upon the knotted branches of the apple-trees, beneath which lay huge pyramids of apples. Truck-loads of them stood at every station. The air was scented by them. Children were pelting one another with them; and here and there, where the orchards had been cleared and the trees stripped, flocks of geese were searching for those scattered among the tufts of grass. The roses were in blossom, and the chrysanthemums were in their first glory. The few countrywomen who got into our carriage were still wearing their snowy muslin caps, as in summer. Nobody appeared cold and pinched yet, and everybody was living out-of-doors.

It was almost like going into a new world, and I breathed more freely the farther we travelled down into the interior. At Falaise we exchanged the train for a small omnibus, which bore the name "Noireau" conspicuously on its door. I had discovered that the little French I knew was not of much service, as I could in no way understand the rapid answers that were given to my questions. A woman came to us, at the door of a café, where the omnibus stopped in Falaise, and made a long and earnest harangue, of which I did not recognize one word. At length we started off on the last stage of our journey.

Where could we be going to? I began to ask myself the question anxiously after we had crept on, at a dog-trot, for what seemed an interminable time. We had passed through long avenues of trees, and across a series of wide, flat plains, and down gently-sloping roads into narrow valleys, and up the opposite ascents; and still the bells upon the horses' collars jingled sleepily, and their hoof-beats shambled along the roads. We were seldom in sight of any house, and we passed through very few villages. I felt as if we were going all the way to Marseilles.

"I'm so hungry!" said Minima, after a very long silence.

I too had been hungry for an hour or two past. We had breakfasted at mid-day at one of the stations, but we had had nothing to eat since, except a roll which Minima had brought away from breakfast, with wise prevision; but this had disappeared long ago.

"Try to go to sleep," I said; "lean against me. We must be there soon."

"Yes," she answered, "and it's such a splendid school! I'm going to stay there four years, you know, so it's foolish to mind being hungry now. 'Courage, Minima!' I must recollect that."

"Courage, Olivia!" I repeated to myself. "The farther you go, the more secure will be your hiding-place." The child nestled against me, and soon fell asleep. I went to sleep myself—an unquiet slumber, broken by terrifying dreams. Sometimes I was falling from the cliffs in Sark into the deep, transparent waters below, where the sharp rocks lay like swords. Then I was in the Gouliot Caves, with Martin Dobrée at my side, and the tide was coming in too strongly for us; and beyond, in the opening through which we might have escaped, my husband's face looked in at us, with a hideous exultation upon it. I woke at last, shivering with cold and dread, for I had fancied that he had found me, and was carrying me away again to his old hateful haunts.

Our omnibus was jolting and rumbling down some steep and narrow streets lighted by oil-lamps swung across them. There were no lights in any of the houses, save a few in the upper windows, as though the inmates were all in bed, or going to bed. Only at the inn where we stopped was there any thing like life. A lamp, which hung over the archway leading to the yard and stables, lit up a group of people waiting for the arrival of the omnibus. I woke up Minima from her deep and heavy sleep.

"We are here at Noireau!" I said. "We have reached our home at last!"

The door was opened before the child was fairly awake. A small cluster of bystanders gathered round us as we alighted, and watched our luggage put down from the roof; while the driver ran on volubly, and with many gesticulations, addressed to the little crowd. He, the chamber-maid, the landlady, and all the rest, surrounded us as solemnly as if they were assisting at a funeral. There was not a symptom of amusement, but they all stared at us unflinchingly, as if a single wink of their eyelids would cause them to lose some extraordinary spectacle. If I had been a total eclipse of the sun, and they a group of enthusiastic astronomers bent upon observing every phenomenon, they could not have gazed more steadily. Minima was leaning against me, half asleep. A narrow vista of tall houses lay to the right and left, lost in impenetrable darkness. The strip of sky overhead was black with midnight.

"Noireau?" I asked, in a tone of interrogation.

"Oui, oui, madame," responded a chorus of voices.

"Carry me to the house of Monsieur Emile Perrier, the avocat," I said, speaking slowly and distinctly.

The words, simple as they were, seemed to awaken considerable excitement. The landlady threw up her hands, with an expression of astonishment, and the driver recommenced his harangue. Was it possible that I could have made a mistake in so short and easy a sentence? I said it over again to myself, and felt sure I was right. With renewed confidence I repeated it aloud, with a slight variation.

"I wish to go to the house of Monsieur Emile Perrier, the avocat," I said.

But while they still clustered round Minima and me, giving no sign of compliance with my request, two persons thrust themselves through the circle. The one was a man, in a threadbare brown greatcoat, with a large woollen comforter wound several times about his neck; and the other a woman, in an equally shabby dress, who spoke to me in broken English.

"Mees, I am Madame Perrier, and this my husband," she said; "come on. The letter was here only an hour ago; but all is ready. Come on; come on."

She put her hand through my arm, and took hold of Minima's hand, as if claiming both of us. A dead silence had fallen upon the little crowd, as if they were trying to catch the meaning of the English words. But as she pushed on, with us both in her hands, a titter for the first time ran from lip to lip. I glanced back, and saw Monsieur Perrier, the avocat, hurriedly putting our luggage on a wheelbarrow, and preparing to follow us with it along the dark streets.

I was too bewildered yet to feel any astonishment. We were in France, in a remote part of France, and I did not know what Frenchmen would or would not do. Madame Perrier, exhausted with her effort at speaking English, had ceased speaking to me, and contented herself with guiding us along the strange streets. We stopped at last opposite the large, handsome house, which stood in the front of the photograph I had seen in London. I could just recognize it in the darkness; and behind lay the garden and the second range of building. Not a glimmer of light shone in any of the windows.

"It is midnight nearly," said Madame Perrier, as we came to a stand-still and waited for her husband, the avocat.

Even when he came up with the luggage there seemed some difficulty in effecting an entrance. He passed through the garden-gate, and disappeared round the corner of the house, walking softly, as if careful not to disturb the household. How long the waiting seemed! For we were hungry, sleepy, and cold—strangers in a very strange land. I heard Minima sigh weariedly.

At last he reappeared round the corner, carrying a candle, which flickered in the wind. Not a word was spoken by him or his wife as the latter conducted us toward him. We were to enter by the back-door, that was evident. But I did not care what door we entered by, so that we might soon find rest and food. She led us into a dimly-lighted room, where I could just make out what appeared to be a carpenter's bench, with a heap of wood-shavings lying under it. But I was too weary to be certain about any thing.

"It is a leetle cabinet of work of my husband," said Madame Perrier; "our chamber is above, and the chamber for you and leetle mees is there also. But the school is not there. Will you go to bed? Will you sleep? Come on, mees."

"But we are very hungry," I remonstrated; "we have had nothing to eat since noon. We could not sleep without food."

"Bah! that is true," she said. "Well, come on. The food is at the school. Come on."

That must be the house at the back. We went down the broad gravel walk, with the pretty garden at the side of us, where a fountain was tinkling and splashing busily in the quiet night. But we passed the front of the house behind it without stopping, at the door. Madame led us through a cart-shed into a low, long, vaulted passage, with doors opening on each side; a black, villanous-looking place, with the feeble, flickering light of the candle throwing on to the damp walls a sinister gleam. Minima pressed very close to me, and I felt a strange quiver of apprehension: but the thought that there was no escape from it, and no help at hand, nerved me to follow quietly to the end.

CHAPTER THE EIGHTH

AT SCHOOL IN FRANCE

The end brought us out into a mean, poor street, narrow even where the best streets were narrow. A small house, the exterior of which I discovered afterward to be neglected and almost dilapidated, stood before us; and madame unlocked the door with a key from her pocket. We were conducted into a small kitchen, where a fire had been burning lately, though it was now out, and only a little warmth lingered about the stove. Minima was set upon a chair opposite to it, with her feet in the oven, and I was invited to do the same. I assented mechanically, and looked furtively about me, while madame was busy in cutting a huge hunch or two of black bread, and spreading upon them a thin scraping of rancid butter.

There was an oil-lamp here, burning with a clear, bright blaze. Madame's face was illuminated by it. It was a coarse, sullen face, with an expression of low cunning about it. There was not a trace of refinement or culture about her, not even the proverbial taste of a Frenchwoman in dress. The kitchen was a picture of squalid dirt and neglect; the walls and ceiling black with smoke, and the floor so crusted over with unswept refuse and litter that I thought it was not quarried. The few cooking-utensils were scattered about in disorder. The stove before which we sat was rusty. Could I be dreaming of this filthy dwelling and this slovenly woman? No; it was all too real for me to doubt their existence for an instant.

She was pouring out some cold tea into two little cups, when Monsieur Perrier made his appearance, his face begrimed and his shaggy hair uncombed. I had been used to the sight of rough men in Adelaide, on our sheep-farm, but I had never seen one more boorish. He stood in the doorway, rubbing his hands, and gazing at us unflinchingly with the hard stare of a Norman peasant, while he spoke in rapid, uncouth tones to his wife. I turned away my head, and shut my eyes to this unwelcome sight.

"Eat, mees," said the woman, bringing us our food. "There is tea. We give our pupils and instructresses tea for supper at six o'clock: after that there is no more to eat."

I took a mouthful of the food, but I could hardly swallow it, exhausted as I was from hunger. The bread was sour and the butter rancid; the tea tasted of garlic. Minima ate hers ravenously, without uttering a word. The child had not spoken since we entered these new scenes: her careworn face was puckered, and her sharp eyes were glancing about her more openly than mine. As soon as she had finished her hunch of black bread, I signified to Madame Perrier that we were ready to go to our bedroom.

We had the same vaulted passage and cart-shed to traverse on our way back to the other house. There we were ushered into a room containing only two beds and our two boxes. I helped Minima to undress, and tucked her up in bed, trying not to see the thin little face and sharp eyes which wanted to meet mine, and look into them. She put her arm round my neck, and drew down my head to whisper cautiously into my ear.

"They're cheats," she said, earnestly, "dreadful cheats. This isn't a splendid place at all. Oh! whatever shall I do? Shall I have to stay here four years?"

"Hush, Minima!" I answered. "Perhaps it is better than we think now. We are tired. To-morrow we shall see the place better, and it may be splendid after all. Kiss me, and go to sleep."

But it was too much for me, far too much. The long, long journey; the hunger the total destruction of all my hopes; the dreary prospect that stretched before me. I laid my aching head on my pillow, and cried myself to sleep like a child.

I was awakened, while it was yet quite dark, by the sound of a carpenter's tool in the room below me. Almost immediately a loud knock came at my door, and the harsh voice of madame called to us.

"Get up, mees, get up, and come on," she said; "you make your toilet at the school. Come on, quick!"

Minima was more dexterous than I in dressing herself in the dark; but we were not long in getting ready. The air was raw and foggy when we turned out-of-doors, and it was so dark still that we could scarcely discern the outline of the walls and houses. But madame was waiting to conduct us once more to the other house, and as she did so she volunteered an explanation of their somewhat singular arrangement of dwelling in two houses. The school, she informed me, was registered in the name of her head governess, not in her own; and as the laws of France prohibited any man dwelling under the same roof with a school of girls, except the husband of the proprietor, they were compelled to rent two dwellings.

"How many pupils have you, madame?" I inquired.

"We have six, mees," she replied. "They are here; see them."

We had reached the house, and she opened the door of a long, low room. There was an open hearth, with a few logs of green wood upon it, but they were not kindled. A table ran almost the whole length of the room, with forms on each side. A high chair or two stood about. All was comfortless, dreary, and squalid.

But the girls who were sitting on the hard benches by the table were still more squalid and dreary-looking. Their faces were pinched, and just now blue with cold, and their hands were swollen and red with chilblains. They had a cowed and frightened expression, and peeped askance at us as we went in behind madame. Minima pressed closely to me, and clasped my hand tightly in her little fingers. We were both entering upon the routine of a new life, and the first introduction to it was disheartening.

"Three are English," said madame, "and three are French. The English are frileuses; they are always sheever, sheever, sheever. Behold, how they have fingers red and big! Bah! it is disgusting."

She rapped one of the swollen hands which lay upon the table, and the girl dropped it out of sight upon her lap, with a frightened glance at the woman. Minima's fingers tightened upon mine. The head governess, a Frenchwoman of about thirty, with a number of little black papillotes circling about her head, was now introduced to me; and an animated conversation followed between her and madame.

"You comprehend the French?" asked the latter, turning with a suspicious look to me.

"No," I answered; "I know very little of it yet."

"Good!" she replied. "We will eat breakfast."

"But I have not made my toilet," I objected; "there was neither washingstand nor dressing-table in my room."

"Bah!" she said, scornfully; "there are no gentlemans here. No person will see you. You make your toilet before the promenade; not at this moment."

It was evident that uncomplaining submission was expected, and no remonstrance would be of avail. Breakfast was being brought in by one of the pupils. It consisted of a teacupful of coffee at the bottom of a big basin, which was placed before each of us, a large tablespoon to feed ourselves with; and a heaped plateful of hunches of bread, similar to those I had turned from last night. But I could fast no longer. I sat down with the rest at the long table, and ate my food with a sinking and sorrowful heart.

Minima drank her scanty allowance of coffee thirstily, and then asked, in a timid voice, if she could have a little more. Madame's eyes glared upon her, and her voice snapped out an answer; while the English girls looked frightened, and drew in their bony shoulders, as if such temerity made them shudder. As soon as madame was gone, the child flung her arms around me, and hid her face in my bosom.

"Oh!" she cried, "don't you leave me; don't forsake me! I have to stay here four years, and it will kill me. I shall die if you go away and leave me."

I soothed her as best I could, without promising to remain in this trap. Would it not be possible in some way to release her as well as myself? I sat thinking through the long cold morning, with the monotonous hum of lessons in my ears. There was nothing for me to do, and I found that I could not return to the house where I had slept, and where my luggage was, until night came again. I sat all the morning in the chilly room, with Minima on the floor at my feet, clinging to me for protection and warmth, such as I could give.

But what could I do either for her or myself? My store of money was almost all gone, for our joint expenses had cost more than I had anticipated, and I could very well see that I must not expect Madame Perrier to refund Minima's fare. There was perhaps enough left to carry me back to England, and just land me on its shores. But what then? Where was I to go then? Penniless, friendless; without character, without a name—but an assumed one—what was to become of me? I began to wonder vaguely whether I should be forced to make myself known to my husband; whether fate would not drive me back to him. No; that should never be. I would face and endure any hardship rather than return to my former life. A hundred times better this squalid, wretched, foreign school, than the degradation of heart and soul I had suffered with him.

I could do no more for Minima than for myself, for I dared not even write to Mrs. Wilkinson, who was either an accomplice or a dupe of these Perriers. My letter might fall into the hands of Richard Foster, or the woman living with him, and so they would track me out, and I should have no means of escape. I dared not run that risk. The only thing I could do for her was to stay with her, and as far as possible shield her from the privations and distress that threatened us both. I was safe here; no one was likely to come across me, in this remote place, who could by any chance know me. I had at least a roof over my head; I had food to eat. Elsewhere I was not sure of either. There seemed to be no other choice given me than to remain in the trap.

"We must make the best of it, Minima," I whispered to the child, through the hum of lessons. Her shrewd little face brightened with a smile that smoothed all the wrinkles out of it.

"That's what father said!" she cried; "he said, 'Courage, Minima. God will take care of my little daughter.' God has sent you to take care of me. Suppose I'd come all the way alone, and found it such a horrid place!"

CHAPTER THE NINTH

A FRENCH AVOCAT

December came in with intense severity. Icicles a yard long hung to the eaves, and the snow lay unmelted for days together on the roofs. More often than not we were without wood for our fire, and when we had it, it was green and unseasoned, and only smouldered away with a smoke that stung and irritated our eyes. Our insufficient and unwholesome food supplied us with no inward warmth. Coal in that remote district cost too much for any but the wealthiest people, Now and then I caught a glimpse of a blazing fire in the houses I had to pass, to get to our chamber over Monsieur Perrier's workshop; and in an evening the dainty, savory smell of dinner, cooking in the kitchen adjoining, sometimes filled the frosty air. Both sight and scent were tantalizing, and my dreams at night were generally of pleasant food and warm firesides.

At times the pangs of hunger grew too strong for us both, and forced me to spend a little of the money I was nursing so carefully. As soon as I could make myself understood, I went out occasionally after dark, to buy bread-and-milk.

Noireau was a curious town, the streets everywhere steep and narrow, and the houses, pell-mell, rich and poor, large and small huddled together without order. Almost opposite the handsome dwelling, the photograph of which had misled me, stood a little house where I could buy rich, creamy milk. It was sold by a Mademoiselle Rosalie, an old maid, whom I generally found solitarily reading a Journal pour Tous with her feet upon a chaufferette, and no light save that of her little oil-lamp. She had never sat by a fire in her life, she told me, burning her face and spoiling her teint. Her dwelling consisted of a single room, with a shed opening out of it, where she kept her milkpans. She was the only person I spoke to out of Madame Perrier's own household.

"Is Monsieur Perrier an avocat?" I asked her one day, as soon as I could understand what she might say in reply. There was very little doubt in my mind as to what her answer would be.

"An avocat, mademoiselle?" She repeated, shrugging her shoulders; "who has told you that? Are the avocats in England like Emile? He is my relation, and you see me! He is a bailiff; do you understand? If I go in debt, he comes and takes possession of my goods, you see. It is very simple. One need not be very learned to do that. Emile Perrier an avocat? Bah!"

"What is an avocat?" I inquired.

"An avocat is even higher than a notaire," she answered; "he gives counsel; he pleads before the judges. It is a high rôle. One must be very learned, very eloquent, to be an avocat."

"I suppose he must be a gentleman," I remarked.

"A gentleman, mademoiselle?" she said; "I do not understand you. There is equality in France. We are all messieurs and mesdames. There is monsieur the bailiff, and monsieur the duke; and there is madame the washer-woman, and madame the duchess. We are all gentlemen, all ladies. It is not the same in your country."

"Not at all," I answered.

"Did my little Emile tell you he was an avocat, mademoiselle?" she asked.

"No," I said. I was on my guard, even if I had known French well enough to explain the deception practised upon me. She looked as if she did not believe me, but smiled and nodded with imperturbable politeness, as I carried off my jug of milk.

So Monsieur Perrier was nothing higher than a bailiff, and with very little to do even in that line of the law! He took off his tasselled cap to me as I passed his workshop, and went up-stairs with the milk to Minima, who was already gone to bed for the sake of warmth. The discovery did not affect me with surprise. If he had been an avocat, my astonishment at French barristers would have been extreme.

Yet there was something galling in the idea of being under the roof of a man and woman of that class, in some sort in their power and under their control. The low, vulgar cunning of their nature appeared more clearly to me. There was no chance of success in any contest with them, for they were too boorish to be reached by any weapon I could use. All I could do was to keep as far aloof from them as possible.

This was not difficult to do, for neither of them interfered with the affairs of the school, and we saw them only at meal times, when they watched every mouthful we ate with keen eyes.

I found that I had no duties to perform as a teacher, for none of the three French pupils desired to learn English. English girls, who had been decoyed into the same snare by the same false photograph and prospectus which had entrapped me, were all of families too poor to be able to forfeit the money which had been paid in advance for their French education. Two of them, however, completed their term at Christmas, and returned home weak and ill; the third was to leave in the spring. I did not hear that any more pupils were expected, and why Madame Perrier should have engaged any English teacher became a problem to me. The premium I had paid was too small to cover my expenses for a year, though we were living at so scanty a cost. It was not long before I understood my engagement better.

I studied the language diligently. I felt myself among foreigners and foes, and I was helpless till I could comprehend what they were saying in my presence. Having no other occupation, I made rapid progress, though Mademoiselle Morel, the head governess, gave me very little assistance.

She was a dull, heavy, yet crafty-looking woman, who had taken a first-class diploma as a teacher; yet, as far as I could judge, knew very much less than most English governesses who are uncertificated. So far from there being any professors attending the school, I could not discover that there were any in the town. It was a cotton-manufacturing town, with a population of six thousand, most of them hand-loom weavers. There were three or four small factories, built on the banks of the river, where the hands were at work from six in the morning till ten at night, Sundays included. There was not much intellectual life here; a professor would have little chance of making a living.

At first Minima, and I took long walks together into the country surrounding Noireau, a beautiful country, even in November. Once out of the vapor lying in the valley, at the bottom of which the town was built, the atmosphere showed itself as exquisitely clear, with no smoke in it, except the fine blue smoke of wood-fire. We could distinguish the shapes of trees standing out against the horizon, miles and miles away; while between us and it lay slopes of brown woodland and green pastures, with long rows of slim poplars, the yellow leaves clinging to them still, and winding round them, like garlands on a May-pole. But this pleasure was a costly one, for it awoke pangs of hunger, which I was compelled to appease by drawing upon my rapidly-emptying purse. We learned that it was necessary to stay in-doors, and cultivate a small appetite.

"Am I getting very thin?" asked Minima one day, as she held up her transparent hand against the light; "how thin do you think I could get without dying, Aunt Nelly?"

"Oh! a great deal thinner, my darling," I said, kissing the little fingers, My heart was bound up in the child. I had been so lonely without her, that now her constant companionship, her half-womanly, half-babyish prattle seemed necessary to me. There was no longer any question in my mind as to whether I could leave her. I only wondered what I should do when my year was run out, and only one of those four of hers, for which these wretches had received the payment.

"Some people can get very thin indeed," she went on, with her shrewd, quaint smile; "I've heard the boys at school talk about it. One of them had seen a living skeleton, that was all skin and bone, and no flesh. I shouldn't like to be a living skeleton, and be made a show of. Do you think I ever shall be, if I stay here four years? Perhaps they'd take me about as a show."

"Why, you are talking nonsense, Minima," I answered.

"Am I?" she said, wistfully, as if the idea really troubled her; "I dream of it often and often. I can feel all my bones now, and count them, when I'm in bed. Some of them are getting very sharp. The boys used to say they'd get as sharp as knives sometimes, and cut through the skin. But father said it was only boys' talk."

"Your father was right," I answered; "you must think of what he said, not the boys' talk."

"But," she continued, "the boys said sometimes people get so hungry they bite pieces out of their arms. I don't think I could ever be so hungry as that; do you?"

"Minima," I said, starting up, "let us run to Mademoiselle Rosalie's for some bread-and-milk."

"You're afraid of me beginning to eat myself!" she cried, with a little laugh. But she was the first to reach Mademoiselle Rosalie's door; and I watched her devouring her bread-and-milk with the eagerness of a ravenous appetite.

Very fast melted away my money. I could not see the child pining with hunger, though every sou I spent made our return to England more difficult. Madame Perrier put no hinderance in my way, for the more food we purchased ourselves, the less we ate at her table. The bitter cold and the coarse food told upon Minima's delicate little frame. Yet what could I do? I dared not write to Mrs. Wilkinson, and I very much doubted if there would be any benefit to be hoped for if I ran the risk. Minima did not know the address of any one of the persons who had subscribed for her education and board; to her they were only the fathers and mothers of the boys of whom she talked so much. She was as friendless as I was in the world.

So far away were Dr. Martin Dobrée and Tardif, that I dared not count them as friends who could have any power to help me. Better for Dr. Martin Dobrée if he could altogether forget me, and return to his cousin Julia. Perhaps he had done so already.

How long was this loneliness, this friendlessness to be my lot? I was so young yet, that my life seemed endless as it stretched before me. Poor, desolate, hunted, I shrank from life as an evil thing, and longed impatiently to be rid of it. Yet how could I escape even from its present phase?

CHAPTER THE TENTH

A MISFORTUNE WITHOUT PARALLEL

My escape was nearer than I expected, and was forced upon me in a manner I could never have foreseen.

Toward the middle of February, Mademoiselle Morel appeared often in tears. Madame Perrier's coarse face was always overcast, and monsieur seemed gloomy, too gloomy to retain even French politeness of manner toward any of us. The household was under a cloud, but I could not discover why. What little discipline and work there had been in the school was quite at an end. Every one was left to do as she chose.

Early one morning, long before daybreak, I was startled out of my sleep by a hurried knock at my door. I cried out, "Who is there?" and a voice, indistinct with sobbing, replied, "C'est moi."

The "moi" proved to be Mademoiselle Morel. I opened the door for her, and she appeared in her bonnet and walking-dress, carrying a lamp in her hand, which lit up her weary and tear-stained face. She took a seat at the foot of my bed, and buried her face in her handkerchief.

"Mademoiselle," she said, "here is a grand misfortune, a misfortune without parallel. Monsieur and madame are gone."

"Gone!" I repeated; "where are they gone?"

"I do not know, mademoiselle," she answered; "I know nothing at all. They are gone away. The poor good people were in debt, and their creditors are as hard as stone. They wished to take every sou, and they talked of throwing monsieur into prison, you understand. That is intolerable. They are gone, and I have no means to carry on the establishment. The school is finished."

"But I am to stay here twelve months," I cried, in dismay, "and Minima was to stay four years. The money has been paid to them for it. What is to become of us?"

"I cannot say, mademoiselle; I am desolated myself," she replied, with a fresh burst of tears; "all is finished here. If you have not money enough to take you back to England, you must write to your friends. I'm going to return to Bordeaux. I detest Normandy; it is so cold and triste."

"But what is to be done with the other pupils?" I inquired, still lost in amazement, and too bewildered to realize my own position.

"The English pupil goes with me to Paris," she answered; "she has her friends there. The French demoiselles are not far from their own homes, and they return to-day by the omnibus to Granville. It is a misfortune without parallel, mademoiselle—a misfortune quite without parallel."

By the way she repeated this phrase, it was evidently a great consolation to her—as phrases seem to be to all classes of the French people. But both the tone of her voice, and the expression of her face, impressed upon me the conviction that it was not her only consolation. In answer to my urgent questions, she informed me that, without doubt, the goods left in the two houses would be seized, as soon as the flight of madame and monsieur became known.

To crown all, she was going to start immediately by the omnibus to Falaise, and on by rail to Paris, not waiting for the storm to burst. She kissed me on both cheeks, bade me adieu, and was gone, leaving me in utter darkness, before I fairly comprehended the rapid French in which she conveyed her intention. I groped to the window, and saw the glimmering of her lamp, as she turned into the cart-shed, on her way to the other house. Before I could dress and follow her, she would be gone.

I had seen my last of Monsieur and Madame Perrier, and of Mademoiselle Morel.

I had time to recover from my consternation, and to see my position clearly, before the dawn came. Leagues of land, and leagues of sea, lay between me and England. Ten shillings was all that was left of my money. Besides this, I had Minima dependent upon me, for it was impossible to abandon her to the charity of foreigners. I had not the means of sending her back to Mrs. Wilkinson, and I rejected the mere thought of doing so, partly because I dared not run the risk, and partly because I could not harden myself against the appeals the child would make against such a destiny. But then what was to become of us?

I dressed myself as soon as the first faint light came, and hurried to the other house. The key was in the lock, as mademoiselle had left it. A fire was burning in the school-room, and the fragments of a meal were scattered about the table. The pupils up-stairs were preparing for their own departure, and were chattering too volubly to one another for me to catch the meaning of their words. They seemed to know very well how to manage their own affairs, and they informed me their places were taken in the omnibus, and a porter was hired to fetch their luggage.

All I had to do was to see for myself and Minima.

I carried our breakfast back with me, when I returned to Minima. Her wan and womanly face was turned toward the window, and the light made it look more pinched and worn than usual. She sat up in bed to eat her scanty breakfast—the last meal we should have in this shelter of ours—and I wrapped a shawl about her thin shoulders.

"I wish I'd been born a boy," she said, plaintively; "they can get their own living sooner than girls, and better. How soon do you think I could get my own living? I could be a little nurse-maid now, you know; and I'd eat very little."

"What makes you talk about getting your living?" I asked.

"How pale you look!" she answered, nodding her little head; "why, I heard something of what mademoiselle said. They've all run away, and left us to do what we can. We shall both have to get our own living. I've been thinking how nice it would be if you could get a place as housemaid and me nurse, in the same house. Wouldn't that be first-rate? You're very poor, aren't you, Aunt Nelly?"

"Very poor!" I repeated, hiding my face on her pillow, while hot tears forced themselves through my eyelids.

"Oh! this will never do," said the childish voice; "we mustn't cry, you know. The boys always said it was like a baby to cry; and father used to say, 'Courage, Minima!' Perhaps, when all our money is gone, we shall find a great big purse full of gold; or else a beautiful French prince will see you, and fall in love with you, and take us both to his palace, and make you his princess; and we shall all grow up till we die."

I laughed at the oddity of this childish climax in spite of the heaviness of my heart and the springing of my tears. Minima's fresh young fancies were too droll to resist, especially in combination with her shrewd, old-womanish knowledge of many things of which I was ignorant.

"I should know exactly what to do if we were in London," she resumed; "we could take our things to the pawnbroker's, and get lots of money for them. That is what poor people do. Mrs. Foster has pawned all her rings and brooches. It is quite easy to do, you know; but perhaps there are no pawn-shops in France."

This incidental mention of Mrs. Foster had sent my thoughts and fears fluttering toward a deep, unutterable dread, which was lurking under all my other cares. Should I be driven by the mere stress of utter poverty to return to my husband? There must be something wrong in a law which bound me captive, body and soul, to a man whose very name had become a terror to me, and to escape whom I was willing to face any difficulties, any distresses. But all my knowledge of the law came from his lips, and he would gladly deceive me. It might be that I was suffering all these troubles quite needlessly. Across the darkness of my prospects flushed a thought that seemed like an angel of light. Why should I not try to make my way to Mrs. Dobrée, Martin's mother, to whom I could tell my whole history, and on whose friendship and protection I could rely implicitly? She would learn for me how far the law would protect me. By this time Kate Daltrey would have quitted the Channel Islands, satisfied that I had eluded her pursuit. The route to the Channel Islands was neither long nor difficult, for at Granville a vessel sailed directly for Jersey, and we were not more than thirty miles from Granville. It was a distance that we could almost walk. If Mrs. Dobrée could not help me, Tardif would take Minima into his house for a time, and the child could not have a happier home. I could count upon my good Tardif doing that. These plans were taking shape in my brain, when I heard a voice calling softly under the window. I opened the casement, and, leaning out, saw the welcome face of Rosalie, the milk-woman.

"Will you permit me to come in?" she inquired.

"Yes, yes, come in," I said, eagerly.

She entered, and saluted us both with much ceremony. Her clumsy wooden sabots clattered over the bare boards, and the wings of her high Norman cap flapped against her sallow cheeks. No figure could have impressed upon me more forcibly the unwelcome fact that I was in great straits in a foreign land. I regarded her with a vague kind of fear.

"So my little Emile and his spouse are gone, mademoiselle," she said, in a mysterious whisper. "I have been saying to myself, 'What will my little English lady do?' That is why I am here. Behold me."

"I do not know what to do," I answered.

"If mademoiselle is not difficult," she said, "she and the little one could rest with me for a day or two. My bed is clean and soft—bah! ten times softer than these paillasses. I would ask only a franc a night for it. That is much less than at the hotels, where they charge for light and attendance. Mademoiselle could write to her friends, if she has not enough money to carry her and the little one back to their own country."

"I have no friends," I said, despondently.

"No friends! no relations!" she exclaimed.

"Not one," I replied.

"But that is terrible!" she said. "Has mademoiselle plenty of money?"

"Only twelve francs," I answered.

Rosalie's face grew long and grave. This was an abyss of misfortune she had not dreamed of. She looked at us both critically, and did not open her lips again for a minute or two.

"Is the little one your relation?" she inquired, after this pause.

"No," I replied; "I did not know her till I brought her here. She does not know of any friends or relations belonging to her."

"There is the convent for her," she said; "the good sisters would take a little girl like her, and make a true Christian of her. She might become a saint some day—"

"No, no," I interrupted, hastily; "I could not leave her in a convent."

Mademoiselle Rosalie was very much offended; her sallow face flushed a dull red, and the wings of her cap flapped as if she were about to take flight, and leave me in my difficulties. She had kindliness of feeling, but it was not proof against my poverty and my covert slight of her religion. I caught her hand in mine to prevent her going.

"Let us come to your house for to-day," I entreated: "to-morrow we will go. I have money enough to pay you."

I was only too glad to get a shelter for Minima and myself for another night. She explained to me the French system of borrowing money upon articles left in pledge and offered to accompany me to the mont de piété with those things that we could spare. But, upon packing up our few possessions, I remembered that only a few days before Madame Perrier had borrowed from me my seal-skin mantle, the only valuable thing I had remaining. I had lent it reluctantly, and in spite of myself; and it had never been returned. Minima's wardrobe was still poorer than my own. All the money we could raise was less than two napoleons; and with this we had to make our way to Granville, and thence to Guernsey. We could not travel luxuriously.

The next morning we left Noireau on foot.

CHAPTER THE ELEVENTH

LOST AT NIGHTFALL

It was a soft spring morning, with an exhilarating, jubilant lightness in the air, such as only comes in the very early spring, or at sunrise on a dewy summer-day. A few gray clouds lay low along the horizon, but overhead the sky was a deep, rich blue, with fine, filmy streaks of white vapor floating slowly across it. The branches of the trees were still bare, showing the blue through their delicate net-work; but the ends of the twigs were thickening, and the leaf-buds swelling under the rind. The shoots of the hazel-bushes wore a purple bloom, with yellow catkins already hanging in tassels about them. The white buds of the chestnut-trees shone with silvery lustre. In the orchards, though the tangled boughs of the apple-trees were still thickly covered with gray lichens, small specks of green among the gray gave a promise of early blossom. Thrushes were singing from every thorn-bush; and the larks, lost in the blue heights above us, flung down their triumphant carols, careless whether our ears caught them or no. A long, straight road stretched before us, and seemed to end upon the skyline in the far distance. Below us, when we looked back, lay the valley and the town; and all around us a vast sweep of country, rising up to the low floor of clouds from which the bright dome of the sky was springing.

We strolled on as if we were walking on air, and could feel no fatigue; Minima with a flush upon her pale cheeks, and chattering incessantly about the boys, whose memories were her constant companions. I too had my companions; faces and voices were about me, which no eye or ear but mine could perceive.

During the night, while my brain had been between waking and sleeping, I had been busy with the new idea that had taken possession of it. The more I pondered upon the subject, the more impossible it appeared that the laws of any Christian country should doom me, and deliver me up against my will, to a bondage more degrading and more cruel than slavery itself. If every man, I had said to myself, were proved to be good and chivalrous, of high and steadfast honor, it might be possible to place another soul, more frail and less wise, into his charge unchallenged. But the law is made for evil men, not for good. I began to believe it incredible that it should subject me to the tyranny of a husband who made my home a hell, and gave me no companionship but that of the vicious. Should the law make me forfeit all else, it would at least recognize my right to myself. Once free from the necessity of hiding, I did not fear to face any difficulty. Surely he had been deceiving me, and playing upon my ignorance, when he told me I belonged to him as a chattel!

Every step which carried us nearer to Granville brought new hope to me. The face of Martin's mother came often to my mind, looking at me, as she had done in Sark, with a mournful yet tender smile—a smile behind which lay many tears. If I could but lay my head upon her lap, and tell her all, all which I had never breathed into any ear, I should feel secure and happy. "Courage!" I said to myself; "every hour brings you nearer to her."

Now and then, whenever we came to a pleasant place, where a fallen tree, or the step under a cross, offered us a resting-place by the roadside, we sat down, scarcely from weariness, but rather for enjoyment. I had full directions as to our route, and I carried a letter from Rosalie to a cousin of hers, who lived in a convent about twelve miles from Noirean; where, she assured me, they would take us in gladly for a night, and perhaps send us on part of our way in their conveyance, in the morning. Twelve miles only had to be accomplished this first day, and we could saunter as we chose, making our dinner of the little loaves which we had bought hot from the oven, as we quitted the town, and drinking of the clear little rills, which were gurgling merrily under the brown hedge-rows. If we reached the convent before six o'clock we should find the doors open, and should gain admission.

But in the afternoon the sky changed. The low floor of clouds rose gradually, and began to spread themselves, growing grayer and thicker as they crept higher into the sky. The blue became paler and colder. The wind changed a point or two from the south, and a breath from the east blew, with a chilly touch, over the wide open plain we were now crossing.

Insensibly our high spirits sank. Minima ceased to prattle; and I began to shiver a little, more from an inward dread of the utterly unknown future, than from any chill of the easterly wind. The road was very desolate. Not a creature had we seen for an hour or two, from whom I could inquire if we were on the high-road to Granville. About noon we had passed a roadside cross, standing where three ways met, and below it a board had pointed toward Granville. I had followed its direction in confidence, but now I began to feel somewhat anxious. This road, along which the grass was growing, was strangely solitary and dreary.

It brought us after a while to the edge of a common, stretching before us, drear and brown, as far as my eye could reach. A wild, weird-looking flat, with no sign of cultivation; and the road running across it lying in deep ruts, where moss and grass were springing. As far as I could guess, it was drawing near to five o'clock; and, if we had wandered out of our way, the right road took an opposite direction some miles behind us. There was no gleam of sunshine now, no vision of blue overhead. All there was gray, gloomy, and threatening. The horizon was rapidly becoming invisible; a thin, cold, clinging vapor shut it from us. Every few minutes a fold of this mist overtook us, and wrapped itself about us, until the moaning wind drifted it away. Minima was quite silent now, and her weary feet dragged along the rough road. The hand which rested upon my wrist felt hot, as it clasped it closely. The child was worn out, and was suffering more than I did, though in uncomplaining patience.

"Are you very tired, my Minima?" I asked.

"It will be so nice to go to bed, when we reach the convent," she said, looking up with a smile. "I can't imagine why the prince has not come yet."

"Perhaps he is coming all the time," I answered, "and he'll find us when we want him worst."

We plodded on after that, looking for the convent, or for any dwelling where we could stay till morning. But none came in sight, or any person from whom we could learn where we were wandering. I was growing frightened, dismayed. What would become of us both, if we could find no shelter from the cold of a February night?

There were unshed tears in my eyes—for I would not let Minima know my fears—when I saw dimly, through the mist, a high cross standing in the midst of a small grove of yews and cypresses, planted formally about it. There were three tiers of steps at its foot, the lowest partly screened from the gathering rain by the trees. The shaft of the cross, with a serpent twining about its base, rose high above the cypresses; and the image of the Christ hanging upon its crossbeams fronted the east, which was now heavy with clouds. The half-closed eyes seemed to be gazing over the vast wintry plain, lying in the brown desolateness of a February evening. The face was full of an unutterable and complete agony, and there was the helpless languor of dying in the limbs. The rain was beating against it, and the wind sobbing in the trees surrounding it. It seemed so sad, so forsaken, that it drew us to it. Without speaking the child and I crept to the shelter at its foot, and sat down to rest there, as if we were companions to it in its loneliness.

There was no sound to listen to save the sighing of the east wind through the fine needle-like leaflets of the yew-trees; and the mist was rapidly shutting out every sight but the awful, pathetic form above us. Evening had closed in, night was coming gradually, yet swiftly. Every minute was drawing the darkness more densely about us. If we did not bestir ourselves soon, and hasten along, it would overtake us, and find us without resource. Yet I felt as if I had no heart to abandon that gray figure, with the rain-drops beating heavily against it. I forgot myself, forgot Minima, forgot all the world, while looking up to the face, growing more dim to me through my own tears.

"Hush! hush!" cried Minima, though I was neither moving nor speaking, and the stillness was profound; "hark! I hear something coming along the road, only very far off."

I listened for a minute or two, and there reached my ears a faint tinkling, which drew nearer and nearer every moment. At last it was plainly the sound of bells on a horse's collar; and presently I could distinguish the beat of a horse's hoofs coming slowly along the road. In a few minutes some person would be passing by, who would be able to help us; and no one could be so inhuman as to leave us in our distress.

It was too dark now to see far along the road, but as we waited and watched there came into sight a rude sort of covered carriage, like a market-cart, drawn by a horse with a blue sheep-skin hanging round his neck. The pace at which he was going was not above a jog-trot, and he came almost to a stand-still opposite the cross, as if it was customary to pause there.

This was the instant to appeal for aid. I darted forward in front of the char à bancs, and stretched out my hands to the driver.

"Help us," I cried; we have lost our way, and the night is come. "Help us, for the love of Christ!" I could see now that the driver was a burly, red-faced, cleanshaven Norman peasant, wearing a white cotton cap, with a tassel over his forehead, who stared at me, and at Minima dragging herself wearily to my side, as if we had both dropped from the clouds. He crossed himself hurriedly, and glanced at the grove of dark, solemn trees from which we had come. But by his side sat a priest, in his cassock and broad-brimmed hat fastened up at the sides, who alighted almost before I had finished speaking, and stood before us bareheaded, and bowing profoundly.

"Madame," he said, in a bland tone, "to what town are you going?"

"We are going to Granville," I answered, "but I am afraid I have lost the way. We are very tired, this little child and I. We can walk no more, monsieur. Take care of us, I pray you."

I spoke brokenly, for in an extremity like this it was difficult to put my request into French. The priest appeared perplexed, but he went back to the char à bancs, and held a short, earnest conversation with the driver, in a subdued voice.

"Madame," he said, returning to me, "I am Francis Laurentie, the curé of Ville-en-bois. It is quite a small village about a league from here, and we are on the road to it; but the route to Granville is two leagues behind us, and it is still farther to the first village. There is not time to return with you this evening. Will you, then, go with us to Ville-en-bois, and to-morrow we will send you on to Granville?"

He spoke very slowly and distinctly, with a clear, cordial voice, which filled me with confidence. I could hardly distinguish his features, but his hair was silvery white, and shone in the gloom, as he still stood bareheaded before me, though the rain was falling fast.

"Take care of us, monsieur?" I replied, putting my hand in his; "we will go with you."

"Make haste then, my children," he said, cheerfully; "the rain will hurt you. Let me lift the mignonne into the char à bancs. Bah! How little she is! Voilà! Now, madame, permit me."

There was a seat in the back of the char à bancs which we reached by climbing over the front bench, assisted by the driver. There we were well sheltered from the driving wind and rain, with our feet resting upon a sack of potatoes, and the two strange figures of the Norman peasant in his blouse and white cotton cap, and the curé in his hat and cassock, filling up the front of the car before us.

It was so unlike any thing I had foreseen, that I could scarcely believe that it was real.

CHAPTER THE TWELFTH

THE CURÉ OF VILLE-EN-BOIS

"They are not Frenchwomen, Monsieur le Curé," observed the driver, after a short pause. We were travelling slowly, for the curé would not allow the peasant to whip on the shaggy cart-horse. We were, moreover, going up-hill, along roads as rough as any about my father's sheep-walk, with large round stones deeply bedded in the soil.

"No, no, my good Jean," was the curé's answer; "by their tongue I should say they are English. Englishwomen are extremely intrepid, and voyage about all the world quite alone, like this. It is only a marvel to me that we have never encountered one of them before to-day."

"But, Monsieur le Curé, are they Christian?" inquired Jean, with a backward glance at us. Evidently he had not altogether recovered from the fright we had given him, when we appeared suddenly from out of the gloomy shadows of the cypresses.

"The English nation is Protestant," replied the curé, with a sigh.

"But, monsieur," exclaimed Jean, "if they are Protestants they cannot be Christians! Is it not true that all the Protestants go to hell on the back of that bad king who had six wives all at one time?"

"Not all at one time, my good Jean," the curé answered mildly; "no, no, surely they do not all go to perdition. If they know any thing of the love of Christ, they must be Christians, however feeble and ignorant. He does not quench the smoking flax, Jean. Did you not hear madame say, 'Help me, for the love of Christ?' Good! There is the smoking flax, which may burn into a flame brighter than yours or mine some day, my poor friend. We must make her and the mignonne as welcome as if they were good Catholics. She is very poor, cela saute aux yeux—"

"Monsieur," I interrupted, feeling almost guilty in having listened so far, "I understand French very well, though I speak it badly."

"Pardon, madame!" he replied, "I hope you will not be grieved by the foolish words we have been speaking one to the other."

After that all was still again for some time, except the tinkling of the bells, and the pad-pad of the horse's feet upon the steep and rugged road. Hills rose on each side of us, which were thickly planted with trees. Even the figures of the curé and driver were no longer well defined in the denser darkness. Minima had laid her head on my shoulder, and seemed to be asleep. By-and-by a village clock striking echoed faintly down the valley; and the curé turned round and addressed me again.

"There is my village, madame," he said, stretching forth his hand to point it out, though we could not see a yard beyond the char à bancs; "it is very small, and my parish contains but four hundred and twenty-two souls, some of them very little ones. They all know me, and regard me as a father. They love me, though I have some rebel sons—Is it not so, Jean? Rebel sons, but not many rebel daughters. Here we are!"

We entered a narrow and roughly-paved village-street. The houses, as I saw afterward, were all huddled together, with a small church at the point farthest from the entrance; and the road ended at its porch, as if there were no other place in the world beyond it.

As we clattered along the dogs barked, and the cottage-doors flew open. Children toddled to the thresholds, and called after us, in shrill notes, "Good-evening, and a good-night, Monsieur le Curé!" Men's voices, deeper and slower, echoed the salutation. The curé was busy greeting each one in return: "Good-night, my little rogue," "Good-night, my lamb." "Good-night to all of you, my friends;" his cordial voice making each word sound as if it came from his very heart. I felt that we were perfectly secure in his keeping.

Never, as long as I live, shall I smell the pungent, pleasant scent of wood burning without recalling to my memory that darksome entrance into Ville-en-bois.

"We drove at last into a square courtyard, paved with pebbles. Almost before the horse could stop I saw a stream of light shining from an open door across a causeway, and the voice of a woman, whom I could not see, spoke eagerly as soon as the horse's hoofs had ceased to scrape upon the pebbles.

"Hast thou brought a doctor with thee, my brother?" she asked.

"I have brought no doctor except thy brother, my sister," answered Monsieur Laurentie, "also a treasure which I found at the foot of the Calvary down yonder."

He had alighted while saying this, and the rest of the conversation was carried on in whispers. There was some one ill in the house, and our arrival was ill-timed, that was quite clear. Whoever the woman was that had come to the door, she did not advance to speak to me, but retreated as soon as the conversation was over; while the curé returned to the side of the char à bancs, and asked me to remain where I was, with Minima, for a few minutes.

The horse was taken out by Jean, and led away to the stable, the shafts of the char à bancs being supported by two props put under them. Then the place grew profoundly quiet. I leaned forward to look at the presbytery, which I supposed this house to be. It was a low, large building of two stories, with eaves projecting two or three feet over the upper one. At the end of it rose the belfry of the church—an open belfry, with one bell hanging underneath a little square roof of tiles. The church itself was quite hidden by the surrounding walls and roofs. All was dark, except a feeble glimmering in four upper casements, which seemed to belong to one large room. The church-clock chimed a quarter, then half-past, and must have been near upon the three-quarters; but yet there was no sign that we were remembered. Minima was still asleep. I was growing cold, depressed, and anxious, when the house-door opened once more, and the curé appeared carrying a lamp, which he placed on the low stone wall surrounding the court.

"Pardon, madame," he said, approaching us, "but my sister is too much occupied with a sick person to do herself the honor of attending upon you. Permit me to fill her place, and excuse her, I pray you. Give me the poor mignonne; I will lift her down first, and then assist you to descend."

His politeness did not seem studied; it had too kindly a tone to be artificial. I lifted Minima over the front seat, and sprang down myself, glad to be released from my stiff position, and hardly availing myself of his proffered help. He did not conduct us through the open door, but led us round the angle of the presbytery to a small outhouse, opening on to the court, and with no other entrance. It was a building lying between the porch and belfry of the church and his own dwelling place. But it looked comfortable and inviting. A fire had been hastily kindled on an open hearth, and a heap of wood lay beside it. A table stood close by, in the light and warmth, on which were steaming two basins of soup, and an omelette fresh from the frying-pan; with fruit and wine for a second course. Two beds were in this room: one with hangings over the head, and a large, tall cross at the foot-board; the other a low, narrow pallet, lying along the foot of it. A crucifix hung upon the wall, and the wood-work of the high window also formed a cross. It seemed a strange goal to reach after our day's wanderings.

Monsieur Laurentie put the lamp down on the table, and drew the logs of wood together on the hearth. He was an old man, as I then thought, over sixty. He looked round upon us with a benevolent smile.

"Madame," he said, "our hospitality is rude and simple, but you are very welcome guests. My sister is desolated that she must leave you to my cares. But if there be any thing you have need of, tell me, I pray you."

"There is nothing, monsieur," I answered; "you are too good to us, too good."

"No, no, madame," he said, "be content. To-morrow I will send you to Granville under the charge of my good Jean. Sleep well, my children, and fear nothing. The good God will protect you."

He closed the door after him as he spoke, but opened it again to call my attention to a thick wooden bar, with which I might fasten it inside if I chose; and to tell me not to alarm myself when I heard the bell overhead toll for matins, at half-past five in the morning. I listened to his receding footsteps, and then turned eagerly to the food, which I began to want greatly.

But Minima had thrown herself upon the low pallet-bed, and I could not persuade her to swallow more than a few spoonfuls of soup. I toot off her damp clothes, and laid her down comfortably to rest. Her eyes were dull and heavy, and she said her head was aching; but she looked up at me with a faint smile.

"I told you how nice it would be to be in bed," she whispered.

"It was not long before I was also sleeping soundly the deep, dreamless sleep which comes to any one as strong as I was, after unusual physical exertion. Once or twice a vague impression forced itself upon me that Minima was talking a great deal in her dreams. It was the clang of the bell for matins which fully roused me at last, but it was a minute or two before I could make out where I was. Through the uncurtained window, high in the opposite wall, I could see a dim, pallid moon sinking slowly into the west. The thick beams of the cross were strongly delineated against its pale light. For a moment I fancied that Minima and I had passed the night under the shelter of the solitary image, which we had left alone in the dark and rainy evening. I knew better immediately, and lay still, listening to the tramp of the wooden sabots hurrying past the door into the church-porch. Then Minima began to talk.

"How funny that is!" she said, "there the boys run, and I can't catch one of them. Father, Temple Secundus is pulling faces at me, and all the boys are laughing." "Well! it doesn't matter, does it? Only we are so poor, Aunt Nelly and all. We're so poor—so poor—so poor!"

Her voice fell into a murmur too low for me to hear what she was saying, though she went on talking rapidly, and laughing and sobbing at times. I called to her, but she did not answer.

What could ail the child? I went to her, and took her hands in mine—burning little hands. I said, "Minima! and she turned to me with a caressing gesture, raising her hot fingers to stroke my face.

"Yes, Aunt Nelly. How poor we are, you and me! I am so tired, and the prince never comes!"

There was hardly room for me in the narrow bed, but I managed to lie down beside her, and took her into my arms to soothe her. She rested there quietly enough; but her head was wandering, and all her whispered chatter was about the boys, and the dominie, her father, and the happy days at home in the school in Epping Forest. As soon as it was light I dressed myself in haste, and opened my door to see if I could find any one to send to Monsieur Laurentie.

The first person I saw was himself, coming in my direction. I had not fairly looked at him before, for I had seen him only by twilight and firelight. His cassock was old and threadbare, and his hat brown. His hair fell in rather long locks below his hat, and was beautifully white. His face was healthy-looking, like that of a man who lived much out-of-doors, and his clear, quick eyes shone with a kindly light. I ran impulsively to meet him, with outstretched hands, which he took into his own with a pleasant smile.

"Oh, come, monsieur," I cried; "make haste! She is ill, my poor Minima!"

The smile faded away from his face in an instant, and he did not utter a word. He followed me quickly to the side of the little bed, laid his hand softly on the child's forehead, and felt her pulse. He lifted up her head gently, and, opening her mouth, looked at her tongue and throat. He shook his head as he turned to me with a grave and perplexed expression, and he spoke with a low, solemn accent.

"Madame," he said, "it is the fever."

CHAPTER THE THIRTEENTH

A FEVER-HOSPITAL

The fever! What fever? Was it any thing more than some childish malady brought on by exhaustion? I stood silent, in amazement at his solemn manner, and looking from him to the delirious child. He was the first to speak again.

"It will be impossible for you to go to-day," he said; "the child cannot be removed. I must tell Jean to put up the horse and char à bancs again. I shall return in an instant to you, madame."

He left me, and I sank down on a chair, half stupefied by this new disaster. It would be necessary to stay where we were until Minima recovered; yet I had no means to pay these people for the trouble we should give them, and the expense we should be to them. Monsieur le Curé had all the appearance of a poor parish priest, with a very small income. I had not time to decide upon any course, however, before he returned and brought with him his sister.

Mademoiselle Thérèse was a tall, plain, elderly woman, but with the same pleasant expression of open friendliness as that of her brother. She went through precisely the same examination of Minima as he had done.

"The fever!" she ejaculated, in much the same tone as his. They looked significantly at each other, and then held a hurried consultation together outside the door, after which the curé returned alone.

"Madame," he said, "this child is not your own, as I supposed last night. My sister says you are too young to be her mother. Is she your sister?"

"No, monsieur," I answered.

"I called you madame because you were travelling alone," he continued, smiling; "French demoiselles never travel alone before they are married. You are mademoiselle, no doubt?"

An awkward question, for he paused as if it were a question. I look into his kind, keen face and honest eyes.

"No, monsieur," I said, frankly, "I am married."

"Where, then, is your husband?" he inquired.

"He is in London," I answered. "Monsieur, it is difficult for me to explain it; I cannot speak your language well enough. I think in English, and I cannot find the right French words. I am very unhappy, but I am not wicked."

"Good," he said, smiling again, "very good, my child; I believe you. You will learn my language quickly; then you shall tell me all, if you remain with us. But you said the mignonne is not your sister."

"No; she is not my relative at all," I replied; "we were both in a school at Noireau, the school of Monsieur Emile Perrier. Perhaps you know it, monsieur?"

"Certainly, madame," he said.

"He has failed and run away," I continued; "all the pupils are dispersed. Minima and I were returning through Granville."'

"Bien! I understand, madame," he responded; "but it is villanous, this affair! Listen, my child. I have much to say to you. Do I speak gently and slowly enough for you?"

"Yes," I answered; "I understand you perfectly."'

"We have had the fever in Ville-en-bois for some weeks," he went on; "it is now bad, very bad. Yesterday I went to Noireau to seek a doctor, but I could only hear of one, who is in Paris at present, and cannot come immediately. When you prayed me for succor last night, I did not know what to do. I could not leave you by the way-side, with the night coming on, and I could not take you to my own house. At present we have made my house into a hospital for the sick. My people bring their sick to me, and we do our best, and put our trust in God. I said to myself and to Jean, 'We cannot receive these children into the presbytery, lest they should take the fever.' But this little house has been kept free from all infection, and you would be safe here for one night, so I hoped. The mignonne must have caught the fever some days ago. There is no blame, therefore, resting upon me, you understand. Now I must carry her into my little hospital. But you, madame, what am I to do with you? Do you wish to go on to Granville, and leave the mignonne with me? We will take care of her as a little angel of God. What shall I do with you, my child?"

"Monsieur," I exclaimed, speaking so eagerly that I could scarcely bring my sentences into any kind of order, "take me into your hospital too. Let me take care of Minima and your other sick people. I am very strong, and in good health; I am never ill, never, never. I will do all you say to me. Let me stay, dear monsieur."

"But your husband, your friends—" he said.

"I have no friends," I interrupted, "and my husband does not love me. If I have the fever, and die—good! very good! I am not wicked; I am a Christian, I hope. Only let me stay with Minima, and do all I can in the hospital."

He stood looking at me scrutinizingly, trying to read, I fancied, if there were any sign of wickedness in my face. I felt it flush, but I would not let my eyes sink before his. I think he saw in them, in my steadfast, tearful eyes, that I might be unfortunate, but that I was not wicked. A pleasant gleam came across his features.

"Be content, my child," he said, "you shall stay with us."

I felt a sudden sense of contentment take possession of me; for here was work for me to do, as well as a refuge. Neither should I be compelled to leave Minima. I wrapped her up warmly in the blankets, and Monsieur Laurentie lifted her carefully and tenderly from the low bed. He told me to accompany him, and we crossed the court, and entered the house by the door I had seen the night before. A staircase of red quarries led up to the second story, and the first door we came to was a long, low room, with a quarried floor, which had been turned into a hastily-fitted-up fever-ward for women and children. There were already nine beds in it, of different sizes, brought with the patients who now occupied them. But one of these was empty.

I learned afterward that the girl to whom the bed belonged had died the day before, during the curé's absence, and was going to be buried that morning, in a cemetery lying in a field on the side of the valley. Mademoiselle Thérèse was making up the bed with homespun linen, scented with rosemary and lavender, and the curé laid Minima down upon it with all the skill of a woman. In this home-like ward I took up my work as nurse.

It was work that seemed to come naturally to me, as if I had a special gift for it. I remembered how some of the older shepherds on the station at home used to praise my mother's skill as a nurse. I felt as if I knew by instinct the wants of my little patients, when they could not put them into coherent words for themselves. They were mostly children, or quite young girls; for the older people who were stricken by the fever generally clung to their own homes, and the curé visited them there with the regularity of a physician. I liked to find for these suffering children a more comfortable position when they were weary; or to bathe their burning heads with some cool lotion; or to give the parched lips the titane Mademoiselle Thérèse prepared. Even the delirium of these little creatures was but a babbling about playthings, and fétes, and games. Minima, whose fever took faster hold of her day after day, prattled of the same things in English, only with sad alternations of moaning over our poverty.

It was probably these lamentations of Minima which made me sometimes look forward with dread to the time when this season of my life should be ended. I knew it could be only for a little while, an interlude, a brief, passing term, which must run quickly to its conclusion, and bring me face to face again with the terrible poverty which the child bemoaned in words no one could understand but myself. Already my own appearance was changing, as Mademoiselle Thérèse supplied the place of my clothing, which wore out with my constant work, replacing it with the homely costume of the Norman village. I could not expect to remain here when my task was done. The presbytery was too poor to offer me a shelter when I could be nothing but a burden in it. This good curé, who was growing fonder of me every day, and whom I had learned to love and honor, could not be a father to me as he was to his own people. Sooner or later there would come an hour when we must say adieu to one another, and I must go out once again to confront the uncertain future.

But for the present these fears were very much in the background, and I only felt that they were lurking there, ready for any moment of depression. I was kept too busy with the duties of the hour to attend to them. Some of the children died, and I grieved over them; some recovered sufficiently to be removed to a farm on the brow of the hill, where the air was fresher than in the valley. There was plenty to do and to think of from day to day.

CHAPTER THE FOURTEENTH

OUTCAST PARISHIONERS

"Madame." said Monsieur Laurentie; one morning, the eighth that I had been in the fever-smitten village, "you did not take a promenade yesterday."

"Not yesterday, monsieur."

"Nor the day before yesterday?" he continued.

"No, monsieur," I answered; "I dare not leave Minima, I fear she is going to die."

My voice failed me as I spoke to him. I was sitting down for a few minutes on a low seat, between Minima's bed and one where a little boy of six years of age lay. Both were delirious. He was the little son of Jean, our driver, and the sacristan of the church; and his father had brought him into the ward the evening of the day after Minima had been taken ill. Jean had besought me with tears to be good to his child. The two had engrossed nearly all my time and thoughts, and I was losing heart and hope every hour.

Monsieur Laurentie raised me gently from my low chair, and seated himself upon it, with a smile, as he looked up at me.

"Voilà, madame," he said, "I promise not to quit the chamber till you return. My sister has a little commission for you to do. Confide the mignonne to me, and make your promenade in peace. It is necessary, madame; you must obey me."

The commission for mademoiselle was to carry some food and medicine to a cottage lower down the valley; and Jean's eldest son, Pierre, was appointed to be my guide. Both the curé and his sister gave me a strict charge as to what we were to do; neither of us was upon any account to go near or enter the dwelling; but after the basket was deposited upon a flat stone, which Pierre was to point out to me, he was to ring a small hand-bell which he carried with him for that purpose. Then we were to turn our backs and begin our retreat, before any person came out of the infected house.

I set out with Pierre, a solemn-looking boy of about twelve years of age, who cast upon me sidelong glances of silent scrutiny. We passed down the village street, with its closely-packed houses forming a very nest for fever, until we reached the road by which I had first entered Ville-en-bois. Now that I could see it by daylight, the valley was extremely narrow, and the hills on each side so high that, though the sun had risen nearly three hours ago, it had but just climbed above the brow of the eastern slope. There was a luxurious and dank growth of trees, with a tangle of underwood and boggy soil beneath them. A vapor was shining in rainbow colors against the brightening sky. In the depth of the valley, but hidden by the thicket, ran a noisy stream—too noisy to be any thing else than shallow. There had been no frost since the sharp and keen wintry weather in December, and the heavy rains which had fallen since had flooded the stream, and made the lowlands soft and oozy with undrained moisture. My guide and I trudged along in silence for almost a kilometre.

"Are you a pagan, madame?" inquired Pierre, at last, with eager solemnity of face and voice. His blue eyes were fastened upon me pityingly.

"No, Pierre," I replied.

"But you are a heretic," he pursued.

"I suppose so," I said.

"Pagans and heretics are the same," he rejoined, dogmatically; "you are a heretic, therefore you are a pagan, madame."

"I am not a pagan," I persisted; "I am a Christian like you."

"Does Monsieur le Curé say you are a Christian?" he inquired.

"You can ask him, Pierre," I replied.

"He will know," he said, in a confident tone; "he knows every thing. There is no curé like monsieur between Ville-en-bois and Paris. All the world must acknowledge that. He is our priest, our doctor, our juge de paix, our school-master. Did you ever know a curé like him before, madame?"

"I never knew any curé before," I replied.

"Never knew any cure!" he repeated slowly; "then, madame, you must be a pagan. Did you never confess? Were you never prepared for your first communion? Oh! it is certain, madame, you are a true pagan."

We had not any more time to discuss my religion, for we were drawing near the end of our expedition. Above the tops of the trees appeared a tall chimney, and a sudden turn in the by-road we had taken brought us full in sight of a small cotton-mill, built on the banks of the noisy stream. It was an ugly, formal building, as all factories are, with straight rows of window-frames; but both walls and roof were mouldering into ruin, and looked as though they must before long sink into the brawling waters that were sapping the foundations. A more mournfully-dilapidated place I had never seen. A blight seemed to have fallen upon it; some solemn curse might be brooding over it, and slowly working out its total destruction.

In the yard adjoining this deserted factory stood a miserable cottage, with a thatched roof, and eaves projecting some feet from the walls, and reaching nearly to the ground, except where the door was. The small casements of the upper story, if there were any, were completely hidden. A row of fleur-de-lis was springing up, green and glossy, along the peak of the brown thatch; this and the picturesque eaves forming its only beauty. The thatch looked old and rotten, and was beginning to steam in the warm sunshine. The unpaved yard about it was a slough of mire and mud. There were mould and mildew upon all the wood-work. The place bore the aspect of a pest-house, shunned by all the inmates of the neighboring village. Pierre led me to a large flat stone, which had once been a horse-block, standing at a safe distance from this hovel, and I laid down my basket upon it. Then he rang his hand-bell noisily, and the next instant was scampering back along the road.

But I could not run away. The desolate, plague-stricken place had a dismal fascination for me. I wondered what manner of persons could dwell in it; and, as I lingered, I saw the low door opened, and a thin, spectral figure standing in the gloom within, but delaying to cross the mouldering door-sill as long as I remained in sight. In another minute Pierre had rushed back for me, and dragged me away with all his boyish strength and energy.

"Madame," he said, in angry remonstrance, "you are disobeying Monsieur le Curé. If you catch the fever, and die while you are a pagan, it will be impossible for you to go to heaven. It would be a hundred times better for me to die, who have taken my first communion."

"But who lives there?" I asked.

"They are very wicked people," he answered, emphatically; "no one goes near them, except Monsieur le Curé, and he would go and nurse the devil himself, if he had the fever in his parish. They became wicked before my time, and Monsieur le Curé has forbidden us to speak of them with rancor, so we do not speak of them at all."

I walked back in sadness, wondering at this misery and solitariness by the side of the healthy, simple society of the lonely village, with its interwoven family interests. As I passed through the street again, I heard the click of the hand-looms in most of the dwellings, and saw the pale-faced weavers, in their white and tasselled caps, here a man and there a woman, look after me, while they suspended their work for a moment. Every door was open; the children ran in and out of any house, playing together as if they were of one family; the women were knitting in companies under the eaves. Who were these pariahs, whose name even was banished from every tongue? I must ask the curé himself.

But I had no opportunity that day. When I returned to the sick-ward, I found Monsieur Laurentie pacing slowly up and down the long room, with Jean's little son in his arms, to whom he was singing in a low, soft voice, scarcely louder than a whisper. His eyes, when they met mine, were glistening with tears, and he shook his head mournfully.

I went on to look at Minima. She was lying quiet, too weak and exhausted to be violent, but chattering all the time in rapid, childish sentences. I could do nothing for her, and I went back to the hearth, where the curé was now standing, looking sadly at the child in his arms. He bade me sit down on a tabouret that stood there, and laid his little burden on my lap.

"The child has no mother, madame," he said; "let him die in a woman's arms."

I had never seen any one die, not even my father, and I shrank from seeing it. But the small white face rested helplessly against my arm, and the blue eyes unclosed for a moment, and gazed into mine, almost with a smile. Monsieur Laurentie called in Jean and Pierre, and they knelt before us in silence, broken only by sobs. In the room there were children's voices talking about their toys, and calling to one another in shrill, feverish accents. How many deaths such as this was I to witness?

"Monsieur le Curé!" murmured the failing voice of the little child.

"What is it, my little one?" he said, stooping over him.

"Shall I play sometimes with the little child Jesus?"

The words fell one by one from the feeble lips.

"Yes, mon chéri, yes. The holy child Jesus knows what little children need," answered the curé.

"He is always good and wise," whispered the dying child; "so good, so wise."

How quickly it was over after that!

CHAPTER THE FIFTEENTH

A TACITURN FRENCHWOMAN

Minima was so much worse that night, that Monsieur Laurentie gave me permission to sit up with Mademoiselle Thérèse, to watch beside her. There was a kindly and unselfish disposition about Monsieur le Curé which it was impossible to resist, or even gainsay. His own share of the trouble, anxiety, and grief, was so large, that he seemed to stand above us all, and be naturally our director and ruler. But to-night, when I begged to stay with Minima, he conceded the point without a word.

Mademoiselle Thérèse was the most silent woman I ever met. She could pass a whole day without uttering a word, and did not seem to suffer any ennui from her silence. In the house she wore always, like the other inhabitants of the village, men and women, soundless felt socks, which slipped readily into the wooden sabots used for walking out-of-doors. I was beginning to learn to walk in sabots myself, for the time was drawing rapidly near when otherwise I should be barefoot.

With this taciturn Frenchwoman I entered upon my night-watch by Minima, whose raving no one could understand but myself. The long, dark hours seemed interminable. Mademoiselle sat knitting a pair of gray stockings in the intervals of attendance upon our patients. The subdued glimmer of the night-lamp, the ticking of the clock, the chimes every quarter of an hour from the church-tower, all conspired to make me restless and almost nervous.

"Mademoiselle," I said, at last, "talk to me. I cannot bear this tranquillity. Tell me something."

"What can I tell you, madame?" she inquired, in a pleasant tone.

"Tell me about those people I saw this morning," I answered.

"It is a long history," she said, her face kindling, as if this were a topic that excited her; and she rolled up her knitting, as though she could not trust herself to continue that while she was talking; "all the world knows it here, and we never talk of it now. Bat you are a stranger; shall I tell it you?"

I had hit upon the only subject that could unlock her lips. It was the night-time too. At night one is naturally more communicative than in the broad light of day.

"Madame," she said, in an agitated voice, "you have observed already that my brother is not like other curés. He has his own ideas, his own sentiments. Everybody knows him at this moment as the good Curé of Ville-en-bois; but when he came here first, thirty years ago, all the world called him infidel, heretic, atheist. It was because he would make many changes in the church and parish. The church had been famous for miracles; but Francis did not believe in them, and he would not encourage them. There used to be pilgrimages to it from all the country round; and crowds of pilgrims, who spend much money. There was a great number of crutches left at the shrine of the Virgin by cripples who had come here by their help, but walked away without them. He cleared them all away, and called them rubbish. So every one said he was an infidel—you understand?"

"I understand it very well," I said.

"Bien! At that time there was one family richer than all the others. They were the proprietors of the factory down yonder, and everybody submitted to them. There was a daughter not married, but very dévote. I have been dévote, myself. I was coquette till I was thirty-five, then I became dévote. It is easier than being a simple Christian, like my brother the curé. Mademoiselle Pineau was accustomed to have visions, ecstasies. Sometimes the angels lifted her from the ground into the air when she was at her prayers. Francis did not like that. He was young, and she came very often to the confessional, and told him of these visions and ecstasies. He discouraged them, and enjoined penances upon her. Bref! she grew to detest him, and she was quite like a female curé in the parish. She set everybody against him. At last, when he removed all the plaster images of the saints, and would have none but wood or stone, she had him cited to answer for it to his bishop."

"But what did he do that for?" I asked, seeing no difference between plaster images, and those of wood or stone.

"Madame, these Normans are ignorant and very superstitious," she replied; "they thought a little powder from one of the saints would cure any malady. Some of the images were half-worn away with having powder scraped off them. My brother would not hold with such follies, and his bishop told him he might fight the battle out, if he could. No one thought he could; but they did not know Francis. It was a terrible battle, madame. Nobody would come to the confessional, and every month or so, he was compelled to have a vicaire from some other parish to receive the confessions of his people. Mademoiselle Pineau fanned the flame, and she had the reputation of a saint."

"But how did it end?" I inquired. Mademoiselle's face was all aglow, and her voice rose and fell in her excitement; yet she lingered over the story as if reluctant to lose the rare pleasure of telling it.

"In brief, madame," she resumed, "there was a terrible conflagration in the village. You perceive that all our houses are covered with tiles? In those days the roofs were of thatch, very old and very dry, and there was much timber in the walls. How the fire began, the good God alone knows. It was a sultry day in July; the river was almost dry, and there was no hope of extinguishing the flames. They ran like lightning from roof to roof. All that could be done was to save life, and a little property. My brother threw off his cassock, and worked like Hercules.

"The Pineaux lived then close by the presbytery, in a house half of wood, which blazed like tinder; there was nothing comparable to it in all the village. A domestic suddenly cried out that mademoiselle was in her oratory, probably in a trance. Not a soul dares venture through the flames to save her, though she is a saint. Monsieur le Curé hears the rumor of it; he steps in through the doorway through which the smoke is rolling; walks in as tranquilly as if he were going to make a visit as pastor; he is lost to their sight; not a man stirs to look after his own house. Bref! he comes back to the day, his brown hair all singed and his face black, carrying mademoiselle in his arms. Good: The battle is finished. All the world adores him."

"Continue, mademoiselle, I pray you," I said, eagerly; "do not leave off there."

"Bien! Monsieur le Curé and his unworthy sister had a small fortune which was spent, for the people. He begged for them; he worked with them; he learned to do many things to help them. He lives for them and them only. He has refused to leave them for better positions. They are not ungrateful; they love him, they lean upon him."

"But the Pineaux?" I suggested.

"Bah! I had forgotten them. Their factory was burnt at the same time. It is more than a kilometre from here; but who can say how far the burning thatch might be carried on the wind? It was insured for a large sum in a bureau in Paris. But there were suspicions raised and questions asked. Our sacristan, Jean, who was then a young boy, affirmed that he had seen some one carrying a lighted torch around the building, after the work-people had all fled to see after their own houses. The bureau refused to pay, except by a process of law; and the Pineaux never began their process. They worked the factory a few years on borrowed money; but they became poor, very poor. Mademoiselle ceased to be dévote, and did not come near the church or the confessional again. Now they are despised and destitute. Not a person goes near them, except my good brother, whom they hate still. There remain but three of them, the old monsieur, who is very aged, a son, and mademoiselle, who is as old as myself. The son has the fever, and Francis visits him almost every day."

"It is a wretched, dreadful place," I said, shuddering at the remembrance of it.

"They will die there probably," she remarked, in a quiet voice, and with an expression of some weariness now the tale was told; "my brother refuses to let me go to see them. Mademoiselle hates me, because in some part I have taken her place. Francis says there is work enough for me at home. Madame, I believe the good God sent you here to help us."

CHAPTER THE SIXTEENTH

SENT BY GOD

I discovered that mademoiselle's opinion was shared by all the people in Ville-en-bois, and Monsieur Laurentie favored the universal impression. I had been sent to them by a special providence. There was something satisfactory and consolatory to them all in my freedom from personal anxieties and cares like their own. I had neither parent, nor husband, nor child to be attacked by the prevailing infection. As soon as Minima had passed safely through the most dangerous stages of the fever, I was at leisure to listen to and sympathize with each one of them. Possibly there was something in the difficulty I still experienced in expressing myself fluently which made me a better listener, and so won them to pour out their troubles into my attentive ear. Jean and Pierre especially were devoted to me, since the child that had belonged to them had died upon my lap.

Through March, April, and May, the fever had its fling, though we were not very long without a doctor. Monsieur Laurentie found one who came and, I suppose, did all he could for the sick; but he could not do much. I was kept too busily occupied to brood much either upon the past or the future, of my own life. Not a thought crossed my mind of deserting the little Norman village where I could be of use. Besides, Minima gained strength very slowly, too slowly to be removed from the place, or to encounter any fresh privations.

When June came there were no new cases in the village, though the summer-heat kept our patients languid. The last person who died of the fever was Mademoiselle Pineau, in the mill-cottage. The old man and his son had died before her, the former of old age, the latter of fever. Who was the heir to the ruined factory and the empty cottage no one as yet knew, but, until he appeared, every thing had to be left as it was. The curé kept the key of the dwelling, though there was no danger of any one trespassing upon the premises, as all the villagers regarded it as an accursed place. Of the four hundred and twenty-two souls which had formed the total of Monsieur le Curé's flock, he had lost thirty-one.

In July the doctor left us, saying there was no fear of the fever breaking out again at present. His departure seemed the signal for mine. Monsieur Laurentie was not rich enough to feed two idle mouths, like mine and Minima's, and there was little for me to do but sit still in the uncarpeted, barely-furnished salon of the presbytery, listening to the whirr of mademoiselle's spinning-wheel, and the drowsy, sing-song hum of the village children at school, in a shed against the walls of the house. Every thing seemed falling back into the pleasant monotony of a peaceful country life, pleasant after the terror and grief of the past months. The hay-harvest was over, and the cherry-gathering; the corn and the apples were ripening fast in the heat of the sun. In this lull, this pause, my heart grew busy again with itself.

"My child," said the curé to me, one evening, when his long day's work was over, "your face is triste. What are you thinking of?"

I was seated under a thick-leaved sycamore, a few paces from the church-porch. Vespers were just ended; the low chant had reached my ears, and I missed the soothing undertone. The women, in their high white caps, and the men, in their blue blouses, were sauntering slowly homeward. The children were playing all down the village street, and not far away a few girls and young men were beginning to dance to the piping of a flute. Over the whole was creeping the golden twilight of a summer evening.

"I am very triste" I replied; "I am thinking that it is time for me to go away from you all. I cannot stay in this tranquil place."

"But wherefore must you leave us?" he asked, sitting down on the bench beside me; "I found two little stray lambs, wandering without fold or shepherd, and I brought them to my own house. What compels them to go into the wide world again?"

"Monsieur, we are poor," I answered, "and you are not rich. We should be a burden to you, and we have no claim upon you."

"You have a great claim," he said; "there is not a heart in the parish that does not love you already. Have not our children died in your arms? Have you not watched over them? spent sleepless nights and watchful days for them? How could we endure to see you go away? Remain with us, madame; live with us, you and my mignonne, whose face is white yet."

Could I stay then? It was a very calm, very secure refuge. There was no danger of discovery. Yet there was a restlessness in my spirit at war with the half-mournful, half-joyous serenity of the place, where I had seen so many people die, and where there were so many new graves in the little cemetery up the hill. If I could go away for a while, I might return, and learn to be content amid this tranquillity.

"Madame," said the pleasant tones of Monsieur Laurentie, "do you know our language well enough to tell me your history now? You need not prove to me that you are not wicked; tell me how you are unfortunate. Where were you wandering to that night when I found you at the foot of the Calvary?"

There, in the cool, deepening twilight, I told him my story, little by little; sometimes at a loss for words, and always compelled to speak in the simplest and most direct phrases. He listened, with no other interruption than to supply me occasionally with an expression when I hesitated. He appeared to understand me almost by intuition. It was quite dark before I had finished, and the deep blue of the sky above us was bright with stars. A glow-worm was moving among the tufts of grass growing between the roots of the tree; and I watched it almost as intently as if I had nothing else to think of.

"Speak to me as if I were your daughter," I said. "Have I done right or wrong? Would you give me up to him, if he came to claim me?"

"I am thinking of thee as my daughter," he answered, leaning his hands and his white head above them, upon the top of the stick he was holding, and sitting so for some moments in silent thought. "Thy voice is not the voice of passion," he continued; "it is the voice of conviction, profound and confirmed. Thou mayst have fled from him in a paroxysm of wrath, but thy judgment and conscience acquit thee of wrong. In my eyes it is a sacrament which thou hast broken; yet he had profaned it first. My daughter, if thy husband returned to thee, penitent, converted, confessing his offences against thee, couldst thou forgive him?"

"Yes," I answered, "yes! I could forgive him."

"Thou wouldst return to him?" he said, in calm, penetrating accents, but so low as to seem almost the voice of my own heart; "thou wouldst be subject to him as the Church is subject to Christ? He would be thy head; wouldst thou submit thyself unto him as unto the Lord?"

"I shivered with dread as the quiet, solemn tones fell upon my ear, poignantly, as if they must penetrate to my heart. I could not keep myself from sobbing. His face was turned toward me in the dusk, and I covered mine with my hands.

"Not now," I cried; "I cannot, I cannot. I was so young, monsieur; I did not know what I was promising. I could never return to him, never."

"My daughter," pursued the inexorable voice beside me, "is it because there is any one whom thou lovest more?"

"Oh!" I cried, almost involuntarily, and speaking now in my own language, "I do not know. I could have loved Martin dearly—dearly."

"I do not understand thy words," said Monsieur Laurentie, "but I understand thy tears and sighs. Thou must stay here, my daughter, with me, and these poor, simple people who love thee. I will not let thee go into temptation. Courage; thou wilt be happy among us, when thou hast conquered this evil. As for the rest, I must think about it. Let us go in now. The lamp has been lit and supper served this half-hour. There is my sister looking out at us. Come, madame. You are in my charge, and I will take care of you."

A few days after this, the whole community was thrown into a tumult by the news that their curé was about to undertake the perils of a voyage to England, and would be absent a whole fortnight. He said it was to obtain some information as to the English system of drainage in agricultural districts, which might make their own valley more healthy and less liable to fever. But it struck me that he was about to make some inquiries concerning my husband, and perhaps about Minima, whose desolate position had touched him deeply. I ventured to tell him what danger might arise to me if any clew to my hiding-place fell into Richard Foster's hands.

"My poor child," he said, "why art thou so fearful? There is not a man here who would not protect thee. He would be obliged to prove his identity, and thine, before he could establish his first right to claim thee. Then we would enter a procés. Be content. I am going to consult some lawyers of my own country and thine."

He bade us farewell, with as many directions and injunctions as a father might leave to a large family of sons and daughters. Half the village followed his char-à-banc as far as the cross where he had found Minima and me, six miles on his road to Noireau. His sister and I, who had ridden with him so far, left him there, and walked home up the steep, long road, in the midst of that enthusiastic crowd of his parishioners.

CHAPTER THE SEVENTEENTH

A MOMENT OF TRIUMPH

The afternoon of that day was unusually sultry and oppressive. The blue of the sky was almost livid. I was weary with the long walk in the morning, and after our mid-day meal I stole away from mademoiselle and Minima in the salon, and betook myself to the cool shelter of the church, where the stone walls three feet thick, and the narrow casements covered with vine-leaves, kept out the heat more effectually than the half-timber walls of the presbytery. A vicaire from a neighboring parish was to arrive in time for vespers, and Jean and Pierre were polishing up the interior of the church, with an eye to their own credit. It was a very plain, simple building, with but few images in it, and only two or three votive pictures, very ugly, hanging between the low Norman arches of the windows. A shrine occupied one transept, and before it the offerings of flowers were daily renewed by the unmarried girls of the village.

I sat down upon a bench just within the door, and the transept was not in sight, but I could hear Pierre busy at his task of polishing the oaken floor, by skating over it with brushes fastened to his feet. Jean was bustling in and out of the sacristy, and about the high altar in the chancel. There was a faint scent yet of the incense which had been burned at the mass celebrated before the curé's departure, enough to make the air heavy and to deepen the drowsiness and languor which were stealing over me. I leaned my head against the wall and closed my eyes, with a pleasant sense of sleep coming softly toward me, when suddenly a hand was laid upon my arm, with a firm, close, silent gripe.

I do not know why terror always strikes me dumb and motionless. I did not stir or speak, but looked steadily, with a fascinated gaze, into my husband's face—a worn, white, emaciated face, with eyes peering cruelly into mine. It was an awful look; one of dark triumph, of sneering, cunning exultation. Neither of us spoke. Pierre I could hear still busy in the transept, and Jean, though he had disappeared into the sacristy, was within call. Yet I felt hopelessly and helplessly alone under the cruel stare of those eyes. It seemed as if he and I were the only beings in the whole world, and there was none to help, none to rescue. In the voiceless depths of my spirit I cried, "O God!"

He sank down on the seat beside me, with an air of exhaustion, yet with a low, fiendish laugh which sounded hideously loud in my ears. His fingers were still about my arm, but he had to wait to recover from the first shock of his success—for it had been a shock. His face was bathed with perspiration, and his breath came and went fitfully. I thought I could even hear the heavy throbbing of his heart. He spoke after a time, while my eyes were still fastened upon him, and my ears listening to catch the first words he uttered.

"I've found you," he said, his hand tightening its hold, and at the first sound of his voice the spell which bound me snapped; "I've tracked you out at last to this cursed hole. The game is up, my little lady. By Heaven! you'll repent of this. You are mine, and no man on earth shall come between us."

"I don't understand you," I muttered. He had spoken in an undertone, and I could not raise my voice above a whisper, so parched and dry my throat was.

"Understand?" he said, with a shrug of his shoulders. "I know all about Dr. Martin Dobrée. You understand that well enough. I am here to take charge of you, to carry you home with me as my wife, and neither man nor woman can interfere with me in that. It will be best for you to come with me quietly."

"I will not go with you," I answered, in the same hoarse whisper; "I am living here in the presbytery, and you cannot force me away. I will not go."

He laughed a little once more, and looked down upon me contemptuously in silence, as if there were no notice to be taken of words so foolish.

"Listen to me," I continued. "When I refused to sign away the money my father left me, it was because I said to myself it was wrong to throw away his life's toil and skill upon pursuits like yours. He had worked, and saved, and denied himself for me, not for a man like you. His money should not be flung away at gambling-tables. But now I know he would rather a thousand times you had the money and left me free. Take it then. You shall have it all. We are both poor as it is, but if you will let me be free of you, you may have it all—all that I can part with."

"I prefer having the money and you," he replied, with his frightful smile. "Why should I not prize what other people covet? You are my wife; nothing can set that aside. Your money is mine, and you are mine; why should I forfeit either?"

"No," I said, growing calmer; "I do not belong to you. No laws on earth can give you the ownership you claim over me. Richard, you might have won me, if you had been a good man. But you are evil and selfish, and you have lost me forever."

"The silly raving of an ignorant girl!" he sneered; "the law will compel you to return to me. I will take the law into my own hands, and compel you to go with me at once. If there is no conveyance to be hired in this confounded hole, we will walk down the road together, like two lovers, and wait for the omnibus. Come, Olivia."

Our voices had not risen much above their undertones yet, but these last words he spoke more loudly. Jean opened the door of the sacristy and looked out, and Pierre skated down to the corner of the transept to see who was speaking. I lifted the hand Richard was not holding, and beckoned Jean to me.

"Jean," I said, in a low tone still, "this man is my enemy. Monsieur le Curé knows all about him; but he is not here. You must protect me."

"Certainly, madame," he replied, his eyes more roundly open than ordinarily—"Monsieur, have the goodness to release madame."

"She is my wife," retorted Richard Foster.

"I have told all to Monsieur le Curé," I said.

"Bon!" ejaculated Jean. Monsieur le Curé is gone to England; it is necessary to wait till his return, Monsieur Englishman."

"Fool!" said Richard in a passion, "she is my wife, I tell you."

"Bon!" he replied phlegmatically, "but it is my affair to protect madame. There is no resource but to wait till Monsieur le Curé returns from his voyage. If madame does not say, 'This is my husband,' how can I believe you? She says, 'He is my enemy.' I cannot confide madame to a stranger."

"I will not leave her," he exclaimed with an oath, spoken in English, which Jean could not understand.

"Good! very good! Pardon, monsieur," responded Jean, laying his iron fingers upon the hand that held me, and loosening its grip as easily as if it had been the hand of a child—"Voilà! madame, you are free. Leave Monsieur the Englishman to me, and go away into the house, if you please."

I did not wait to hear any further altercation, but fled as quickly as I could into the presbytery. Up into my own chamber I ran, drew a heavy chest against the door, and fell down trembling and nerveless upon the floor beside it.

But there was no time to lose in womanish terrors; my difficulty and danger were too great. The curé was gone, and would be away at least a fortnight. How did I know what French law might do with me, in that time? I dragged myself to the window, and, with my face just above the sill, looked down the street, to see if my husband were in sight. He was nowhere to be seen, but loitering at one of the doors was the letter-carrier, whose daily work it was to meet the afternoon omnibus returning from Noireau to Granville. Why should I not write to Tardif? He had promised to come to my help whenever and wherever I might summon him. I ran down to Mademoiselle Thérèse for the materials for a letter, and in a few minutes it was written, and on the way to Sark.

I was still watching intently from my own casement, when I saw Richard Foster come round the corner of the church, and turn down the street. Many of the women were at their doors, and he stopped to speak to first one and then another. I guessed what he wanted. There was no inn in the valley, and he was trying to hire a lodging for the night. But Jean was following him closely, and from every house he was turned away, baffled and disappointed. He looked weary and bent, and he leaned heavily upon the strong stick he carried. At last he passed slowly out of sight, and once more I could breathe freely.

But I could not bring myself to venture downstairs, where the uncurtained windows were level with the court, and the unfastened door opened to my hand. The night fell while I was still alone, unnerved by the terror I had undergone. Here and there a light glimmered in a lattice-window, but a deep silence reigned, with no other sound than the brilliant song of a nightingale amid the trees which girdled the village. Suddenly there was the noisy rattle of wheels over the rough pavement—the baying of dogs—an indistinct shout from the few men who were still smoking their pipes under the broad eaves of their houses. A horrible dread took hold of me. Was it possible that he returned, with some force—I knew not what—which should drag me away from my refuge, and give me up to him? What would Jean and the villagers do? What could they do against a body of gendarmes?

I gazed shrinkingly into the darkness. The conveyance looked, as far as I could make out of its shape, very like the char-à-banc, which was not to return from Noireau till the next day. But there was only the gleam of the lantern it carried on a pole rising above its roof, and throwing crossbeams of light upon the walls and windows on each side of the street. It came on rapidly, and passed quickly out of my sight round the angle of the presbytery. My heart scarcely beat, and my ear was strained to catch every sound in the house below.

I heard hurried footsteps and joyous voices. A minute or two afterward, Minima beat against my barricaded door, and shouted gleefully through the key-hole:

"Come down in a minute, Aunt Nelly," she cried; "Monsieur Laurentie is come home again!"

CHAPTER THE EIGHTEENTH

PIERRE'S SECRET

I felt as if some strong hand had lifted me out of a whirl of troubled waters, and set me safely upon a rock. I ran down into the salon, where Monsieur Laurentie was seated, as tranquilly as if he had never been away, in his high-backed arm-chair, smiling quietly at Minima's gambols of delight, which ended in her sitting down on a tabouret at his feet. Jean stood just within the door, his hands behind his back, holding his white cotton cap in them: he had been making his report of the day's events. Monsieur held out his hand to me, and I ran to him, caught it in both of mine, bent down my face upon it, and burst into a passion of weeping, in spite of myself.

"Come, come, madame!" he said, his own voice faltering a little, "I am here, my child; behold me! There is no place for fear now. I am king in Ville-en-bois—Is it not so, my good Jean?"

"Monsieur le Curé, you are emperor," replied Jean.

"If that is the case," he continued, "madame is perfectly secure in my castle. You do not ask me what brings me back again so soon. But I will tell you, madame. At Noireau, the proprietor of the omnibus to Granville told me that an Englishman had gone that morning to visit my little parish. Good! We do not have that honor every day. I ask him to have the goodness to tell me the Englishman's name. It is written in the book at the bureau. Monsieur Fostère. I remember that name well, very well. That is the name of the husband of my little English daughter. Fostère! I see in a moment it will not do to proceed, on my voyage. But I find that my good Jacques has taken on the char-à-banc a league or two beyond Noireau, and I am compelled to await his return. There is the reason that I return so late."

"O monsieur!" I exclaimed, "how good you are—"

"Pardon, madame," he interrupted, "let me hear the end of Jean's history."

Jean continued his report in his usual phlegmatic tone, and concluded with the assurance that he had seen the Englishman safe out of the village, and returning by the road he came.

"I could have wished," said the curé, regretfully, "that we might have shown him some hospitality in Ville-en-bois; but you did what was very good, Jean. Yet we did not encounter any stranger along the route."

"Not possible, monsieur," replied Jean; "it was four o'clock when he returned on his steps, and it is now after nine. He would pass the Calvary before six. After that, Monsieur le Curé, he might take any route which pleased him."

"That is true, Jean," he said, mildly; "you have done well. You may go now. Where is Monsieur the Vicaire?"

"He sleeps, monsieur, in the guest's chamber, as usual."

"Bien! Good-evening, Jean, and a good-night."

"Good-night, Monsieur le Curé, and all the company," said Jean.

"And you also, my child," continued Monsieur Laurentie, when Jean was gone, "you have great need of rest. So has this baby, who is very sleepy."

"I am not sleepy," protested Minima, "and I am not a baby."

"You are a baby," said the curé, laughing, "to make such rejoicing over an old papa like me. But go now, my children. There is no danger for you. Sleep well and have pleasant dreams."

I slept well, but I had no pleasant dreams, for I did not dream at all. The curé's return, and his presence under the same roof, gave me such a sense of security as was favorable to profound, unbroken slumber. When the chirping of the birds awoke me in the morning, I could not at first believe that the events of the day before were not themselves a dream. The bell rang for matins at five o'clock now, to give the laborers the cool of the morning for their work in the fields, after they were over. I could not sleep again, for the coming hours must be full of suspense and agitation to me. So at the first toll of the deep-toned bell, I dressed myself, and went out into the dewy freshness of the new day.

Matins were ended, and the villagers were scattered about their farms and households, when I noticed Pierre loitering stealthily about the presbytery, as if anxious not to be seen. He made me a sign as soon as he caught my eye, to follow him out of sight, round the corner of the church. It was a mysterious sign, and I obeyed it quickly.

"I know a secret, madame," he said, in a troubled tone, and with an apprehensive air—"that monsieur who came yesterday has not left the valley. My father bade me stay in the church, at my work; but I could not, madame, I could not. Not possible, you know. I wished to see your enemy again. I shall have to confess it to Monsieur le Curé, and he will give me a penance, perhaps a very great penance. But it was not possible to rest tranquil, not at all. I followed monsieur, your enemy, à la dérobée. He did not go far away."

"But where is he, then?" I asked, looking down the street, with a thrill of fear.

"Madame," whispered Pierre, "he is a stranger to this place, and the people would not receive him into their houses—not one of them. My father only said, 'He is an enemy to our dear English madame,' and all the women turned the back upon him. I stole after him, you know, behind the trees and the hedges. He marched very slowly, like a man very weary, down the road, till he came in sight of the factory of the late Pineaux. He turned aside into the court there. I saw him knock at the door of the house, try to lift the latch, and peep through the windows. Bien! After that, he goes into the factory; there is a door from it into the house. He passed through. I dared not follow him, but in one short half-hour I saw smoke coming out of the chimney. Bon! The smoke is there again this morning. The Englishman has sojourned there all the night."

"But, Pierre," I said, shivering, though the sun was already shining hotly—"Pierre, the house is like a lazaretto. No one has been in it since Mademoiselle Pineau died. Monsieur le Curé locked it up, and brought away the key."

"That is true, madame," answered the boy; "no one in the village would go near the accursed place; but I never thought of that. Perhaps monsieur your enemy will take the fever, and perish."

"Run, Pierre, run," I cried; "Monsieur Laurentie is in the sacristy, with the strange vicaire. Tell him I must speak to him this very moment. There is no time to be lost."

I dragged myself to the seat under the sycamore-tree, and hid my face in my hands, while shudder after shudder quivered through me. I seemed to be watching him again, as he strode wearily down the street, leaning, with bent shoulders, on his stick, and turned away from every door at which he asked for rest and shelter for the night. Oh! that the time could but come back again, that I might send Jean to find some safe place for him where he could sleep! Back to my memory rushed the old days, when he screened me from the unkindness of my step-mother, and when he seemed to love me. For the sake of those times, would to God the evening that was gone, and the sultry, breathless night, could only come back again!

CHAPTER THE NINETEENTH

SUSPENSE

I felt as if I had passed through an immeasurable spell, both of memory and anguish, before Monsieur Laurentie came to me, though he had responded to my summons immediately. I told him, in hurried, broken sentences, what Pierre had confessed to me. His face grew overcast and troubled; yet he did not utter a word of his apprehensions to me.

"Madame," he said, "permit me to take my breakfast first; then I will seek Monsieur Foster without delay. I will carry with me some food for him. We will arrange this affair before I return; Jean shall bring the char à bancs to the factory, and take him back to Noireau."

"But the fever, monsieur? Can he pass a night there without taking it?"

"He is in the hands of his Creator," he answered; "we can know nothing till I have seen him. We cannot call back the past."

"Ought I not to go with you?" I asked.

"Wherefore, my child?"

"He is my husband," I said, falteringly; "if he is ill, I will nurse him."

"Good! my poor child," he replied, "leave all this affair to me; leave even thy duty to me. I will take care there shall be no failure in it, on thy part."

We were not many minutes over our frugal breakfast of bread-and-milk, and then we set out together, for he gave me permission to go with him, until we came within sight of the factory and the cottage. We walked quickly and in foreboding silence. He told me, as soon as he saw the place, that I might stay on the spot where he left me, till the church-clock struck eight; and then, if he had not returned to me, I must go back to the village, and send Jean with the char à bancs. I sat down on the felled trunk of a tree, and watched him, in his old threadbare cassock, and sunburnt hat, crossing the baked, cracked soil of the court, till he reached the door, and turned round to lift his hat to me with a kindly gesture of farewell. He fitted the key into the lock, passed out of my sight; but I could not withdraw my eyes from the deep, thatched eaves, and glossy fleur-de-lis growing along the roof.

How interminable seemed his absence! I sat so still that the crickets and grasshoppers in the tufted grass about me kept up their ceaseless chirruping, and leaped about my feet, unaware that I could crush their merry life out of them by a single movement. The birds in the dusky branches overhead whistled their wild wood-notes, as gayly as if no one were near their haunts. Now and then there came a pause, when the silence deepened until I could hear the cones, in the fir-trees close at hand, snapping open their polished scales, and setting free the winged seeds, which fluttered softly down to the ground. The rustle of a swiftly—gliding snake through the fallen leaves caught my ear, and I saw the blunted head and glittering eyes lifted up to look at me for a moment; but I did not stir. All my fear and feeling, my whole life, were centred upon the fever-cottage yonder.

There was not the faintest line of smoke from the chimney, when we first came in sight of it. Was it not quite possible that Pierre might have been mistaken? And if he had made a mistake in thinking he saw smoke this morning, why not last night also? Yet the curé was lingering there too long for it to be merely an empty place. Something detained him, or why did he not come back to me? Presently a thin blue smoke curled upward into the still air. Monsieur Laurentie was kindling a fire on the hearth. He was there then.

What would be the end of it all? My heart contracted, and my spirit shrank from the answer that was ready to flash upon my mind. I refused to think of the end. If Richard were ill, why, I would nurse him, as I should have nursed him if he had always been tender and true to me. That at least was a clear duty. What lay beyond that need not be decided upon now. Monsieur Laurentie would tell me what I ought to do.

He came, after a long, long suspense, and opened the door, looking out as if to make sure that I was still at my post. I sprang to my feet, and was running forward, when he beckoned me to remain where I was.

He came across to the middle of the court, but no nearer; and he spoke to me at that distance, in his clear, deliberate, penetrating voice.

"My child," he said, "monsieur is ill! attacked, I am afraid, by the fever. He is not delirious at present, and we have been talking together of many things. But the fever has taken hold upon him, I think. I shall remain with him all the day. You must bring us what we have need of, and leave it on the stone there, as it used to be."

"But cannot he be removed at once?" I asked.

"My dear," he answered, "what can I do? The village is free from sickness now; how can I run the risk of carrying the fever there again? It is too far to send monsieur to Noireau. If he is ill of it, it is best for us all that he should remain here. I will not abandon him; no, no. Obey me, my child, and leave him to me and to God. Cannot you confide in me yet?"

"Yes," I said, weeping, "I trust you with all my heart."

"Go, then, and do what I bid you," he replied. "Tell my sister and Jean, tell all my people, that no one must intrude upon me, no one must come nearer this house than the appointed place. Monsieur le Vicaire must remain in Ville-en-bois, and officiate for me, as though I were pursuing my journey to England. You must think of me as one absent, yet close at hand: that is the difference. I am here, in the path of my duty. Go, and fulfil yours."

"Ought you not to let me share your work and your danger?" I ventured to ask.

"If there be any need, you shall share both," he answered, in a tranquil tone, "though your life should be the penalty. Life is nothing in comparison with duty. When it is thy duty, my daughter, to be beside thy husband, I will call thee without fail."

Slowly I retraced my steps to the village. The news had already spread, from Pierre—for no one else knew it—that the Englishman, who had been turned away from their doors the day before, had spent the night in the infected dwelling. A group of weavers, of farmers, of women from their household work, stopped me as I entered the street. I delivered to them their curé's message, and they received it with sobs and cries, as though it bore in it the prediction of a great calamity. They followed me up the street to the presbytery, and crowded the little court in front of it.

When mademoiselle had collected the things Monsieur Laurentie had sent me for—a mattress, a chair, food, and medicine—every person in the crowd wished to carry some small portion of them. We returned in a troop to the factory, and stood beyond the stone, a group of sorrowful, almost despairing people. In a few minutes we saw the curé open the door, close it behind him, and stand before the proscribed dwelling. His voice came across the space between us and him in distinct and cheerful tones.

"My good children," he said, "I, your priest, forbid any one of you to come a single step nearer to this house. It may be but for a day or two, but let no one venture to disobey me. Think of me as though I had gone to England, and should be back again among you in a few days. God is here, as near to me under this roof, as when I stand before him and you at his altar."

He lifted up his hands to give them his benediction, and we all knelt to receive it. Then, with unquestioning obedience, but with many lamentations, the people returned to their daily work.

CHAPTER THE TWENTIETH

A MALIGNANT CASE

For three days, morning after morning, while the dew lay still upon the grass, I went down, with a heavy and foreboding heart, to the place where I could watch the cottage, through the long, sultry hours of the summer-day. The first thing I saw always was Monsieur Laurentie, who came to the door to satisfy me that he was himself in good health, and to tell me how Richard Foster had passed the night. After that I caught from time to time a momentary glimpse of his white head, as he passed the dusky window. He would not listen to my entreaties to be allowed to join him in his task. It was a malignant case, he said, and as my husband was unconscious, I could do him no good by running the risk of being near him.

An invisible line encircled the pestilential place, which none of us dare break through without the permission of the curé, though any one of the villagers would have rejoiced if he had summoned them to his aid. A perpetual intercession was offered up day and night, before the high altar, by the people, and there was no lack of eager candidates ready to take up the prayer when the one who had been praying grew weary. On the third morning I felt that they were beginning to look at me with altered faces, and speak to me in colder accents. If I were the means of bringing upon them the loss of their curé, they would curse the day he found me and brought me to his home. I left the village street half broken-hearted, and wandered hopelessly down to my chosen post.

I thought I was alone, but as I sat with my head bowed down upon my hands, I felt a child's hand laid upon my neck, and Minima's voice spoke plaintively in my ear.

"What is the matter, Aunt Nelly?" she asked. "Everybody is in trouble, and mademoiselle says it is because your husband is come, and Monsieur Laurentie is going to die for his sake. She began to cry when she said that, and she said, 'What shall we all do if my brother dies? My God! what will become of all the people in Ville-en-bois?' Is it true? Is your husband really come, and is he going to die?"

"He is come," I said, in a low voice; "I do not know whether he is going to die."

"Is he so poor that he will die?" she asked again. "Why does God let people be so poor that they must die?".

"It is not because he is so poor that he is ill," I answered.

"But my father died because he was so poor," she said; "the doctors told him he could get well if he had only enough money. Perhaps your husband would not have died if he had not been very poor."

"No, no," I cried, vehemently, "he is not dying through poverty."

Yet the child's words had a sting in them, for I knew he had been poor, in consequence of my act. I thought of the close, unwholesome house in London, where he had been living. I could not help thinking of it, and wondering whether any loss of vital strength, born of poverty, had caused him to fall more easily a prey to this fever. My brain was burdened with sorrowful questions and doubts.

I sent Minima back to the village before the morning-heat grew strong, and then I was alone, watching the cottage through the fine haze of heat which hung tremulously about it. The song of every bird was hushed; the shouts of the harvest-men to their oxen ceased; and the only sound that stirred the still air was the monotonous striking of the clock in the church-tower. I had not seen Monsieur Laurentie since his first greeting of me in the early morning. A panic fear seized upon me. Suppose he should have been stricken suddenly by this deadly malady! I called softly at first, then loudly, but no answer came to comfort me. If this old man, worn out and exhausted, had actually given his life for Richard's, what would become of me? what would become of all of us?

Step by step, pausing often, yet urged on by my growing fears, I stole down the parched and beaten track toward the house, then called once more to the oppressive silence.

Here in the open sunshine, with the hot walls of the mill casting its rays back again, the heat was intense, though the white cap I wore protected my head from it. My eyes were dazzled, and I felt ready to faint. No wonder if Monsieur Laurentie should have sunk under it, and the long strain upon his energies, which would have overtaxed a younger and stronger man. I had passed the invisible line which his will had drawn about the place, and had half crossed the court, when I heard footsteps close behind me, and a large, brown, rough hand suddenly caught mine.

"Mam'zelle'" cried a voice I knew well, "is this you!"

"O Tardif! Tardif!" I exclaimed. I rested my beating head against him, and sobbed violently, while he surrounded me with his strong arm, and laid his hand upon my head, as if to assure me of his help and protection.

"Hush; hush! mam'zelle," he said; "it is Tardif, your friend, my little mam'zelle; your servant, you know. I am here. What shall I do for you? Is there any person in yonder house who frightens you, my poor little mam'zelle? Tell me what I can do?"

He had drawn me back into the green shade of the trees, and set me down upon the felled tree where I had been sitting before. I told him all quickly, briefly—all that had happened since I had written to him. I saw the tears start to his eyes.

"Thank God I am here!" he said; "I lost no time, mam'zelle, after your letter reached me. I will save Monsieur le Curé; I will save them both, if I can. Ma foi! he is a good man, this curé, and we must not let him perish. He has no authority over me, and I will go this moment and force my way in, if the door is fastened. Adieu, my dear little mam'zelle."

He was gone before I could speak a word, striding with quick, energetic tread across the court. The closed door under the eaves opened readily. In an instant the white head of Monsieur Laurentie passed the casement, and I could hear the hum of an earnest altercation, though I could not catch a syllable of it. But presently Tardif appeared again in the doorway, waving his cap in token of having gained his point.

I went back to the village at once to carry the good news, for it was the loneliness of the curé that had weighed so heavily on every heart, though none among them dare brave his displeasure by setting aside his command. The quarantine was observed as rigidly as ever, but fresh hope and confidence beamed upon every face, and I felt that they no longer avoided me, as they had begun to do before Tardif's arrival. Now Monsieur Laurentie could leave his patient, and sit under the sheltering eaves in the cool of the morning or evening, while his people could satisfy themselves from a distance that he was still in health.

The physician whom Jean fetched from Noireau spoke vaguely of Richard's case. It was very malignant, he said, full of danger, and apparently his whole constitution had been weakened by some protracted and grave malady. We must hope, he added.

Whether it was in hope or fear I awaited the issue, I scarcely know. I dared not glance beyond the passing hour; dared not conjecture what the end would be. The past was dead; the future yet unborn. For the moment my whole being was concentrated upon the conflict between life and death, which was witnessed only by the curé and Tardif.

CHAPTER THE TWENTY-FIRST

THE LAST DEATH

It seemed to me almost as if time had been standing still since that first morning when Monsieur Laurentie had left my side, and passed out of my sight to seek for my husband in the fever-smitten dwelling. Yet it was the tenth day after that when, as I took up my weary watch soon after daybreak, I saw him crossing the court again, and coming toward me.

"What had he to say? What could impel him to break through the strict rule which had interdicted all dangerous contact with himself? His face was pale, and his eyes were heavy as if with want of rest, but they looked into mine as if they could read my inmost soul.

"My daughter," he said, "I bade you leave even your duty in my keeping. Now I summon you to fulfil it. Your duty lies yonder, by your husband's side in his agony of death."

"I will go," I whispered, my lips scarcely moving to pronounce the words, so stiff and cold they felt.

"Stay one moment," he said, pityingly. "You have been taught to judge of your duty for yourself, not to leave it to a priest. I ought to let you judge now. Your husband is dying, but he is conscious, and is asking to see you. He does not believe us that death is near; he says none but you will tell him the truth. You cannot go to him without running a great risk. Your danger will be greater than ours, who have been with him all the time. You see, madame, he does not understand me, and he refuses to believe in Tardif. Yet you cannot save him; you can only receive his last adieu. Think well, my child. Your life may be the forfeit."

"I must go," I answered, more firmly; "I will go. He is my husband."

"Good!" he said, "you have chosen the better part. Come, then. The good God will protect you."

He drew my hand through his arm, and led me to the low doorway. The inner room was very dark with the overhanging eaves, and my eyes, dilated by the strong sunlight, could discern but little in the gloom. Tardif was kneeling beside a low bed, bathing my husband's forehead. He made way for me, and I felt him touch my hand with his lips as I took his place. But no one spoke. Richard's face, sunken, haggard, dying, with filmy eyes, dawned gradually out of the dim twilight, line after line, until it lay sharp and distinct under my gaze. I could not turn away from it for an instant, even to glance at Tardif or Monsieur Laurentie. The poor, miserable face! the restless, dreary, dying eyes!

"Where is Olivia?" he muttered, in a hoarse and labored voice.

"I am here, Richard," I answered, falling on my knees where Tardif had been kneeling, and putting my hand on his; "look at me. I am Olivia."

"You are mine, you know," he said, his fingers closing round my wrist with a grasp as weak as a very young child's—"She is my wife, Monsieur le Curé."

"Yes," I sobbed, "I am your wife, Richard."

"Do they hear it?" he asked, in a whisper.

"We hear it," answered Tardif.

A strange, spasmodic smile flitted across his ghastly face, a look of triumph and success. His fingers tightened over my hand, and I left it passively in their clasp.

"Mine!" he murmured.

"Olivia," he said, after a long pause, and in a stronger voice, "you always spoke the truth to me. This priest and his follower have been trying to frighten me into repentance, as if I were an old woman. They say I am near dying. Tell me, is it true?"

The last words he had spoken painfully, dragging them one after another, as if the very utterance of them was hateful to him. He looked at me with his cold, glittering eyes, which seemed almost mocking at me, even then.

"Richard," I said, "it is true."

"Good God!" he cried.

His lips closed after that cry, and seemed as if they would never open again. He shut his eyes weariedly. Feebly and fitfully came his gasps for breath, and he moaned at times. But still his fingers held me fast, though the slightest effort of mine would have set me free. I left my hand in his cold grasp, and spoke to him whenever he moaned.

"Martin," he breathed between his set teeth, though so low that only my ear could catch the words, "Martin—could—have saved—me."

There was another long silence. I could hear the chirping of the sparrows in the thatched roof, but no other sound broke the deep stillness. Monsieur Laurentie and Tardif stood at the foot of the bed, looking down upon us both, but I only saw their shadows falling across us. My eyes were fastened upon the face I should soon see no more. The little light there was seemed to be fading away from it, leaving it all dark and blank; eyelids closed, lips almost breathless; an unutterable emptiness and confusion creeping over every feature.

"Olivia!" he cried, once again, in a tone of mingled anger and entreaty.

"I am here," I answered, laying my other hand upon his, which was at last relaxing its hold, and falling away helplessly. But where was he? Where was the voice which half a minute ago called Olivia? Where was the life gone that had grasped my hand? He had not heard my answer, or felt my touch upon his cold fingers.

Tardif lifted me gently from my place beside him, and carried me away into the open air, under the overshadowing eaves.

CHAPTER THE TWENTY-SECOND

FREE

The rest of that day passed by like a dream. Jean had come down with the daily supply of food, and I heard Monsieur Laurentie call to him to accompany me back to the presbytery, and to warn every one to keep away from me, until I could take every precaution against spreading infection. He gave me minute directions what to do, and I obeyed them automatically and mechanically. I spent the whole day in my room alone.

At night, after all the village was silent, with the moon shining brilliantly down upon the deserted streets, the sound of stealthy footsteps came to me through my window. I pulled the casement open and looked out. There marched four men, with measured steps, bearing a coffin on their shoulders, while Monsieur Laurentie followed them bareheaded. It was my husband's funeral; and I sank upon my knees, and remained kneeling till I heard them return from the little cemetery up the valley, where so many of the curé's flock had been buried. I prayed with all my heart that no other life would be forfeited to this pestilence, which had seemed to have passed away from us.

But I was worn out myself with anxiety and watching. For three or four days I was ill with a low, nervous fever—altogether unlike the terrible typhoid, yet such as to keep me to my room. Minima and Mademoiselle Thérèse were my only companions. Mademoiselle, after talking that one night as much as she generally talked in twelve months, had relapsed into deeper taciturnity than before. But her muteness tranquillized me. Minima's simple talk brought me back to the level of common life. My own nervous weeping, which I could not control, served to soothe me. My casement, almost covered by broad, clustering vine-leaves, preserved a cool, dim obscurity in my room. The village children seemed all at once to have forgotten how to scream and shout, and no sound from the street disturbed me. Even the morning and evening bell rang with a deep, muffled tone, which scarcely stirred the silence. I heard afterward that Jean had swathed the bell in a piece of sackcloth, and that the children had been sent off early every morning into the woods.

But I could not remain long in that idle seclusion. I felt all my strength returning, both of body and mind. I began to smile at Minima, and to answer her childish prattle, with none of the feeling of utter weariness which had at first prostrated me.

"Are we going to stay here forever and ever?" she asked me, one day, when I felt that the solitary peace of my own chamber was growing too monotonous for me.

"Should you like to stay, Minima?" I inquired in reply. It was a question I must face, that of what I was going to do in the future.

"I don't know altogether," she said, reflectively. "The boys here are not so nice as they used to be at home. Pierre says I'm a little pagan, and that's not nice, Aunt Nelly. He says I must be baptized by Monsieur Laurentie, and be prepared for my first communion, before I can be as good as he is. The boys at home used to think me quite as good as them, and better. I asked Monsieur Laurentie if I ought to be baptized over again, and he only smiled, and said I must be as good a little girl as I could be, and it did not much matter. But Pierre, and all the rest, think I'm not as good as them, and I don't like it."

I could not help laughing, like Monsieur Laurentie, at Minima's distress. Yet it was not without foundation. Here we were heretics amid the orthodox, and I felt it myself. Though Monsieur le Curé never alluded to it in the most distant manner, there was a difference between us and the simple village-folk in Ville-en-bois which would always mark us as strangers in blood and creed.

"I think," continued Minima, with a shrewd expression on her face, which was beginning to fill up and grow round in its outlines, "I think, when you are quite well again, we'd better be going on somewhere to try our fortunes. It never does, you know, to stop too long in the same place. I'm quite sure we shall never meet the prince here, and I don't think we shall find any treasure. Besides, if we began to dig they'd all know, and want to go shares. I shouldn't mind going shares with Monsieur Laurentie, but I would not go shares with Pierre. Of course when we've made our fortunes we'll come back, and we'll build Monsieur Laurentie a palace of marble, and put Turkey carpets on all the floors, and have fountains and statues, and all sorts of things, and give him a cook to cook splendid dinners. But we wouldn't stay here always if we were very, very rich; would you, Aunt Nelly?"

"Has anybody told you that I am rich?" I asked, with a passing feeling of vexation.

"Oh, no," she said, laughing heartily, "I should know better than that. You're very poor, my darling auntie, but I love you all the same. We shall be rich some day, of course. It's all coming right, by-and-by."

Her hand was stroking my face, and I drew it to my lips and kissed it tenderly. I had scarcely realized before what a change had come over my circumstances.

"But I am not poor any longer, my little girl," I said; "I am rich now.".

"Very rich?" she asked, eagerly.

"Very rich," I repeated.

"And we shall never have to go walking, walking, till our feet are sore and tired? And we shall not be hungry, and be afraid of spending our money? And we shall buy new clothes as soon as the old ones are worn out? O Aunt Nelly, is it true? is it quite true?"

"It is quite true, my poor Minima," I answered.

She looked at me wistfully, with the color coming and going on her face. Then she climbed up, and lay down beside me, with her arm over me and her face close to mine.

"O Aunt Nelly!" she cried, "if this had only come while my father was alive!"

"Minima," I said, after her sobs and tears were ended, "you will always be my little girl. You shall come and live with me wherever I live."

"Of course," she answered, with the simple trustfulness of a child, "we are going to live together till we die. You won't send me to school, will you? You know what school is like now, and you wouldn't like me to send you to school, would you? If I were a rich, grown-up lady, and you were a little girl like me, I know what I should do."

"What would you do?" I inquired, laughing.

"I should give you lots of dolls and things," she said, quite seriously, her brows puckered with anxiety, "and I should let you have strawberry-jam every day, and I should make every thing as nice as possible. Of course I should make you learn lessons, whether you liked it or not, but I should teach you myself, and then I should know nobody was unkind to you. That's what I should do, Aunt Nelly."

"And that's what I shall do, Minima," I repeated.

We had many things to settle that morning, making our preliminary arrangements for the spending of my fortune upon many dolls and much jam. But the conviction was forced upon me that I must be setting about more important plans. Tardif was still staying in Ville-en-bois, delaying his departure till I was well enough to see him. I resolved to get up that evening, as soon as the heat of the day was past, and have a conversation with him and Monsieur Laurentie.

CHAPTER THE TWENTY-THIRD

A YEAR'S NEWS

In the cool of the evening, while the chanting of vespers in the church close by was faintly audible, I went downstairs into the salon. All the household were gone to the service; but I saw Tardif sitting outside in my own favorite seat under the sycamore-tree. I sent Minima to call him to me, bidding her stay out-of-doors herself; and he came in hurriedly, with a glad light in his deep, honest eyes.

"Thank God, mam'zelle, thank God!" he said.

"Yes," I answered, "I am well again now. I have not been really ill, I know, but I felt weary and sick at heart. My good Tardif, how much I owe you!"

"You owe me, nothing, mam'zelle," he said, dropping my hand, and carrying the curé's high-backed chair to the open window, for me to sit in it, and have all the freshness there was in the air. "Dear mam'zelle," he added, "if you only think of me as your friend, that is enough."

"You are my truest friend," I replied.

"No, no. You have another as true," he answered, "and you have this good Monsieur le Curé into the bargain. If the curés were all like him I should be thinking of becoming a good Catholic myself, and you know how far I am from being that."

"No one can say a word too much in his praise," I said.

"Except," continued Tardif, "that he desires to keep our little mam'zelle in his village. 'Why must she leave me?' he says; 'never do I say a word contrary to her religion, or that of the mignonne. Let them stay in Ville-en-bois.' But Dr. Martin, says: 'No, she must not remain here. The air is not good for her; the village is not drained, and it is unhealthy. There will always be fever here.' Dr. Martin was almost angry with Monsieur le Curé."

"Dr. Martin?" I said, in a tone of wonder and inquiry.

"Dr. Martin, mam'zelle. I sent a message to him by telegraph. It was altered somehow in the offices, and he did not know who was dead. He started off at once, travelled without stopping, and reached this place two nights ago."

"Is he here now?" I asked, while a troubled feeling stirred the tranquillity which had but just returned to me. I shrank from seeing him just then.

"No, mam'zelle. He went away this morning, as soon as he was sure you would recover without his help. He said that to see him might do you more harm, trouble you more, than he could do you good by his medicines. He and Monsieur le Curé parted good friends, though they were not of the same mind about you. 'Let her stay here,' says Monsieur le Curé. 'She must return to England,' says Dr. Martin. 'Mam'zelle must be free to choose for herself,' I said. They both smiled, and said yes, I was right. You must be free."

"Why did no one tell me he was here? Why did Minima keep it a secret?" I asked.

"He forbade us to tell you. He did not wish to disquiet you. He said to me: 'If she ever wishes to see me, I would come gladly from London to Ville-en-bois', only to hear her say, 'Good-morning, Dr. Martin.' 'But I will not see her now, unless she is seriously ill.' I felt that he was right, Dr. Martin is always right."

I did not speak when Tardif paused, as if to hear what I had to say. I heard him sigh as softly as a woman sighs.

"If you could only come back to my poor little house!" he said; "but that is impossible. My poor mother died in the spring, and I am living alone. It is desolate, but I am not unhappy. I have my boat and the sea, where I am never solitary. But why should I talk of myself? We were speaking of what you are to do."

"I don't know what to do," I said, despondently; "you see Tardif, I have not a single friend I could go to in England. I shall have to stay here in Ville-en-bois."

"No," he answered; "Dr. Martin has some plan for you, I know, though he did not tell me what it is. He said you would have a home offered to you, such as you would accept gladly. I think it is in Guernsey."

"With his mother, perhaps," I suggested.

"His mother, mam'zelle!" he repeated; "alas! no. His mother is dead; she died only a few weeks after you left Sark."

I felt as if I had lost an old friend whom I had known for a long time, though I had only seen her once. In my greatest difficulty I had thought of making my way to her, and telling her all my history. I did not know what other home could open for me, if she were dead.

"Dr. Dobrée married a second wife only three months after," pursued Tardif, "and Dr. Martin left Guernsey altogether, and went to London, to be a partner with his friend, Dr. Senior."

"Dr. John Senior?" I said.

"Yes, mam'zelle," he answered.

"Why! I know him," I exclaimed; "I recollect his face well. He is handsomer than Dr. Martin. But whom did Dr. Dobrée marry?"

"I do not know whether he is handsomer than Dr. Martin," said Tardif, in a grieved tone. "Who did Dr. Dobrée marry? Oh! a foreigner. No Guernsey lady would have married him so soon after Mrs. Dobrée's death. She was a great friend of Miss Julia Dobrée. Her name was Daltrey."

"Kate Daltrey!" I ejaculated. My brain seemed to whirl with the recollections, the associations, the rapid mingling and odd readjustment of ideas forced upon me by Tardif's words. What would have become of me if I had found my way to Guernsey, seeking Mrs. Dobrée, and discovered in her Kate Daltrey? I had not time to realize this before Tardif went on in his narration.

"Dr. Martin was heart-broken," he said; "we had lost you, and his mother was dead. He had no one to turn to for comfort. His cousin Julia, who was to have been his wife, was married to Captain Carey three weeks ago. You recollect Captain Carey, mam'zelle?"

Here was more news, and a fresh rearranging of the persons who peopled my world. Kate Daltrey become Dr. Dobrée's second wife; Julia Dobrée married to Captain Carey; and Dr. Martin living in London, the partner of Dr. Senior! How could I put them all into their places in a moment? Tardif, too, was dwelling alone, now, solitarily, in a very solitary place.

"I am very sorry for you," I said, in a low tone.

"Why, mam'zelle?" he asked.

"Because you have lost your mother," I answered.

"Yes, mam'zelle," he said, simply; "she was a great loss to me, though she was always fretting about my inheriting the land. That is the law of the island, and no one can set it aside. The eldest son inherits the land, and I was not her own son, though I did my best to be like a real son to her. She died happier in thinking that her son, or grandson, would follow me when I am gone, and I was glad she had that to comfort her, poor woman."

"But you may marry again some day, my good Tardif," I said; "how I wish you would!"

"No, mam'zelle, no," he answered, with a strange quivering tone in his voice; "my mother knew why before she died, and it was a great comfort to her. Do not think I am not happy alone. There are some memories that are better company than most folks. Yes, there are some things I can think of that are more and better than any wife could be to me."

Why we were both silent after that I scarcely knew. Both of us had many things to think about, no doubt, and the ideas were tumbling over one another in my poor brain till I wished I could cease to think for a few hours.

Vespers ended, and the villagers began to disperse stealthily. Not a wooden sabot clattered on the stones. Mademoiselle and Monsieur Laurentie came in, with a tread as soft as if they were afraid of waking a child out of a light slumber.

"Mademoiselle," I cried, "monsieur, behold me; I am here."

My voice and my greeting seemed to transport them with delight. Mademoiselle embraced me, and kissed me on both cheeks. Monsieur le Curé blessed me, in a tremulously joyous accent, and insisted upon my keeping his arm-chair. We sat down to supper together, by the light of a brilliant little lamp, and Pierre, who was passing the uncurtained window, saw me there, and carried the news into the village.

The next day Tardif bade me farewell, and Monsieur Laurentie drove him to Granville on his way home to Sark.

CHAPTER THE TWENTY-FOURTH

FAREWELL TO VILLE-EN-BOIS

The unbroken monotony of Ville-en-bois closed over me again. The tolling of the morning bell; the hum of matins; the frugal breakfast in the sunlit salon; the long, hot day; vespers again; then an hour's chat by twilight with the drowsy curé and his sister, whose words were so rare. Before six such days had passed, I felt as if they were to last my lifetime. Then the fretting of my uneasy woman's heart began. There was no sign that I had any friends in England. What ought I to do? How must I set about the intricate business of my affairs? Must I write to my trustees in Melbourne, giving them the information of my husband's death, and wait till I could receive from them instructions, and credentials to prove my identity, without which it was useless, if it were practicable, to return to London? Was there ever any one as friendless as I was? Monsieur Laurentie could give me no counsel, except to keep myself tranquil; but how difficult it was to keep tranquil amid such profound repose! I had often found it easier to be calm amid many provocations and numerous difficulties.

A week has glided by; a full week. The letter-carrier has brought me no letter. I am seated at the window of the salon, gasping in these simmering dog-days for a breath of fresh air; such a cool, balmy breeze as blows over the summer sea to the cliffs of Sark. Monsieur Laurentie, under the shelter of a huge red umbrella, is choosing the ripest cluster of grapes for our supper this evening. All the street is as still as at midnight. Suddenly there breaks upon us the harsh, metallic clang of well-shod horse-hoofs upon the stony roadway—the cracking of a postilion's whip—the clatter of an approaching carriage.

It proves to be a carriage with a pair of horses.

Pierre, who has been basking idly under the window, jumps to his feet, shouting, "It is Monsieur the Bishop!" Minima claps her hands, and cries, "The prince, Aunt Nelly, the prince!"

Monsieur Laurentie walks slowly down to the gate, his cotton umbrella spread over him, like a giant fungus. It is certainly not the prince; for an elderly, white-haired man, older than Monsieur Laurentie, but with a more imposing and stately presence, steps out of the carriage, and they salute one another with great ceremony. If that be Monsieur the Bishop, he has very much the air of an Englishman.

In a few minutes my doubt as to the bishop's nationality was solved. The two white-headed men, the one in a glossy and handsome suit of black, the other in his brown and worn-out cassock, came up the path together, under the red umbrella. They entered the house, and came directly to the salon. I was making my escape by another door, not being sure how I ought to encounter a bishop, when Monsieur Laurentie called to me.

"Behold a friend for you madame," he said, "a friend from England—Monsieur, this is my beloved English child."

I turned back, and met the eyes of both, fixed upon me with that peculiar half-tender, half-regretful expression, with which so many old men look upon women as young as I. A smile came across my face, and I held out my hand involuntarily to the stranger.

"You do not know who I am, my dear!" he said. The English voice and words went straight to my heart. How many months it was since I had heard my own language spoken thus! Tardif had been too glad to speak in his own patois, now I understood it so well; and Minima's prattle had not sounded to me like those few syllables in the deep, cultivated voice which uttered them.

"No," I answered, "but you are come to me from Dr. Martin Dobrée."

"Very true," he said, "I am his friend's father—Dr. John Senior's father. Martin has sent me to you. He wished Miss Johanna Carey to accompany me, but we were afraid of the fever for her. I am an old physician, and feel at home with disease and contagion. But we cannot allow you to remain in this unhealthy village; that is out of the question. I am come to carry you away, in spite of this old curé."

Monsieur Laurentie was listening eagerly, and watching Dr. Senior's lips, as if he could catch the meaning of his words by sight, if not by hearing.

"But where am I to go?" I asked. "I have no money, and cannot get any until I have written to Melbourne, and have an answer. I have no means of proving who I am."

"Leave all that to us, my dear girl," answered Dr. Senior, cordially. "I have already spoken of your affairs to an old friend of mine, who is an excellent lawyer. I am come to offer myself to you in place of your guardians on the other side of the world. You will do me a very great favor by frankly accepting a home in my house for the present. I have neither wife nor daughter; but Miss Carey is already there, preparing rooms for you and your little charge. We have made inquiries about the little girl, and find she has no friends living. I will take care of her future. Do you think you could trust yourself and her to me?"

"Oh, yes!" I replied, but I moved a little nearer to Monsieur Laurentie, and put my hand through his arm. He folded his own thin, brown hand over it caressingly, and looked down at me, with something like tears glistening in his eyes.

"Is it all settled?" he asked, "is monsieur come to rob me of my English daughter? She will go away now to her own island, and forget Ville-en-bois and her poor old French father!"

"Never! never!" I answered vehemently, "I shall not forget you as long as I live. Besides, I mean to come back very often; every year if I can. I almost wish I could stay here altogether; but you know that is impossible, monsieur. Is it not quite impossible?"

"Quite impossible!" he repeated, somewhat sadly, "madame is too rich now; she will have many good friends."

"Not one better than you," I said, "not one more dear than you. Yes, I am rich; and I have been planning something to do for Ville-en-bois. Would you like the church enlarged and beautified, Monsieur le Curé?"

"It is large enough and fine enough already," he answered.

"Shall I put some painted windows and marble images into it?" I asked.

"No, no, madame," he replied, "let it remain as it is during my short lifetime."

"I thought so," I said, "but I believe I have discovered what Monsieur le Curé would approve. It is truly English. There is no sentiment, no romance about it. Cannot you guess what it is, my wise and learned monsieur?"

"No, no, madame," he answered, smiling in spite of his sadness.

"Listen, dear monsieur," I continued: "if this village is unhealthy for me, it is unhealthy for you and your people. Dr. Martin told Tardif there would always be fever here, as long as there are no drains and no pure water. Very well; now I am rich I shall have it drained, precisely like the best English town; and there shall be a fountain in the middle of the village, where all the people can go to draw good water. I shall come back next year to see how it has been done, Voilà, monsieur! There is my secret plan for Ville-en-bois."

Nothing could have been more effectual for turning away Monsieur Laurentie's thoughts from the mournful topic of our near separation. After vespers, and before supper, he, Dr. Senior, and I made the tour of Ville-en-bois, investigating the close, dark cottages, and discussing plans for rendering them more wholesome. The next day, and the day following, the same subject continued to occupy him and Dr. Senior; and thus the pain of our departure was counterbalanced by his pleasure in anticipating the advantages to be obtained by a thorough drainage of his village, and more ventilation and light in the dwellings.

The evening before we were to set out on our return to England, while the whole population, including Dr. Senior, were assisting at vespers, I turned my feet toward the little cemetery on the hill-side, which I had never yet visited—The sun had sunk below the tops of the pollard-trees, which grew along the brow of the hill in grotesque and fantastic shapes; but a few stray beams glimmered through the branches, and fell here and there in spots of dancing light. The small square enclosure was crowded with little hillocks, at the head of which stood simple crosses of wood; crosses so light and little as to seem significant emblems of the difference between our sorrows, and those borne for our sakes upon Calvary. Wreaths of immortelles hung upon most of them. Below me lay the valley and the homes where the dead at my feet had lived; the sunshine lingered yet about the spire, with its cross, which towered above the belfry; but all else was in shadow, which was slowly deepening into night. In the west the sky was flushing and throbbing with transparent tints of amber and purple and green, with flecks of cloud floating across it of a pale gold. Eastward it was still blue, but fading into a faint gray. The dusky green of the cypresses looked black, as I turned my splendor-dazzled eyes toward them.

I strolled to and fro among the grassy mounds, not consciously seeking one of them; though, very deep down in my inmost spirit, there must have been an impulse which unwittingly directed me. I did not stay my feet, or turn away from the village burial-place, until I came upon a grave, the latest made among them. It was solitary, unmarked; with no cross to throw its shadow along it, as the sun was setting. I knew then that I had come to seek it, to bid farewell to it, to leave it behind me for evermore.

The next morning Monsieur Laurentie accompanied us on our journey, as far as the cross at the entrance to the valley. He parted with us there; and when I stood up in the carriage to look back once more at him, I saw his black-robed figure kneeling on the white steps of the Calvary, and the sun shining upon his silvery head.

CHAPTER THE TWENTY-FIFTH

TOO HIGHLY CIVILIZED

For the third time I landed in England. When I set foot upon its shores first I was worse than friendless, with foes of my own household surrounding me; the second time I was utterly alone, in daily terror, in poverty, with a dreary, life-long future stretching before me. Now every want of mine was anticipated, every step directed, as if I were a child again, and my father himself was caring for me. How many friends, good and tried and true, could I count! All the rough paths were made smooth for me.

It was dusk before we reached London; but before the train stopped at the platform, a man's hand was laid upon the carriage-door, and a handsome face was smiling over it upon us. I scarcely dared look who it was; but the voice that reached my ears was not Martin Dobrée's.

"I am here in Martin's place," said Dr. John Senior, as soon as he could make himself heard; "he has been hindered by a wretch of a patient—Welcome home, Miss Martineau!"

"She is not Miss Martineau, John," remarked Dr. Senior. There was a tinge of stateliness about him, bordering upon formality, which had kept me a little in awe of him all the journey through. His son laughed, with a pleasant audacity.

"Welcome home. Olivia, then!" he said, clasping my hand warmly. "Martin and I never call you by any other name."

A carriage was waiting for us, and Dr. John took Minima beside him, chattering with her as the child loved to chatter. As for me, I felt a little anxious and uneasy. Once more I was about to enter upon an entirely new life; upon the untried ways of a wealthy, conventional, punctilious English household. Hitherto my mode of life had been almost as wandering and free as that of a gypsy. Even at home, during my pleasant childhood, our customs had been those of an Australian sheep-farm, exempt from all the usages of any thing like fashion. Dr. John's kid gloves, which fitted his hand to perfection, made me uncomfortable.

I felt still more abashed and oppressed when we reached Dr. Senior's house, and a footman ran down to the carriage, to open the door and to carry in my poor little portmanteau. It looked miserably poor and out of place in the large, brilliantly-lit hall. Minima kept close beside me, silent, but gazing upon this new abode with wide-open eyes.

Why was not Martin here? He had known me in Sark, in Tardif's cottage, and he would understand how strange and how unlike home all this was to me.

A trim maid was summoned to show us to our rooms, and she eyed us with silent criticism. She conducted us to a large and lofty apartment, daintily and luxuriously fitted up, with a hundred knick-knacks about it, of which I could not even guess the use. A smaller room communicated with it which had been evidently furnished for Minima. The child squeezed my hand tightly as we gazed into it. I felt as if we were gypsies, suddenly caught, and caged in a splendid captivity.

"Isn't it awful?" asked Minima, in a whisper; "it frightens me."

It almost frightened me too. I was disconcerted also by my own reflection in the long mirror before me. A rustic, homely peasant-girl, with a brown face and rough hands, looked back at me from the shining surface, wearing a half-Norman dress, for I had not had time to buy more than a bonnet and shawl as we passed through Falaise. What would Miss Carey think of me? How should I look in Dr. John's fastidious eyes? Would not Martin be disappointed and shocked when he saw me again?

I could not make any change in my costume, and the maid carried off Minima to do what she could with her. There came a gentle knock at my door, and Miss Carey entered. Here was the fitting personage to dwell in a house like this. A delicate gray-silk dress, a dainty lace cap, a perfect self-possession, a dignified presence. My heart sank low. But she kissed me affectionately, and smiled as I looked anxiously into her face.

"My dear," she said, "I hope you will like your room. John and Martin have ransacked London for pretty things for it. See, there is a painting of Tardifs cottage in Sark. Julia has painted it for you. And here is a portrait of my dear friend, Martin's mother; he hung it there himself only this morning. I hope you will soon feel quite at home with us, Olivia."

Before I could answer, a gong sounded through the house, with a sudden clang that startled me.

We went down to the drawing-room, where Dr. Senior gave me his arm, and led me ceremoniously to dinner. At this very hour my dear Monsieur Laurentie and mademoiselle were taking their simple supper at the little round table, white as wood could be made by scrubbing, but with no cloth upon it. My chair and Minima's would be standing back against the wall. The tears smarted under my eyelids, and I answered at random to the remarks made to me. How I longed to be alone for a little while, until I could realize all the change that had come into my life!

We had been in the drawing-room again only a few minutes, when we heard the hall-door opened, and a voice speaking. By common consent, as it were, every one fell into silence to listen. I looked up for a moment, and saw that all three of them had turned their eyes upon me; friendly eyes they were, but their scrutiny was intolerable. Dr. Senior began to talk busily with Miss Carey.

"Hush!" cried Minima, who was standing beside Dr. John, "hush! I believe it is—yes, I am sure it is Dr. Martin!"

She sprang to the door just as it was opened, and flung her arms round him in a transport of delight. I did not dare to lift my eyes again, to see them all smiling at me. He could not come at once to speak to me, while that child was clinging to him and kissing him.

"I'm so glad," she said, almost sobbing; "come and see my auntie, who was so ill when you were in Ville-en-bois. You did not see her, you know; but she is quite well now, and very, very rich. We are never going to be poor again. Come; she is here. Auntie, this is that nice Dr. Martin, who made me promise not to tell you he was at Ville-en-bois, while you were so ill."

She dragged him eagerly toward me, and I put my hand in his; but I did not look at him. That I did some minutes afterward, when he was talking to Miss Carey. It was many months since I had seen him last in Sark. There was a great change in his face, and he looked several years older. It was grave, and almost mournful, as if he did not smile very often, and his voice was lower in tone than it had been then. Dr. John, who was standing beside him, was certainly much gayer and handsomer than he was. He caught my eye, and came back to me, sitting near enough to talk with me in an undertone.

"Are you satisfied with the arrangements we have made for you?" he inquired.

"Quite," I said, not daring either to thank him, or to tell him how oppressed I was by my sudden change. Both of us spoke as quietly, and with as much outward calm, as if we were in the habit of seeing each other every day. A chill came across me.

"At one time," he continued, "I asked Johanna to open her home to you; but that was when I thought you would be safer and happier in a quiet place like hers than anywhere else. Now you are your own mistress, and can choose your own residence. But you could not have a better home than this. It would not be well for you, so young and friendless, to live in a house of your own."

"No," I said, somewhat sadly.

"Dr. Senior is delighted to have you here," he went on; "you will see very good society in this house, and that is what you should do. You ought to see more and better people than you have yet known. Does it seem strange to you that we have assumed a sort of authority over you and your affairs? You do not yet know how we have been involved in them."

"How?" I asked, looking up into his face with a growing curiosity.

"Olivia," he said, "Foster was my patient for some months, and I knew all his affairs intimately. He had married that person—"

"Married her!" I ejaculated.

"Yes. You want to know how he could do that? Well, he produced two papers, one a medical certificate of your death, the other a letter purporting to be from some clergyman. He had, too, a few lines in your own handwriting, which stated you had sent him your ring, the only valuable thing left to you, as you had sufficient for your last necessities. Even I believed for a few hours that you were dead. But I must tell you all about it another time."

"Did he believe it?" I asked, in a trembling voice.

"I do not know," he answered; "I cannot tell, even now, whether he knew them to be forgeries or not. But I have no doubt, myself, that they were forged by Mrs. Foster's brother and his partner, Scott and Brown."

"But for what reason?" I asked again.

"What reason!" he repeated; "you were too rich a prize for them to allow Foster to risk losing any part of his claim upon you, if he found you. You and all you had were his property on certain defined conditions. You do not understand our marriage laws; it is as well for you not to understand them. Mrs. Foster gave up to me to-day all his papers, and the letters and credentials from your trustees in Melbourne to your bankers here. There will be very little trouble for you now. Thank God! all your life lies clear and fair before you."

I had still many questions to ask, but my lips trembled so much that I could not speak readily. He was himself silent, probably because he also had so much to say. All the others were sitting a little apart from us at a chess-table, where Dr. Senior and Miss Carey were playing, while Dr. John sat by holding Minima in his arm, though she was gazing wistfully across to Martin and me.

"You are tired, Olivia," said Martin, after a time, "tired and sad. Your eyes are full of tears. I must be your doctor again for this evening, and send you to bed at once. It is eleven o'clock already; but these people will sit up till after midnight. You need not say good-night to them—Minima, come here."

She did not wait for a second word, or a louder summons; but she slipped under Dr. John's arm, and rushed across to us, being caught by Martin before she could throw herself upon me. He sat still, talking to her for a few minutes, and listening to her account of our journey, and how frightened we were at the grandeur about us. His face lit up with a smile as his eyes fell upon me, as if for the first time he noticed how out of keeping I was with the place. Then he led us quietly away, and up-stairs to my bedroom-door.

"Good-night, Olivia," he said; "sleep soundly, both of you, for you are at home. I will send one of the maids up to you."

"No, no," I cried hastily, "they despise us already."

"Ah!" he said, "to-night you are the Olivia I knew first, in Sark. In a week's time I shall find you a fine lady."

CHAPTER THE TWENTY-SIXTH

SEEING SOCIETY

Whether or no I was transformed into a finer lady than Martin anticipated, I could not tell, but certainly after that first evening he held himself aloof from me. I soon learned to laugh at the dismay which had filled me upon my entrance into my new sphere. It would have been difficult to resist the cordiality with which I was adopted into the household. Dr. Senior treated me as his daughter; Dr. John was as much at home with me as if I had been his sister. We often rode together, for I was always fond of riding as a child, and he was a thorough horseman. He said Martin could ride better than himself; but Martin never asked me to go out with him.

Minima, too, became perfectly reconciled to her new position; though for a time she was anxious lest we were spending our riches too lavishly. I heard her one day soundly rating Dr. John, who seldom came to his father's house without bringing some trinket, or bouquet, or toy, for one or other of us.

"You are wasting all your money," she said, with that anxious little pucker of her eyebrows, which was gradually being smoothed away altogether, "you're just like the boys after the holidays. They would buy lots of things every time the cake-woman came—and she came every day—till they'd spent all their money. You can't always have cakes, you know, and then you'll miss them."

"But I shall have cakes always." answered Dr. John.

"Nobody has them always," she said, in an authoritative tone, "and you won't like being poor. We were so poor we daren't buy as much as we could eat; and our boots wore out at the toes. You like to have nice boots, and gloves, and things, so you must learn to take care of your money, and not waste it like this."

"I'm not wasting my money, little woman," he replied, "when I buy pretty things for you and Olivia."

"Why doesn't Dr. Martin do it then?" she asked; "he never spends his money in that sort of way. Why doesn't he give auntie as many things as you do?"

Martin had been listening to Minima's rebukes with a smile upon his face; but now it clouded a little, and I knew he glanced across to me. I appeared deeply absorbed in the book I held in my hand, and he did not see that I was listening and watching attentively.

"Minima," he said, in a low tone, as if he did not care that even she should hear, "I gave her all I had worth giving when I saw her first."

"That's just how it will be with you, Dr. John," exclaimed Minima, triumphantly, "you'll give us every thing you have, and then you'll have nothing left for yourself."

But still, unless Martin had taken back what he gave to me so long ago, his conduct was very mysterious to me. He did not come to Fulham half as often as Dr. John did; and when he came he spent most of the time in long, professional discussions with Dr. Senior. They told me he was devoted to his profession, and it really seemed as if he had not time to think of any thing else.

Neither had I very much time for brooding over any subject, for guests began to frequent the house, which became much gayer, Dr. Senior said, now there was a young hostess in it. The quiet evenings of autumn and winter were gone, and instead of them our engagements accumulated on our hands, until I very rarely met Martin except at some entertainment, where we were surrounded by strangers. Martin was certainly at a disadvantage among a crowd of mere acquaintances, where Dr. John was quite at home. He was not as handsome, and he did not possess the same ease and animation. So he was a little apt to get into corners with Dr. Senior's scientific friends, and to be somewhat awkward and dull if he were forced into gayer society. Dr. John called him glum.

But he was not glum; I resented that, till Dr. John begged my pardon. Martin did not smile as quickly as Dr. John, he was not forever ready with a simper, but when he did smile it had ten times more expression. I liked to watch for it, for the light that came into his eyes now and then, breaking through his gravity as the sun breaks through the clouds on a dull day.

Perhaps he thought I liked to be free. Yes, free from tyranny, but not free from love. It is a poor thing to have no one's love encircling you, a poor freedom that. A little clew came to my hand one day, the other end of which might lead me to the secret of Martin's reserve and gloom. He and Dr. Senior were talking together, as they paced to and fro about the lawn, coming up the walk from the river-side to the house, and then back again. I was seated just within the drawing-room window, which was open. They knew I was there, but they did not guess how keen my hearing was for any thing that Martin said. It was only a word or two here and there that I caught.

"If you were not in the way," said Dr. Senior, "John would have a good chance, and there is no one in the world I would sooner welcome as a daughter."

"They are like one another," answered Martin; "have you never seen it?"

What more they said I did not hear, but it seemed a little clearer to me after that why Martin kept aloof from me, and left me to ride, and talk, and laugh with his friend Jack. Why, they did not know that I was happier silent beside Martin, than laughing most merrily with Dr. John. So little did they understand me!

Just before Lent, which was a busy season with him, Monsieur Laurentie paid us his promised visit, and brought us news from Ville-en-bois. The money that had been lying in the bank, which I could not touch, whatever my necessities were, had accumulated to more than three thousand pounds, and out of this sum were to come the funds for making Ville-en-bois the best-drained parish in Normandy. Nothing could exceed Monsieur Laurentie's happiness in choosing a design for a village fountain, and in examining plans for a village hospital. For, in case any serious illness should break out again among them, a simple little hospital was to be built upon the brow of the hill, where the wind sweeps across leagues of meadow-land and heather.

"I am too happy, madame," said the curé; "my people will die no more of fever, and we will teach them many English ways. When will you come again, and see what you have done for us?"

"I will come in the autumn," I answered.

"And you will come alone?" he continued.

"Yes, quite alone," I answered, "or with Minima only."

CHAPTER THE TWENTY-SEVENTH

BREAKING THE ICE

Yet while I told Monsieur Laurentie seriously that I should go alone to Ville-en-bois in the autumn, I did not altogether believe it. We often speak in half-falsehoods, even to ourselves.

Dr. Senior's lawn, in which he takes great pride, slopes gently down to the river, and ends with a stone parapet, over which it is exceedingly pleasant to lean, and watch idly the flowing of the water, which seems to loiter almost reluctantly before passing on to Westminster, and the wharves and docks of the city. On the opposite bank grows a cluster of cedars, with rich, dark-green branches, showing nearly black against the pale blue of the sky. In our own lawn there stand three fine elms, a colony for song-birds, under which the turf is carefully kept as smooth and soft as velvet; and seats are set beneath their shadow, where one can linger for hours, seeing the steamers and pleasure-boats passing to and fro, and catching now and then a burst of music or laughter, softened a little by the distance. My childhood had trained me to be fond of living out-of-doors; and, when the spring came, I spent most of my days under these elm-trees, in the fitful sunshine and showers of an English April and May, such as I had never known before.

From one of these trees I could see very well any one who went in or out through the gate. But it was not often that I cared to sit there, for Martin came only in an evening, when his day's work was done, and even then his coming was an uncertainty. Dr. John seldom missed visiting us, but Martin was often absent for days. That made me watch all the more eagerly for his coming, and feel how cruelly fast the time fled when he was with us.

But one Sunday afternoon in April I chose my seat there, behind the tree where I could see the gate, without being too plainly seen myself. Martin had promised Dr. Senior he would come down to Fulham with Dr. John that afternoon, if possible. The river was quieter than on other days, and all the world seemed calmer. It was such a day as the one in Sark, two years ago, when I slipped from the cliffs, and

Tardif was obliged to go across to Guernsey to fetch a doctor for me. I wondered if Martin ever thought of it on such a day as this. But men do not remember little things like these as women do.

I heard the click of the gate at last, and, looking round the great trunk of the tree, I saw them come in together, Dr. John and Martin. He had kept his promise then! Minima was gone out somewhere with Dr. Senior, or she would have run to meet them, and so brought them to the place where I was half-hidden.

However, they might see my dress if they chose. They ought to see it. I was not going to stand up and show myself. If they were anxious to find me, and come to me, it was quite simple enough.

But my heart sank when Martin marched straight on, and entered the house alone, while Dr. John came as direct as an arrow toward me. They knew I was there, then! Yet Martin avoided me, and left his friend to chatter and laugh the time away. I was in no mood for laughing; I could rather have wept bitter tears of vexation and disappointment. But Dr. John was near enough now for me to discern a singular gravity upon his usually gay face.

"Is there any thing the matter?" I exclaimed, starting to my feet and hastening to meet him. He led me back again silently to my seat, and sat down beside me, still in silence. Strange conduct in Dr. John!

"Tell me what is the matter," I said, not doubting now that there was some trouble at hand. Dr. John's face flushed, and he threw his hat down on the grass, and pushed his hair back from his forehead. Then he laid his hand upon mine, for a moment only.

"Olivia," he said, very seriously, "do you love me?"

The question came upon me like a shock from a galvanic battery. He and I had been very frank and friendly together; a pleasant friendship, which had seemed to me as safe as that of a brother. Besides, he knew all that Martin had done and borne for my sake. With my disappointment there was mingled a feeling of indignation against his treachery toward his friend. I sat watching the glistening of the water through the pillars of the parapet till my eyes were dazzled.

"I scarcely understand what you say," I answered, after a long pause; "you know I care for you all. If you mean, do I love you as I love your father and Monsieur Laurentie, why, yes, I do."

"Very good, Olivia," he said.

That was so odd of him, that I turned and looked steadily into his face. It was not half as grave as before, and there was a twinkle in his eyes as if another half minute would make him as gay and light-hearted as ever.

"Whatever did you come and ask me such a question for?" I inquired, rather pettishly.

"Was there any harm in it?" he rejoined.

"Yes, there was harm in it," I answered; "it has made me very uncomfortable. I thought you were going out of your mind. If you meant nothing but to make me say I liked you, you should have expressed yourself differently. Of course, I love you all, and all alike."

"Very good," he said again.

I felt so angry that I was about to get up, and go away to my own room; but he caught my dress, and implored me to stay a little longer.

"I'll make a clean breast of it," he said; "I promised that dear old dolt Martin to come straight to you, and ask you if you loved me, in so many words. Well, I've kept my promise; and now I'll go and tell him you say you love us all, and all alike."

"No," I answered, "you shall not go and tell him that. What could put it into Dr. Martin's head that I was in love with you?"

"Why shouldn't you be in love with me?" retorted Dr. John; "Martin assures me that I am much handsomer than he is—a more eligible parti in every respect. I suppose I shall have an income, apart from our practice, at least ten times larger than his. I am much more sought after generally; one cannot help seeing that. Why should you not be in love with me?"

I did not deign to reply to him, and Jack leaned forward a little to look into my face.

"Olivia," he continued, "that is part of what Martin says. We have just been speaking of you as we came down to Fulham—never before. He maintains he is bound in honor to leave you as free as possible to make your choice, not merely between us, but from the number of fellows who have found their way down here, since you came. You made one fatal mistake, he says, through your complete ignorance of the world; and it is his duty to take care that you do not make a second mistake, through any gratitude you might feel toward him. He would not be satisfied with gratitude. Besides, he has discovered that he is not so great a prize as he fancied, as long as he lived in Guernsey; and you are a richer prize than you seemed to be then. With your fortune you ought to make a much better match than with a young physician, who has to push his way among a host of competitors. Lastly, Martin said, for I'm merely repeating his own arguments to you: 'Do you think I can put her happiness and mine into a balance, and coolly calculate which has the greater weight? If I had to choose for her, I should not hesitate between you and me.' Now I have told you the sum of our conversation, Olivia."

Every word Dr. John had spoken had thrown clearer light upon Martin's conduct. He had been afraid I should feel myself bound to him; and the very fact that he had once told me he loved me, had made it more difficult to him to say so a second time. He would not have any love from me as a duty. If I did not love him fully, with my whole heart, choosing him after knowing others with whom I could compare him, he would not receive any lesser gift from me.

"What will you do, my dear Olivia?" asked Dr. John.

"What can I do?" I said.

"Go to him," he urged; "he is alone. I saw him a moment ago, looking out at us from the drawing-room window. The old fellow is making up his mind to see you and me happy together, and to conceal his own sorrow. God bless him! Olivia, my dear girl, go to him."

"O Jack!" I cried, "I cannot."

"I don't see why you cannot," he answered, gayly. "You are trembling, and your face goes from white to red, and then white again; but you have not lost the use of your limbs, or your tongue. If you take my arm, it will not be very difficult to cross the lawn. Come; he is the best fellow living, and worth walking a dozen yards for."

Jack drew my hand through his arm, and led me across the smooth lawn. We caught a glimpse of Martin looking out at us; but he turned away in an instant, and I could not see the expression of his face. Would he think we were coming to tell him that he had wasted all his love upon a girl not worthy of a tenth part of it?

The glass doors, which opened upon the lawn, had been thrown back all day, and we could see distinctly into the room. Martin was standing at the other end of it, apparently absorbed in examining a painting, which he must have seen a thousand times. The doors creaked a little as I passed through them, but he did not turn round. Jack gave my hand a parting squeeze, and left me there in the open doorway, scarcely knowing whether to go on, and speak to Martin, or run away to my room, and leave him to take his own time.

I believe I should have run away, but I heard Minima's voice behind me, calling shrilly to Dr. John, and I could not bear to face him again. Taking my courage in both hands, I stepped quickly across the floor, for if I had hesitated longer my heart would have failed me. Scarcely a moment had passed since Jack left me, and Martin had not turned his head, yet it seemed an age.

"Martin," I whispered, as I stood close behind him, "how could you be so foolish as to send Dr. John to me?"

CHAPTER THE TWENTY-EIGHTH

PALMY DAYS

We were married as soon as the season was over, when Martin's fashionable patients were all going away from town. Ours was a very quiet wedding, for I had no friends on my side, and Martin's cousin Julia could not come, for she had a baby not a month old, and Captain Carey could not leave them. Johanna Carey and Minima were my bridesmaids, and Jack was Martin's groomsman.

On our way home from Switzerland, in the early autumn, we went down from Paris to Falaise, and through Noireau to Ville-en-bois. From Falaise every part of the road was full of associations to me. This was the long, weary journey which Minima and I had taken, alone, in a dark November night; and here were the narrow and dirty streets of Noireau, which we had so often trodden, cold, and hungry, and friendless. Martin said little about it, but I knew by his face, and by the tender care he lavished upon me, that his mind was as full of it as mine was.

There was no reason for us to stay even a day in Noireau, and we hurried through it on our way to Ville-en-bois. This road was still more memorable to me, for we had traversed it on foot.

"See, Martin!" I cried, "there is the trunk of the tree still, where Minima and I sat down to rest. I am glad the tree is there yet. If we were not in a hurry, you and I would sit there now; it is so lonely and still, and scarcely a creature passes this way. It is delicious to be lonely sometimes. How foot-sore and famished we were, walking along this rough part of the road! Martin, I almost wish our little Minima were with us. There is the common! If you will look steadily, you can just see the top of the cross, against the black line of fir-trees, on the far side."

I was getting so excited that I could speak no longer; but Martin held my hand in his, and I clasped it more and more tightly as we drew nearer to the cross, where Minima and I had sat down at the foot, forlorn and lost, in the dark shadows of the coming night. Was it possible that I was the same Olivia?

But as we came in sight of the little grove of cypresses and yews, we could discern a crowd of women, in their snow-white caps, and of men and boys, in blue blouses. The hollow beat of a drum reached our ears afar off, and after it the shrill notes of a violin and fife playing a merry tune. Monsieur Laurentie appeared in the foreground of the multitude, bareheaded, long before we reached the spot.

"O Martin!" I said, "let us get out, and send the carriage back, and walk up with them to the village."

"And my wife's luggage?" he answered, "and all the toys and presents she has brought from Paris?"

It was true that the carriage was inconveniently full of parcels, for I do not think that I had forgotten one of Monsieur Laurentie's people. But it would not be possible to ride among them, while they were walking.

"Every man will carry something," I said. "Martin, I must get out."

It was Monsieur Laurentie who opened the carriage-door for me; but the people did not give him time for a ceremonious salutation. They thronged about us with vivats as hearty as an English hurrah.

"All the world is here to meet us, monsieur," I said.

"Madame, I have also the honor of presenting to you two strangers from England," answered Monsieur Laurentie, while the people fell back to make way for them. Jack and Minima! both wild with delight. We learned afterward, as we marched up the valley to Ville-en-bois, that Dr. Senior had taken Jack's place in Brook Street, and insisted upon him and Minima giving us this surprise. Our procession, headed by the drum, the fife, and the violin, passed through the village street, from every window of which a little flag fluttered gayly, and stopped before the presbytery, where Monsieur Laurentie dismissed it, after a last vivat.

The next stage of our homeward journey was made in Monsieur Laurentie's char à bancs, from Ville-en-bois to Granville—Jack and Minima had returned direct to England, but we were to visit Guernsey on the way. Captain Carey and Julia made it a point that we should go to see them, and their baby, before settling down in our London home. Martin was welcomed with almost as much enthusiasm in St. Peter-Port as I had been in little Ville-en-bois.

From our room in Captain Carey's house I could look at Sark lying along the sea, with a belt of foam encircling it. At times, early in the morning, or when the sunset light fell upon it, I could distinguish the old windmill, and the church breaking the level line of the summit; and I could even see the brow of the knoll behind Tardifs cottage. But day after day the sea between us was rough, and the westerly breeze blew across the Atlantic, driving the waves before it. There was no steamer going across, and Captain

Carey's yacht could not brave the winds. I began to be afraid that Martin and I would not visit the place, which of all others in this half of the world was dearest to me.

"To-morrow," said Martin one night, after scanning the sunset, the sky, and the storm-glass, "if you can be up at five o'clock, we will cross to Sark."

I was up at four, in the first gray dawn of a September morning. We had the yacht to ourselves, for Captain Carey declined running the risk of being weather-bound on the island—a risk which we were willing to chance. The Havre Gosselin was still in morning shadow when we ran into it; but the water between us and Guernsey was sparkling and dancing in the early light, as we slowly climbed the rough path of the cliff. My eyes were dazzled with the sunshine, and dim with tears, when I first caught sight of the little cottage of Tardif, who was stretching out his nets, on the stone causeway under the windows. Martin called to him, and he flung down his nets and ran to meet us.

"We are come to spend the day with you, Tardif," I cried, when he was within hearing of my voice.

"It will be a day from heaven," he said, taking off his fisherman's cap, and looking round at the blue sky with its scattered clouds, and the sea with its scattered islets.

It was like a day from heaven. We wandered about the cliffs, visiting every spot which was most memorable to either of us, and Tardif rowed us in his boat past the entrance of the Gouliot Caves. He was very quiet, but he listened to our free talk together, for I could not think of good old Tardif as any stranger; and he seemed to watch us both, with a far-off, faithful, quiet look upon his face. Sometimes I fancied he did not hear what we were saying, and again his eyes would brighten with a sudden gleam, as if his whole soul and heart shone through them upon us. It was the last day of our holiday, for in the morning we were about to return to London, and to work; but it was such a perfect day as I had never known before.

"You are quite happy, Mrs. Martin Dobrée?" said Tardif to me, when we were parting from him.

"I did not know I could ever be so happy," I answered.

"We saw him to the last moment standing on the cliff, and waving his hat to us high above his head. Now and then there came a shout across the water. Before we were quite beyond ear-shot, we heard Tardif's voice calling amid the splashing of the waves:

"God be with you, my friends. Adieu, mam'zelle!"

CHAPTER THE TWENTY-NINTH

A POSTSCRIPT BY MARTIN DOBRÉE

You may describe to a second person, with the most minute and exact fidelity in your power, the leading and critical events in your life, and you will find that some trifle of his own experience is ten times more vivid to his mind. You narrate to your friend, whom you have not met for many years, the incident that has turned the whole current of your existence; and after a minute or two of musing, he asks you, "Do you remember the day we two went bird-nesting on Gull's Cliff?" That day of boyish daring and of narrow escapes is more real to him than your deepest troubles or keenest joys. The brain receives but slightly second-hand impressions.

I had told Olivia faithfully all my dilemmas with regard to Julia and the Careys; and she had seemed to listen with intense interest. Certainly it was during those four bewildering and enchanted months immediately preceding our marriage, and no doubt the narrative was interwoven with many a topic of quite a different character. However that might be, I was surprised to find that Olivia was not half as nervous and anxious as I felt, when we were nearing Guernsey on our visit to Julia and Captain Carey. Julia had seen her but once, and that for a few minutes only in Sark. On her account she had suffered the severest mortification a woman can undergo. How would she receive my wife?

Olivia did not know, though I did, that Julia was somewhat frigid and distant in her manner, even while thoroughly hospitable in her welcome. Olivia felt the hospitality; I felt the frigidity. Julia called her "Mrs. Dobrée." It was the first time she had been addressed by that name; and her blush and smile were exquisite to me, but they did not thaw Julia in the least. I began to fear that there would be between them that strange, uncomfortable, east-wind coolness, which so often exists between the two women a man most loves.

It was the baby that did it. Nothing on earth could be more charming, or more winning, than Olivia's delight over that child. It was the first baby she had ever had in her arms, she told us; and to see her sitting in the low rocking-chair, with her head bent over it, and to watch her dainty way of handling it, was quite a picture. Captain Carey had an artist's eye, and was in raptures; Julia had a mother's eye, and was so won by Olivia's admiration of her baby, that the thin crust of ice melted from her like the arctic snows before a Greenland summer.

I was not in the least surprised when, two days or so before we left Guernsey, Julia spoke to us with some solemnity of tone and expression.

"My dear, Olivia," she said, "and you, Martin, Arnold and I would consider it a token of your friendship for us both, if you two would stand as sponsors for our child."

"With the greatest pleasure, Julia," I replied; and Olivia crossed the hearth to kiss her, and sat down on the sofa at her side.

"We have decided upon calling her Olivia," continued Julia, stroking my wife's hand with a caressing touch—"Olivia Carey! That sounds extremely well, and is quite new in the island. I think it sounds even better than Olivia Dobrée."

As we all agreed that no name could sound better, or be newer in Guernsey, that question was immediately settled. There was no time for delay, and the next morning we carried the child to church to be christened. As we were returning homeward, Julia, whose face had worn its softest expression, pressed my arm with a clasp which made me look down upon her questioningly. Her eyes were filled with tears, and her mouth quivered. Olivia and Captain Carey were walking on in front, at a more rapid pace than ours, so that we were in fact alone.

"What is the matter?" I asked, hastily.

"O Martin!" she exclaimed, "we are both so happy, after all! I wish my poor, darling aunt could only have foreseen this! but, don't you think, as we are both so happy, we might just go and see my poor uncle? Kate Daltrey is away in Jersey, I know that for certain, and he is alone. It would give him so much pleasure. Surely you can forgive him now."

"By all means let us go," I answered. I had not heard even his name mentioned before, by any one of my old friends in Guernsey. But, as Julia said, I was so happy, that I was ready to forgive and forget all ancient grievances. Olivia and Captain Carey were already out of sight; and we turned into a street leading to Vauvert Road.

"They live in lodgings now," remarked Julia, as we went slowly up the steep street, "and nobody visits them; not one of my uncle's old friends. They have plenty to live upon, but it is all her money. I do not mean to let them got upon visiting terms with me—at least, not Kate Daltrey. You know the house, Martin?"

I knew nearly every house in St. Peter-Port, but this I remembered particularly as being the one where Mrs. Foster had lodged when she was in Guernsey. Upon inquiring for Dr. Dobrée, we were ushered at once, without warning, into his presence.

Even I should scarcely have recognized him. His figure was sunken and bent, and his clothes, which were shabby, sat in wrinkles upon him. His crisp white hair had grown thin and limp, and hung untidily about his face. He had not shaved for a week. His waistcoat was sprinkled over with snuff, in which he had indulged but sparingly in former years. There was not a trace of his old jauntiness and display. This was a rusty, dejected old man, with the crow's-feet very plainly marked upon his features.

"Father!" I said.

"Uncle!" cried Julia, running to him, and giving him a kiss, which she had not meant to do, I am sure, when we entered the house.

He shed a few tears at the sight of us, in a maudlin manner; and he continued languid and sluggish all through the interview. It struck me more forcibly than any other change could have done, that he never once appeared to pluck up any spirit, or attempted to recall a spark of his ancient sprightliness. He spoke more to Julia than to me.

"My love," he said, "I believed I knew a good deal about women, but I've lived to find out my mistake. You and your beloved aunt were angels. This one never lets me have a penny of my own: and she locks up my best suit when she goes from home. That is to prevent me going among my own friends. She is in Jersey now; but she would not hear a word of me going with her, not one word. The Bible says: 'Jealousy is cruel as the grave; the coals thereof are coals of fire, which hath a most vehement flame.' Kate is jealous of me. I get nothing but black looks and cold shoulders. There never lived a cat and dog that did not lead a more comfortable life than Kate leads me."

"You shall come and see Arnold and me sometimes, uncle," said Julia.

"She won't let me," he replied, with fresh tears; "she won't let me mention your name, or go past your house. I should very much like to see Martin's wife—a very pretty creature they say she is—but I dare not. O Julia! how little a man knows what is before him!"

We did not prolong our visit, for it was no pleasure to any one of us. Dr. Dobrée himself seemed relieved when we spoke of going away. He and I shook hands with one another gravely; it was the first time we had done so since he had announced his intention of marrying Kate Daltrey.

"My son," he said, "if ever you should find yourself a widower, be very careful how you select your second wife."

These were his parting words—words which chafed me sorely as a young husband in his honeymoon. I looked round when we were out of the house, and caught a glimpse of his withered face, and ragged white hair, as he peeped from behind the curtain at us. Julia and I walked on in silence till we reached her threshold.

"Yet I am not sorry we went, Martin," she observed, in a tone as if she thus summed up a discussion with herself. Nor was I sorry.

A few days after our return to London, as I was going home to dinner, I met, about half-war along Brook Street, Mrs. Foster. For the first time since my marriage I was glad to be alone; I would not have had Olivia with me on any account. But the woman was coming away from our house, and a sudden fear flashed across me. Could she have been annoying my Olivia?

"Have you been to see me?" I asked her, abruptly.

"Why should I come to see you?" she retorted.

"Nor my wife?" I said.

"Why shouldn't I go to see Mrs. Dobrée?" she asked again.

I felt that it was necessary to secure Olivia, and to gain this end I must be firm. But the poor creature looked miserable and unhappy, and I could not be harsh toward her.

"Come, Mrs. Foster," I said, "let us talk reasonably together. You know as as well as I do you have no claim upon my wife; and I cannot have her disturbed and distressed by seeing you; I wish her to forget all the past. Did I not fulfil my promise to Foster? Did I not do all I could for him?"

"Yes," she answered, sobbing, "I know you did all you could to save my husband's life."

"Without fee?" I said.

"Certainly. We were too poor to pay you."

"Give me my fee now, then," I replied. "Promise me to leave Olivia alone. Keep away from this street, and do not thrust yourself upon her at any time. If you meet by accident, that will be no fault of yours. I can trust you to keep your promise."

She stood silent and irresolute for a minute. Then she clasped my hand, with a strong grip for a woman's fingers.

"I promise," she said, "for you were very good to him."

She had taken a step or two into the dusk of the evening, when I ran after her for one more word.

"Mrs. Foster," I said, "are you in want?"

"I can always keep myself," she answered, proudly; "I earned his living and my own, for months together. Good-by, Martin Dobrée."

"Good-by," I said. She turned quickly from me round a corner near to us; and have not seen her again from that day to this.

Dr. Senior would not consent to part with Minima, even to Olivia. She promises fair to take the reins of the household at a very early age, and to hold them with a tight hand. Already Jack is under her authority, and yields to it with a very droll submission. She is so old for her years, and he is so young for his, that—who can tell? Olivia predicts that Jack Senior will always be a bachelor.

SARAH SMITH (writing as Hesba Stretton) – A CONCISE BIBLIOGRAPHY

Short Stories & Periodicals
The Lucky Leg (19th March 1859)
The Ghost in the Clock Room (Christmas, 1859)
The Postmaster's Daughter (All the Year Round, 5th November 1859)
A Provincial Post Office (All the Year Round, 28 February 1863)
Jessica's First Prayer (Sunday at Home, July 1866)
The Travelling Post-Office (All the Year Round, Mugby Junction, December 1866)
Jessica's Mother (1867)

Books
Fern's Hollow (1864)
Enoch Roden's Training (1865)
The Children of Cloverley (1865)
Jessica's First Prayer (Sunday at Home, July 1866)
The Fishers of Derby Haven (1866)
Jessica's Mother (Periodical 1867, book 1904)
Pilgrim Street (1867)
Little Meg's Children (1868)
Alone in London (1869)
Nellie's Dark Days (1870)
The Doctor's Dilemma (1872)
The King's Servants (1873)
Lost Gip (1873
Cassy (1874)
Brought Home (1875)

In Prison and Out (1878)
Two Secrets (1882)
The Lord's Purse-Bearers (1883)
Sam Franklin's Savings Bank (1888)
Little Meg's Children (1905)
The Christmas Child (1909 in US)

Other Works
Brought Home
Cobwebs And Cables